A PITYING OF DOVES

A BIRDER MURDER MYSTERY

STEVE BURROWS

POINT BLANK

A Point Blank Book

First published in Great Britain and the Commonwealth by Point Blank, an imprint of
Oneworld Publications, 2016

First published in English by Dundurn Press Limited, Canada. This edition published by
Oneworld Publications in arrangement with Dundurn Press Limited

ISBN 978-1-78074-897-9
ISBN 978-1-78074-898-6 (ebook)

Printed and bound in Great Britain by Clays Ltd, St Ives plc

Visit our website for a reading guide
and exclusive content on THE BIRDER MURDER SERIES
www.oneworld-publications.com

Oneworld Publications
10 Bloomsbury Street
London WC1B 3SR
England

ACKNOWLEDGEMENTS

I would like to thank my editor, Allison Hirst, and the staff at Dundurn for their continuing support and enthusiasm for the Birder Murder series. I am grateful, too, for the guidance and advice of Bruce Westwood and Lien de Nil at Westwood Creative Artists. Ray Popkie kindly shared the secrets of bird carving and showed me some wonderful examples of his art. Doug Gibson has pointed me in the right direction on more than one occasion, and the same is true of my many birding companions. My thanks to all of them.

And, as always, love and thanks go to my beautiful wife, Resa, who from the very beginning was convinced that there would be a second Birder Murder Mystery. Once again, darling, I have no hesitation in stating, in print, that you were absolutely ... not incorrect.

For Mark, Andrew and Matthew
May your stories always have happy endings

PROLOGUE
AUTUMN 2006

It was like driving into death; a grey maelstrom of ferocious rain and roiling storm clouds that cloaked the landscape with their dark menace. The storm of the century, they were calling it, worse even than '53.

It had been building for days, hunkering offshore, marshalling its power as it waited for that one perfect confluence of weather systems. In the previous hours there had been a couple of tentative incursions over the land — high winds and swift, angry rain squalls — but at 9:32 that morning, as the tide rose to its highest point in fifteen years, the storm began to unleash its full fury on the north Norfolk coastline. By now it had built to its peak, bringing evening to the afternoon in a sinister twilight of bruised skies and vast, swirling sheets of rain. The low-lying coastal lands were being inundated by the deluge from above and the storm-driven tidal surges from the sea. And now the floodwaters were headed this way.

The man urged the tiny car onward, a shiny sliver of light creeping over the oily blackness of the road. He wondered how long it would be before he saw the first evidence of flooding in the fields on either side. The river had already burst its banks, according to the latest report that had come over the car radio. Soon the waters would begin creeping insidiously across the flat black earth of the farms, swallowing up every feature, every hollow of the land. It was no wonder the radio announcers had started rolling out the Noah's ark references, even if they didn't know what they were talking about. *Two by two?* He had turned the radio off in a fit of exasperation at that point. How could you trust their storm updates when they couldn't even get basic scripture right? Seven: that was the number of clean beasts God had commanded Noah to take on the ark. Seven and seven, of each species, the male and the female. Not two.

At least somebody knew his Bible.

A momentary wave of lightheadedness passed over him. This snail's pace driving and those earlier diversions had taken him long past his scheduled time to eat. Still, a glass of orange juice and a couple of digestives when he got home …

The man blinked hard to clear his blurred vision and concentrated on the narrow country lane in front of him. The incessant hammering of the rain on the roof seemed to fill the car. In the feeble headlights, he could see the manic devil-dance of raindrops falling so hard they were bouncing back up from the surface of the road. All around him, the storm was attacking the land with such terrifying ferocity that it seemed almost to have one single purpose: to obliterate Saltmarsh from the map. When the storm finally passed, thought the man, the destruction left in its wake would be devastating. It would take the local communities a long time to recover from the day this veil of misery descended upon them. Perhaps some never would.

Violent gusts of wind tore at the tops of the overgrown hedgerows along both sides of the narrow lane, scattering leaves like tiny wet messages of the storm's destruction. A burst of wind-driven rain came out of the darkness like an ambush, rattling against the driver's window and startling the man into a momentary oversteer. *Careful. Get stuck in a ditch tonight, with the north Norfolk countryside disappearing beneath this storm of biblical proportions, and who knows when they'll be out to rescue you.* According to the radio reports, the emergency services were already stretched to the limit, clearing people from the path of the relentless brown tide that was bearing down on them.

And besides, there was his precious cargo. He didn't want to have to explain that to any potential rescuers. He patted the lid of the large cardboard box on the seat next to him and wiped the back of a clammy hand across his forehead, blinking his eyes once more to clear his vision.

There were those in his church, he knew, who would argue that this storm was a punishment from above; divine retribution for Saltmarsh's sins, past and present. He wondered if his actions counted among them. He had committed a crime, yes. He was prepared to admit that much. A perfect crime, as a matter of fact; but not a sin, surely. After all, he had acted with the best of intentions — compassion and mercy and pity. There could be no sin in that. The sky lit up as tendrils of lightning clawed their way across the towering bank of cloud on the horizon. The thunder that followed threatened to tear the swollen sky apart with its force. Somewhere over the noise of the storm, he heard the splintering crack of wood and saw the severed arm of an ancient oak crash onto the road ahead of him in an explosion of leaves and debris. Motive: that was what made it a sin. The man understood that now. His act of kindness had only ever had one real motive: his own gain. He knew it. And God knew it, too.

He steered cautiously around the fallen limb, gripping the steering wheel tightly as he feathered the accelerator. Silver sprays cascaded up against the bodywork as the wheels found a deeper patch of water near the edge of the road. He felt tired;

the constant focus, the concentration, was taking its toll. And all the time, the metronomic beat of the wipers slapping back and forth against the wet windscreen filled his senses, as measured and constant as a heartbeat, lulling him toward the rest he so badly needed.

In the dark, he almost missed the driveway. The little yellow carriage lamp had been torn off the gatepost by the wind and lay shattered across the road. What a shame. Maggie loved that lamp. An irrational sadness moved him almost to the point of weeping. He pulled into the driveway and parked. His body was bathed in sweat and he was shaking.

He sat in the car, watching the rain stream down the windows. The house beyond was dark. His mind fogged with confusion. *Where was Maggie?* Of course. Working. He would call her from the house; make sure she had arrived safely at the hospital. But first he needed to rest, to close his eyes. Just for a few minutes. Not in his bed. Too far away. Here in the car, next to his prize, the spoils of his perfect crime. He fumbled in his jacket for a pen and scrawled a spidery note on the top of the box: *For my Turtle D...* The pen slipped from his grasp and fell to the floor. Too far away. The drumming of the rain on the roof of the car was almost deafening now. He felt the weariness, the overwhelming weariness, pressing down upon him. He needed food, but it was in the kitchen. Too far away in this storm. Too far away. Just rest, then.

Maggie knew before she reached the car. Not when she alighted from the bus, stopped so thoughtfully by the driver a few feet past the actual bus stop, so she could avoid the massive puddle: not as she was walking along the lane, with its vegetation still dripping and heaving from the effects of last night's storm. But by the time she turned into the driveway, she knew.

The threat of death had been a constant in their lives ever since his diagnosis all those years before. Though it sometimes drifted to the back of their consciousness, it never really left them. So she approached the car with a strange mix of reluctance and haste, pressing in to look through the passenger window, through the clearing morning mist on the glass, where she saw her husband slumped against the steering wheel. She opened the door and put a finger to his neck. Even to her, it seemed a cold, professional gesture. Perhaps it was best that she was still in her nursing mindset. Sometimes it took her hours to switch off after a shift, especially after a night like last night, with all the stress and trauma of the storm-related injuries. She withdrew her hand, noticing for the first time the box lying on the passenger seat, and the words, his last words, scrawled on the top. She gently lifted the lid, peered in, and then replaced the lid and carried the box into the house.

Inside, she set the box on the floor and sat for a moment at the kitchen table in the cold, empty house. Then she crossed to the computer, typed out a short note, and printed it off. Folding and refolding the paper a couple of times, she opened a drawer of a battered old filing cabinet and stuffed the note into the middle of an untidy sheaf of papers, closing the drawer again with exaggerated care.

By the time she had swept the seat and floor of the passenger side of the car with a dustpan and brush, and emptied the dustpan onto a flowerbed, the shock was starting to set in. Back in the house, now barely aware of her actions, she put away the dustpan and brush and picked up the telephone. And then, having called the police to report the death of her husband of thirty-five years, Margaret Wylde sat down on her living-room couch and cried.

1
SPRING 2014

The thing about death is, it never taunts you with false hope. There is never any chance that things will reverse course, or get better, or even change. So in that respect, death never disappointed Danny Maik. Only life could do that. Still, even a detective sergeant as familiar with death as Danny was entitled to wonder, just for a second, whether encountering this scene the second time around would make it any easier. But when he re-entered the room, he was greeted by the same frozen tableau of horror; the silent, empty absence of life that was witness to the violence that had gone before it. And so Danny's own reaction was the same, too; an overwhelming sense of sadness. It came upon him whenever he encountered death, but perhaps this time the feeling was even a little stronger than usual, now that he could properly take in the pathetic innocence of the girl in the cage, and the peaceful repose of the man lying at her feet.

It was hard to believe that anyone's first reaction to the news of these murders could have been optimism. But if Lindy Hey could have witnessed this room for herself, experienced the blood, the stench of soiled feathers, the grotesque posture of the girl's body, Danny suspected that her response would not have been quite so upbeat.

"I don't suppose he's there," Maik had asked when Lindy answered the phone.

"Weather like this? Peak migration season? Nothing wrong with your detective skills, is there, Sergeant?"

"I thought perhaps if you knew where he was, we could send a car. It might be faster."

"Sorry, he could be anywhere along the coast at this time of year. Texting is your best bet. His phone will be off, but he's pretty good at checking his messages. Is it a bad one?"

Danny could imagine Lindy cringing at the seeming insensitivity of her question. She knew that, for him, there were no levels to murder. For Danny Maik, it was only ever the extinction of life, terrible in its finality, no matter who the victim was, or what the circumstances. But he knew Lindy wasn't being callous. Murder had once again intruded into her partner's life. She was simply trying to gauge how it would affect him, them, their relationship.

"If he calls, can you tell him to come to the Free to Fly Sanctuary on Beach Road?"

"Really, that bird rescue place?"

It wasn't just his imagination, that note of hope in her voice. He was sure of it now, considering it for a second time. Lindy was thinking that the presence of birds could possibly turn this into the one case that finally engaged Domenic Jejeune. And she might be right. A murder in a bird sanctuary might just capture the inspector's interest in a way that previous cases had so obviously failed to do. Whether it would be enough to ultimately convince Jejeune to commit himself to the career everybody seemed to believe was his destiny, well, that was another question altogether. As the title of one of Maik's beloved Motown titles might have put it: "Yes, No, Maybe So."

Danny returned to the present and swept his eyes over the scene once again. Two rows of floor-to-ceiling cages lined the breeze block walls of the sparse room, separated by a narrow walkway. In every cage but one, birds huddled silently in the farthest corner, away from the light. The survival instinct, he recognized. Sit still and avoid drawing attention to yourself. In another life, Danny had employed the same tactics himself, when his own survival had depended on it.

Detective Constable Tony Holland approached and nodded toward the bodies on the other side of the wire. "Murders in a bird cage," he said. "He's going to love this one, isn't he? Where is he, anyway? Off communing with his feathered friends somewhere, I suppose."

Maik ignored the question. "Uniforms made sure they left the scene exactly as it was? Keys hung in exactly the same place?"

Holland's look told Maik that even the uniforms had enough experience in dealing with a Domenic Jejeune crime scene to know what was expected of them. They would have disturbed nothing during their initial inspection, relocking the cage and replacing the keys carefully. The DCI would see everything just as it was when they first arrived on the scene. If any messages had been left, intentional or otherwise, Jejeune would be able to interpret them *in situ* before SOCO started sifting through things.

Maik asked for the background on the victims and Holland did his best to provide what they knew so far. It wasn't much.

"The kneeler is Phoebe Hunter. She runs the shelter. Ran. Him, we have no idea. No ID or phone, either on the body or in the car. Nice *shine*, though." Holland indicated an expensive watch and ring on the man's left hand.

"There's a car?" Maik couldn't remember seeing anything other than familiar police vehicles when he arrived.

"Round the back, tucked away in the corner. It's a local rental from Saxon's Garage. I've called Old Man Saxon. He'll pull the file and get us an ID as soon as he gets in." Maik's silence unnerved Holland and the constable checked the time on a flashy new iPhone. "I could go and get him if you like…"

Maik dismissed the idea with a wave of his hand. He peered into the cage once more, forcing himself to look beyond the carnage to take in the details. The body of a young woman knelt in a pool of her own blood. She had slumped far enough in death that her knees were resting on the concrete floor of the cage. But her upper torso remained suspended upright, impaled on a broken branch that protruded like a spear point from a dead tree limb that had been stretched across the cage as a makeshift perch. Her head rested against her chest in an attitude Maik remembered from the crucifixes of his church-going youth. Beneath her, almost at her feet, lay the body of a man. He wore an expensive-looking turtleneck sweater, finely tailored trousers, and high-quality leather shoes, all in black. The man looked almost peaceful, curled on one side as though sleep had suddenly overtaken him. Maik wondered if it was the serenity of the man's pose that made the girl's own situation seem so grotesque by comparison. But no, Phoebe Hunter's death really needed no point of contrast to appal anyone.

Maik looked at the dark blood pooled on the floor around the girl. He had seen blood spilled on many surfaces, but only on cement did it seem to settle like this, flowing outwards and then drawing back slightly from the edges, as if shrinking back in revulsion at its own progress. In that strange way of things, the blood had flowed to within inches of the man's body, but had not touched it. There was not a trace of blood anywhere on the man's black clothing.

Maik considered the girl's clothes carefully: well-worn shoes, a short skirt, and a skimpy baby-blue top with tiny embroidered flowers around the neck. The top was bunched and one of the spaghetti straps had been torn as her killer grabbed her and thrust her onto the branch. Maik wondered what she had been thinking about when she got dressed the previous morning. These birds? The tasks that awaited her? Excitement about what the new day might bring? All for it to end like this, kneeling on the floor of a locked cage, amid bird droppings and spilled seed, in a pool of her own blood. *Yes, Lindy, it was a bad one.*

To Maik's right, Detective Constable Lauren Salter was pressing her face against the cage, gripping the wire with her fingers. She seemed unable to pull her eyes away from the scene inside, terrible as it was.

"Everything all right, Constable?"

"He's not from around here," said Salter, "I'm sure of it." She seemed distant, distracted. Sometimes, the nervous system put mechanisms in place to shield a person from shock. But Salter had seen her share of traumatic deaths. Maik wondered if it might be something else. She nodded toward the well-dressed man with his dark complexion and jet-black hair. Even in death, he was startlingly handsome. "Trust me, quality like that would have stuck out a mile from the local gene pool."

Tony Holland readied himself for a response, but he seemed to think better of it. Sergeant Maik liked a bit of decorum around his murder scenes, and he could get very testy if he thought people weren't taking things seriously enough.

"An out-of-towner and a local, then," mused Maik. "So what were they doing here together, I wonder."

Holland smirked. "You're kidding, right? He's away from home, meets plain Jane here; game over."

Holland held up his hand to fend off the looks he was getting from both Maik and Salter. "What? I'm just saying, a no-frills number like her, with her *maybe* outfit on, just to let you know it was a possibility. If he had the chat to go with his looks, it would be a foregone conclusion. I'm just saying," he repeated.

Maik was silent, which was probably the safest response Holland could have hoped for from him. But Salter wasn't in the mood to indulge Tony Holland's singular view of the world. "And they chose this place why, exactly, Tony? The ambiance? Believe it or not, there are other reasons a man and a woman could be together. That is, unless the man is a complete brain-dead moron with a one-track mind. Oh, wait ..." said Salter with heavy irony.

Salter's outburst was so out of keeping with her normal demeanour around Danny Maik that both he and Holland shot her a surprised look. But while Maik had always put her previous self-control down to simple professionalism, Holland had long ago identified a different cause. When you had been striving as long as Salter had to get Maik to even notice your attentions, let alone respond to them, you didn't want something as unattractive as a temper tantrum spoiling your chances.

"What's up with you, then?" asked Holland. "Touch of the hot flushes?"

"Oh, for God's sake, grow up."

Both fell silent under the sergeant's stony stare. In his present mood, if Danny Maik decided to start banging heads together, the lab team would have more than one mess to clean up when they got here.

"I'll go see if I can light a fire under that lazy bugger, Saxon," announced Salter, striding off angrily toward the doorway. Maik stared after her retreating form, but neither she nor the silent Tony Holland met his gaze.

Maik considered the bodies carefully once again; the man's smart black attire, the girl's clothing. What had Holland called it, her *maybe* outfit? A little low up top; a little high down below. At this stage anything was possible, but a romantic pairing looked off to him. Death was the ultimate leveller, but appearances suggested that in life these two would have inhabited very different worlds. Still, Danny Maik was hardly an expert on what attracted people to each other. More the opposite, truth be told. And he had known stranger relationships in his time. If somebody came up with a sighting of the two of them huddled together over G and Ts in the local bar, he wouldn't dismiss it out of hand.

But, regardless of why these two people had come here together, or what they intended to do, one thing was clear. They hadn't been alone. Someone had killed them both, then deliberately manipulated the evidence before fleeing the scene. As to whom that someone might have been, the only person Maik knew who might be capable of working that out was currently occupied with other matters — specifically, the spring migration of birds along the north Norfolk coast.

2

Chief Inspector Domenic Jejeune flattened himself against the wall as the forensic team squeezed past him in the narrow passageway. He watched the team enter the cage, ready to begin their work as soon as he gave the word.

Jejeune leaned forward to peer into the cage, and felt something seep from him, like fluid escaping from a wound. The transition from the scene he had just left — the bright, fecund promise of a spring bird migration, to this theatre of fluorescent-lit tragedy — was almost overwhelming. Perhaps if they had been with him, the sergeant, the forensic team, the constables now staring at him with such expectation, perhaps if they had been there to witness that glorious sunrise breaking over the coast, the soft light of morning dappling the north Norfolk countryside, with the calls of a thousand birds filling the air, perhaps then they would understand his reluctance to be here, to be a part of this world. But he'd been alone that morning, as alone as he felt now, despite the presence of the others.

He stepped back from the cage and sighed inwardly. He knew that it was his job to make sense of these senseless killings, to provide answers as to why two people should die amongst discarded bird feathers and overturned seed dishes. And he knew, too, that regardless of his personal desolation, these two people deserved the attentions of someone who was engaged, focused on the task, determined to pursue it to a result. So Domenic Jejeune quietly folded away the pleasures of the previous hours and resigned himself once more to the job that life had chosen for him.

Sergeant Maik approached cautiously. "Anonymous tip," he said. "A note left on the windscreen of a car in the hotel car park down the road."

Jejeune looked dubious.

"The side door was open when we got here," said Maik. "We're thinking some local roustabout probably found it like that and had a wander in, looking to help himself to anything that was lying about. Found this scene and wanted to let us know, without having to explain what he was doing in here in the first place."

"Still, they could have called from a pay phone. Just how good do they think the voice-recognition skills of the switch-board operators are?"

"I don't think they wanted to find out. Criminals in these parts tend to have what the American talk shows call 'trust issues' with coppers who have sent them away in the past," said Maik drily. "The girl's flat is upstairs, whenever you like," he said, though he knew the inspector would want to look around a bit more down here first. "Her name is Phoebe Hunter," continued Maik. "Constable Salter has gone to the car rental company to see if we can get an ID on the man." He knew Jejeune liked to have identifications as soon as possible. It was obvious enough that these people were victims without having to constantly refer to them as such.

Jejeune nodded. He saw the emotion behind Maik's eyes, in sharp contrast to the dry, measured statements of fact he was delivering. He was aware that he was yet to offer any meaning-ful contribution of his own, but he seemed unable to find any words worth saying.

"Uniforms weren't able to find any wounds on the man. Not that that means very much, of course."

Jejeune made a face to acknowledge Maik's point. There were plenty of ways to kill a man without leaving any obvious signs. He regarded the bodies carefully again. He knew that he was expected to shut out the horror, to push it aside, so that only the facts remained. For him, this was the worst travesty of all, to consider these deaths only as an event, a crime, simply because you couldn't allow your judgment to be clouded by emotion. As if reacting to scenes like this was evidence itself, of weakness, or an inability to do your job. As if expressing sadness at the sight of a young woman kneeling in her own blood was somehow a bad thing, a negative thing. So he would do it the way his police training had taught him, filtering out the revulsion, the horror, even if he would never offer that final insult to these people; that of treating them merely as cases. He would pay a price for offering them his compassion, for continuing to regard them as people, this young girl, this handsome man before him. He knew that. But with murder, everybody paid a price.

Jejeune spent another silent moment staring at the bodies before waving in the forensics team. With Danny Maik in the building, nobody would have to remind them to show the victims the proper respect.

Tony Holland approached carrying a book. "Uniforms found it under the front seat of the car," he told Maik, handing him the book. "Oh, hello, sir," he said, feigning to notice Jejeune for the first time. "You found us okay, then? Pity this lot aren't parrots, eh? Might have been able to tell us what happened."

"You'll be wanting to see this." Maik handed the book to Jejeune. It was a well-worn bird guide with a bookmark protruding from between the pages. "Two birders? A meeting of the minds?" asked Maik. "Perhaps he was interested in whatever work she was doing here, and she invited him to see it first-hand."

"Possibly," said Jejeune. "Did you find anything about a meeting in her diary?"

Maik's expression suggested that if they had come across a detail of such significance, he may just have thought to mention by now. Jejeune riffled through the book with his thumb. Next to some of the images were notes: dates, locations, weather conditions. He turned to the bookmarked page. Maik peered over his shoulder, then looked up into one of the cages.

"So these are Turtledoves, then?" he asked.

Jejeune nodded absently. "Yes. Turtledoves." He once again turned his attention to the bodies. "In every cage but this one. Locked from the outside, with the keys on the hook." A thoughtful expression clouded his features.

Holland looked at Maik incredulously and then back at Jejeune. And this was supposed to be the star of the North Norfolk Constabulary? "We were thinking that might have been the third party, sir. You know, after he killed them. Locked the cage and hung up the keys again. Just an idea, mind."

Jejeune nodded. It was impossible to tell if he had missed the sarcasm or was choosing to ignore it. "Not the work of somebody in a hurry, though, is it? Or somebody surprised in the act?"

"And yet they didn't bother to take the man's jewellery," said Maik, nodding to acknowledge Jejeune's point. "But if robbery wasn't the motive here ..."

"Then they came for something else."

"Came for?" Holland looked at Jejeune carefully, as if trying to read where exactly the DCI might have come up with the idea that somebody had entered these premises with the intention of taking something. And anyway, what else was there here to steal, other than ... no, surely he wasn't suggesting ...

"Juan Perez," announced Salter from the doorway. She pronounced it *Ju-an*. "Saxon's description of him is an exact match. I can get a photo over to him, if you like, but it's definitely our victim. He gave his address as The Pheasant. It's that hotel just down the road. I told you he wasn't local."

Jejeune was silent. He seemed to be playing his mind over the information Salter had just brought them. "Juan Perez is the equivalent of John Smith in many parts of Latin America. If he has no ID on him, perhaps it's because he's trying to hide his real identity."

"There are actually people called John Smith, you know," said Salter testily. She seemed annoyed that her information hadn't met with the gratitude she expected from Jejeune. "And people do occasionally leave home without their wallets."

Maik shot Salter a glance. She was normally among the more circumspect of the constables when confronted with the oblique meanderings of Jejeune's mind. But today she seemed to have little patience for the inspector's outside-the-box musings. Or anything else, for that matter.

"Well, I suppose I had better get over to his room and see if he left any ID laying around, fake or otherwise," said Holland, unable to keep a note of amusement from his voice. Maik watched him leave. A quick smoke, a chat to the housemaids, a casual look around the hotel room to confirm what he had already decided — that the Chief Inspector was completely on the wrong track. It was a job made for Tony Holland. If he played it right, it would be worth an hour away from the crime scene, at least.

"The rental car," Jejeune said to Salter, as if returning from another place, "was Mr. Perez the only named driver?"

"Yes." She seemed to hesitate. *Falter* would have been Maik's word.

"Your views on the John Smiths of the world notwithstanding, Constable, is there anything else you'd like to share with us?"

Perhaps it was Holland's departure, or just Maik's encouraging tone, but something seemed to free Salter of her burden.

"I, I had a call, yesterday. From this woman, Phoebe Hunter. She told me Wild Maggie had been making threatening phone calls. Something about the shelter having Maggie's doves. She didn't sound worried, but she said she thought she should report it anyway …"

"Wild Maggie?"

It was unclear to whom Jejeune had directed the question, but it was Maik who supplied the answer. "Margaret Wylde. Local character. She's a bit off, a serial complainer." His tone seemed to imply that if he had taken the call himself, he would have taken the investigation no further either. But it didn't seem to be doing much to relieve Salter's sense of guilt.

Jejeune thought for a moment. "Did she work here?"

"I doubt it," said Maik. "She used to be a nurse, I believe, but she has been unable to hold down a job ever since her husband died some years back. Serious mental health issues. It takes some that way, I understand, the death of a loved one."

"I see. Can we find out? Any history of employment at this sanctuary or any other facility like it?" Jejeune turned to Salter. "Phoebe Hunter said this woman was asking about *her* birds? That the sanctuary had *her* birds?" There was no admonition in Jejeune's tone, no hint that Salter should have reacted differently to the phone call, pursued matters, made further inquiries. But then, it was clear from Salter's expression that there was no need for anyone to try to make her feel any worse than she already did.

She nodded.

Wordlessly, Jejeune began a slow walk down the corridor, peering into each of the cages in turn. He appeared to be studying the birds intently. Maik and the constable stood in an uncomfortable silence, suspended between the DCI's absence and the uncertainty of his return. Tears weren't Salter's style, but she found something other than the sergeant's intense gaze to occupy her eyes as she spoke.

"I was going to contact the animal rescue service to see if they had even brought Maggie's birds to this shelter. You know how she is; it wouldn't have been unlike her to get her story completely backward. But I ... Max had a doctor's appointment. I was going to get onto it as soon as I got in this morning." Salter touched her fingers to her lips, but their tremor only mirrored the one she was trying to disguise.

Jejeune returned along the corridor and paused once more in front of the cage where the forensic team was working around the bodies.

"We need to bring in Maggie, I take it," said Maik. He reached for his phone.

"I can do it," said Salter quickly.

It was obvious to Maik that it meant a lot to her, but if it was as obvious to Jejeune, he chose to ignore it. "Uniforms can handle it," he said. "What I'd like you to do is contact the British Trust for Ornithology. Ask them for any recent reports of ringed birds sent in from this sanctuary." Jejeune checked his watch. "Their offices should be open by now. In the meantime, the sergeant and I will be upstairs."

Danny Maik had spent a lifetime disguising his surprise at orders from his superiors, but judging from the expression on Salter's face, she either had less practice, or less interest, in masking her true feelings. Both watched the departing form of Domenic Jejeune in silence. Based on past experience, they knew the reasons for the inspector's unusual request would eventually become clear. But just at that moment, neither one of them would have cared to speculate quite when that might be.

3

Danny Maik stood on the landing and looked around. "Well, you could hardly fault her for variety."

Jejeune nodded in agreement. The four rooms above the sanctuary that together constituted Phoebe Hunter's living quarters opened off the landing. From the detectives' vantage point at the top of the stairs, it was possible to see into each of the rooms. From the startling tiger-stripes of the bedroom to the stark white Scandinavian economy of the living area to the delicate pastels of the kitchen, each room presented a bold, dramatic alternative in décor. *Exploring her boundaries*, thought Jejeune; the exuberant self-discovery of someone emerging from the chrysalis of youth. It was yet another reminder of what had been taken away by the killer; an unfolding life, now stilled forever, one floor below them, kneeling in a pool of still-drying blood.

Salter arrived on the landing behind them. "No answer at the BTO, so I've texted them." She consulted her smartphone. "According to Phoebe Hunter's Facebook page, she was doing post-grad research on bird migrations. Tracking Turtledoves. Running the shelter was a volunteer position, but it came with these digs."

Jejeune looked around at the slight disarray, the coffee cup in the kitchen sink, the half-opened post on the dresser, the general lived-in feel of the rooms. It was as if Phoebe Hunter had just stepped out for a moment. Which, of course, she had. Only she would never be stepping back in.

Jejeune headed into the living room while Maik took the kitchen. Salter hesitated uncertainly on the landing, watching. Maik, methodical as ever, lifting and replacing items with precision, making his notes as he went; the DCI, wandering around aimlessly, dragging a fingernail absently across the spine of a book now and then, but mostly just letting his eyes do the work. *Opposites attract*, thought Salter, but surely, you had to bring them together first. From what she could see, these two were about as distant as it was possible to be in the confines of this small upstairs flat.

Salter wandered into the bedroom and opened a drawer beside the bed. A pile of erotic lingerie lay in an untidy bundle. Perhaps Tony Holland, with his unerring eye for the possibility, had not been wrong. The thought irritated her, enough that she didn't bring the items to the attention of either Jejeune or Maik. Both knew what they were doing when they searched a location. One of them would eventually find the lingerie without any help from her.

For now, Danny was still examining the contents of the kitchen cabinets, but Jejeune's mercurial attention had already alighted elsewhere; on an academic paper lying on the desk. Beneath the title, the author's name, David Nyce, had been scratched out and Phoebe Hunter's name pencilled in above it. Jejeune spent some time leafing through the paper, studying the occasional passage closely. He flipped to the bibliography and made a face.

"If Mr. Nyce did author this paper, he certainly seems to enjoy quoting from his own work."

"To anybody who knows him, sir, that would hardly come as a surprise," said Salter, coming over to join him, "and I think you'll find it's *Dr.* Nyce. I may as well mention it, because he certainly will."

"You know him well, Constable?"

Salter nodded, "Most people around here know David Nyce. He makes it his business to ensure we are all well aware of his genius."

"Then perhaps we should seek an audience ourselves. Can you set it up, please, Sergeant?"

Maik's expression suggested it wasn't going to be the most pleasant task he faced that day, but he said nothing. His phone rang. He answered it and listened without speaking before hanging up. "Wild Maggie appears to have gone to ground. Her car is missing, too."

"She'll turn up," said Salter. "I'll stay on it until she does."

"This Margaret Wylde, would you say she's a strong woman? Physically, I mean?"

Salter seemed to tense at Jejeune's question. "I know it would have taken some strength to shove that poor girl back onto that branch, sir, but believe me, I've seen Maggie in action. She can get really worked up." There was a moment's hesitation. "Sir, if I could just say … well, I know you like to look at all angles, the Latin American thing, for example, but I don't think we should ignore the obvious here, I mean, you know, Occam's razor and all that."

Maik managed to keep his sigh internal, but only just. Occam's razor was all over the Internet and the popular media these days, so he had known it was only a matter of time before somebody tried to introduce it into a murder inquiry. *Enter Lauren Salter, Saltmarsh Division's resident expert in trending topics and other related idiocy.*

Occam's razor! The idea that the simplest explanation was usually the correct one. Common sense, they used to call it in Maik's day. But, of course, now everything had to have its own marketing label. Maik would have bet a good portion of his meagre sergeant's salary that Salter knew only the barest details about Occam's razor — the pop culture, ten-second sound-byte version. But that didn't change the fact that she had a point. Latin America was a long way to come to end up murdered in a bird cage in north Norfolk. On the other hand, it made sense that Salter would be looking to push Maggie as a suspect. She wanted to punish herself for her failure to protect Phoebe Hunter, and Maik knew only too well how easy it was to rush to judgment in those circumstances. A musical note from the constable's phone stopped Maik from having to come down on one side or the other on the question of Maggie's guilt, at least for the moment.

Salter read the text message herself before wordlessly handing over the phone to Jejeune. The BTO received banding reports now and again from the Free to Fly Sanctuary, but since one in early February of a Snow Bunting previously banded in the Netherlands, there had been nothing.

Something in Jejeune's expression seemed to suggest that the news from the BTO had changed things. It was hard to put into words exactly, but the inspector's focus seemed to have shifted. Jejeune was now looking in a different direction.

"Sergeant, can you make sure SOCO collect feathers from that cage," he said, as if it had suddenly become important. Maik suppressed a grimace. The DCI had an annoying habit of requesting things in a way that suggested that, without his guidance, other people would forget to perform the most basic of tasks. The SOCO boys were good, and they knew their job. Any blood-stained feathers would be collected, labelled, and recorded without any reminder from him. Or Jejeune.

"I'll see to it," said Salter. She disappeared down the stairs hurriedly, as if she was anxious to get away from this flat, this living place of a dead person.

The men continued to sift through Phoebe's belongings, the skeleton of a human life about whom they knew nothing, and perhaps would never know anything. If possible, the information that she was a post-graduate, poised on the cusp of recouping some of the investment she had made in her future, seemed only to heighten the sense of loss.

They looked up simultaneously as Tony Holland appeared on the landing. Some of the bounce appeared to have gone from his demeanour. Maik recognized the signs. It rarely sat well with Holland, having to confirm one of Jejeune's outlandish theories. You would have thought with all the practice it might have become a bit easier, but the constable was obviously still struggling with it.

"I … er … conducted a search of the victim's hotel room, sir," he said formally. "There *was* documentation that indicated another name. Photo ID, in fact. The victim's real name was Ramon Santos."

"I see," said Jejeune. He seemed utterly unimpressed with his own shrewdness. *But what was Jejeune doing with knowledge like this Juan Perez business rattling around in his head anyway?* wondered Maik. It wasn't the sort of thing you picked up on pub trivia night down at The Boatman's Arms.

"Have a Canadian suspect do a runner down that way one time, did you?" he asked.

"Something like that," said Jejeune quietly.

"The thing is," continued Holland. He hesitated, "Well, I'm afraid the DCS is not going to like it much."

Danny Maik straightened up and raised an eyebrow.

"That photo ID. It was a diplomatic pass. Apparently, Mr. Santos was a diplomatic attaché with the Mexican Consulate."

A flicker passed across Jejeune's features. Holland was right. DCS Shepherd wasn't going to like it. Not at all.

4

It was still before noon when Jejeune arrived back at the station, but Detective Chief Superintendent Colleen Shepherd was already wearing the expression of someone who had been waiting a long time. And none too patiently.

Shepherd followed him into his office but left the door open behind her. It was a signal they would both be leaving soon. Jejeune set the well-used birding book on his desk, but did not bother taking a seat. Despite Tony Holland's dire predictions, Shepherd did not seem particularly distraught that they were going to be dealing with the death of a senior foreign diplomat on her patch. She was unusually animated, perhaps, but there was none of the hand-wringing angst that such an event might have occasioned in a less ambitious DCS.

"I understand Sergeant Maik's been running background checks on Maggie Wylde. This complaint lodged by one of the victims against her," said Shepherd, "anything to it?"

"It's one lead," said Jejeune flatly.

But not one I like, his look told Shepherd.

She gestured him out of the office and they made their way along the corridor side by side, the brisk clack of Shepherd's heels matching Jejeune's loping stride step for step. She spoke in low, urgent tones as they walked. It was her way of indicating that this was important, and that Jejeune should pay attention.

"At this point, I'm sure Señor Hidalgo is merely looking for assurances that we know what we're doing, that this case hasn't fallen into the laps of some bumbling village coppers who are in over their heads. So let's try to give him those assurances, shall we, Domenic? On cue?"

Shepherd had worked with Jejeune long enough to know that his silence during these exchanges was not necessarily tacit agreement. She stopped outside the door to her office and turned to look at him directly.

"It goes without saying that the eyes of some very important people are going to be upon us as soon as the identity of the victim gets out. In order for us to get the kind of breathing room we will need, we have to convince the Mexican Counsellor for Culture and Heritage that the right people are on the job. For the record, that's us, Domenic, you and me, and this whole team that I have assembled here at Saltmarsh Division. So let's get in there and do some convincing. Okay? Follow my lead."

She ushered Jejeune into her office to find a distinguished-looking man sitting in a chair.

"Counsellor Hidalgo. Allow me to introduce my Chief Inspector, Domenic Jejeune. The counsellor has kindly come down here to discuss how the Mexican authorities can assist us in our enquiries," said Shepherd.

Efren Hidalgo rose with dignity and offered a well-manicured hand. The counsellor was not a tall man, but his slightly rotund figure was skillfully disguised by an exquisitely tailored suit. He smoothed the jacket now with a downward stroke of one hand as he resumed his seat. "Your reputation precedes you, Inspector," said Hidalgo. "This reassures me. This morning, I concluded a very difficult telephone call with Ramon's wife back in Mexico. I ended by suggesting that I would be able to provide her with some details in the near future. I would like also to be able to pass along some news of progress in this case as soon as possible."

Jejeune nodded in understanding. Without facts, Santos's death was nothing more than an empty, senseless event, a swirling cloud of pain that cast a shadow of confusion and anger. If Jejeune could at least offer some meaning, some context to the man's death, it would be a starting point for the family to begin the process of grieving.

Hidalgo continued. "Due to the nature of Ramon's work at the consulate, there may be areas where special permission will be necessary in order for you to pursue your enquiries." The clipped economy of his dismissive hand gesture had its own special elegance. "But rest assured, we are prepared to provide any assistance you may require. You must know, we are as anxious as you are yourselves to see the person who committed this dreadful crime brought to justice."

"Well, I'm sure Inspector Jejeune appreciates the need for such diplomatic restrictions, but I don't think we are anticipating any enquiries in that direction at the moment, are we, Domenic?"

Jejeune addressed them both.

"Mr. Santos journeyed all the way from London to north Norfolk and stayed in accommodation as close to the sanctuary as possible. It seems reasonable to assume that it was his intended destination."

"I think it goes without saying, Domenic, that if Mr. Santos was at the sanctuary on official business, Señor Hidalgo would have already brought it to our attention."

Jejeune wasn't overly fond of having other people hijack his questions, especially those he had not intended asking in the first place, but he supposed that Shepherd was anxious to avoid the unedifying spectacle of having him directly interrogate a foreign dignitary in her office. Still, if this was the way all enquiries were going to go in this case, it was not going to make Jejeune's job any easier.

Hidalgo tilted his head slightly to show he was unoffended by even the faintest suggestion that he would withhold such information.

"I can confirm that Ramon was not at the sanctuary as a representative of the Mexican Consulate. To the best of my knowledge, no one at the consulate has had any dealings with this organization, this sanctuary, nor, indeed, was anyone even aware of its existence before the terrible events of today."

"Can you think of any reason Mr. Santos would have wanted to keep the consulate from knowing his whereabouts?"

Shepherd fired a warning glance at Jejeune, and for a second time she hurried in to spare the counsellor's feelings. "We are aware, of course, that there could be any number of reasons a travelling foreign diplomat might want to use an alias. It is not a criminal offence, provided there is no illegal motive. I'm sure Inspector Jejeune simply wants to eliminate that as a possibility."

Failing to receive the reassurance she sought, Shepherd used the half-beat of uncomfortable silence to flash an apologetic smile toward Hidalgo. But Hidalgo inclined his head amiably again to dismiss the awkwardness.

"You must obviously establish Ramon's motives for checking into the hotel under an alias, if you feel it is important. However, I doubt it would be to conceal his movements from us. All consular staff members have tracking devices in their phones these days, as a security precaution. I understand Ramon left his phone at the hotel?" Hidalgo spread his hands, palms upward. "We could have found out exactly where he was if we had wanted to. Again, for the record, we did not."

The effort of politesse seemed to weigh upon Hidalgo and he sighed deeply. While he carried his sadness with dignity, it was clear to see the counsellor had been devastated by the loss of one of his staff. Hidalgo's grief had its own bittersweet charm. It was the kind of quality the DCS would respond to, thought Jejeune.

Shepherd stared at the chief inspector intently. "So, any early thoughts, Domenic?"

Her inviting tone puzzled Jejeune at first. *The woman*, he realized. *Maggie.* She wants to show Hidalgo we are off and running already. But there were far too many inconsistencies for Jejeune to put Maggie Wylde forward as a viable suspect. And surely Shepherd knew his methods well enough by now to know he was unlikely to be stampeded into a rash course of action merely because she wanted to show off in front of her dignitary.

"Nothing concrete," he said cautiously.

As far as Jejeune was concerned, his expression could have only reflected his unwillingness to reveal anything about Maggie, but whatever it was that Shepherd imagined she could see in his face seemed to please her.

"First impressions, then? I expect the counsellor would be interested to hear any preliminary thoughts you may have." *What is it that makes you doubt Maggie's involvement?* she meant. For reasons Jejeune couldn't even begin to understand, Shepherd seemed to be enjoying their little sub rosa conversation, revelling in it, almost.

"It would just be speculation, at this point," he said warily.

"I'm sure Señor Hidalgo will appreciate that, in the absence of any firm evidence yet, speculation is going to be one of our best approaches."

Jejeune tried to convey to Shepherd with a laden glance just how dubious he thought this line of conversation was, but Shepherd was simultaneously returning his gaze and avoiding the import of it with such practised skill, he was left with little alternative but to accept her invitation.

"The scene suggests that this was not a pre-planned attack. There were no weapons, no signs of ambush. It doesn't look like the work of somebody who went there with the intention of

killing people. Rather, it suggests that things happened spon-
taneously, a situation that got out of control and escalated. In
circumstances like that, especially where there is a lot of blood,
most people would panic, be confused, terrified even. Yet the
cage was locked and the keys returned to their hook. That
suggests we're dealing either with someone who could keep
calm and clear-headed at such a horrific scene, or someone
for whom locking the door and re-hanging the keys was an
automatic response, the sort of action you might resort to if
you were in a state of shock."

Hidalgo sat forward. "You know of this type of person?"

"Perhaps someone who worked at this sanctuary, or another
one like it, where locking cages and hanging up keys becomes
a habit, an ingrained action."

Jejeune stopped. Shepherd would already know, as he did,
that Maik's inquiries had shown Maggie Wylde to have had
no such background. At the very least, Jejeune might have
expected a reprimanding look from his DCS for effectively
eliminating their only suspect in such a cavalier manner. More
likely would be the spectacle of Shepherd rushing into the
breach, trying to convince Hidalgo that Jejeune's ideas were
tenuous, at best, and without any foundation whatsoever. But
when Jejeune did finally meet Shepherd's gaze, he saw only a
strange look of contentment waiting for him.

On cue. Follow my lead.

This wasn't about his theories, he realized. It was about
him, Chief Inspector Domenic Jejeune, property of Saltmarsh
Division, *her* Saltmarsh Division, on display and full of ideas,
even at this early stage. Domenic Jejeune, DCS Colleen
Shepherd's reluctant show pony, trotted out to reassure Hidalgo
that the right people were on the case. It occurred to Jejeune
that if he had given voice to some of his other early thoughts,
Shepherd's response might not have been quite so enthusiastic.

But it was a moot point. Because no matter what other party tricks the DCS had in mind for her prize asset, Domenic Jejeune was done speculating for the moment.

"I see," said Hidalgo after a thoughtful pause.

"I wonder, can you remember what time you received the news of Mr. Santos's death?" asked Jejeune politely.

"At approximately five forty-five this morning."

"Can I ask where you were at the time?"

Hidalgo turned to Jejeune. If he had noticed Shepherd's horrified expression, he chose to ignore it. Instead, he allowed himself a faint smile. "I was asleep in my London residence when I was awoken by a call from a member of your Foreign Office. You may verify this with my duty secretary. In fact, I insist upon it."

Jejeune gave a non-committal tilt of the head, but his expression assured Hidalgo they were on the same page. If the counsellor was in London, more than three hours away, when he received the news, he could not have committed two murders that preliminary examinations had already set at between 4:00 and 5:00 a.m.

Hidalgo stood up with an elegant flourish and turned to extend a hand first to DCS Shepherd and then to Jejeune. "If there is nothing else, I must return to the consulate. There will be much sadness today. Ramon was well-liked. His colleagues will need support. I welcome your earlier reassurance, Superintendent. I can ask for no more."

Shepherd turned to explain to Jejeune. "I have assured Señor Hidalgo that this will be receiving our top priority."

"The entire case, you mean, presumably?" confirmed Jejeune.

Shepherd looked momentarily puzzled. But Hidalgo got it. He straightened and acknowledged Jejeune's comment with an apologetic smile.

"Ah, yes, the poor young woman who died alongside Ramon."

"Phoebe Hunter," supplied Jejeune, just to emphasize that her name hadn't come up in the conversation to this point.

"You are quite right, Inspector. Given his diplomatic status, it is inevitable that Ramon's death will be the focus of attention, but we must make sure that this does not overshadow the other unfortunate victim. It would be wrong to imply this young lady is somehow less deserving of justice."

Not least because their deaths are almost certainly linked in some way, thought Jejeune. And it was clear from their troubled expressions that Hidalgo and Shepherd were now struggling with the same idea. Hidalgo had already turned to leave and was approaching Shepherd's door when Jejeune's question stopped him in his tracks.

"I was wondering, Counsellor, did Mr. Santos have any mobility problems? Trouble walking, for example, anything like that?"

Hidalgo's face clouded with puzzlement. He gave his head a short shake. "I don't believe so, no. The health of all consular staff is closely monitored. Such an infirmity may have affected Ramon's ability to perform his duties, so I would have been informed. To the best of my knowledge, Ramon was a fit and healthy young man. Is that important?"

Jejeune wasn't saying, but as the counsellor left her office, Shepherd already knew the answer. By the time Domenic Jejeune was ready to voice an idea out loud, he was long past the stage of dismissing it as irrelevant.

5

Jejeune craned his neck as he tracked the flight of a tightly packed flock of shorebirds heading north, out toward the coast. The bright morning sky backlit the birds, washing out any diagnostic markings, but a telltale call drifted down to him, definitive, unmistakable. He smiled. Yet, did it really matter? Was he really able to enjoy the sight more just because he knew they were Grey Plovers? The truth was, of course, that it was the spectacle of the fast-flying shorebirds itself that counted; a glorious vignette of the natural world that was enough to raise the spirits, to remind him of all the positives life held, all the possibilities for happiness and pleasure outside of this career.

Danny Maik shifted impatiently by the inspector's side. In truth, Jejeune doubted the identity of the birds mattered much to him, either. They were on one of Saltmarsh's older streets, lined on both sides with rows of houses with cars parked in front of them, two wheels up on the curb. Just ahead of them sat a new Jaguar F-Type, its flawless British racing green coachwork glinting in the morning light. For Jejeune, the number plate was as good as a sign pointing to the house: AVES. "This one, I believe," he said, mounting the steps and knocking on the door.

To Maik's jaundiced eye, David Nyce had just the kind of fading golden-boy looks that would have the female undergraduates swooning over their notebooks. His sharp features had a slight swell of age on them, and there were flecks of grey in the lavish, swept-back locks, but his tight, faded jeans and tailored denim shirt suggested he hadn't yet completely given up trying to be Saltmarsh's rock-star academic.

Nyce was on his mobile phone when he answered the door. He motioned them in as he continued his conversation and pointed them to a small study at the front of the house with a bay window overlooking the street. And the car.

"Yes, I have actually got a calendar of my own," he said into the phone with heavy sarcasm. "Know how to use it, too, order of the months and everything." He turned to wander away again and it gave the men a chance to look around the room. Nyce's desk was cluttered with papers and books, but there was still room for a couple of sumptuously appointed plaques bearing his name. Behind the desk, a built-in bookshelf was untidily jammed with various journals and reference books. Maik could see Nyce's name prominently displayed on the spines of a number of them. He couldn't really see the point himself. If you had authored the books in the first place, presumably you would already know any information that was in them.

Nyce wandered back in. "Well, how about this for an idea? You lot sit around staring at one another, and I'll send it over to you when it's ready." He curtly ended the call without waiting for a reply. "For God's sake, you'd think they were publishing a sequel to the Bible," he said with frustration, "rather than some obscure academic journal no one is going to read."

He took his seat behind the desk and motioned to a couple of empty chairs with an open palm. Maik took a seat, but, predictably, Jejeune declined, preferring to wander around the room and take in the view from the window. Maik recognized it as his cue to start proceedings.

"The reason we're here, Dr. Nyce, is because your name came up during our enquiries into the death of Phoebe Hunter. It was on an academic paper found in her room."

"Yes, I hardly thought you were calling as part of a scheme to canvas the whole of Saltmarsh at random, Sergeant," said Nyce impatiently. He began sorting distractedly through the papers on his desk. "But there's not much I can tell you about her, really. Parents gone, no sibs. A few old college friends scattered here and yon, I imagine." He paused and shook his head slowly, as if taking in for the first time the import of what he had just said. "Add that to no publications, a worthless degree, and a half-finished thesis, and it's not much of a legacy to leave for your twenty-four years on this planet, is it? Hardly seems worth the trouble of being here at all."

In Maik's experience, insensitivity was a common response to murder, perhaps a way some people found to deal with the numbing shock. But he got the impression that Nyce's off-handedness was no act. From the way Jejeune looked over from the bookshelf he was perusing, it was clear he found the academic's comments equally cold.

"Can you tell us the nature of your own relationship with Ms. Hunter?"

Nyce toyed with one of the plaques on his desk. "Relationship? Now there's an interesting choice of word, Sergeant. Perjorative, loaded with nuance. Right, well, my *relationship* with her was that of a thesis supervisor to a graduate student. As such, I effectively controlled the direction of her academic life. I reviewed her methodology, read and evaluated her findings, generally set her in the right direction whenever she wandered off track — which was fairly often."

It occurred to Maik that of all the people you would want controlling the direction of your life, academic or otherwise, David Nyce would probably be at the bottom of most people's lists. Danny had never been one to take an instant dislike to a person, but in Nyce's case, he imagined he could probably make an exception. Just what Jejeune thought about David Nyce wasn't immediately clear, since the inspector was still immersed in reading the spines of the books in Nyce's collection. Given that he was obviously not ready to ask any questions of his own just yet, Maik realized it was up to him to press on.

"What about Phoebe Hunter as a person?" Maik was hoping the use of the word might remind Nyce of the young woman of twenty-four whose life he had just so summarily dismissed.

Nyce shrugged. "Competent, though not overly so. Her mind was a bit all over the shop, to be frank. You've seen her place, I take it? The tiger stripes, the pastels, the patterns? Classic signs of someone who's never properly settled the question of who they intend to be in this world. That was Phoebs, though, ten directions at once, which is probably why she lacked the focus for real academic success."

"Can you tell me what she was researching, exactly?"

"Her exact area of research would be a bit abstruse for a non-specialist, I should imagine, but I can give you the Idiot's Guide version for the purposes of being able to fill out your copper's forms. Phoebe was attempting to identify the specific wintering grounds of the Turtledoves that arrive in north Norfolk in the spring."

"And she would do this through bird ringing?"

No wonder Jejeune flashed Maik a look. It wasn't like the sergeant to supply the answers himself when he was questioning somebody. Maik was angry with himself for falling into the trap of trying to justify that he was bright enough to be worthy of questioning Nyce. He returned Jejeune's look with one that told the DCI he should feel free to jump in at any time. After all, this *was* about birds.

"She couldn't rely on information from ringed birds, surely," said Jejeune. "It would be far too unpredictable. She could go entire monitoring seasons without ever netting a ringed Turtledove, let alone one from specific wintering grounds she had been monitoring."

"And a round of applause for the inspector," said Nyce. He leaned across the table toward Maik and nodded in Jejeune's direction, dropping his voice to a stage aside. "That's why he's the boss, you see." He leaned back in his chair, resting one foot on an open drawer. "Phoebe was using stable isotopes to track the birds. Hydrogen isotopes, or deuterium, to be more precise, come from the rainwater, carbon isotopes you get from the plants, and those of nitrogen from any fertilizers used in the area. Isotope levels vary and are quite specific to a location. Anything the birds eat contains these isotopes, so by recovering feathers from birds once they get here, and measuring the isotope levels, you can tell where the bird was when it was growing its feathers."

"As long as you have already identified the various isotope levels at their wintering sites," Jejeune added.

"Yes, Inspector, full marks again. There are numerous projects all over North America doing the same kind of thing: American Redstarts in Jamaica, for example. But Phoebe's was one of the first in that part of Africa. It was considerably more difficult, mega-probs with logistics, infrastructure, et cet."

Maik could understand a twonk like this having to play to an invisible audience, awarding marks and rounds of applause and such. Given the choice, most real people would doubtless give David Nyce a very wide berth indeed. "Any reason she would have chosen Turtledoves, specifically?" he asked, more to show he had recovered his composure than because he had any real interest in the answer. But Nyce flashed Jejeune a look, as if he thought someone as obviously interested in birds as the DCI might have already covered a topic this important in a case involving Turtledoves.

"Turtledove populations in the U.K. are going off a cliff, Sergeant. Reason enough for you? They've declined by about seventy-five percent in the past forty years. Here in Norfolk, we still see more than most places, but those heady days of fifty-strong flocks are long gone, I'm afraid. A sighting now is worthy of a note on the Norfolk birding websites."

"So Phoebe Hunter was doing important work, then?" asked Maik with the kind of emphasis designed to remind Nyce of her worth.

Nyce nodded reluctantly. "Inasmuch as it's certainly true to say that unless somebody does something, the extinction of Turtledoves in our lifetime is a very real possibility."

Maik must have looked dubious.

"Sad to say, we have let it happen before." Nyce looked at Jejeune. "Will you tell him, Inspector, or shall I?" He turned back to Maik. "There is a well-known report from the inspector's homeland. A single flock of Passenger Pigeons in southern Ontario took fourteen hours to pass overhead. Imagine it, Sergeant, fourteen hours, birds darkening the sky and filling the air with the thunder of their wing beats. One hundred and fifty years ago, the estimated North American population of Passenger Pigeons was three and a half billion. Would you care to hazard a guess at the population today?"

Even a card-carrying non-birder like Maik knew the answer to that one. For a moment the enormity of the loss seemed to grip all three men. The silence was finally broken by Jejeune.

"What will happen to Phoebe Hunter's research project now?" he asked, with that deceptive casualness that Maik had learned to pay attention to.

Nyce seemed surprised by the question. "Hard to say. For one thing, she left matters in a right old state — unfinished data sets, half-written papers, notes all over the place." He nodded at his phone lying on his desk. "That was her mess I was clearing up just now. For the time being, I suppose everything will be put into the deep freeze while we see if we can find someone else to take up the mantle." Nyce shook his head ruefully. "It's unlikely, to say the least. Pity really, given how much time we've already spent on this project."

So at least there is something about this whole affair that he finds regrettable, then, thought Maik with contempt. "Had Phobe Hunter been working on anything in particular since she returned to the U.K.?" he asked.

"Trying to arrange set-asides, mostly. Turtledoves feed mainly on weed seeds, but today's intensive farming methods don't leave much room for weeds, so she was asking the local farmers to set-aside portions of farmland as a food source for the doves."

"Why unlikely?" Jejeune's question seemed so impulsive, both Nyce and Maik turned to look at him. "You said it's unlikely you'll find someone to take the project on?"

Nyce leaned back and ran his fingers through his hair, locking them behind his head. "It would require an unusual suite of skills: post-grad in conservation biology, a solid understanding of bird behaviour, plus, of course, the intellectual wherewithal to put it all together."

From what Maik could remember, it sounded like Nyce was reading extracts from Jejeune's CV, but the DCI offered no response beyond a look of interest that had been noticeably absent during the rest of the interview.

"I take it those papers from Phoebe's flat will be released sooner rather than later?" Nyce challenged Maik with a stare. "I'm just worried some idiot down at the station will file them under *D* for documents or some such and that'll be the last we'll ever see of them."

"If they're important, they usually go under *I*," said Maik.

Nyce tried a smile, but he was long out of practice, and it looked forced and awkward. He turned to Jejeune. "Beware of this one, Inspector. We come across them at the uni every now and again. No time for us clever clogs with our book-learnin' and such. Prefer their own brand of home-spun wisdom, born of experience in the real-world. Am I right, Sergeant?" Nyce smiled again to show it was all nice and playful. He rose from behind the desk. "Now, if that's all …"

"I wonder," said Jejeune, stepping firmly on Nyce's attempt to bring the interview to a close, "is there any specific identifier that researchers might use to tell Turtledoves apart? House Sparrows have those black bibs, for example, but I'm not aware of anything like that with Turtledoves."

Nyce nodded slowly. "Ah, those black bibs, *varying in size according to a sparrow's rank within the flock, thus making individual birds easily identifiable.*" Nyce seemed to be reciting something from memory. "Field observer's dream, those bibs are. With Turtledoves…?" He shook his head. "There's hardly any variation in the plumage at all. Size possibly, in males, but generally, assuming they haven't picked up any distinguishing features — missing eyes, broken toes — Turtledoves are more or less physically homogenous. Means they all look the same," Nyce confided in the same stage aside for Maik's benefit. He checked his watch. "Look, I really have to get on with some work here. If there is anything further, perhaps an email might suffice?"

Nyce walked them to the door and opened it for them. The detectives paused on the top step for another appreciative look at the Jaguar. "Writing the definitive university text on *Con Bio* does have its benefits," said Nyce, affecting a modesty that was rusty with lack of use.

"Interesting number plate, that," said Maik.

"AVES? It's Latin for birds. I take it you don't share your boss's obvious interest."

"More of an *'ave not*, truth be told," said Maik dryly.

The two detectives left Nyce on the top step and walked away from the house in silence.

They were some way along the street before Jejeune finally spoke. "Tell me, Sergeant," he said quietly, "how many female graduate students do you imagine Dr. Nyce has supervised over the years?"

"Pretty boy, recognized authority in his field and a celebrated author to boot? Dozens, I should imagine. They would seek him out in droves." Maik paused for a moment on the pavement and smiled to himself. "And now you're going to ask me for how many of those would he be able to tell us the colour of their bedroom walls."

Jejeune smiled. There was apparently something to be said for home-spun wisdom, after all. He looked across at his sergeant. Danny Maik didn't seem to be suffering any lasting wounds from the good doctor's antagonism. Like Jejeune, he would have already recognized that if you could get a couple of coppers looking at each other, they might just forget to focus on you.

6

Jejeune was sitting at his desk in the study, staring intently at his computer screen, when Lindy came in.

"I trust that's not porn," she said. She came around behind him and saw a grainy picture of rock-strewn ground displayed on the screen.

"It's a live feed from one of the cameras Phoebe Hunter set up in Burkina Faso to monitor Turtledoves. I did just see a couple of Bronze Munias mating, though," conceded Domenic, "if that counts."

"Pornithology, maybe?" said Lindy. She leaned in over Domenic's shoulder, the scent of that wonderfully fragrant shampoo she used hovering between them. "It looks like a pretty desolate place. She must have really loved her work to put up with conditions like those."

"She seems to have thought about little else." Jejeune waved a few sheets of paper from his desk. "She logged over seven hundred hours of research time during her last eight-week spell over there. That's more than twelve hours a day, seven days a week."

Lindy drew back and shot him a glance. Lindy had seen his modus operandi on enough investigations to recognize that his interest in Phoebe's efforts was going far beyond his usual thoroughness. Checks of what he called the "background noise" were part of what had earned Jejeune his reputation. Armed with the small details of the person's life, Domenic had more permutations to try, more information to fit into his theories, as he tried to piece together the larger picture. But it never took him this long to review one aspect of a victim's background. His interest in Phoebe Hunter's research was about something more than merely finding a reason for her murder. Lindy suspected that she knew what that might be, and if she was right, she knew that Domenic's scrutiny of Phoebe Hunter's research methodology was a long way from being over.

"Fancy a walk before dinner?"

They often went for an early evening stroll along the bluffs near their cottage, but it was usually Domenic who proposed it, when he had finished work for the day. It might just have crossed the mind of a Domenic Jejeune less absorbed in Phoebe Hunter's field notes, too, that there was a forced casualness to Lindy's sudden suggestion.

By the time he pushed his chair back from the computer and stood up, arching his back to relieve the stress, Lindy was already waiting at the door, wearing a light cardigan.

They walked slowly along the path, side by side, shoulders occasionally touching like boats bobbing on gentle swells, both immersed in their own thoughts. Along the edges of the narrow clifftop path, small knots of early spring flowers, common daisies and yellow hop trefoils, poked their heads tentatively between the pale tussocks of grass. It would be a while yet before Lindy's favourites, the sea pinks — *thrift* as the locals called them — emerged. Out over the sea, the call of a Kittiwake pealed through the soft evening air.

"You never mentioned how the migration watch went the other day," said Lindy. "I usually get chapter and verse but this time, not a dicky bird. *Word*, Dom," she offered to Jejeune's puzzled expression. "Rhyming slang. Remember, your crash course with Robin?"

"Ah." Jejeune and Lindy had hosted a dinner recently for Robin and Melissa, friends of Lindy's from college. Robin was an affable East Ender who had delighted in introducing Jejeune to the colourful world of cockney rhyming slang. But *dicky bird*, for *word*, hadn't been among the lessons. Jejeune was pretty sure he would have remembered that one.

"So? How was it?"

"Wonderful," said Jejeune simply.

Lindy knew that Domenic chose his adjectives carefully, and he was using this one in the literal sense: full of wonder. Wonder at the swirling flocks of birds flying by, at the thought of the vast distances they had travelled — from Africa and beyond — and at the mechanisms of nature that set them on their way, and guided them, in ways that humans could, even now, only barely understand. How much more wonderful, then, might it be for someone with Domenic's interest in birds to study them on a full-time basis? To continue the research that Phoebe Hunter had been working on when she died? Lindy knew Phoebe Hunter's project represented everything Domenic would have wanted to do, in another life. She couldn't imagine he was seriously considering pursuing it now, but when you were as unsettled in your career as Domenic Jejeune was, even dreams could be dangerous.

"Where did you go?" asked Lindy, more to drive away other, more troubling thoughts than because she had any real interest. "Did you take that same stretch of the coastal path you usually do?"

Jejeune nodded "Burnham Overy to Brancaster Staithe, and then inland to the Downs."

Lindy shook her head. "Blimey, Robert Frost wouldn't have made much of a birder, would he? No road less travelled with you lot. Why do birders always follow the same route when they go somewhere?"

Jejeune hadn't really thought about it, but as usual there was some truth to Lindy's observation. He shrugged. "There's always a temptation to try a new path when you go to a place you've been before, but there's a pull, a tension that seems to drag you to the places you've already had success. Birders can remember the exact tree, the exact branch where they saw a good bird. If you saw it there once ..."

"You see a bird on a twig and then five years later you expect the same bird to reappear in the same spot? You know you birders are all mad, right? The lot of you. Certifiable."

Jejeune smiled at Lindy's exasperated expression and raised his binoculars to watch the Kittiwake carving the air with its graceful, effortless glide. Once, he would have automatically announced what the bird was, but he had stopped doing that lately. Perhaps he was waiting for Lindy to ask, or perhaps he had simply come to terms with the fact that it really didn't matter to her.

Lindy began walking slowly along the path again, head down, as if measuring her progress. Domenic fell in beside her.

"Melissa says there are some pretty good deals to St. Lucia coming up," she said with studied nonchalance. "They have endemics there, birds not found anywhere else."

"That's my definition of endemics, too," said Jejeune guardedly. The demands of their respective careers meant that holidays required some advance planning, and Lindy had made no secret of the fact that she had already started the process. Apart from being cockney Robin's better half, Melissa was also, by the strangest of coincidences, a travel agent.

"I know that friend of yours from college is down there. The one with the strange name. I thought it might be nice for you to see him again." Lindy tried one of her smiles on him, but Jejeune's initial caginess had been replaced now by something else she couldn't quite identify. For a man who supposedly wasn't exactly in love with his job, it could be remarkably difficult sometimes to get him to consider taking a break from it. But this time, there seemed to be even more resistance than usual. All she knew was the destination had suddenly become a little more distant.

"C'mon Dom, it would be nice to go somewhere warm."

"It's warming up here," said Jejeune.

"It's spring in north Norfolk, which means it's slightly less cold and grey than winter in north Norfolk. I'm talking about proper sunshine. Caribbean sunshine."

Jejeune shook his head slightly. "There's a lot going on right now. Maybe we could talk about this later?"

It sounded like a reasonable enough request, unless you knew Domenic Jejeune. Then you realized this was about as close as his Canadian politeness ever came to letting him slam the door on an idea completely. Lindy drew the cardigan around her and turned to stare out to sea, letting the breeze tousle her hair.

"Well, just promise me you'll think about it, when you've finished with this case." She turned to him. "Do you really think it's about somebody wanting to steal a few doves?"

A while ago, she might have phrased it differently; told him how preposterous the idea was, how ridiculous. But Domenic had posited other unlikely birding connections in another case, and they had proven to be eerily accurate. That knowledge stopped her now from being too quick to disregard what seemed, on the face of it, a ludicrous theory. She suspected it would stop a lot of other people, too.

"It's called a pitying," said Jejeune. "A pitying of doves. And yes, I think it's related."

"But you don't think it was this woman, Maggie Wylde?"

Jejeune shook his head slowly. "No."

Lindy sighed. This was how things were now. Dom would tell her just enough so that they could chat about the case, bounce around a few ideas, but she wasn't going to be privy to all the details. It had been different once, when they first met, and she was reporting on his investigation into what had come to be known as the *Home Sec's Daughter Case*. But once he had gotten — they both had gotten — their big breaks, things had changed. He had been promoted, she had taken another job, and they had hashed out a new set of rules of engagement over laughter and spaghetti and a couple of bottles of Chianti on the back porch. And chief among those new rules was that she wouldn't ask anymore, and he wouldn't tell. Suspects, lines of enquiry, the internal workings of Domenic Jejeune's labyrinthine mind — all off limits until he had solved the case. And even for the celebrated Chief Inspector Jejeune, the evening of the third day was a bit early for that.

"She did call, though, this woman, and accuse the sanctuary of having her birds. Perhaps it could just be as easy as it looks for once," said Lindy reasonably.

"Occam's razor?"

Lindy's look of surprise seemed to please Jejeune. He recounted Salter's reference at the sanctuary. Lindy arched an eyebrow. "My, my, if the North Norfolk Constabulary keeps indulging in heuristics, they're going to do irreversible damage to my notion of the thick local copper. Come on, dinner will be ready."

They turned to begin making their way back along the path to the cottage, crunching up the gravel to the porch, where the storm lantern bounced in the freshening breeze and the wind chimes dripped their music into the evening air. They paused for a moment, looking out over the water. An afternoon rainstorm had rolled out toward the horizon, leaving the sky a mottled mosaic of Monet shades, a blue-grey ephemera shot through with shafts of light. Lindy smiled. If anything would keep Dom from trekking to Africa to measure isotopes in bird feathers, it would be this: these skies, this sea, the glorious unfettered openness of the north Norfolk coastline. And the birds.

"I'm sure you'll solve this case soon," she said. "I mean, if it wasn't this Maggie Wylde person, there can't possibly be that many other people who would be interested in stealing Turtledoves from a shelter, can there?"

"No," said Jejeune. He paused, as if hesitant to give further voice to his thoughts, even out here, where only nature and his partner could hear. "But I think there were at least two."

7

Whether by design or happenstance, the incident room at the Saltmarsh police station was at the opposite end of the corridor from DCS Shepherd's office — far enough away that the occupants could usually hear the early warning system of the DCS's heels power-walking their way toward them. But today, Shepherd wasn't here to check up on them. She was on tour guide duty, marching her charge through the facilities herself, solicitous hand on elbow, while she rhapsodized over her team and the latest technological advancements that had allowed her station to become one of the most forward-thinking and innovative in the country.

Her audience of one was a tall man, lean and fit, with quick eyes. He seemed to know instinctively when to express a keen interest and where a bright smile of appreciation would do.

Danny Maik was standing in his customary position at the front of the room, conducting a survey of the progress on the case, when the door opened. To say that the interruption took him off guard would be no small understatement.

"You wouldn't know it," said Shepherd, "but the man perched on the desk at the back is actually the one in charge here. Chief Inspector Domenic Jejeune, this is Guy Trueman. Guy is head of external security for the Mexican Consulate. Señor Hidalgo has asked him to act as liaison, get us what we need in terms of information."

Jejeune crossed the floor quickly and shook the man's hand. He was immediately drawn to Trueman's easy self-assurance and warm smile. But no amount of warmth was going to completely disguise the man's steel core.

Shepherd turned toward Maik and extended an open palm, "And I understand you already know …"

"Danny Maik," supplied Trueman. "Yes, DCS, the sergeant and I are well acquainted. Aren't we, Danny?"

He gripped Maik's extended hand warmly, resting his other hand on the sergeant's elbow. Between other men, the greeting might have morphed into a shoulder hug, but even if the group did not yet know Guy Trueman, they were familiar enough with Danny Maik to know it was unlikely, to say the least. Nevertheless, it was clear that the sergeant was genuinely pleased to see Trueman, and the onlookers were treated to the rare sight of a sincere Danny Maik smile as he turned to address them.

"Major Trueman was my commanding officer," he said. "I count myself lucky to have served under him."

"You know, the first time I saw this man, he was up before me on charges," announced Trueman to the room at large. "Insubordination, of all things."

"Please do go on," said Shepherd. Like many in the room, she was enjoying this momentary peek into the sergeant's guarded past. It was rare to find Danny Maik in any kind of revealing situation, and she was keen to exploit the moment.

"About that Latin quote, wasn't it, Danny. Remember?"

"Dulce et decorum est, Pro patria mori," said Maik. "It is a sweet and noble thing to die for one's homeland." If he had to be reminiscing about this incident at all, his look seemed to say, about the last place he wanted to do it was in front of his fellow police officers. But Trueman was clearly a man comfortable on the big stage,

and Maik had apparently decided, with an effort of will that was almost visible, that the best way to get this over with was to try to enter into the spirit of the thing as much as his dignity would allow.

Trueman nodded. "It was a favourite of Danny's old staff sergeant," he told the audience. "He used to greet all the new recruits with it. Only this time, Danny insisted on adding his own bit — 'But it is sweeter to live for the homeland, and sweetest to drink for it. Therefore, let us drink to the homeland instead.'"

Maik shrugged. "It's from an old drinking toast. I just didn't want the kids thinking it was okay to go off and get themselves killed just because some Roman poet said so." He was clearly uncomfortable being reminded that he had ever shown anything approaching disloyalty toward a superior officer, and everyone in the room realized that it would have to be a formidable individual indeed who had earned Maik's respect to the point where he would allow them to take such liberties as this.

"So there he is before me," said Trueman, "and I'm thinking to myself, 'I'm supposed to discipline the man. Trouble is, they tell me he's one of the best soldiers in the unit, and what's more, I agree with him.'"

"So what did you do?" asked Shepherd. She turned to Maik, but he left Trueman to supply the answer himself.

"Issued a blanket ban on quoting classical literature on base," announced Trueman, "and as a punishment, I set Sergeant Maik the task of having the men in the unit write their own poems about army life. We read them out loud to each other in my office over a couple of beers. Remember, Danny? Laughed till the tears rolled down our cheeks."

The two men drifted to a place of memories from which the others were excluded until Trueman brought them back to the present brightly. "Sergeant Danny Maik," he said, as if he could not quite believe it. "Still driving everybody mad with that Motown music of yours, I suppose."

"Night and day," confirmed Tony Holland from the front row, emboldened by the casual familiarity of the moment to add a theatrical eye roll.

"Right," said Shepherd in a way that was designed to suggest to one and all that, nice as Danny's reunion with his old army comrade had been, it was time to get down to business again. "Perhaps you can bring us all up to speed, Sergeant."

Jejeune's wasn't the only face to express surprise at Shepherd's willingness to discuss the case in front of their guest. They all understood her obvious desire to show they were making progress, but when the consulate's liaison officer was getting information at the same time as the investigating officers, it might be time to point out that it was supposed to be the consulate sharing information with the police, rather than the other way around.

"There seem to be four possible scenarios," began Maik tentatively, flicking a glance in Jejeune's direction as if to say, *that suggest themselves to us mere mortals, at least.* But if Jejeune, now perched impassively on the desk at the back of the room again, had at first appeared set to make a contribution, he seemed to think better of it. Maik took a heartbeat to register Jejeune's expression and moved on. "The first possibility is that it was a burglary gone wrong. The victims stumbled in and it all went haywire from there. Second is that the girl, Phoebe Hunter, was the target and Santos was just an unlucky witness who had to be dealt with. Killed," he corrected himself. "Third, vice versa, and number four," Maik paused significantly, "is that someone went there with the intention of killing them both. So far, we've found no evidence of any connection between the victims, and nothing to suggest anybody even knew Santos was going to be at the sanctuary, so we're concentrating on the first two theories, that either it was a burglary, or it was Phoebe Hunter the killer was after, especially since we have a suspect calling to threaten her the day before."

Like the others, Lauren Salter had picked up on the inspector's reluctance to discuss matters of evidence in front of an outsider. But this particular outsider was held in high esteem by Danny Maik, and that was good enough for her.

"There's a fingerprint and a partial palm print on the filing cabinet that don't match any of the others in the sanctuary. The thing is, they could belong to Maggie Wylde. Her prints aren't on file with us."

Shepherd pinned Jejeune with a look that seemed to ask just when he was planning on getting around to telling them his views on that theory. "I believe the inspector has some misgivings about Margaret Wylde as a suspect," she said.

The silence of disapproval is perhaps the most eloquent silence of all. Jejeune's audience looked at one another uneasily. Maggie had disappeared immediately after the crime, and they all knew that sudden flight was about as clear a sign of guilt as you were likely to get in the early stages of a murder inquiry. And that was without even considering the fact that she had called and threatened one of the victims the day before the murder.

Unable to avoid discussing it in front of Trueman without appearing to have something to hide, Jejeune went over the same ideas he had expressed in Shepherd's office. He had barely finished speaking before Salter rushed in.

"Sir, with respect, you don't know Maggie. It would be just like her to do a bit of tidying up afterward, locking the cages and such." She looked around the room, seeking support for her claims.

"It isn't just that," said Jejeune carefully. He drew a breath, as if readying himself for an inevitable battle. "The records indicate there were thirteen doves at the sanctuary, in six different cages. The cage from which the two doves were taken, the one where the bodies were found, was at the far end of the corridor. I think whoever took the doves targeted the ones in that cage specifically."

"Surely that points even more squarely at Maggie," said Salter, still aggressively defending her ground.

"The problem is," said Jejeune, "BTO confirmed none of the birds at the sanctuary were banded."

Salter and the others looked puzzled, but off to Jejeune's side, Maik slowly nodded his head. "And according to David Nyce, Turtledoves have no distinguishing features."

"So?" Salter was louder now, belligerent, not least because she was aware that she was missing the point, and doing so in front of her DCS and Maik's old army pal.

"So how could Maggie have known which ones were hers?" asked Maik reasonably. "You've seen those birds, Constable. Could you tell one from the other?"

"So she just grabbed a couple of birds, any birds." Salter's tone was strident, her frustration increasing to the point that it now threatened to get the better of her judgment.

"Then why go all the way to the end of the corridor instead of just taking the pair nearest the door?" asked Jejeune.

He seemed to be completely unaware of the effect each blithe rebuttal was having on Salter. *This is the downside of Jejeune's detachment,* thought Shepherd, *his inability to see, no, to appreciate the passion that cases sometimes aroused in others — like detective constables who felt that by ignoring a young girl's telephone call, they were somehow responsible for her death.* To Jejeune, Salter's objections were just academic problems, to be considered and answered. He didn't seem to understand that Salter *wanted* it to be Maggie, *needed* it to be, so that by bringing her to justice, she could somehow absolve herself of her error and gain her own forgiveness. Most of the people in the room could have told her things didn't necessarily work like that, but Constable Salter didn't seem to be in any mood to listen to this, or any other, counsel.

"Maggie Wylde was involved. I know it."

Her certainty seemed to cut through the anger, the frustration, so much so that Maik finally stirred.

"And how might you know a thing like that, Constable?" he asked calmly.

She spun the computer monitor on her desk around toward the room. "Because her old man worked for the Obregóns, that's how." She stood up and turned on Jejeune. "Unless you want to try to *clever* us all out of that, too." she said. "So if nobody minds, perhaps I'll just get on with the job of finding her."

When the eyes in the room returned from watching Salter's angry exit, they fell universally upon Shepherd. Those used to dealing with the DCS on a regular basis might have noted the slight tensing of her frame and the working of her jaw muscle, but her outward appearance otherwise gave nothing away. Her voice, too, when it came, was as light as a spring breeze, and betrayed no trace of any internal agitation she might have been feeling.

"It's a stretch," she said carefully, "but we can have a look into it. Sergeant, perhaps you can fill the inspector in on the details. In the meantime, we must be getting on. I am taking Guy for a bite to eat at The Boatman's Arms, but you know what that place is like. If we don't beat the lunchtime crowd, we'll be waiting an hour to get a table. Ready, Guy?"

She ushered Trueman from the room with undisguised haste.

As soon as they had left, Holland looked around the room. "Blimey, what's up with her? I've whipped suspects off to the cells with more ceremony than that. I half-expected her to put her hand on his collar next."

Jejeune, too, had watched the hurried departure with interest, no doubt putting Shepherd's discomfort down to the fact that all the disharmony had been played out in front of their visitor. But Sergeant Maik knew differently.

"Victor Obregón was a prominent local resident," he told Jejeune cautiously. "He went missing, be about eight years ago now. Left a wife and a son. No signs of foul play; a walk-off, we think. Among the things he left behind, in addition to his family, was the largest private bird aviary in north Norfolk."

"I see," said Jejeune. But Maik knew he didn't. Not the whole picture, anyway.

"The thing is," said Holland, enjoying Jejeune's obvious incomprehension, "the name Obregón, sir, it's Mexican. They're Mexican nationals."

Jejeune nodded his head thoughtfully. "I see," he said again. And this time, both Maik and Holland were fairly sure that he did.

8

L indy looked up from the bird guide resting on her lap. "You know, I've seen Turtledoves lots of times, but until you study them closely you don't realize what a lovely shade of pink that is on their chests. I'm thinking that would look good in our living room."

Jejeune allowed himself a small head shake and resumed his scan of the passing countryside. They were in his Land Rover, nicknamed The Beast, and he had been using the extra height to peer over the hedgerows into the fields. He, too, enjoyed the beauty of Turtledoves, but more as a welcome sign of spring than as an animated paint chip for the living-room wall.

The landscape was bathed in the subtle shadows of early morning, and the tangled hedgerows were alive with bird activity on both sides of the narrow lane. Jejeune particularly loved this time of year for the promise it held; a new season, new migrants arriving daily, and always, always in north Norfolk, the possibility of a rarity — a Mediterranean overshoot, perhaps, or a vagrant driven inland by the erratic North Sea winds. Add to this a country drive with Lindy by his side, albeit a Lindy in spring decorating mode, and the opportunity to chat to a seriously fine woodcarver and birding expert once he reached his destination, and life on this soft spring morning seemed about as perfect as it could get for Domenic Jejeune. As long as you ignored the fact that the reason for his visit was to further his enquiries into a horrific double murder.

Lindy riffled through the book. "Santos made pretty detailed notes. I suppose that's what makes you think he's a good birder?"

"Partly, but it's more *what* he notes. Chiffchaff and Willow Warbler, for example, in the same place, on the same date. Those two are virtually inseparable in the field. The only sure way to tell them apart is by their calls. And if he was birding by ear, I'd say that takes him out of the realm of a novice."

"Unless he was just trying to convince himself they were different species. You know, just to pad his list," said Lindy.

Jejeune shook his head. "I doubt it. People deceive themselves in a lot of ways, but they rarely lie to themselves in print, I find."

Lindy considered it for a while. "Fair point, I suppose, but if he's such a good birder, why did he need a book to identify a Turtledove at the shelter? Even I could do that one."

Jejeune inclined his head. "Another fair point. Let's find out if Carrie Pritchard has any ideas." He wheeled the Land Rover into a driveway half-hidden by a clump of gorse.

"And I thought you only came out here to look at her bird carvings," said Lindy. But she didn't smile. She, too, had not forgotten the real reason for their visit.

At the far end of the rutted track was a small cottage that appeared from this distance to be perched on the edge of the world. The building was surrounded on three sides by low, flat land, across which the views seemed to go on forever. On the far side of the dwelling, the land fell away to a wide estuary that sloped gently out toward the sea. There was not another building or man-made structure anywhere in sight. Lindy knew that Domenic loved their own home, an older cottage overlooking a rock-strewn bay farther south, but as Jejeune wheeled The Beast to a stop, she knew that this place would be a strong contender for his second choice.

Carrie Pritchard was standing by the side of the house and waved them over. She had apparently tracked their approach along the long driveway. "Domenic, how nice to see you again. No trouble finding me, then, out here on the edge of civilization? And you must be Lindy. I'm Carrie," she said, resting a delicate hand against the binoculars on her chest. "I was planning to show you around the studio, but I hear there may be some interesting visitors coming this way. In numbers."

While Domenic returned to The Beast to retrieve his own bins, Lindy took the opportunity to cast a quick eye over Pritchard. Her mid-length blonde hair was tied back in a simple ponytail. She wore no make-up at all, beyond the natural rouge bestowed by the elements on those who spent their time outdoors in these parts. Nor did her outfit — a loose, billowy blouse and simple belted peasant skirt — lend her willowy frame any particular glamour. But she possessed an indefinable inner sensuality, and she carried it with such casual elegance that Lindy knew Carrie Pritchard would rarely want for male company when she sought it.

When Jejeune rejoined them, the party descended a stony path toward the shore, coming to rest behind a small stand of gorse that served as both a windbreak and hide. Out on the horizon, a low bank of cloud was gathering. The onshore breeze brought the promise of change to the soft, bright morning they were now enjoying.

"If this is what I think it is, it's going to be worth waiting for," whispered Jejeune to Lindy, his voice taut with anticipation. And then, as if from nowhere, it was there, high and fast, mid-point between the shore and the horizon and heading toward land.

"What is that?" asked Lindy. "Smoke? Rain?"

"Knots," said Pritchard, snapping up her binoculars to follow the swirling, dipping flock. "I only get the dregs in this estuary, of course, a few hundred at most. Snettisham gets the best shows. I have seen flocks of forty thousand up there at times. If there is a more breathtaking spectacle in birdwatching, I would be hard pressed to come up with it."

Binoculars raised, she and Jejeune watched for a while in silence as the birds switched and swooped over the water in a mesmerizing ballet of precision and complexity. Lindy, too, watched them, their silvery forms highlighted against the gathering bank of dark clouds approaching from the horizon. The storm, when it came, was going to be a good one. With a final flourish, the Knots banked and descended on the muddy shore, coming to rest like the gentle pattering of raindrops.

"Watch them now," said Carrie without lowering her bins. "They will work this shoreline like a military operation. They're fuelling up, you see, for their trip up to their breeding grounds."

On cue, the birds began a measured, methodical march along the muddy flats. Jejeune and Pritchard watched in quiet rapture, eyes glued to their binoculars.

"Such incredible numbers here," said Jejeune, "and yet in North America the *rufa* subspecies is under such threat."

Pritchard nodded. "Yes. A predictable pattern. Horseshoe crabs become vital to the medical profession and the subsequent overharvesting leaves no crabs' eggs for the birds. The irony is, of course, that humans need healthy horseshoe crab populations every bit as much as Red Knots do." She shook her head sadly. "Everything is so interconnected, and yet so often we poor humans fail to realize it."

Not Dom, thought Lindy. *He sees those interconnections. It's his job to see them, those tendrils that tie our lives together. To see them, and unravel them, to follow them wherever they lead. Especially when they lead to murder.*

She watched them now, these strangers, united by their passion for birding, leaving her alone to seek the bleak consolation of this windswept landscape. "What is the collective noun for Knots, I wonder?" she asked of no one in particular. "A tangle, maybe? Or how about a rate?"

Pritchard lowered her glasses and smiled. "A rate of Knots. Oh, well done, Lindy. That's very good."

Behind the birds, the grey hue was deepening in the cloudbank on the horizon.

"How about a cloud?" Jejeune suggested.

Pritchard turned to look at him. "Yes, Inspector, a cloud. A cloud of Knots. Perfect."

Lindy noticed the delicate resting of the other woman's fingertips on his forearm, even if Domenic appeared not to.

Jejeune and Pritchard continued to watch the birds as they probed and prodded the mudflats for food. Lindy sat nearby chewing a stalk of grass, knees gathered to her chest, only occasionally glancing out over the estuary. Eventually, Jejeune lowered his binoculars and shifted his body position to face Pritchard.

"As the chair of the board of trustees of the sanctuary, you were, in effect, Phoebe Hunter's landlord. Did you know her well?"

Pritchard shook her head. "Hardly at all. I rarely go there myself, but since it was part of the original plan to have the project's researcher use the sanctuary's facilities whenever they were back in the U.K., I made it clear to David that I would need some input into the selection process. That quickly morphed into my conducting first interviews. David doesn't really enjoy the HR side of things. People aren't really his strong suit. Anyway, from his shortlist of potential candidates, I recommended Phoebe, and he accepted her without a second glance. After that, I had very little to do with her."

"And nothing came up when you were interviewing her?" asked Jejeune. He raised his binoculars to check on the Knots once more.

"No red flags that I remember," said Pritchard. "Phoebe struck me as being somewhat, well, unassuming at the interview, but since then I've heard she could be quite a force of nature when she wanted something. This business with the set-asides, for example. I'm quite sure it never would have gotten as far as it did without her relentless efforts. David will miss her tremendously, of course. In so many ways. I know he was quite taken with Phoebe Hunter. Quite taken."

"It didn't seem that way," said Jejeune.

"Ah, that's David, you see. He is…, well, let's just say he's a very complex individual. He's not particularly good at sharing his emotions."

"I think the phrase you're looking for is 'He's a man,'" said Lindy, earning a soft smile from Pritchard.

"You seem to know David Nyce quite well." The abruptness of Jejeune's question suggested he had already recognized that there wasn't really any way to disguise its implications.

"We used to see quite a lot of each other at one time." Pritchard curled a strand of hair behind her ear with an elegant finger. "Oh, they're up," she said suddenly.

The Knots had lifted as one, alarmed by some invisible threat, and Pritchard and Jejeune watched as the birds circled in unison and began a slow, majestic sweep out over the estuary, heading north. "Possibly the last good numbers of them I will see until autumn," said Pritchard wistfully, almost to herself.

With the departure of the birds, the estuary took on a forlorn emptiness, and the small party scrambled back up the bank.

As they emerged at the top, a thought seemed to strike Jejeune. "I imagine your involvement with the sanctuary brings you into contact with the owners of the Obregón aviary every now and again," he said. "It's now run by Ms. Obregón, I believe?"

Pritchard stiffened. Behind her, the skies over the estuary had started to darken as the storm rolled still closer. It struck

Lindy that the scene was not a million miles from the expression on the Pritchard's face.

"I'm afraid I can't help you, Inspector," she said coldly. "I barely know the woman, and I've certainly never been permitted to visit her aviary. We hardly have very much in common, after all. The ultimate goal of the Free to Fly program is to ensure wild birds remain exactly that. Other than the Turtledoves Phoebe Hunter kept for her research purposes, we cage birds only so they can recover from injuries or other trauma and be released back into the wild. Luisa Obregón is a collector, nothing more. People like that are interested only in possessions. It could be cars, watches, wine," continued Pritchard. "In Luisa Obregón's case, it happens to be birds."

Lindy noticed that Dom was paying particular attention. Mention possessions and you were halfway toward a motive for murder.

"The rumour was that there was a shopping list," continued Pritchard. "Luisa Obregón let it be known that she would be interested in acquiring any of the species on it. Beyond that, I know nothing about her. Nor do I particularly wish to."

Jejeune used the awkward silence that followed Pritchard's comments to offer his thanks one more time. The promised trip to her studio hadn't materialized, and Lindy was under no illusions that it would now. She and Domenic climbed into the Range Rover and drove off, leaving their hostess staring out at the now empty mudflats and the coming storm.

The Beast had negotiated most of the rutted drive before Lindy broke the silence. "Blimey, Dom. You don't want to get on the wrong side of that one. From Miss Congeniality to Madame Defarge in the blink of a mascara-less eye. And if she can get that kind of a hate on for a woman she barely knows, can you imagine what she'd be like if she had a genuine reason for disliking somebody?" *Like a manipulative twenty-four-year-old post-graduate competitor for David Nyce's affections, for example,* Lindy didn't say. She didn't need to. She knew a detective as bright as Domenic was perfectly capable of getting there all by himself.

9

"And if you could avoid dropping us in it with the DCS this time, it would be greatly appreciated." Tony Holland set a mug of tea on Salter's desk and resumed his seat without further eye contact.

"It's a lead, Tony. Can I help it if Obregón was a bloody Mexican?" As much as anything, Salter was annoyed about the way Holland was carrying on, as if he had understood the situation all along, when really, until Maik had walked them both through the potential ramifications of Salter's announcement, Tony Holland had been as clueless about the whole thing as she was.

Jejeune had already left the incident room by the time Danny Maik delivered his considered wisdom on the subject; the sergeant clearly not deeming it necessary to include the inspector in his explanation. "It's got a nasty feel to it, looking at other Mexicans, especially before we've even explored any other leads. Like we're suggesting this is a problem between foreigners, and we'd rather wash our hands of it." Maik spread his hands. "At least, the DCS is concerned that's how the Mexican Consulate will see it, if it gets back to them."

And so, by the time Shepherd returned from her lunch at The Boatman's Arms to deliver her fire and brimstone state of the union, pointing out that, while they may indeed follow the Obregón link, they would have to tread very carefully indeed, or risk this blowing up into a major diplomatic incident, Tony was already nodding knowingly as if to say, *I'm glad somebody is finally pointing out the facts of life to this poor naïf sitting beside me.* And when the time came for the DCS to conclude her address by driving home her point with her customary sledgehammer subtlety that there was to be no discussion about Mexican suspects within earshot of the public, the media, or other interested parties, *for which please read Mr. Guy Trueman*, she didn't need to say, the suitably chastened Constable Salter felt about as isolated and alone as she had ever felt in this department.

"So where's DCI Twitcher, then?" asked Holland, sipping his tea. "Morning briefings beneath him now, are they?"

Maik was standing at the front of the room holding a sheet of paper, ready to begin the meeting whenever the DCI arrived. He checked a chunky wristwatch. "The briefing is not due to start for another couple of minutes. Detective Chief Inspector Jejeune, as he is to you, will be here. Anybody hear how his interview with Carrie Pritchard went? Did he get anything interesting?"

"Possibly more than he bargained for," said Salter archly, "if the rumours about her are true."

"Carrie Pritchard? The woman who does those bird carvings?" asked Holland, stirring with interest. "Perhaps I should interview her next time. We seem to have this connection, older women and me. The last one I was with kept saying how much more stimulating my company was compared to the crowd she usually hung around with."

"Really?" said Salter. "What was her name, Jane Goodall?"

Maik looked like he was already about to put an end to any further discussions about Tony Holland's cross-generational conquests when the entrance of Jejeune and DCS Shepherd abruptly did it for him. He recognized Shepherd's presence here as evidence of her agitation; a sign that she couldn't leave them alone to get on with things. As was the fact that she had gone to the trouble of getting advance copies of the medical examiner's report.

"The ME found something interesting, I see," she said, nodding at the sheet in Maik's hand. "A puncture wound in Santos's neck?"

"From a large-bore syringe, they think," said Maik. "The wound was hidden by the collar of his sweater, which is why the officers on the scene missed it."

Shepherd made a face that suggested that this did not in any way mean she would be exonerating them for this oversight. "Embolism to the brain," she said, "a nasty way to go."

Both she and Maik waited for some sort of response from Jejeune, who was standing beside them reading the ME's report for himself. But he apparently had nothing to say. He really could seem maddeningly disconnected from events at times.

"Anything on the fingernail yet?" A tiny fragment of fingernail had been found in the fabric of Phoebe Hunter's baby-blue top, torn away as her killer shoved her back onto the branch.

Salter fielded the enquiry. "No matches in our DNA database. But uniforms might have a lead on wild Maggie. They're off down to Yarmouth to check it out now. As soon as they bring her in, we'll have her typed and see if it's hers."

Shepherd nodded and turned to Jejeune. "Speaking of DNA testing, I've had Procurement bending my ear about frivolous requests. Priority codes are there for a purpose, Domenic, and bird feathers rank somewhat lower than human tissue on that scale. I understand they have farmed the work out to a local lab."

"But it could be a long time before we hear anything from an outside lab," objected Jejeune. "DNA sequencing involves a lot of steps. There's extraction, purification, staining, separation, sequencing. They all take time, and in between, an independent lab might put the samples aside to take on other work."

Somebody's been doing their homework, thought Maik. Despite his constantly rising opinion of the inspector, he realized not even Jejeune would be likely to carry this kind of information around in his head. He wondered why he would have found it necessary to look into the process of DNA testing so deeply, when, really, it was only the results that they were interested in. But regardless of the reason, it was exactly the wrong time to be delivering a lecture like this to Shepherd, and it was a sign of the frustration Jejeune was feeling that he failed to recognize this.

"I'm sorry, Domenic, but wise use of resources is a departmental mantra these days, and I'm afraid I just can't see myself standing before the assistant chief constable trying to justify the use of highly sophisticated police equipment to test bird feathers." She offered him a placatory smile. "I'm sure you'll get your results soon enough."

She turned to the room in general. "Right, well, I'll leave you to get on with it then, unless there's anything else I should know. Anything on the fingerprints on the filing cabinet, for example. I assume we have already tested the volunteers to see if they belong to any of them?"

The assembled crowd looked at one another sheepishly, making it clear that the report wasn't going to make happy listening for the DCS. It was no surprise to anyone that Tony Holland rushed into the breach. He had a rare skill for reporting events in a way that simultaneously suggested that he had not been involved, and that if he had, things would have turned out immeasurably better.

"The volunteer system seems to have operated on a drop-in basis, ma'am. They were on first-name terms only, if they ever even saw each other. No insurance clearances required, so no need for any records. Nobody seems really sure of who was there and who wasn't, let alone how they could be contacted."

"For God's sake," said Shepherd, barely keeping her temper in check. "Is that what you people expect Guy Trueman to be taking back to the Mexican Consulate as evidence of our progress? Find out who these people were and get them printed. And do it quickly."

If this was leaving them to get on with it, Maik couldn't imagine what it would be like if she decided to take an active interest. But just as she did appear about to leave, finally, Jejeune's question stopped her in her tracks.

"I wonder," he said, so quietly Maik could barely hear the words, though he was only a few feet away. "Have we checked the prints against Ramon Santos?"

The silence was so profound, for a moment it seemed as if Jejeune's question had taken away the group's collective powers of speech. Anger darkened Shepherd's features. Trying to open locked filing cabinets suggested only one thing, and it was very much at odds with a status as an innocent bystander.

"It's the rental car," said Jejeune simply. "Santos tucked it away round the back of the building, even though there were plenty of spaces by the side and even at the front."

"Perhaps he was just ashamed of it. If I had to drive one of Saxon's pieces of crap around town, I would be, too," said Holland. He had noted Shepherd's expression and clearly decided now might not be a bad time to become her attack dog.

"It's quite obvious he didn't want people to see it, Domenic," said Shepherd, her voice registering the strain of keeping herself in check. "But there could be any number of reasons. A discreet business meeting. An anonymous donation." She spread her hands in an appeal for reason.

"Then why bring a car at all? It was a nice night, ten minutes' walk from the hotel. He was fit and healthy. The only explanation is that he was intending to take something from the sanctuary when he left, something that he couldn't afford to be seen carrying down the street."

Shepherd sighed irritably, as if she found Jejeune's inclusion of the word *only* particularly galling. "I thought we were looking at shelter volunteers and former employees," she said, "this business about re-locking the cage and what-not. And now, all of a sudden, you think Santos was there to steal the birds? You'll have a reason, of course, why a senior Mexican diplomat would want to break into a shelter to take a couple of birds you could find just about anywhere in Norfolk."

Her tone suggested she didn't particularly want Jejeune to offer one.

"Santos and Phoebe Hunter were killed in that cage, and birds were taken from it. I think those birds were the specific target of both Santos and the person who killed him. Beyond that, I don't have any answers at the moment."

Until now, Shepherd had been doing a serviceable job of keeping her emotions in check, obviously unwilling to berate Jejeune in front of the others. But it was clear that he wasn't going to leave this line of enquiry alone just because it might make people uncomfortable. She spun on her heel, unable to contain her rising anger any longer. "Domenic, a word, please. My office."

Jejeune followed her from the room. Their departure left a vacuum that Tony Holland was only too eager to fill.

"Somebody needs to call his girlfriend and tell her to get her needle and thread ready. She's going to be sewing a couple of things back on after Shepherd's finished with him." He didn't sound too dismayed at the prospect. "You realize what he's saying," Holland continued, addressing the room at large. "Not only did Santos go to the shelter with the intent of stealing those birds, 'cause that wouldn't be bizarre enough. No, in this case there was a second person who came in, and this person killed Santos, killed two people, in fact, so *they* could steal the birds instead."

Holland slipped into a contented silence and Salter resumed her study of Maggie Wylde's case file, leaving Maik to mull over this new development. Despite Holland's obvious delight at Jejeune's situation, it was hard to disagree with the constable's point. It was doubtful that there was one person in the country who would want to steal Turtledoves, let alone two. And as for such a theft being a viable motive for murder, even for the sometimes unconventional theories of Domenic Jejeune, this one seemed a bit of a stretch. And yet, Danny Maik had seen the inspector pull solutions like this out of the air before, and be right, so he wasn't prepared to write anything off just yet. He doubted DCS Shepherd was, either. And that, no doubt, was contributing to her mood just now; the thought that Domenic Jejeune's nightmarish scenario might just have some merit.

10

Colleen Shepherd stared carefully at the two men. Guy Trueman had perched his lean ex-soldier's frame on the corner of Danny Maik's desk and the two men were engaged now in easy conversation. How similar they were, she thought, these men who could reach out and make the world do their bidding, instead of having it drag them around on its whims, as it seemed to be doing so often with her these days.

Things had moved even faster than Shepherd had anticipated once she and Jejeune had gotten back to her office. The DCI's steadfast defence of his position concerning Santos's involvement had resulted in a moment's indecisive silence followed by a curt, if polite, dismissal. It had taken less than fifteen minutes from the time of her call to the Deputy Assistant Commissioner for Sir Michael Hillier's office to call and ask for Domenic Jejeune to be sent over first thing in the morning. And, the minister's secretary had added, it would be appreciated if neither the inspector nor anyone else at the station mentioned Jejeune's suspicions in the meantime.

Shepherd regretted having to send Domenic to the headmaster's office like this, but the directive from the DAC had been clear. Any attempt to link the crime back to the Mexican Consulate was to be reported immediately. The murder of a diplomat was sensitive enough without the senior investigating officer claiming that Santos may have been in some way complicit in his own death. Shepherd would have thought Jejeune would have been astute enough to see that for himself. Now, it would be up to Sir Michael Hillier, MP for Norfolk North, to explain the Home Office's point of view, presumably in terms that even the celebrated Domenic Jejeune would find impossible to ignore.

Maik noticed Shepherd watching them. Before Trueman's arrival, she had addressed the troops informally, making her point in terms that left no room for misinterpretation: the Obregón's were now fair game, but the name of Ramon Santos was not to come up under any circumstances as being on the sharp end of their investigations. Maik knew that on the numerous occasions the DCS had catalogued the admirable qualities of the team she had assembled here at the North Norfolk Constabulary, loyalty was always near the top of the list. She had used the word more than once in her address this morning. But if she had to be down here now, shadowing Guy Trueman to make sure no one got close enough to whisper in his ear or pass him a clandestine note, then the quality she so prized among her team wasn't loyalty in any way that Danny Maik understood it.

Tony Holland shut off his phone and addressed the room. "They're bringing Maggie Wylde in now," he said. "She was in a clinic in Yarmouth. Apparently, she had an episode when she was down visiting her sister."

"I thought you had contacted all the relatives," said Maik to Salter. It seemed inconceivable that she could have missed such a rudimentary check. He knew she had been doing everything possible to contribute to the case since she left Phoebe Hunter's flat, even staying beyond the time she normally left to make her son, Max, his evening meal. Maik could have told her that regret wasn't something you could erase with an increased workload, but he wasn't normally in the habit of offering unsolicited advice, and besides, he found those most in need of it rarely took heed anyway.

Holland delivered Salter's confirmation for her. "She asked everyone the same two questions: Was Maggie there? Had they seen her recently?" He turned to Salter. "But by the time you called the sister's house, Maggie had already been taken into care, so, literally, she wasn't there. And by recently, she apparently thought you meant within the previous ten minutes or so." He shook his head. "And this is supposed to be the sane sister?"

"Have we heard anything from Inspector Jejeune yet?"

Shepherd had been asking Maik, but again Tony Holland was first in with the response. "Still slumming it over at Hillier's office, as far as we know, ma'am. Probably into the second bottle of sherry by now."

Shepherd regarded Holland dubiously, as if unsure of his information, or perhaps his motives. "Yes, well, I hope he gets back soon. I want to be able to question Maggie Wylde as soon as we get her in here." She turned to Maik. "Perhaps you should get the ball rolling, Sergeant. If she is our killer, I want this thing wrapped us as quickly as possible."

It wasn't a request, but Maik wasn't a man to undertake inadvisable actions just because a superior was getting twitchy. Jejeune would be the best person to interview Maggie, and Maik would do what he could to see that the interview was delayed until the inspector got back.

"Probably best to let Constable Salter handle the preliminaries before we move on to the questioning proper," he said. Danny had long ago realized that in policing, as in most things in life, the more people who were involved in a process, the longer it took. And he was fairly confident that with the right sort of coaching, Salter could string out Maggie Wylde's initial booking for as long as he needed her to.

A slight commotion in the corridor announced the arrival of Maggie Wylde. All eyes turned to the doorway as two officers escorted a frail-looking woman into the room and settled her in a chair at Salter's desk, directly across from the constable.

At first, Maggie Wylde seemed bewildered by the booking process. From time to time, a spark of realization seemed to jolt within her, as if she was awakening to her surroundings. But then she would be gone again, retreating into her detached monotone as she confirmed the details for Salter, speaking in a quiet voice, at times so low that the detective constable had to lean forward to catch her words. Yes, her husband had worked at Victor Obregón's private aviary. Yes, after Obregón had disappeared, the family had let Norman Wylde stay on. He had worked there until his death, the night of that terrible storm.

Later, the inquiry put it down to guilt: Salter's feeling that if she had followed up on Phoebe Hunter's original complaint about Maggie, she might somehow have been able to prevent the later events. That was why she was so willing, eager even, to put Maggie at her ease. In itself, the actual breach of protocol was nothing, really. They had all done it, letting somebody put something on the desk between them — a book, a pair of gloves. With her bag up there on the desk where she could see it, Maggie would feel more comfortable, perhaps less disoriented by the strangeness of the police station and its constant hum of unfamiliar activity. That's what the review board settled on, and for all anyone knew, perhaps that was the truth.

The official report stopped short of assigning any blame to Detective Constable Lauren Salter, though it went to great lengths to point out, in its dispassionate, damning tone, that things should have been handled differently. Perhaps. But the report was authored by a review committee ensconced in the comfortable womb of an administrative block somewhere. And review committees were detached, disinterested, self-important entities concerned with ideal situations and optimum responses. Lauren Salter, on the other hand, was a human being. And human beings make mistakes. Having the bag where it was meant that when Maggie reached into the side pocket, the detective constable couldn't even see what Maggie had pulled out, much less react, until it was too late.

Perhaps Trueman had already detected something; a sudden change in the atmosphere, a shimmer in the ambient noise of the station. Certainly, in everybody's later recollection, it seemed that he was already turning off his perch on the corner of Danny's desk, half-standing even, by the time the heavy steel scissors reached Salter's throat.

The rest of the room turned as one, alerted by the wild scraping of the chairs and the crash of items falling from Salter's desk as Maggie's dramatic lunge swept them to the floor.

"I want my babies back," said Maggie, as quietly and calmly as if she was answering another of Salter's questions. "They belong to me. I've got the paper."

From every corner of the room, frozen figures stared at the scene in silence, afraid to make the noise that might startle the scissor-wielding woman into catastrophic action. Maggie was leaning across the desk, supporting herself unsteadily on one trembling, mottled hand while the other jabbed the point of the scissors into Salter's skin with each word she spoke.

"Those birds are mine. I've got the paper to prove it." As words, they were benign. But Maggie was getting agitated now. She reached up with her spare hand and snatched a handful of Salter's blonde hair, dragging the constable's head closer to the scissors. A small bead of blood appeared at their point, threading its way over the pale skin of Salter's throat like a teardrop. She gave a small sob and it seemed to spur Maggie into further action. She pulled Salter's head closer now, tilting it, jerking her hair cruelly. She came around the desk and began to drive the scissors deeper, forcing Salter to crane her neck back, expose her throat, to prevent the steel points from piercing deeper into the flesh. More blood flowed.

Behind Maggie, Maik was up and moving. Holland, too. But they were behind desks, farther to go. Trueman was closer. Trueman, first among alphas, there so swiftly you wondered how he had covered so much ground without anyone noticing.

"They took them away," said Maggie. Now her voice began to rise, shrill with anger, control sliding away. "They can't do that. Those birds belong to me. They are my property. I've got the paper." She steadied herself to plunge the scissors in.

With a blur of action, Trueman reached one arm inside Maggie's extended weapon hand and slid his other under her other arm, spinning her rapidly toward him in a move of almost ballet-like grace. A clump of Salter's blonde hair came away, trapped between Maggie's fingers. With a deft flick of Maggie's wrist, Trueman romanced the scissors from the woman's hand, closing a restraining arm around the frail body at the same time, pinning her arms to her side. Maggie looked confused, eyes darting wildly around, as if seeing her surroundings for the first time. She made no attempt to free herself from Trueman's hold, futile as that would have been.

"All right, my love, you just settle down," said Trueman softly. "You go with these nice people. They are going to help you work things out." He nodded for two officers to come forward and handed Maggie's unresisting, limp form to them. Each placed a restraining hand on one arm and Maggie was shuffled out of the room toward the holding cells.

In the collective exhalation of pent-up breath and excited conversation, it would have been easy to miss what happened next, but Maik was watching for it. Trueman was beside Salter in seconds. She was still wide-eyed with fear, her skin pale and paling, except for two red blotches on her cheeks.

"I didn't ... I didn't see it coming," she said. "I should have ..."

Maik knew it wasn't the assault that had unnerved her. In her job, Salter was well used to the occasional bout of violence, and was more than capable of defending herself. It was the irrationality of the attack, the unpredictability. One minute you're having a conversation with somebody, the next you have pointed steel digging into your throat. No amount of training can prepare you for that. Maik would have told Salter this, and more, but Trueman was already there, leaning in close, comforting her.

"All I could think about was Max," said Salter, in a voice far removed from the present.

"Of course," said Trueman. He dabbed at the thin trail of blood from her neck with a tissue. "Listen, Lauren is it? If you had thought of anything else, you wouldn't be normal. So tell me about this Max. This him here?" He picked up a photograph that had fallen to the floor in the struggle and set it back on her desk.

She nodded. "My son, he's seven." She breathed deeply, trying to get herself back under control.

"I'll bet he's a handful. They're into everything at that age, aren't they? Has he got a favourite football team yet? I hope it's not Norwich. You tell him from me he's in for a world of disappointment if he chooses to follow that lot."

And more of the same, as he helped her to her feet and walked her over to the doorway, hand on her shoulder, the reassurance of physical contact. At the door, Trueman handed her off to a female officer, to lead her, hand on arm, to the cafeteria, for the magic elixir of a restorative cup of tea while they awaited the arrival of the medical officer.

Maik had seen it before. Keep engaging. The mind, the verbals, then the kinetics — the standing, the walking, the holding — all the normal things, to re-establish balance, put the trauma back in its box. It happened, it's over, let's get back to normal. Still, as a piece of performance art, it was impressive, and Colleen Shepherd, in particular, seemed to look at Trueman with new eyes as he resumed his seat at Maik's desk.

"Well, I suppose this answers the question of whether Maggie Wylde could have killed someone," she said.

Maik was fairly sure that if Inspector Jejeune was here he would have pointed out that the question was not whether Maggie could have killed the two people in the sanctuary, but whether she did.

"All this over a couple of doves," said Holland to nobody in particular.

Trueman rolled his bottom lip between his thumb and forefinger. He wasn't saying anything. But such was the bond between himself and Danny Maik, he didn't need to.

11

Sir Michael Hillier attended to his constituency matters from a suite of lavishly appointed offices overlooking the main square of Saltmarsh. Though Jejeune doubted that many of Hillier's constituents knew the extent of this luxury, he suspected few would have begrudged the MP his comforts. He was popular with the local voters, and an enthusiastic supporter of all things Saltmarsh and north Norfolk. This included its police force.

Hillier was standing at the window, seemingly absorbed by the Saltmarsh skyline, when Jejeune entered. He turned to greet the detective. Though Jejeune could not imagine the number of people Hillier would see on any given day, the MP had mastered that upper class affectation of implying that his guest's arrival was of singular importance.

"Inspector, thank you so much for coming," he said in a deep voice, rich with breeding. He had a long, distinguished face, framed by white hair, cut to a shaggy length just the right side of unruly. Exuberant grey eyebrows that seemed to have a life of their own sprouted from behind a pair of heavy, black-rimmed glasses that were perched on the end of Hillier's nose, as if to emphasize the idea that he didn't normally wear such contraptions. Hillier was wearing a navy blue suit with a broad white pinstripe that merely served to further define his thin, over-tall frame. As he approached in greeting, Jejeune noted the politician's slight stoop, seeming to begin around the shoulder blades. The early onset of scoliosis, he suspected.

"Would you care for coffee?"

In eschewing the traditional offering of tea, the MP was no doubt trying to accommodate what he imagined to be Jejeune's Canadian tastes. But in the detective's experience, institutional coffee in Britain was always an adventure, and at its frequent worst it could be a deeply regrettable experience. If Hillier had any thoughts about Jejeune's refusal, he gave no sign.

"I have been asked to convey personal greetings from the Home Secretary, and his daughter. She's doing wonderfully well, these days, I understand. Thankfully, she seems to have been able to put the whole terrible business behind her. Engaged now, as you may have heard."

Jejeune had, through the dailies, though he wasn't expecting an invitation to the wedding. Reminding everybody on her wedding day of the debt the bride owed to another man hardly seemed like the ideal way to start a happy marriage.

Hillier seemed to read the thought in Jejeune's face. "I can assure you, Inspector, no one in the government is likely to forget your efforts in bringing about that young lady's safe return. Believe it or not, politicians see themselves as something of a family. A bit like the police, in a way, I suppose. A little more self-absorbed, perhaps, and a damn sight pettier, I shouldn't wonder. But in the end, when it's one of our own, we all rally round. Her ordeal affected us all greatly."

Jejeune acknowledged the comments about the case that had first brought him national recognition, but said nothing further. He was still trying to assess the man standing across from him. Having achieved the knighthood he had doubtless spent the better part of his career chasing, Sir Michael Hillier seemed content to dedicate himself to the common good these days, largely because he had nothing else left to occupy his time. Jejeune suspected that Hillier's new role would provide more than enough opportunities. He had been appointed assistant minister with the Department of Environment, Food, and Rural Affairs: an "emeritus position," the less kind newspaper reports said. But they may not have been entirely wrong. The new minister, a raw recruit with good looks in place of any actual political experience, had made a sure-footed start to the DEFRA portfolio, and the political commentators suspected they could already detect Hillier's steadying hand at work in the shadows.

Hillier sat at his desk and extended a hand that invited Jejeune to do likewise. "I do apologize for your having to come over like this. The DAC thought it might be wise to have a word. Bit of an Intro to Politics course, if you like."

Hillier flashed a smile to rob the words of any offence. To some, the inspector's meteoric rise through ranks might have suggested Jejeune already had a rudimentary grasp of politics, at least those of the U.K. police service. What was of more interest to Jejeune was the fact that Hillier was taking great pains to point out that this meeting being held at the deputy assistant commissioner's behest, when DCS Shepherd had indicated the summons had come directly from Hillier's office. In Jejeune's experience, any time someone in authority was unwilling to take ownership for something, it didn't bode well for those lower down the food chain.

"Regarding this business of the murders in the bird sanctuary. There are a couple of ground rules Her Majesty's government would like to lay down, if we may."

Even after so many years in England, the exquisite politeness of those in high office was something that still occasionally took Jejeune by surprise. The nation's statesmen spent so much time polishing their manners to a blinding sheen that it was a wonder they had ever found the time to establish a global empire. But politely stated or not, Hillier's meaning was clear.

And Ramon Santos, the inspector was sure, was going to be one of the principal ground rules, possibly the only one.

"Frankly, diplomatic matters involving crimes on foreign soil are such a dog's dinner. The boundaries can be remarkably fuzzy in matters like this. For that reason, we usually err on the side of caution. So perhaps you could walk me through this, Inspector. You seem to believe the diplomatic attaché was involved in criminal activity when he met his death?"

Matters like this? Usually? How often did this sort of thing happen? But even if Hillier's statement raised some questions, there was one word that the detective had no trouble understanding: *caution.*

Jejeune reviewed his misgivings about the rental car and the false ID, careful not to give any one detail the extra significance that might cause Hillier to seize upon it. As he spoke, Jejeune watched the MP's features carefully, looking for signs that might betray a reaction — disapproval, surprise, anger even. Instead, he got the impression that Hillier had already heard it all before. Jejeune ended his summary by stressing he had nothing specific linking Santos to the attempted theft of the doves.

Hillier nodded thoughtfully. "And whether or not he was involved in any criminal activity, that's not to say the poor chap deserved what he got, of course. His death is still a tragic and deeply regrettable incident."

The MP slipped into the detached cadence of his profession so naturally Jejeune wondered whether he would still be even capable of tapping into his own emotions anymore, much less expressing them.

"D'you think the girl was involved, too?" he asked, looking up at Jejeune.

"There's nothing to suggest so."

Hillier shook his head. "She was quite driven, I understand. I wonder, is there anything more tragic than a young life robbed of its chance to reach its full potential?"

Jejeune's expression suggested that he, too, had visited this question. He knew that, in a way, his work was society's attempt to redress losses like this, to seek compensation for what had been taken from it. But for him, solving Phoebe Hunter's murder would not restore any kind of balance. What could counteract the lost promise of this girl's life, of any life?

"The Mexican press is portraying the murder of Ramon Santos as further proof that our once great empire is slipping into terminal decline," said Hillier suddenly. "Murderous psychopaths on every street corner, cities degenerating into dens of violence and drug-fuelled mayhem. Nothing personal in it, of course. We're just as bad when a British citizen dies overseas. Any time a nation can focus attention on the ills of another, it takes the spotlight off its own domestic problems." Hillier sighed. "To exploit the death of a young man like this no doubt appears unseemly. In truth, you are probably right. The more immediate concern, however, is of some weak, or worse, overly ambitious, politician, theirs or ours, getting stampeded into an ill-advised course of action just to satisfy public opinion."

Hillier had a disconcerting way of slipping into silence after making a point, as if considering it with a view to convincing himself of its validity. Jejeune, who also knew a thing or two about the value of staying silent, tried to exude an eternity of patience as he waited for Hillier to resume his comments. Through the window behind the politician, Jejeune could see the light clouds scudding across a grey sky. On the far side of the square, the steeple of Saltmarsh's fifteenth-century church dominated the skyline. "The point is," said Hillier finally, "any suggestion that Santos was involved in criminal activity would obviously be subject to the most intense scrutiny. We would need to be absolutely certain of our ground if we were to make such a claim. *Absolutely* certain."

Jejeune did not need the repetition to understand Hillier's point. But absolute certainty was not a fantasy that even sentencing judges allowed themselves to indulge in, much less police detectives. Was Hillier advising Jejeune to discontinue this line of enquiry? Or was he encouraging him to gather more evidence, in an attempt to prove the connection beyond all reasonable doubt? It was perhaps a testament to the other man's finely honed political skills that Jejeune really wasn't sure.

Sir Michael Hillier was far too experienced a politician to be thrown by Jejeune's studied silence. Whether or not it was the reaction he had been aiming for, it seemed to suit him. He rose from his desk and went to stand at the window, his back to Jejeune. "D'you know, I've been thinking about this dove business," he said without turning around. "I'm wondering if there could possibly be anything symbolic in it. As you may or may not be aware, Inspector, doves feature quite prominently in classical literature, eternal symbols of love and peace and all that."

How they loved their classics, thought Jejeune. It was understandable, he supposed, this link with the past, especially in this part of the world. In the square below, people walked in the shadow of that church's centuries-old steeple without a second thought. Perhaps Hillier could be forgiven for his disparaging view of the education system in Canada, a country whose constitution was barely a single generation old.

The horizon apparently no longer worthy of his attention, Hillier turned around. "Anyone looking into that aspect of things, I wonder?"

Jejeune managed to hide his exasperation. In his experience, members of the public could rarely refrain from offering a theory on a murder case. The difference was, those in high office expected theirs to be actively considered. On this occasion, Jejeune suspected that Hillier was offering out of a genuine desire to be helpful rather than any self-aggrandizement. But that did not make it easier for Jejeune to look like he was taking it seriously. "I'll certainly have someone check it out," he said, in a tone that those familiar with the detective might recognize as signifying it would not be a priority.

"Just a thought, mind," concluded Hillier, flapping a dismissive hand. He shifted gears once again. Jejeune was used to such disconcerting lurches in interviews. It was just that he was usually the one employing them. "You see, any allegation of criminal activity on the part of Santos would profoundly change the narrative. Now, no doubt both governments would find it easier to reach a clear-minded solution without the sort of background noise the Mexican media is currently providing. So, of course, the right sort of result in this case would certainly be most welcome."

The right sort, noted Domenic. Not even a particular result, just as long as certain others were avoided. Through the window behind Hillier, he could still see the dappled rooftops of Saltmarsh. But it was another landscape that occupied Jejeune's thoughts, one of warm, earthy tones and red soil and dazzling African sunlight. One where the challenges were overt and the requirements were clear, unfettered by vested interests and dangerous, veiled agendas. *What would it be like to operate in such a landscape?* he wondered.

There was a discreet knock at the door and an assistant entered meekly. "Your eleven o'clock, Minister."

The choreography was not lost on Jejeune. Hillier rounded the desk with a suitably resigned expression. He extended a hand to shake Jejeune's. "Thank you for coming, Inspector. Do let me know if this business about dove symbolism turns out to be anything," he said. "And be sure you tell DCS Shepherd from whence it came. We can't have you claiming it was all your idea, can we?"

"Oh, no worries there," Jejeune assured the other man honestly. "I doubt anyone would believe I could come up with an idea like that all on my own."

12

In the general adrenaline crash that followed Maggie Wylde's standoff with Lauren, few people would have raised an eyebrow at Trueman's suggestion of a drink, even if they had been within hearing distance. But it was the reason that tipped Danny off. A stiff brandy, just to settle the nerves, said Trueman, fixing Danny with a significant look.

After what? Disarming an ageing, disoriented civilian wielding a pair of scissors? Certainly there had been plenty of tension. And for Lauren Salter, the danger, too, had been real enough. But Danny Maik had seen Trueman handle worse situations, far worse, without the need to worry about settling his nerves afterward. Unless he had lost a lot more than just a couple of inches from his hairline since they last met, Guy Trueman wasn't going to get so much as an elevated pulse rate over an incident like this, much less have the need for a strong brandy. It was enough to tip Maik off that it would need to be a private chat, and that he would need to find Tony Holland something to do to prevent him from offering to join them, stand them a round even, while he paid homage to his new-found hero and encouraged Trueman to divulge more stories from Maik's army days. Which was why Maik now found himself here, alone, on the raised outdoor patio of The Boatman's Arms, overlooking the wharf, waiting for Guy Trueman to return from the bar.

Trueman slid a pint toward Danny and settled in across the table from the sergeant. Maik noticed that for his ex-CO, a large whisky was going to be standing in for that medicinal brandy.

"DC Holland not joining us then?" asked Trueman mischievously. "He's a live wire, that one. Bugger for the women, too, I imagine," he added, smiling. Trueman had a similar reputation himself, as Danny recalled, and in the sergeant's experience it was not necessarily the sort of behaviour that a man tended to grow out of as he got older.

"Sends his regrets," said Maik. "You'll have to make do with me."

Trueman took a sip of his whisky and set down the glass. "I was hoping they'd have some of that St. George. Seemed appropriate, a nice glass of England's only single malt, right in the county where they make it. Only the bartender said they don't sell it in pubs."

"It's around," said Maik. "You just have to know which pubs to go to."

Trueman let his eyes play over a group of young men who had settled at a table just over Danny's shoulder.

"I gave a bottle of it to Jimmy McCall as a present when it first came out, just to wind him up," said Trueman, smiling to himself. "Remember Jimmy, the Mad Jock? He said being a true Scotsman, he could never bring himself to drink an English whisky, but he might keep the bottle, seeing as it was such a nice shape." Trueman shook his head. "He's gone now. Roadside bomb on the outskirts of Lashkar Gah." Trueman took a long drink of his whisky and shook his head. "We lost so many of them over the years, Danny."

"They're not lost. Not to the people who knew them."

"True enough," said Trueman. He held up his glass. "To them, every last one of 'em."

A stillness settled between them and they sat with their own thoughts; two hard men who knew the dark side of the world, who had seen the human animal at its worst, and yet somehow still managed to make their peace with it.

"Anyway, that was then. And this is now," said Trueman, brightening. "And here we are, you and me, still doing our bit to make the world a better place, eh, Danny? Safer, anyway."

"Diplomatic protection group? I did a bit of that myself, once, on secondment." Maik took a sip of his beer. "I could see why they called it DPG."

"Doors, Posts, and Gates, you mean?" Trueman shook his head. "It's not all standing around anymore. They even let us carry sharp objects now and again. As long as we promise not to run with them, of course. Besides, we're not the police DPG. We're private. We get to make our own rules."

Maik pulled a face. "You say that like it's a good thing."

"Come on, Danny," said Trueman amicably. "No-nothing soldiers like us pulling down ninety large a year, a company car, and a flat on the South Bank." Trueman spread his hands. "Where did it all go wrong, eh? Listen, you should come and join us. Get the kind of respect you deserve. As you say, you've already got a bit of background. I would imagine you've kept a sly edge on those special skills the army paid all that good money to provide you with. I could slide the diplomatic clearances through for you. Sign you up for a bit of upgrading and you'd be ready to go."

Danny wondered briefly if Trueman had picked up any signals that he was not getting the kind of respect he deserved at the moment, something he had failed to pick up on himself — one of Holland's smirky expressions, perhaps, as he was listening to the sergeant's briefings?

Low strains of music were drifting up to them from one of the boats moored below in the harbour, but the volume was cranked up as a new song came on. Maik smiled; somebody else who approved of the close harmonies of the Isley Brothers' early Motown days.

Maik listened, an expression somewhere between sadness and empathy spreading across his features as Ronald Isley told him how his old heart had been broke a thousand times.

Yours too, Ronald?

Trueman knew better than to interrupt, so he looked out over the wharf, at the flat grey light bouncing off the calm waters, and the gulls wheeling and calling above. Like many towns along the coast, Saltmarsh had been a vibrant port in earlier times. Harbours like these had seen goods and people from all over the world in their time. What commerce must have taken place on the boards below, what deals made, intrigues woven, secrets traded.

When the song ended, Trueman turned to Maik. "Danny and his Motown," he said, shaking his head. "Part of the legend that was. Motown Maik, they used to call you."

"Amongst other things," said Danny. By his count, this was now four topics his ex-CO had broached. If there was a pattern, something bringing them ever closer to the real reason Trueman wanted to be here, it had eluded him up to now.

Trueman gestured at the group of young men sitting behind Maik, teasing the waitress with their overloud, good-natured boisterousness. "That's why we did it, you know. So kids like that can come and have a nice mid-afternoon pint, share a laugh with their mates, and give the waitress a bit of grief that she can't get enough of. Look at them; they're just babies, no older than the new recruits you used to train. No wonder you used to frighten them half to death."

Maik glanced over. He knew most of them, or their families, at least. Small-town policing was like that.

"Would Jordan Waters be among that group? I wonder."

Maik was unable to keep the look of surprise from his face, but he didn't need a second glance at the group before shaking his head.

"You know him then, this Waters?" Trueman asked, without taking his own eyes off the group.

Maik shrugged. "Local layabout. Drugs, mostly. And the usual nonsense that goes along with them."

"Drugs," said Trueman sadly. "I don't know why they bother. You know what I heard? The average drug dealer could make more with a job at a fast-food restaurant."

Maik nodded. He had heard that, too, but he wasn't about to let Trueman sidetrack this conversation into the economics of the Saltmarsh drug trade.

"Do you want me to handle the introductions, or should I just point you in the right direction?"

"Me? A bit above my pay grade, Danny." Trueman leaned in slightly toward his listener. "The thing is, supposing somebody at the consulate, from, oh, say, the military side, had asked a private firm, at arms length from anything official, shall we say, to keep tabs on somebody, a quick *shufti* at the phone traffic now and then. I mean, they wouldn't necessarily want to go bothering anyone for permission, just a few lukewarm enquiries like that, would they?"

"I can see that," said Maik equitably. He took a drink of his beer. "The only problem might be if they came across something they shouldn't have, say about somebody like Jordan Waters. Then it might be a bit late to backtrack and inform the authorities that they had been commissioning illegal phone surveillance on British soil."

"Still as sharp as ever, Danny," said Trueman with an appreciative smile. "That's why I used to go straight to you with anything important, back in the day."

"I'm listening," said Maik.

"Now, I don't know this area well myself, of course, but I'll bet with a bit of careful police work, somebody like that clever inspector of yours could come up with a short, shortlist of people around here who the Mexican Consulate might have an interest in keeping an eye on."

Maik's expression suggested that the talents of clever Inspector Jejeune might not even be necessary in this instance. "Waters called the Obregóns?"

Trueman took a sip of his whisky and looked out over the water. "Wherever did you get an idea like that?"

"I don't suppose we have any idea what the call was about?"

"I don't think there was anybody standing by taking it down in shorthand, if that's what you mean," said Trueman, "but at least a couple of possibilities suggest themselves once you know the date of the phone call. April 29th, in case you're interested."

"The day before the murders?"

"The day before the murders."

The two men sat in silence for a moment, their separate thoughts cocooning them from each other and from the wider world beyond. The noises of the pub, the mewling of the gulls, the clanking of the lanyards as the moored boats rocked on the gentle mercury swells in the harbour, none of it seemed to penetrate the inner silence of the two men. They drained their drinks simultaneously and Trueman stood up to leave. "No interview," he said. "No hoops to jump through. One call and you'd be straight in. Just promise me you'll think about it, Danny, that's all."

Danny watched Trueman leave, having given him an assurance that, in the absence of any other things to keep him awake at night, he would give his ex-CO's offer some consideration.

13

It doesn't take long to lose touch with the rhythms of London, and Jejeune found he could no longer judge the travel times across the city with any accuracy. As a result, he arrived for his meeting at Regent's Park more than half an hour early.

"The Clarence Gate entrance," Hidalgo had said, "near Baker Street." Jejeune realized he had time for a coffee and strolled through the pedestrian traffic, past the shops with their Sherlock Holmes paraphernalia and the small knots of early-morning tourists destined for disappointment in their search for a real-life number 221B. He took a table on the outside patio of a café called The Blue Parrot and ordered a small cappuccino. The blackboard menu on the wall beside the doorway featured an exquisite chalk drawing of a Blue-and-Yellow Macaw. The proportions and plumage of the bird were rendered perfectly. It seemed a shame that someone with such obvious artistic talent should be working at a café. A shame, too, perhaps, that they didn't know their parrots from their macaws.

As Jejeune sipped his coffee, a steady stream of pedestrians passed by a few yards from his table, each immersed in an internal world from which everything and everyone else were excluded. It was unusual for Jejeune to have time like this, to simply sit and observe the passing parade of life. If he had free time, he spent it birding, or musing on his current case. Or both.

What would the famous Sleuth of Baker Street have made of this case? he wondered. Would Holmes have brought his own brand of Occam's razor to bear, the now-famous axiom that when you had eliminated the impossible, whatever remained must be the truth? Well, Jejeune had eliminated the impossible, and he was fairly sure that a lot of what remained was not the truth, or anything close to it. *So, any other thoughts, Sherlock?*

A group of people stopped in front of the café, as if weighing whether or not to go in. The men were dressed in exquisitely tailored suits, but the women wore traditional African dress — billowing garments in bold, earthy colours. Jejeune looked at the men. They said that once Africa got into your veins, it never really left you. Had it stayed with them, he wondered, when they had sloughed off their old skins and donned the garb of the London businessman? And what about Phoebe Hunter? Had she died clinging to the faint exotic tang of her field research, the scent of Africa in her nostrils, the red earth buried into her skin? He drained his coffee and checked his watch. Hidalgo, he knew, would be a punctual man, and it was Jejeune's habit, also, to arrive on time.

Hidalgo was on the bridge staring at the water when Jejeune approached. His expression when he turned reflected a genuine pleasure to see the detective. "Thank you for meeting me here, Inspector. Please understand, we have no secrets at the consulate, but your presence, while the sorrow is still ..."

Jejeune nodded. "Of course. I understand you had a service yesterday."

"A small ceremony in the consulate chapel. A larger, more formal service is to be held at Westminster Cathedral. The archbishop himself has kindly offered to preside." Hidalgo shrugged. "Perhaps it will help the staff to come to terms with things a little.

Some will also find distraction in their work, others with their private memories. But grief is like water, Inspector. No matter how many diversions you put in its path, it will find an outlet eventually." He sighed deeply. "Sometimes I do not know what to do with this sadness. To know I am responsible for Ramon's death."

Jejeune tensed, unable to keep from staring at Hidalgo.

"In this foreign land, I was responsible for his life," said Hidalgo simply. "So I must be responsible for his death, also. How could it be otherwise? But I apologize. Not *responsible*. Perhaps there is a better word in English. I had a duty of care. I failed in that. I brought him from his homeland as a healthy young man. I will return him to his family in a coffin. It is a burden I must live with forever." He addressed Jejeune with a new urgency. "You must find this person who killed him, Inspector."

Jejeune was not in the habit of offering the consolation of empty guarantees that the killer would be brought to justice, but all the same he would have liked to have been able to provide Hidalgo with some assurance that progress was being made. But was it? What leads was he following, exactly, other than the one that Hidalgo would least like to hear — that Santos may have died while committing a crime?

Hidalgo began to move off along the path. "I thought we could walk around the park," he said. "I understand you are a birdwatcher. Perhaps you will see something interesting."

More likely if I'd brought binoculars, thought Jejeune. Still, it was a perfect morning for birding, soft and calm, and a park, even one as expansive as Regent's Park, generally brought birds close enough for identification. If not, perhaps he could still work on his bird calls.

They followed a path along the edge of the lake and paused near the bandstand to look out over the water, spangling in the morning light. Jejeune saw the dark shapes of small ducks. Pochard, probably, though they were just too far out to be sure.

"Your first university degree was in conservation biology, I understand, Inspector. I, too, was interested in this as a young man. But, like you, I suspect, I came to realize my talents lay in other areas."

He waited, but Jejeune did not seem predisposed to comment either way. Hidalgo shrugged philosophically. "In the end, I turned my attention to the study of economics. It gives the mind the structure to take on other subjects more easily. As a career decision, it was a wise one. It has brought me great success."

Hidalgo stopped abruptly, as if chastising himself for letting his thoughts stray from the crushing sadness of his subordinate's death. The two men strolled on, pausing on the Long Bridge. Hidalgo spent a long time looking out over the water. "Despite its much-admired cosmopolitanism, London can make a person feel very alone at times, especially outsiders like you and I. Do you not think so, Inspector?"

Jejeune did not answer. He scanned the waters carefully, but there were no birds in sight. "Did you know Santos used to come birdwatching in this park?" he asked. "His book has a number of records from here."

Hidalgo's eyes opened wide. "But I would have thought Hyde Park, surely? It is not far from the consulate. A nice walk at lunchtime."

"There are a few records from there, but this park seems to have been a particular favourite of his." Jejeune fell silent and scanned the water once again in a slow, careful pass. When he returned his gaze to Hidalgo, the older man was waiting, half-turned toward him, an eternity of patience in his eyes.

"You are looking for something in particular, perhaps?"

Jejeune offered an apologetic smile. "Santos recorded a Smew out there, a duck of the high Arctic. It's a very good sighting. I imagine he would have been pretty pleased with it." He continued to let his eyes rest on Hidalgo.

"If you are wondering whether he ever mentioned it, I can tell you, Inspector, with my hand on my heart, he did not. Ramon may have enjoyed looking at birds, but he said nothing of this to me, or, as far as I am aware, to any of his colleagues."

Was it possible? Jejeune never discussed his own birding with his work colleagues, at least not anymore. Not unless it was in response to some cryptic comment from Maik, or more likely, Shepherd. But did acquaintances not come to know about your hobbies simply by being around you, by picking up on hints, absorbing the clues almost by osmosis? Jejeune thought about Eric, Lindy's larger-than-life boss at the magazine. The two men had met numerous times, but there were still vast open oceans of Eric's life that were completely unknown to Jejeune. But he didn't work with Eric, did he? Danny Maik, then? Hardly a fair example, either, really. Maik could be awarded a knighthood and the first you would know of it would be when you saw it on the six o' clock news. So perhaps it was possible to work closely beside someone and be completely unaware of their personal life — their passions, their interests — if they decided they wanted it to be that way. Like so many things in this case, it left Jejeune with a vague feeling of uncertainty, as disconcerting as it was distracting.

"I understand you met with Sir Michael Hillier earlier. He is well?"

Jejeune said nothing, but he didn't try to hide his surprise. Hidalgo smiled. "He is a good man, but he has a job to do. We must both protect the interests of our countries. Such a case as this, it can test friendships to the limit, I think."

They walked on again in silence, passing the plantation and the playing fields, empty now in the middle of a weekday morning. Jejeune could hear the gentle burble of a Blackbird coming from the large stand of trees framing Winfield House in front of them. He peered closer and found the bird working the ground beneath a large pine. From somewhere up in the tree, the distinctive wheezy song of a Greenfinch drifted down. Once the calls had been unfamilar to him, but now he thought of them as the birds of his everyday world. In truth, Jejeune no longer felt like an outsider in this country. Despite the best efforts of Holland, and others, he felt at home here; if not British exactly, then a part of the British identity. But if that was true, why were thoughts of Africa consuming his every waking moment?

Jejeune suddenly realized where they had stopped. "This seems to have been another favourite spot of Mr. Santos's. He recorded Chiffchaff and Willow Warbler right over there, in fact," he said, pointing. He casually scanned the treetops for any sign of movement, but there was none.

"You read all of the entries in this book of his?" Hidalgo asked in surprise.

"Not all, no. But those I saw gave me some sense of the man. He seems to have been meticulous, precise in his records. And perhaps a little cautious. Many of his sightings were tagged with question marks."

"Yes." Hidalgo gave a thoughtful nod. "Yes," he said again, "Ramon was all of these things. Perhaps it was his military background that encouraged these qualities, this precision. Your sergeant, he, too, possesses them?"

Jejeune nodded. Along with loyalty and trustworthiness, other qualities Hidalgo had praised in Ramon Santos. Another wave of introspection seemed to take hold of Hidalgo and neither man spoke for a time as they continued their stroll along the edge of the lake. They walked unhurriedly, just two men in the watery sunshine of a spring morning in London, lost in their own thoughts, about loyalty, about loss, about murder.

Back at the bridge, Hidalgo reached out to grab Jejeune's hand. The DCI could feel the dry warmth of the other man's skin, and it seemed to add sincerity to his words. "I am comforted to know you are on this case, Inspector. It is strange, is it not, how we both abandoned our early career choices in favour of more pragmatic ones? And yet, here we are. I still work in conservation, but now it is the Mexican culture I hope to conserve, wherever I can. And you, too, are still protecting the world from those who would do it harm, if perhaps in a different way than you once intended. I wonder, sometimes, if it is not the career that chooses the man, rather than the other way around."

It occurred to Jejeune that of all the people to whom Hidalgo might have chosen to address this observation, few would be as well-qualified to comment as himself. But he said nothing, and after shaking hands one last time, the two men went their own separate ways without a backward glance.

14

Jejeune was hunched over the computer when Lindy entered the tiny nook they had set aside as a home office. From behind, she draped her arms over his shoulders. An image of a barren, sun-baked landscape flickered on the screen.

Oh, Dom, she thought, *how I wish you wouldn't wish.* Surely he could see it was too late to start all over again, too late to start chasing rainbows, stomping through the wilderness of Burkina Faso in search of the career that had eluded him. She leaned forward and popped a piece of something into his mouth.

"Norfolk dried biffin. Pressed baked apples, basically," said Lindy. "I found the recipe in an old Norfolk cookbook."

"How old?" asked Jejeune.

"Be careful, young Domenic, or I might just start asking what *again* means, when used by somebody like Carrie Pritchard. As in, 'so nice to see you again, Domenic.'"

"It means we had met before," said Jejeune simply. "We've both been birding the same bit of coast recently."

"You never mentioned it," said Lindy casually.

"There didn't seem any point," said Jejeune. "You didn't know her at the time."

Jejeune's naiveté in matters of relationships still took away Lindy's breath at times. What woman wouldn't want to know that her partner had been alone on the wild shores of north Norfolk with Carrie Pritchard and her pulsating sexuality? Surely even Dom could not be that oblivious to her charms. Could he?

"Cosy was it, out there, with just the two of you? Share a skin of wine with the bohemian Ms. Pritchard, perhaps?"

"I told her I never touch alcohol, having seen its terrible effects on my booze-hag of a girlfriend."

Lindy pulled a face, signalling the end of the contest, but not of her interest in the subject. How much had Carrie Pritchard's presence added to the sense of "wonder" he had referred to earlier. Perhaps it was she who was behind this nonsense of Dom's assuming Phoebe Hunter's research project. Pritchard was responsible for finding a replacement. If she really felt Dom was a suitable candidate, who knew where it could lead? Had they already talked about it, perhaps, at another meeting that he had failed to mention because he didn't think it would be of interest to Lindy?

She navigated back to the safer waters of the case, concentrating on the victims, rather than the suspects, just as she knew Domenic was. "Were you ever able to locate any of Phoebe Hunter's relatives?" Lindy knew it bothered Dom particularly that he could not find even a single family member to mourn this girl's passing.

He shook his head. "It's funny, but even the few friends who knew her all seem to have a different opinion — Phoebe the meek, Phoebe the driven, the manipulative, the caring." He spread his hands. "Take your pick."

"There's nothing sinister in that, though, surely," said Lindy. "We are all different things to different people. You, me, everybody. None of us lives our lives so we can have a nice, consistent obituary."

Jejeune shook his head again. "The thing is, it's all based around her professional life. On a personal level, she seems to have gone through her life without meaning very much to anyone at all. Phoebe Hunter appears to have barely existed beyond her work."

The overwhelming sadness of Jejeune's comment hung in the silence between them for a moment.

"I must say, Carrie was right about her success with set-asides, though," said Jejeune, as if trying to redeem the memory of Phoebe Hunter in some way. "She seems to have had a knack for getting local landowners to commit to the idea."

Carrie! Lindy was thoughtful for a moment. "You know, appropriating farmland is still a sensitive issue in these parts. Could Phoebe Hunter have upset somebody with her efforts?"

Jejeune shrugged. "It's hard to see how. Set-asides are entirely voluntary. Still, I suppose it wouldn't hurt to look into it." He nodded appreciatively. "Thanks."

"Glad to oblige," said Lindy. "The sooner you get this case wrapped up, the sooner I get to lie on a beach somewhere."

Jejeune's response, if he was going to offer one, was stilled by a knock at the door.

Lindy opened the door to find Danny Maik blocking out the light from the almost full moon behind him.

"Danny, come in. Domenic didn't say you were coming over. Still, that's my man, mind like a steel sieve sometimes. Fancy a cuppa?"

Domenic had told her once that her use of the sergeant's first name made Maik uncomfortable. Lindy had smiled to herself at the time, at the very thought of making a granite wall like Danny Maik uncomfortable about anything. Maik stepped inside uncertainly.

"I just stopped by on the off-chance the inspector might be in. I thought it might be a bit dark for birding by now."

"You've heard of owls, I take it?" said Lindy with a lopsided grin. "He's in the back. Go on through. Do you want me to put on some Motown? I've probably got some Stevie Wonder on my iPod somewhere. He's no Biggie Smalls, but I've heard he's okay."

The sergeant's wan smile seemed to suggest he could live with the pain of her jibe, and he went along the hallway to the office. Jejeune greeted him with a certain caution. Good policemen, the best ones, knew enough to separate their private lives from the job. If Maik had been prepared to risk breaching that delicate membrane, it could only be because he had something significant to report.

"Sorry to bother you at home, sir, but a couple of things have come up."

From somewhere, the unmistakable vocals of a young Stevie Wonder emerged from hidden speakers, telling them that everything was alright. Uptight. Clean outta sight.

Lindy appeared in the doorway. "This okay?" She was swinging her long blonde hair from side to side in time with the music, bouncing lightly from one foot to another in a way that made Maik feel every moment of his age.

Yes, Stevie, tonight everything is definitely alright. And uptight. And clean outta sight.

Maik turned back to Jejeune. "The prints from the filing cabinet are not Maggie Wylde's. Neither is the fingernail fragment. But this paper she was talking about, it's a receipt. Unsigned, but it says Victor Obregón sold a pair of doves to Norman Wylde. It was stuffed in a drawer in her filing cabinet."

Jejeune nodded. In and of itself, the news was nowhere near important enough for Maik to have made the journey out here, especially at this time of night. "A couple of things?"

"The employee roster at the sanctuary has yielded a viable suspect. In fact, better than viable — a local drug dealer, Jordan Waters."

Alright.

"Was he a volunteer?" asked Jejeune.

"Not a voluntary volunteer, no. It was a parole job, which is the only reason there is any record he was working there. Looks like you were right, sir. He would have been in the habit of locking the cages as a matter of course."

Uptight.

"And," continued Maik, "I have come across a source who says he was in contact with Luisa Obregón at least once by phone."

Clean outta sight.

Maik allowed himself a satisfied smile. "The interesting thing is, this phone call …"

"It was placed before the theft."

Maik was startled. "The day before."

Jejeune nodded. "It crossed my mind that whoever took those birds wouldn't have done so without a buyer in place. Whatever it is that makes these birds special, there would be a very exclusive market for them. If this Waters was prepared to risk violating his parole to get mixed up in something like this, it would only be because he had a pre-arranged buyer out there. It makes sense."

"Of course it makes sense," said Lindy sarcastically. "As long as you ignore the fact that pathetic get-rich-quick schemes are a drug dealer's stock in trade."

Both Maik and Jejeune looked puzzled. For reasons neither of them could understand, Jejeune's response seemed to have upset Lindy. Both men were conscious of the awkwardness of the sergeant's presence here, but it didn't seem to have anything to do with that.

Jejeune nodded thoughtfully. "I suppose it's unlikely that a parolee like Waters is going to lock up the cage and then leave prints all over a filing cabinet."

"I would certainly hope all these television police dramas are teaching our young criminals better than that," said Maik flatly.

"We won't get a warrant for Obregón's phone records based on a single unsubstantiated report," said Jejeune. He looked up at Maik. "I wonder … if it came to it, would your source be willing to go on record about this call?"

Maik thought for a moment. "Let's say no, for the time being. But the call did take place. I have no doubt about that."

He shut up suddenly. Danny Maik's skepticism was legendary. If he said anymore, he may as well identify Trueman by name, though he suspected from Jejeune's expression that the DCI may have already gotten there anyway.

Even for a book as closed as Jejeune, the reaction was less enthusiastic than Maik had been anticipating. As he saw things, it pretty much nailed Waters with regards to time and place for the theft, at the very least. He talks to Obregón one day, and the next he's in the sanctuary stealing some birds that used to belong to her husband. Identifying Jordan Waters represented a fairly significant step in the right direction in this case, and linking him to Obregón was a step still further. But from his expression, Jejeune apparently didn't share that view. Lindy saw the confusion on Maik's face and felt badly for him.

"Are you sure you won't stay for a cuppa, Sarge? There's a dried biffin with your name on it in the kitchen, too."

"As spiced shoe leather goes, it's not too bad," said Jejeune, trying to reduce the odd tension that was pulsing through the room. But neither Maik nor Lindy seemed willing to let him, though he had no idea why.

"Thanks all the same, but I'd better be getting back. Leave you two to enjoy the rest of your evening together."

"Fat chance of that, now you've brought him a viable suspect. Still, you've done brilliantly. Hasn't he, Dom?"

Jejeune snapped back from his thoughts. "What? Yes, excellent, Sergeant."

As soon as she had closed the door on the sergeant's retreating figure, Lindy rounded on Jejeune. "You don't *have* to be so clever all the time. You can have a day off, you know. You don't have to constantly keep showing us how easy it all is for you, this case, this profession, how it all so manifestly fails to offer you any sort of challenge whatsoever."

Jejeune looked puzzled. Lindy sometimes unleashed these

tirades and he had learned from past experience that the best way to handle them was to let them run their course and then try to find the root cause afterward. Usually, though, there was some sort of warning, a gathering of clouds before the storm. This attack was so sudden and so intense that Jejeune offered a defence almost as a reflex.

"I told him he had done well."

"Eventually, yes. But you had already done better, hadn't you? Gotten there anyway, worked it all out in advance. Sergeant Maik was obviously well chuffed to bring you the news about Waters, but you had to show him you already knew the suspect would be looking to sell the birds. Couldn't you have waited, at least a little bit, just nodded and thanked him?"

Jejeune looked perplexed. It wasn't really a giant leap of logic that the person who had stolen the doves would already have a buyer in place. These were live creatures that would need care and shelter and food and water every day. They weren't the kind of commodity you kept hanging around on the half-chance you were going to be able to unload them on eBay. Was she asking him to have delayed pointing all that out, just for the sake of massaging Danny Maik's ego?

"We get it, Dom. This is all so easy for you. You come up with the answers before most of us have even figured out the questions. But just so you know, there are few things as satisfying to the rest of us mere mortals as watching some smug prat get his comeuppance. You'd do well to remember that, Inspector Domenic bloody Jejeune."

She stormed out of the room, leaving the residue of her anger suspended in the void created by her departure. But whether or not he had intended sending out the message, it occurred to Jejeune that if it was so clear that this profession held no challenges for him, then there was one very obvious solution. It was interesting that someone as perceptive as Lindy had failed to point it out.

15

Jejeune stared out at the high hedgerows passing in a blur. He had found them intimidating when he first began driving out here, but now he found them more of a comforting presence, sheltering the laneways from the exposed, flat land that lay on either side. Beside him, Danny Maik guided the Mini along in quiet contentment. Somebody called Tammi Terrell had accompanied them on their journey all the way from the Saltmarsh station, singing wistfully about how wonderful it was to be in love, despite the terrible things people did to those who loved them. Even if it wasn't quite to Jejeune's taste, he could still appreciate a good tune well sung, and it did provide a pleasant, soothing background for him to conduct his roadside birding.

A large sign marked PRIVATE signalled the entrance they were looking for. Maik drove through the open gateway over the cattle grid and drew to a stop in the courtyard of a modest two-storey farmhouse. On the far side, an old barn showed the signs of age Jejeune had seen in many similar properties out here, but the house itself looked fairly new. It had been constructed with modern materials, albeit in a faux-Tudor style, with heavy black timbers dressing its smart white façade. From the look of them, neither the timbers nor the façade had weathered the trials and tribulations of very many north Norfolk decades.

On the ground in front of the barn, an exultation of Skylarks was feeding industriously. Jejeune gave them no more than a passing glance. Flocking was unusual behaviour this close to the breeding season, but the birds seemed particularly plump and healthy, as if life out here agreed with them. As Maik and Jejeune got out of the car, the birds exploded in a flurry of wings, coming to rest on a telephone wire stretched between the house and the barn.

A thin young man was sitting on a fence beside the barn. Across his knees lay an air rifle. He was staring down, studying it intently. He spoke without looking up as the two men approached.

"Can you read?" he said unpleasantly. His voice was hoarse and rough, much older than his young years.

"As a matter of fact, I can," said Maik pleasantly. "What words are you having trouble with?"

"This is private property," said the man. "So that means get lost." He looked up finally. His face was startlingly pale, accented by the jet black hair that shrouded it. His eyes were as dark and dangerous as his attitude. He turned his attention back to the air rifle, raising it slightly in his hands.

"Put down the weapon, sir," said Maik carefully.

"This?" The man waved it about. "It's a toy. It's not even loaded."

Jejeune introduced himself and the sergeant with careful civility, and explained the purpose of their visit. "We need to ask Ms. Obregón a few questions."

The young man shook his head. "No, I don't think so," he said conversationally.

Jejeune looked at the man carefully. He was probably about twenty, but he looked younger and had not yet developed a man's body. His chest was sunken and his thin arms were pale and hairless. Only in those eyes, and the husky, unnatural voice, could Jejeune detect any trace of adulthood.

"This is a murder inquiry," he said. "We can conduct the interview back at the station if we have to, but I'm sure it will be better for all of us if we don't have to do that."

"You won't be taking her anywhere," said the man, still absorbed with the air rifle. "I can guarantee that."

Maik had been taking in the scenery, with his arms folded loosely across his chest. "You'll have heard about a police officer's right to meet an imminent threat with appropriate force," he said evenly, without letting his attention wander from the surrounding fields. "And about how it's at the officer's discretion to decide what might constitute *appropriate*."

The man looked at the sergeant as squarely as before. There were times when Danny Maik exuded a raw power that suggested he could snap a person in half if he wanted to, especially a frail, sickly man-boy like this. But the man seemed utterly unconcerned about Danny Maik's menace, or anything else. He stood up, letting the air rifle dangle loosely from his hand, and took a step toward the detectives.

"Is this imminent enough for you?"

He was almost as tall as Maik, but he was so slightly built that Danny could have left nearly half of his considerable bulk at home and still outweighed him by plenty. Jejeune understood that his sergeant would be reluctant to use force on such a fragile individual as this. He knew, too, though, that despite his reservations, Maik would not let the man get any closer without acting.

"You've been asked to put that weapon down," said Maik with ominous control. "You won't be asked again."

"Is that because you're leaving?" asked the man, his arrogant, defiant stare challenging Danny Maik to action.

Jejeune could sense that Maik was unsettled by the man's unnatural detachment, his air of complete indifference. They had both seen courage before, real and feigned, but this was something different. No matter how confident you were, you had to know you would not be emerging from the other side of a physical confrontation with Danny Maik without some damage to show for it. But the man seemed to have no concern at all for the consequences of his provocation. None whatsoever.

In the razor-edged silence of the moment, the high-pitched whine seemed unnaturally loud; an over-revving engine, nearby and approaching fast. Both Maik and Jejeune snapped their heads around at the same time as the four-wheel ATV skidded around the corner of the barn and began approaching them full on. For a brief second Jejeune wondered if the rider's intention was to drive directly into the group. At the last moment, engine still roaring, the rider slewed the machine around, dragging the front wheels so they came to rest between Maik and the young man. The machine was close enough that Jejeune could feel the heat off the exposed engine.

It was not until the rider turned off the ignition and dismounted that the two detectives got a proper sense of scale. The ATV was low to the ground, but even then, the figure standing beside it seemed tiny.

"Basta!" said Luisa Obregón, taking off her helmet and tossing her hair to free it of the tangles. She hurled some rapid-fire instructions in Spanish and the man backed away. Another volley of orders followed and he cradled the air rifle and walked off.

"It is not what you think, Sergeant. It is not my son's fault. He has no fear."

"It's never too late to learn," said Maik, who despite himself was still unnerved by both the man's actions and Luisa Obregón's dramatic intervention. He, too, had been unsure of her intentions when she had been speeding toward them on the ATV.

"No, it is not possible. He cannot learn." She looked at Jejeune. "The sergeant I remember from before. You are a policeman, also, I think."

Maik let his eyes rest on the young man unconcernedly ambling back toward the barn. So this was the son. He had been sent to stay with neighbours the last time Maik was here, no doubt to protect him from the sight of all these police officers enquiring into his father's disappearance. The only time he had crossed Maik's radar since was on an arrest report a couple of years back. But it hadn't been Maik's case, and the details wouldn't come to him readily now. He cast a look at Jejeune, but he would have no memory of the incident, either. It had happened long before the DCI arrived in Saltmarsh.

Luisa Obregón watched her son until he had resumed his position on the fence near the barn. "Come," she said, "we can speak inside."

16

Luisa Obregón shrugged off her black jacket in the hallway and turned to face them. For the first time, Jejeune was able to properly take in her appearance. Her long black hair framed a face of high cheekbones and finely defined features, set off with a pair of glittering grey-blue eyes. She would once have been a stunningly attractive woman, but her face had been robbed of its light by sadness. It was still with her now, laying upon her like a blanket, smothering any signs of joy with its heaviness.

"I can offer you coffee, or tea. No alcohol." Whether she didn't have any, or simply wouldn't be offering it was unclear, but neither man was a drinking-on-duty type anyway. Her offer declined, Luisa Obregón crossed the open-plan living room and settled on a large leather couch that seemed to dwarf her small frame. She moved with a dancer's grace. Combined with her looks, a career striding the runways of the world as a fashion model would surely have been a possibility if she had been a few inches taller. But perhaps not. Luisa Obregón did not strike Jejeune as the kind of woman who would allow others to tell her what to wear, or how to walk. Or what to say.

"My son," she said, "he cannot control his actions." She shifted awkwardly. Like many people who are unwilling to admit fault, she would offer up an explanation instead, but it was clear that even this contrition was unfamiliar territory for her, and the men suspected that this was about as close as they were going to get to an apology.

A faint flicker danced across Maik's memory. "That medical condition." He vaguely remembered hearing something about it at the time of the original investigation, but again, he couldn't recall the details. Perhaps he should start drinking some of that ginko tea that Lauren Salter was always trying to push on him to improve his memory.

"Urbach-Wiethe," said Obregón. "A very rare disease. A part of his brain has been damaged, the part that allows a person to experience fear. My son cannot recognize a threatening situation, nor read such expressions in people's faces, so no threat of violence or danger registers with him."

A complete absence of fear was not a condition either man could easily imagine, and for a few seconds they sat quietly with their thoughts.

"You came today because you wished to speak to me about my aviary," said Luisa Obregón matter-of-factly, jarring them from their silence. It was clear that the subject of her son's illness was behind them now. She was expecting neither sympathy nor any further comments about it.

"We are making enquiries about the provenance of some birds," said Jejeune. "It seems your husband sold the birds to a former employee, a man named Wylde."

"My husband sold no birds to that man," said Obregón firmly.

"Mrs. Wylde has a receipt showing that your husband sold them to him."

Obregón waved a hand dismissively. "My husband did not sell those birds. They disappeared in the storm of 2006, many months after my husband … left. The roof of the aviary was torn off by the winds. I had assumed all the birds escaped, but this man Wylde must have found these birds somehow, stolen them. Where are the birds now? They are still my property, I believe."

"The birds may be evidence in a murder inquiry," said Jejeune.

Not exactly what Luisa Obregón asked, though, was it, noted Maik. Whether it would be as clear to someone whose first language wasn't English, he didn't know. Either way, Luisa Obregón apparently wasn't going to press her enquiry any farther.

Since Jejeune had taken the unusual step of opening the questioning himself, Maik felt free to do some wandering around. His attention was drawn to an immense glass room that was secured to the back of the house. Through large plate glass windows set in the rear wall, he could see that the house was set on the edge of a steep ravine. From far below a central pole rose up and supported a spiderweb of thin metal ribs. Large sheets of glass covered the whole structure, forming an enclosed aviary that ran off the back off the house as far as he could see in all directions. At eye-level, the tops of several trees marked the end of a climb from the aviary floor. Craning slightly to look down, he could see a dense tangle of foliage, all but impenetrable, some twenty feet below.

"I'd forgotten just how big this thing is," he said.

"Ten thousand square feet," said Obregón, with the certainty of someone who did not deal in approximations. "My husband chose the location for this house only after he had selected the place where he would build his aviary. Being on the edge of the ravine allowed him to work where he could be surrounded by his birds in all directions."

Maik could see a stilt-supported wooden walkway leading from the back door of the house and stretching out into the centre of the aviary. At the end was a circular deck surrounded by a low wooden railing and a built in bench seat, the entire structure looking for all the world as if it was suspended in mid-air, high above the mass of vegetation below.

"Do you mind?" Jejeune stood and joined Maik at one of the large plate glass windows that looked out into the aviary. He spent some moments standing motionless, letting his eyes flicker in all directions, taking it all in.

"They go through much food," said Luisa Obregón, standing behind the two men. She indicated the well-stocked feeding trays and water dishes arranged around the edge of the platform. It was the only evidence of upkeep Jejeune could see in the entire aviary. Obregón seemed to sense the sentiment.

"My husband planted tropical vegetation. He wanted the birds to have the exact habitat they were used to in their home countries. But ..."

But it would require careful management to keep it in check. And that hadn't happened. Not since Victor Obregón walked out of her life and disappeared forever. The tropical vegetation had grown out of control now; a dense mass of ferns and palm fronds covered the ground, and the trees and shrubs had grown together in a jumble of intertwined trunks and leafy branches.

Jejeune was watching the birds as they flitted in from the trees to visit the feeding trays around the platform. He seemed engrossed by what he saw. Transfixed.

"I wonder," he said without turning, "do you know Ramon Santos?"

No context, no mention of his position, thought Maik. Present tense, too. Inspector Jejeune was on a roll today. Perhaps it was this bird business, the aviary and all, that was inspiring this new level of engagement.

"It is my business to know the Mexican officials in the U.K. After all, the Mexican government was responsible for the disappearance of my husband. But I have never had any dealings personally with Señor Santos."

When she reverted to formal language, Obregón's accent betrayed no trace of her mother tongue. Like many of those expensively educated in English, it was the clipped, slang nuances of a native speaker that she lacked. But there had been nothing lost in this translation. Obregón's statement was worthy of Jejeune's eye contact. He turned to look at her.

"The Mexican authorities were involved in your husband's disappearance? In what way?"

"You must ask them," she said. It was clear she would say nothing more on the subject. Nevertheless, it seemed to Maik that this might be an avenue of investigation worth pursuing, not least because they didn't have many others. But if Jejeune's mind was also mulling over this possibility, the DCI seemed to feel, for the moment at least, that they would take it no farther.

"You have a fair-sized farm property here," said Jejeune. "Can I ask, were you ever contacted by a woman called Phoebe Hunter about the possibility of setting aside some of your land as habitat for Turtledoves?"

Obregón nodded. "She came to see us some months ago. I told her this may be possible. It would be what my husband would have wanted. We had done this before, but I know he was concerned particularly about the declining numbers of Turtledoves."

Jejeune looked puzzled. "Before?"

"A bird called the Corn Bunting. The project had been successful in other parts of the country, and they wanted to try at a site in Norfolk."

Jejeune's face registered an expression Maik didn't recognize. Disappointment? Anger? With whom? Himself? If Luisa Obregón also noted Jejeune's expression, she chose to ignore it.

"The earlier set-aside was troublesome," she said. "Even for an organic farm, to have to grow spring barley in this way and not clear the stubble fields over the winter caused many hardships and extra work for us. The compensation did not cover this. But it was my husband's wish, and I know it made him happy to help these birds. For this reason, if this woman had wanted us to do it again, for Turtledoves, I would have agreed."

"Apart from Phoebe Hunter, have you had any contact with any of the staff who worked at the sanctuary where the birds were being held?" Jejeune had not identified the sanctuary, or Waters, by name, Maik noticed. Somehow, the DCI always seemed to give his interviewees the chance to offer answers to questions he hadn't asked.

It would have been easy for Obregón to lie. Instead, she looked at Jejeune frankly with her piercing grey-blue eyes.

"A man called to tell me he could return some property of ours. He was supposed to contact me when he had acquired this property. But I did not hear from him again." She said it coldly, simply, in a way that people sometimes do when they suspect their truths will be disbelieved.

"And you have no idea who this man was?"

She shook her head firmly. "No. And now, I must return to my work. There is always much to do on an organic farm."

"Your son" said Jejeune as he turned to leave. "It might be well to advise him that we may have to come back here again."

"Do you think it will be necessary?"

"Oh, I would imagine so," said Jejeune. "Thank you for your time."

As they walked across the courtyard, Jejeune halted to stare at the flock of small brown birds again. They had returned to the ground and were feeding busily on the wheat chaff on the concrete pad in front of the barn. Corn Buntings. He had not bothered examining them closely enough, and had taken them for Skylarks, consigning them to irrelevance with barely a second thought. But now he noted the subtle details that had troubled him before, the slight difference in size, in colouration. He watched as one of the birds flew up to the wire and threw its head back to sing, a wonderful rolling trill. How many other small brown birds like this were misindentified or, worse still, overlooked completely in such a cavalier manner? In his defence, there had been distractions. A man who could not know fear holding an air rifle across his knees for one. But it was not good enough, not for someone who considered himself a birder, who was considering, even, a career in bird studies.

From his seat on the fence, Gabriel Obregón watched as Jejeune studied the birds. As the inspector and his sergeant walked past, he raised the empty air rifle and took a bead on the bird on the wire.

"Vermin," he said. He closed one eye and made a clicking sound with his tongue as he fired off his imaginary pellet.

Jejeune paused at the passenger side of Maik's Mini. "Corn Buntings are a red-listed species in Britain, Mr. Obregón," he said, "meaning they are fully protected. Harming them or harassing them in any way is a criminal offence. It could result in a prison sentence."

To Maik, threatening a man who was incapable of fear with a jail sentence for shooting some birds on his own property seemed beyond ludicrous. He had expected sarcasm in response, or defiance. But Obregón appeared to take Jejeune's comments seriously.

"We suffered season after season of losses for these birds," the young man said. "And then this woman comes to ask if we would do it all again. Should humans suffer hardships so life will be kinder to a few birds?" He shook his head. "I don't think so."

Obregón was still looking up at the bird on the wire as the two policemen got in the car.

"Vermin," he said again as they drove away.

17

The low early-morning sun cast long shadows across the flat meadows as Jejeune wheeled The Beast into the car park at Snettisham and pulled up beside a battered hatchback. A man stood beside it, arranging a variety of boxes and blankets. He was about Jejeune's height but his raw muscularity made him seem larger. He was about Jejeune's age, too, but his features had the telltale signs of an outdoor life on them. He had leathery brown skin and a spiderweb of tiny lines tracing from the corners of his eyes, like someone who had spent a long time squinting in bright sunlight.

"Morning, Inspector." Gavin Churchill straightened from his task and looked around him briefly, taking in the flat lands that surrounded them on all sides. In a field on the far side of the lane, thin green margins of vegetation traced a waterway along the edge of ploughed earth. Jejeune introduced Lindy, and Churchill shook hands politely with both of them.

"Thanks for agreeing to come all the way out here. I know you're investigating something pretty serious, but there's a situation over at the beach that probably can't wait." His Canadian accent was stronger than Domenic's, but it could just have been that Lindy was more familiar with Dom's. Or perhaps Gavin simply hadn't been over here as long. "Do you mind if we walk while we talk?" He gathered his long brown hair and tied it into an untidy ponytail before picking up a cardboard box and setting off at a brisk pace. Jejeune and Lindy fell into step behind him.

They mounted the wooden steps over the first of the grassy berms and fell into a single-file line as they began to follow the narrow track between the raspberry bushes and brambles. Gavin moved with the easy gait of a man with a strong internal rhythm, but even so it was clear he was in a hurry to cover the ground between himself and the animal in need of his help.

"Jejeune," said Gavin over his shoulder. "There used to be a guy back home with that name who led bird tours. Had a good rep., too. It wasn't you, was it?"

Lindy had somehow manoeuvred her way up to second in the procession, leaving Jejeune to call his answer from the back of the line. "No."

"Unusual name, though …"

"It wasn't me," said Jejeune in that polite tone Lindy recognized as the one he used when he wanted to end a conversation. He called forward his own question. "I was wondering if you could remember anything special about the pair of doves you recovered two weeks ago from Margaret Wylde's place. Were they ringed, for example, or did they have any distinguishing marks?"

From behind, Jejeune watched Gavin's head move slowly from side to side. "Nope. They were just doves, you know. Kept in terrible conditions though. That's why we had to confiscate them. But definitely not ringed."

With conversation difficult in this single-file arrangement and Gavin's pace picking up a little, the party proceeded in silence. It wasn't until the path widened out as they began to make their way beside the river that Jejeune was able to come alongside Gavin.

"You must have met Phoebe Hunter on occasion, given your line of work. Anything particular strike you about her?"

Gavin didn't slow his urgent stride at all, but he looked across at Jejeune as they walked, as if aware the DCI must have already asked this question of other people, meaning that it was not information he was looking for, but his impressions of her.

"It's too bad, what happened to her. She was a nice person. She really loved those birds. Their welfare, protecting them, that was pretty much all she talked about. That and her set-aside projects. If somebody was going to injure those birds, or steal them, I could see her putting herself in harm's way."

Jejeune seemed to take in Gavin's answer before asking his next question. "You'd never seen those doves before? You weren't doing this rescue work when all those birds escaped from the Obregón aviary in the storm of 2006?"

Gavin shook his head. "Nope, still at uni back in Canada then. You think that family is involved in that girl's death?"

Behind them Lindy was having trouble keeping up, her sandals no match for the pebbles on the gravel path. But even from her distance, Lindy could pick up on Jejeune's sudden interest. She redoubled her efforts to catch up with the two men.

"Why would you ask that?" inquired Jejeune.

Gavin seemed to hesitate a little, though his pace remained constant. "I've been up to their property a couple of times. Animals get into trouble there the same as anywhere else. Last time was a Tawny Owl with a broken wing. I picked it up but it didn't make it. The lady, she was okay. You could tell she felt bad for the bird, wanted to help it, you know, like most people. But the guy, her son, I guess it is, he told me just to leave the owl, let the foxes and crows have their fun with it." Gavin turned to Lindy who had just arrived, as if perhaps he had had more luck with these kinds of explanations with women in the past. "I mean, I get that some people are not really into animals, but I got the impression if one crossed this guy's path, he would alter his stride just so he could step on it." He shook his head. "It was kind of unnerving, that's all. That sort of coldness."

Jejeune had no more questions, and dropped back to walk next to Lindy, who was finding it impossible to match Gavin's pace along the trail. By the time they emerged from the footpath at the edge of Snettisham Bay, Gavin had already assessed the situation and was removing things from the cardboard box: a large beach towel; a small, lint-free cloth; and a spray bottle half-filled with what looked to be water.

"Black Guillemot," he said as Jejeune and Lindy approached. "Badly oiled. If we can't get to him soon, he won't make it."

Jejeune peered into a small tide pool that had collected on the leeward side of a rocky outcrop. A pair of Black-headed Gulls were perched on the overhanging rocks, and a couple of Dunlin were working the outer fringes of the shallow pool, but in the centre Jejeune could see a bird struggling to stay afloat.

Gavin looked at Jejeune. "I guess the local birders are going to be mad, huh?"

Jejeune nodded. A mega-rarity like this showing up on these shores and they would have no chance to see it. Of course, whether a distress case like this even counted as a legitimate record was by no means certain. For Jejeune himself, it wouldn't, but he knew other birders had different criteria for what was permitted to appear on their lists.

Gavin seemed to be considering the situation. "If you're okay with it, I could use your help. I'm going to circle around and try to grab him in the water, but, if he finds the strength to make a run for it, throw this over him." He handed the large towel to Jejeune. "Keep it in front of your legs, though. I'm told these birds have a habit of trying to run right between them if they can." He gave a thin smile. "You tell me where on the evolutionary timeline they picked up that little survival trick."

Lindy headed down toward the shoreline, ready to drive
the bird back inland if it came her way. Gavin moved stealthily
through the water until he was directly behind the bird. Then
with a rush, he approached, missing with his attempted grab.
The bird was startled into an ungainly flap-run across the water
surface and continued at pace across the rocky beach. Jejeune's
first throw was unsuccessful, but his second was a direct hit,
before the bird had even had time to turn and head back in
Lindy's direction. The mass beneath the towel stopped moving
instantly. Jejeune was unsure if he should approach and secure
the bird, but Gavin was beside him in a moment. "Thanks, I
can take it from here."

He swiftly wrapped the towel around the bird and folded it
back to reveal a forlorn, bedraggled head, matted with thick oil.
He shook his head sadly. "You see that spray bottle anywhere?"

Lindy handed it to him. "Will it be okay?"

Jejeune imagined he could detect hope in Lindy's voice, even
though she could surely see, as clearly as he could, the dismal
state of the bird's head and neck.

"It's not good," said Gavin. "He's pretty weak. He's been here
all night. Somebody noticed him last night but they didn't call
it in until this morning. Can you believe it?" he asked bitterly.
"I guess they were too busy watching the show."

The sunset, he meant. Locals gathered at the north end of the
bay each evening to watch the sun paint the sky with a spectacular palette of reds and oranges. Sometimes, if the tide was out,
the glistening mudflats could look like they were ablaze with
the tiny fires of a thousand reflecting pools. It was the reason a
suggestion by Dom for an evening birding trip to Snettisham
rarely met with any resistance from Lindy.

Gavin gently sprayed the bird's face and used the cloth to
carefully wipe oil from the bird's eyes and nostrils. The bird
attempted a couple of feeble, half-hearted jabs with its beak,

but the efforts seemed too much for it and eventually it simply remained still while Gavin worked on it.

"Good nictitating membrane response, at least," he said. He looked up at Lindy. "Third eyelid. Means he's got a chance. But I need to get him back to the rescue centre quickly so they can begin to clean him up."

He replaced the towel over the bird's head and lifted the shrouded form carefully. He set it gently in the cardboard box and closed the flaps. Without speaking, Gavin struck off along the beach, cradling the box in both arms.

No one spoke as they made their way in single file, in the same order as before, back up from the beach and onto the narrow trail. As the cars came in sight, Lindy eased ahead of Gavin on the path and ran to open the rear hatch of his car, where Gavin was able to nestle the box into a pile of old blankets to prevent it rocking around. Only a slight scrabbling sound gave any indication that there was life inside the box.

"He seems a little livelier, at least," said Lindy, without any real justification that Jejeune could see.

"Maybe," said Gavin, "but it's hard to tell. Sometimes, they do okay for a while, respond to treatment even, and then they just seem to go sour on us, for no apparent reason. It's like they lose the will to live."

"How sad," said Lindy.

"Yeah, I mean it's not like we're piping Leonard Cohen music into their cages or anything." Gavin gave a lop-sided grin. "I hope this one makes it, though. It shouldn't even be here. Probably way out to sea somewhere, on its way to a breeding ground, when it got hit by the oil." He paused for a moment. "Makes you wonder how many others are out there that didn't make it in to shore." He turned and extended his hand to Jejeune. "Listen, thanks for your help. I just feel bad that you came all the way out here and I wasn't able to give you any answers. Those doves. Can I ask what it was you were looking for?"

"To be honest, I'm not sure," said Jejeune. "They seem to have been targeted, so whoever took them must have been able to tell them from the others. It would obviously have to be something external. Nothing the DNA is going to tell us would have been visible to the naked eye."

The news seemed to take Gavin by surprise. "You're having DNA testing done? How is that possible? I thought the birds had been stolen."

"We're testing the feathers," said Jejeune simply.

Gavin seemed to pause, considering this information. And then, there it was: a momentary halt, a heartbeat of hesitancy betraying an inner thought. Even Lindy noticed it. *This is what Domenic does,* she thought. *He picks up on these things, these flickers, these interruptions in the normal patterns of human behaviour, perhaps even something as subtle as a change in a person's breathing rhythm. He registers these involuntary telltale signs, as he had registered this one. And then he closes in.*

Jejeune posed the question with a raised eyebrow only.

Gavin shook his head slowly. "That ringing business. It is kind of strange when you think about it," he said. "I mean, given that they must have been from a breeder."

"Why do you say that?"

"Well, how else is a pair of exotic birds going to show up here together? I mean one, maybe. This is north Norfolk, after all. You never know what might drop in. But a pair arriving together naturally?" He shook his head again disbelievingly.

"Exotics?" Jejeune made no attempt to disguise the surprise in his voice. "You mean the birds you took from Margaret Wylde's weren't Turtledoves?"

"Turtledoves?" Gavin gave a hearty laugh. "No way. I would have almost gone for good old North American Mourning Doves, but there was something a bit off about them."

"Are you sure?"

"I carried them out by hand, Inspector. I might not be any Tom Gullick on bird ID, but I'm pretty sure I could tell a Turtledove. No, these were definitely something else. Listen, I gotta get this guy to the rescue centre right away. The research suggests transportation time is a key factor in survival rates. But if you need anything else from me, identify those birds from a line-up, anything like that, just give me a shout. Okay?"

Gavin waved through the open window of his car as he drove away, but by then Jejeune was a long way from paying attention. He was quiet as he and Lindy climbed into The Beast. "It was your brother who led those birding tours, wasn't it?" she asked as reached for the seatbelt. "You never talk about him, Dom. Why is that?"

Jejeune shrugged, "There's not much to say. He used to be a birder, and now he isn't."

Domenic didn't do innocent misunderstanding very well at the best of times, and it was perfectly clear he knew a discussion of his brother's birding career wasn't what Lindy meant. But it was equally clear that he didn't want to discuss the subject. To this point, Lindy had tolerated this off-limits approach, indulged it even. But they had been together for long enough now that she was starting to feel entitled to some insights, especially into something that had obviously played such a significant role in Domenic's past. But he wasn't ready to talk about it yet, and she'd let it go. For now.

She realized that they were not moving, and looked over at Jejeune. He had Santos's bird guide open on his lap and he was studying the page on Turtledoves intently. When he closed the book, a look of quiet satisfaction spread across his face. Lindy's own world might be filled with unanswered questions at the moment, but to Domenic Jejeune, at least, some things were apparently starting to make sense.

18

The sound of raised voices reached the detectives even before they rounded the corner, causing them to quicken their pace, as police officers do when they sense some disturbance to the equilibrium of daily life. Halfway down the street, David Nyce was standing on his doorstep conducting a strident discussion with a man in a business suit below him on the pavement.

"Well, there are obviously a number of recourses open to you. Feel free to pursue whichever of them you see fit. In fact, why not give all of 'em a try; perhaps develop some sort of ranking system for them. For now, though, I've given this matter all the time I am prepared to give it, so I suggest you just toddle off and let me get on with my day."

The man turned on his heel and brushed angrily past the detectives as they approached. A glimmer of familiarity airbrushed Danny Maik's memory as he passed.

"Ah, the rozzers," said Nyce, noticing them for the first time. "Wish you could have been spared such an unedifying spectacle, but that's the way some people apparently prefer to conduct their business these days." He gestured for the two men to come inside.

"Anything we should know about?" asked Maik.

Nyce affected a shrug. "Disgruntled parent, unhappy that his little darling is not quite the intellectual giant he, and she, imagined she would be. University signals the death knell of so many dreams, I find. They come here, fresh from being the stars of their little village schools, heads filled with notions that they can achieve anything, that the world is theirs for the taking, only to be shown that they are really no more than just average, not really special at all." Nyce gave a contemptuous sneer. "Hard to take, I suppose — all those hopes and ambitions disappearing into thin air like that. But it's hardly my fault, and I have no intention of letting anyone take out their frustrations on me."

"Nevertheless, sir, until we're sure what went on at the sanctuary, I would suggest you avoid antagonizing the locals as much as possible."

"Really? Pity. A bit of a hobby of mine, as it happens." Nyce settled behind his desk. "So, more questions? About Turtledoves again? Or sparrows. Can't help you with murder, I'm afraid. Not really my field at all." He gave a thin smile that neither of the detectives matched.

The room had undergone a transformation since the last time they were there. Books and magazines lay open everywhere, strewn about untidily as if someone had desperately been searching them for information.

"Carrie Pritchard said Phoebe Hunter was surprisingly successful in getting support for a plan for set-asides for Turtledoves," said Jejeune.

Taking the lead again? thought Maik. Pity there couldn't be a birding element in all their cases, if DCI Jejeune was going to show this level of engagement.

Nyce offered Jejeune an indulgent smile. "Ah, been chatting to old Carrie, have you? Well, she certainly has her talents, the delightful Ms. P., but keeping her finger on the pulse of the Saltmarsh community is hardly one of them. Artist type, you see. Need I say more? Barely function in the real world, can they, let alone keep abreast of its various doings? What is she suggesting, that one of the local farmers might have had a touch too much cider one night and finished poor old Phoebe off because we were going to pinch a little corner of his land?" Nyce shook his head emphatically. "Absolute tosh."

"So you don't think the set-aside proposal would have posed a threat to Phoebe Hunter?" asked Jejeune with the sort of careful tone that Maik had learned to pay particular attention to.

"Why should it? I have spent much of my time — time I won't get back, I should add — in the company of the leather-necked sons of the soil in these parts, and I can tell you quite categorically, if there is one thing they like more than a government handout to grow their agro-chemicals, it is the prospect of a bung that will allow them to sit at home and do nothing instead."

Outside of Jejeune and his girlfriend, Maik could think of no one locally who could not trace some farming lineage in their family background. It crossed his mind that if Nyce ever reported receiving death threats, they were going to need more memory on the computers at the station to store the list of potential suspects.

"Besides, it was far from certain that I was going to give the project the go-ahead."

Jejeune looked surprised. "What was the delay? Most of those agreements were reached weeks ago, in some cases, months. I mean set-asides worked well enough for the Linnet and Corn Bunting in these parts," he said reasonably.

Nyce nodded. "Indeed, but the jury is still very much out as to whether it would work for Turtledoves. We also could not say with any certainty that a set-aside would not have a negative impact on some as-yet-unidentified ecosystem within the designated areas. It was simply not good science to proceed at this time. We need to follow, in a word, the golden rule of conservation."

"Do no harm," said Jejeune.

Maik couldn't get over the impression that Jejeune was continually looking for a chance to impress Nyce with his background in all this stuff. Though why his DCI should care one way or the other about the opinion of a patronizing tool like Nyce was beyond him. The phone rang but Nyce ignored it, letting it go to voicemail, and reaching over to turn the volume to silent.

"So you and Phoebe Hunter disagreed about these set-asides then?" asked Maik, anxious to make something approaching actual progress in their investigations amid all this birding talk.

"No, Sergeant," said Nyce, reaching deep for some inner level of condescension, "the student lacked sufficient knowledge in the subject to fully appreciate her supervisor's position."

"Getting back to Carrie Pritchard for a moment," said Jejeune. "I was wondering if you could shed any light on the conflict that appears to exist between her and Luisa Obregón."

Maik allowed himself a faint smile. It was no accident, he was sure, that Jejeune had happened to ask this of a person who would delight in the disagreements of others and be more than ready to report on them.

"Whole thing stems from when the Obregón's aviary was destroyed by the storm of '06," said Nyce confidently. "Luisa Obregón refused to supply the local birders with a list of the birds she'd lost."

Maik looked faintly puzzled. *Why would birders care what species had been in Obregón's aviary?* He asked the question aloud, to see who wanted to field it.

It was his boss. "Without a stock list from Obregón, every time a rarity showed up for months afterward, no one could be sure if it was a wild bird, in other words, a legitimate rarity, or an escapee," said Jejeune.

Nyce nodded. "Full marks, once again, Inspector. Obregón's

lack of co-operation was seen as sheer bloody-mindedness and caused a great deal of resentment in the birding community as a whole. Made Carrie's job as recorder for the Rare Birds Committee hell, I can tell you."

"But there must be more to it than that," said Maik. He looked at the others uneasily. What Jejeune and Nyce were describing sounded like the material for a dispute at a birdwatching society meeting, but hardly something to fuel a feud as deep as this one seemed to go.

"My, my, the North Norfolk Constabulary does have some swifties in its ranks, doesn't it? Any more like you two down there and you'll be able to enter a team in University Challenge. Yes, Sergeant, there is more to it. A few weeks after the storm, a Mourning Dove was sighted in Hunstanton. It had no bands and no signs of feather abrasion — the usual telltales for captive birds. The sighting was just far enough away from the aviary to raise the possibility that this was a wild bird. As you can imagine, there was a fair amount of optimism that it would be accepted as a legitimate record. Nevertheless, as Rare Bird Recorder, it was still Carrie's job to check for the possibility of an escape, and after a short time she came back to declare definitively that Luisa Obregón's aviary stock had included Mourning Doves, and the sighting, therefore, could not be validated. Disappointed a lot of prominent birders in this area, I can tell you — Quentin Senior and Cameron Brae among them. Only, as soon as she made the announcement, up pops Luisa Obregón to categorically deny she had ever confirmed one way or the other whether her aviary had contained Mourning Doves. Furthermore, she claimed she had never even been contacted by Carrie about it. Whatever the truth of it, it was egg-on-face for Carrie, I'm afraid. *Molto* embarrassment, and a quick vote off the Rare Birds Committee. Carrie, as you will have already surmised, is not a woman to take that sort of thing lying down. From that moment on, the relationship between the two women went downhill. I daresay it hasn't hit bottom yet."

Maik greeted Nyce's report with a stony silence. Nyce's mobile sounded, but he turned it off without checking it. Jejeune flapped an academic paper he had picked up from a side table.

"This paper, the copy we found at Phoebe Hunter's flat had your name crossed out and hers written in as lead author."

Nyce rolled his eyes dramatically. "Oh, God, Inspector, please don't tell me I have to walk you through the tedious world of academic publishing. She'd done some good work on that paper, and I decided to give her some recognition: the lead credit. Only some idiot at the journal got the wrong end of the stick and put me on as lead instead. Force of habit, I suppose. Anyway, I told Phoebe to change it and send it back, along with a nice note asking them if they could possibly manage to get it right this time. Speaking of which, those other papers of Phoebe's, they will be released soon, I take it? I can't understand the delay. I mean, presumably they're not evidence."

"Is there any reason they should be?" asked Jejeune.

"Damned if I know. You're the detective." Nyce spread his hands to indicate his desk. "As you can see, I've got quite enough to do tidying up her mess. Can't be doing your job for you, as well, can I?"

The chirrup of an incoming email sounded from Nyce's laptop, but again he ignored it. "Apologies, Inspector." Nyce tried one of his underused smiles. "I'm under a bit of pressure at the moment."

Jejeune hesitated for a second before asking, "Did Phoebe ever mention anyone in particular she may have been close to at the sanctuary?"

The sudden interest in Nyce's expression was in such marked contrast to his earlier ambivalence that it would have been impossible to miss it. "You suspect she was killed by one of the volunteers?" He seemed to consider the prospect briefly, before shrugging. "She may have mentioned one or two of them now and again in passing, but I doubt she would have come down in favour of anyone in particular. Not good with the big questions, our Phoebe. Her generation seems to struggle so much with the kinds of decisions our own took as a matter of course, don't they, Inspector?"

Maik would have put Nyce closer to his own generation than to Jejeune's, but he supposed when you were in the habit of preying on younger women, a bit of self-deception about your age came with the territory.

"There is an unidentified print from the scene," said Maik. "I wonder if you would you mind coming down to the station with us to be fingerprinted? So we can officially eliminate you from our enquiries."

"I hardly think so," said Nyce with a distainful laugh. "You have noticed my desk, I take it? Do you have any idea how incredibly inconvenient it would be for me to leave and go down the station at the moment?"

"Yes," said Maik simply. "I do."

With another man he might have pointed out that it would help move the search for Phoebe's killer forward, but Nyce was intelligent enough to fully appreciate the consequences of his actions. Yet Maik simply couldn't accept that Nyce was as disconnected from Phoebe Hunter's death as he was trying to act. What the connection was, the sergeant couldn't say, but judging from Jejeune's own measured silence, the inspector had sensed it, too.

"Thank you, Dr. Nyce. If anything else comes to mind, let us know," said Jejeune abruptly, bringing the interview to a close on his own terms, as he always did.

Nyce had not walked them to the door this time, so the men were alone as they stood on the pavement admiring his shiny green toy. But Jejeune suspected from his sergeant's expression that Maik's mind might be elsewhere.

"Everything all right?"

"That man who Nyce was arguing with," Maik said slowly. "I've just remembered who he is. He might well be a disgruntled parent, but he's also chair of the university's Faculty Conduct Committee. I wonder why Dr. Nyce failed to mention that. Perhaps it just slipped his mind," he said with a slight smile. "You know, what with all this pressure he's under and everything."

19

Shepherd entered the incident room with Guy Trueman a respectful half-step behind her. He was playing his supporting role to perfection, and if Shepherd was aware that there might be an element of calculation about it, she didn't seem to mind. Those familiar with Domenic Jejeune, however, might have detected something of the inspector's own views on Trueman's presence by the way he abruptly abandoned his customary desk-perch at the back of the room to take up an awkward hovering off to the side of Danny Maik as the sergeant delivered his morning briefing.

"As you all know, the focus of our investigations has now switched to one Jordan Waters. Now I know one or two of you are familiar with Mr. Waters already, Constable Holland in particular, but for those of you who have not yet had the pleasure, I can tell you that he is most often to be found where drugs are being sold, when he is not trying to get the money to buy them."

"We're talking B and E, stolen goods ..." offered Holland, "basically, anything that would help him avoid doing an honest day's work."

"Are we thinking he's our killer, Sarge?" asked Salter from the front row. The only visible sign of her previous ordeal with Maggie Wylde was a small bandage on her neck, but that wasn't to say there weren't other, internal scars. She was looking at Maik in a way that seemed to suggest his answer mattered a lot to her. *Are we giving up on Maggie?* she was asking. *Are we closing the book on my last chance to redeem myself?*

"He is, I would say, someone we would be extremely interested in speaking to about the murders." Maik looked across at Jejeune for confirmation that he didn't need. Despite plenty of practice, Maik still wasn't comfortable running the briefings to this extent, less so when Shepherd was in attendance, let alone his ex-CO. But if Jejeune saw no reason to relieve the sergeant of his burden just yet, Shepherd apparently did.

"While we are out beating the bushes trying to locate said Mr. Waters, it might be nice to have a solid motive in place for when we do eventually bring him in. Do we happen to know, for example, whether he was stealing the birds to order? I hear Luisa Obregón posted a list of birds she would be willing to purchase for her aviary. Anything in that, do you think?"

Shepherd studiously avoided looking at Trueman. Jejeune suspected that, like him, she had little doubt about the identity of Maik's source, but she also suspected Trueman would be unwilling to confirm the details of illegal phone surveillance conducted at the behest of Mexican officials while he was in front of a roomful of police officers. Nevertheless, Jejeune and Maik could hardly be expected to keep the rest of the investigative team in the dark about the fact that Waters had telephoned Obregón. So now Shepherd was apparently casting around for another way to introduce the Obregóns into their collective consciousness. Not for the first time, Holland was in quickly to take up his DCS's lead.

"Most of us here remember what a tearaway the son was in his younger days," said Holland, casting a sly glance in Jejeune's direction.

Salter nodded. "It wasn't just teenager temper tantrums either," she said. "That assault on the photographer was vicious." She turned to offer an explanation to Jejeune. "He caught him sneak-ing around on their property, trying to get pictures of his mother. A follow-up story to the father's disappearance; you know what they're like — 'the grieving wife, two years on.' Gabriel Obregón attacked him with an iron bar, sent him to the hospital. In the end, it all went away. The photographer was trespassing. I suppose it could have gotten messy for the newspaper ..." She shrugged.

"The boy *is* very protective of his mother," Maik said thoughtfully. "If somebody had upset her in some way ..." he made a *who knows* face. "Still, she seems to have him on a pretty tight rein these days."

"A mummy's boy with a hair-trigger temper," said Holland. "Put a lid on a simmering pot like that, and something's bound to blow."

"I wonder," said Jejeune, casting a significant glance in Trueman's direction, "does anyone know what Victor Obregón's area of study was?"

"Something to do with genetic engineering," said Trueman. "He was very highly regarded, I believe."

Shepherd nodded. "That's right. I remember reading at the time that it was something of a coup for North Norfolk University to get him." She cast an inviting glance around the room, seeking others to confirm her recollections.

"So, have we been overthinking this thing, then?" Holland asked the room at large. "A genetic engineer, a Mexican. I mean, hello, let's connect the dots here. I can think of a cou-ple of Mexican organizations who might be very interested in Obregón's line of work. And I'm not talking about increasing the yield of their avocados, either."

"I'm not sure the north Norfolk climate would be the ideal place to do genetic engineering on avocado trees, in any case," said Maik, grateful that Salter in the front row had dropped her gaze to avoid eye contact with him.

"No," said Shepherd quickly. "There's no evidence to support that at all. I think that's at least one avenue of investigation we can safely shut down. Agreed, Domenic? No traction there?"

She seemed keen to not only kill off Holland's line of enquiry, but to bury it in a lead coffin. Her furtive glance in Trueman's direction confirmed what Jejeune suspected. With Anglo-Mexican detente dangling from an ever more tenuous thread these days, stereotypical theories involving Mexican drug cartels were not the sorts of ideas DCS Shepherd wanted Guy Trueman taking back with him to the consulate. Having scoured the room with a glance that dared anyone else to postulate any connection between Obregón's disappearance and this case, Shepherd switched gears with her customary élan.

"Did you come across anything of significance at the Obregón's aviary, Domenic?"

"Possibly," he said warily. "Did you notice anything about the birds in that aviary, Sergeant?"

"They had wings?" said Maik. Although Jejeune suspected there might not be quite as much ambivalence as there once had been, Maik clearly wasn't going to admit to any interest in birds today, especially in front of his former CO.

"They were all doves. The Mourning, Inca, and Zenaida doves I could recognize, but there were a couple of other species I couldn't identify — possibly hybrids of the other three."

He looked at Shepherd as if anticipating some sort of protest. Instead, all he got was a dead-eyed stare. "The thing is, they're pretty drab birds. I mean, I don't particularly advocate keeping birds in an aviary anyway, but if you were going to, there are some fairly spectacular species you could choose: monmots, turacos, rollers. Even if you wanted to stick to pigeons and doves, you could have Luzon Bleeding-heart Doves, for example, or Splendid Fruit Doves. They are astonishingly beautiful, exotic-looking, just the kind of thing you might expect a private collector to want in an aviary. But to set up such an elaborate arrangement and then stock it with dowdy birds like these, well, it just doesn't seem to make sense."

If Jejeune was waiting for anyone in the room to contradict him, it seemed like he might be waiting a very long time.

"I've also looked into the species Luisa Obregón was looking to buy," continued Jejeune. "Again, all doves. Pacific, Galapagos, and Eared."

"I didn't know doves had ears," said Holland, to relieve the silent astonishment of the room.

Jejeune ignored the interruption. "I think somebody should look into all these species of doves, the ones she has, the ones on her list. Let's see if we can find anything that connects them all."

Maik stepped back slightly, although whether it was to distance himself from the suggestion or to make way for the avalanche of volunteers he expected for this task wasn't entirely clear. As it was, the suggestion hung loosely in the air, unclaimed, uncomfortable, unwelcome. The sound that escaped Shepherd's lips could have signified any number of things. To most in the room, exasperation could most definitely have been one of them.

"Well, an interesting idea, certainly," she said with an enthusiasm that sounded just a little bit forced. "But in the meantime, it does seem that Jordan Waters is our best suspect. For now, at least, finding him should be our number one priority."

"Right then," said Maik briskly. "We all know what needs to be done, so let's get out there and do it. If there's nothing else?"

Possibly there was. Amid the general scraping of chairs and low mutterings as the group collected their belongings and began to file slowly from the room, Jejeune appeared ready to say something to his sergeant. But Maik was already sharing a laugh with Trueman, and at the last moment the DCI seemed to think better of it. Whatever it was that Domenic Jejeune was going to say, it could apparently wait for another time.

20

The clouds hung low over the estuary behind Carrie Pritchard's house, as if the sky had descended to meet the land. It had rained earlier in the day, and was threatening to do so again, but for now, patches of bright blue sky peered through the clouds and the sun was shining. North Norfolk weather was a transient, temporal thing. Predicting how it would change in the course of a day was something of a preoccupation with the locals, but it seemed to Lindy that if you went with a forecast that it was going to be rainy with sunny breaks, or vice versa, you would be right more often than not.

Carrie Pritchard was tending to some potted plants on her window ledge when Jejeune and Lindy approached. "Ah, Inspector, I just had a call about you, as it happens."

Jejeune looked interested, Lindy more so.

"The lab called. Apparently, they think they might have mixed up the feather samples submitted by your department with some sent in from the sanctuary earlier."

"Phoebe Hunter sent materials to a lab for analysis?"

"Yes. The sanctuary obviously doesn't have the resources to do its own lab work, so we outsource it all to a local firm. They were asking if I could send back Phoebe's results so they could check them against these new ones. They're in quite a state about it, actually. But I told them the police were not allowing anyone access to the sanctuary at the moment, so I wouldn't be able to get to Phoebe's results."

"There were no lab results at the sanctuary," said Jejeune definitely. "I need to call them right away."

"Use my phone. You can 1471 it," said Carrie.

Jejeune excused himself as he disappeared past the two women into the hallway.

"There is such an intensity about him," said Carrie, with a smile. "I wonder, is that a Canadian thing, do you think?"

"I couldn't say," said Lindy. "He's the only one I know. Actually, I did meet another one the other day. I could get his number from Dom, if you'd like to find out for yourself."

Carrie laughed. "Thank you. I have quite enough going on at the moment without the added complication of a man in my life. And they do so complicate things, don't they?" She curled her hair behind her ear and turned her attention back to tending her plants. "There, done," she said, standing back to admire her handiwork. "A glass of wine, while we're waiting for the inspector to finish his call? Come on, we can go into my studio."

Lindy followed her into a large, low-ceilinged room at the back of the house. A picture window stretched the entire length of the rear wall, presenting a sweeping vista of the estuary. Lindy could see a multitude of tiny black dots on the muddy shores, but the presence of a high-powered telescope on a tripod suggested that Carrie didn't have to rely on the naked eye to watch the birds.

"Some view," said Lindy.

"It lets me get a good look at my models, at least," said Carrie. She made a gesture with her hand and Lindy dragged her eyes from the scene outside to take in the interior of the room. A well-lit work desk arrayed with an impressive-looking display of carving tools stood near the window, affording it maximum exposure to natural light. Set off to one side of the bench, an elaborate exhaust fan assembly was vented out through the wall. All around the room were wooden carvings of birds. To Lindy they seemed impeccably rendered; the proportions, the painted plumage. She was sure they would be instantly recognizable to anyone who knew anything about birds. Like Domenic, for instance.

Carrie pointed to a large fridge in the corner of the room. "Would you mind grabbing the wine? There's ice in the freezer, too, but you must promise not to scream if you look in there."

She watched, knowing that Lindy wouldn't be able to resist, and smiled at the look of horror that spread across Lindy's face as she opened the freezer door. "Sorry. My little joke. I know it seems macabre, but bird skins can be incredibly useful to check for plumage details, feather arrangements, that sort of thing. Try as you might, you can't always get fine details from field observations, especially for the more enigmatic species like that Greenshank or the Arctic Skua in there. A lot of research and preparation goes into a bird carving. We don't just pick up a hunk of wood and start hacking away, you know," she said, playfully defending herself against a charge no one who saw her work would ever have made. "I suppose I like to think that, in some way, I am giving some meaning to their deaths, too, using them like this. Probably a bit fanciful, I know, but they are such beautiful creatures, it seems such a shame to let their carcasses just rot away on a beach somewhere."

Carrie took the wine and poured two glasses, handing one to Lindy before settling on a large velour couch, her feet tucked beneath her. "I don't suppose you know what it was Domenic wanted to ask me," she said casually.

Lindy's long blonde locks swayed a negative.

"Then I suggest we just settle in with our wine," said Carrie. She sipped her drink with affected relish. "You know, I might not have another all day, but there seems to be such a delicious decadence to a glass of wine in the morning, don't you think?"

"I consider decadence the height of a civilized existence, myself," said Lindy.

Jejeune entered the room, ducking instinctively beneath the black timber beams. "Apparently, the lab realized after they completed their tests that they had already run a DNA analysis on the same material. I hope you don't mind, I asked them to bring the results here. They're sending a driver." He took in his surroundings for the first time and allowed himself a delighted smile.

"These are superb," he said. "Do you enter them in competitions?"

"Sometimes. I usually send a couple to the Ward 'Worlds' in Maryland. I used to get the odd ribbon or two, though lately not as often. The judges seem as interested in habitat settings as they are in bird carvings these days, and unfortunately that's not really my forte."

"That doesn't seem right," said Lindy. "Still, it's a sign of the times, I suppose. The packaging is as important as the product for a lot of things these days."

Carrie nodded in agreement. "In fairness, many wood-carvers have taken realistic renditions of birds about as far as they can be taken, so I suppose the judges have to have some other criteria to distinguish them. I can't say I agree with it, but I suppose it does help to distinguish the true wood sculptors from the mere carvers."

"Sorts the Wheatears from the Chaffinches, you might say."

Carrie clapped her hands twice in delight. "Oh, I say, Lindy, well done you. But I don't really have time this year anyway, what with trying to find a suitable candidate to assume Phoebe Hunter's research project."

Jejeune crossed to the workbench and picked up a small round-handled tool, rolling it between his fingers to examine its long, needle-like point.

"Do be careful with that Swiss riffler, Inspector. The point is extremely sharp."

Jejeune laid down the instrument carefully and bent down to peer intently at the unpainted model on the workbench. It was a shorebird with a delicately curved bill. He picked it up for a closer examination, turning it slowly in his hands.

"Carrie was wondering what it was you wanted to ask her," said Lindy, in an effort to reel him back into the present. "I told her I didn't know."

"It was about your dispute with Luisa Obregón," said Jejeune, looking up from the model. "I understand it stems from a Mourning Dove sighting a few years ago."

"That? Oh, really, Inspector. Stuff and nonsense." She fashioned an artistic wave of her hand from the wrist to show how preposterous the idea was. At times, she had the air of an art school teacher about her, though with Carrie Pritchard's voluptuous figure leaning over their shoulders, Lindy was sure any teenage boys in her class would have considerably more on their minds than *chiaroscuro*.

"I'm a big girl. I can handle a little personal criticism. No, Inspector, it is Free to Fly that Luisa Obregón really objects to. She suspects the entire organization is directed at her specifically. It isn't, of course, but the storm of '06 does highlight some of the concerns we have about people keeping caged birds. I don't know if you are aware how often exotic birds escape from private collections, but they do so with astonishing frequency. For the most part, these birds cannot hope to survive in the wild. At best, they face starvation or death from the elements. Most, though, would undoubtedly be taken by predation of one sort or another. In any event, the dreadful fates that awaited Luisa Obregón's birds can really only be laid at the feet of the person who chose to keep them in captivity in the first place."

"This shopping list of hers," asked Jejeune, "do you have any idea who her suppliers might have been?"

"Not specifically, but I can make a few enquiries and see if anyone knows who she's done business with. I believe for the most part she simply let it be known in certain circles that she would be willing to pay handsomely for specific species. One can only presume the higher the price, the fewer questions about the birds' origins."

"Certain circles?"

"Internet sites, commercial breeders. Anywhere and everywhere." Pritchard affected a shrug. "I have it on good authority that a number of birds in her collection are of dubious provenance, to say the least. But *specific* does seem to have been the operative word. Apparently she made it quite clear she was not interested in any birds not on her list, no matter how desirable they may be to other collectors. It appears she has discriminating tastes, even if she lacks the morals to go with them."

Jejeune nodded to show he had been listening, though he was still turning the unfinished model around in his hands. "Is this one accurate?" He seemed embarrassed by his question and hurried into an explanation. "It's just that I don't recognize it. I would have said a Whimbrel, but it's too small, and its bill is too short and straight."

Carrie held out her hand and Jejeune passed it to her. "Then I shall let you stew on it for a while, Inspector. It'll be good practice for you. To the best of my knowledge, it is accurate in every detail: proportions, bill length to body ratio, et cetera. Of course, it won't really come to life until I paint it. The plumage is a critical part of the overall model. A great bird sculptor told me when I started, if you can't paint, you'd better choose a different subject than birds. I will say, though, that you should perhaps be looking to your part of the world for clues to this one." The doorbell rang. "That'll be your results, I expect."

Lindy watched Carrie Pritchard carefully as she unfurled herself from the couch to answer the door: the hairstyle that covered the nape of her neck, then revealed it; the wrap-around skirt that showed, if she moved her leg the right way, the briefest flash of thigh; the gathered fabric top, just tight enough to make an impressionable mind like Domenic's dance with the possibilities of what it might conceal. There was an effortless sensuality about the woman, which Lindy knew was, for many men, by far the most alluring kind.

"I was telling her about Gavin," said Lindy when Carrie had left the room. "I thought she might be interested. He's quite tasty in a rugged lumberjack kind of way, *sans* the putting on women's clothing and hanging around in bars, of course. You did get Monty Python in Canada, I take it?"

"I think my grandparents used to watch it," said Jejeune, deadpan.

Lindy stuck out her tongue.

"Was she?" asked Jejeune. "Interested?"

Lindy managed a look, but nothing more, before Carrie returned to the room. She handed the envelope to Jejeune and settled back in on the couch. If she had heard their conversation, she gave no indication. Lindy complimented her on the wine.

"Thank you, Lindy. Your name contracts so beautifully, by the way. From Belinda, isn't it? My first name is Candis, but people kept shortening it to Candy, which made me sound like a stripper. Carrie sounds infinitely more *proper*, don't you think?" she said with a carefree laugh.

Simultaneously, both women realized Domenic had gone very quiet and they turned to look at him. Silently, he handed the paper to Pritchard.

She read it. "But that's.... How is that possible? There must be some mistake."

Jejeune shook his head. "They have tested two separate samples — the ones I submitted and the ones from Phoebe Hunter. There is no mistake. The feathers come from Socorro Doves."

Pritchard and Jejeune looked at each other significantly. Lindy turned from one to the other. "What? Is there something special about Socorro Doves?"

"You could say that," said Jejeune. "They're extinct."

21

"Well, I clearly still have quite a few things to learn about this birding business," said Colleen Shepherd, "such as, how extinct birds can end up in a cage in a north Norfolk bird sanctuary. Or in any cage anywhere, come to that, I suppose."

They were standing in Shepherd's office; the smell of perfume hanging heavy in the air. The DCS was riffling through her desk drawer for something Jejeune couldn't see. But that didn't mean her attention was elsewhere. She paused momentarily in her treasure hunt to look up at Jejeune for an explanation.

"Socorro Doves are extinct in the wild, but there are probably a couple of hundred in captivity," he said. "A few zoos have birds for captive breeding programmes, but there are also some in private hands."

"But you're telling me the DNA suggests these birds are special?" Shepherd parked her work shoes neatly beneath the long dresser behind her desk and stepped into a pair of high-heels that showed off her shapely calves to good effect. Jejeune watched his DCS's performance with interest.

"About half of the Socorro Doves they know of are hybrids, interbred with other species. These two are pure Socorros. It's an incredibly rare find. It probably increases the pure Socorro

Dove gene pool by about two percent. The impact on reducing inbreeding depression will be immense."

Shepherd cast him one of her special glances. "It would be, you mean, if we could locate them." She closed the drawer, having apparently found what she was looking for. "Well, that certainly settles motive. Those birds would be worth a fortune to a collector, I take it. Black or red?" She pointed to the necklace she was wearing and then to one she was holding up in her hand. Jejeune stared frankly at the bold contrast between the black one and the crisp white blouse she was wearing, but flicked his eyes away, unwilling to follow the necklace as it plunged down toward the DCS's cleavage. He missed the faint smile that flickered at the corners of Shepherd's mouth. "Well, does the black one go?"

"Yeah, you know. Er, nice," he said awkwardly. "The birds would be worth a few thousand pounds on the legal market, I would guess. Perhaps double if you didn't have to prove where they came from. It's not a lot of money to commit a double murder for."

"To a small-time drug dealer who has just come out of prison and has no other immediate means of income?" Shepherd looked directly at him, pinning him with her gaze. "If I can just recap, here, for my own sanity: We have Waters, who is, I think you'll agree, a viable suspect in these murders. And now we have a motive, which also, to some police officers at least, seems more than plausible. But you're not happy with either of these. Perhaps you have your own theory? Or someone else's?"

Jejeune looked puzzled.

"Michael Hillier wanted to know what I thought about his notion of the theft of the doves being in some way symbolic. Anything else you failed to pass on to me from your audiences with the great and the good, Domenic? Plans for my retirement, for example?" She asked it casually, playfully almost, as she tucked away the rejected necklace and turned her attentions to earrings. But Jejeune knew he needed to treat the accusation with the seriousness it deserved.

He had often wondered about the British propensity to store up archaic knowledge like Latin phrases and quotes from fourteenth-century poets, but it undeniably had its uses. An afternoon with Lindy had left him in no doubt about the dove's ambivalent role in classical literature. "Blimey, Dom. Take your pick. The ancient Egyptians thought doves were a symbol of purity, but the Greeks thought they were the lustful birds of Venus. Pliny said they were the symbol of fidelity and chastity, while Homer thought they were timid. And that's to say nothing of the dove's place in Christian and Jewish faiths."

Jejeune patiently related all this to Shepherd now, saving perhaps the most telling objection, from his perspective, until last. It didn't come from classical literature or religious symbolism, but from mere common sense. "Besides, if you want somebody to appreciate the symbolism of something," he said reasonably, "you need to leave it for them to see. You don't take a symbol with you when you go."

"Yes, well, put like that ..." said Shepherd, suitably chastened. "Still, if you wouldn't mind keeping me in the loop on these things. The department still does run through me, you know, nominally at least."

Earrings clipped on, she began rummaging in her handbag, emerging with a tube of lipstick. "So what exactly is your objection, then, to the idea that Waters murdered the two victims so he could steal valuable birds?"

"I'm not discounting Waters's involvement at all," said Jejeune, eying Shepherd warily. "The problem is, in every scenario — Waters, the set-asides, Obregón — Ramon Santos is the extra piece, the part that won't fit. I can't accept that he was just an innocent bystander. There's too much that suggests otherwise."

Jejeune might have expected one of Shepherd's patented looks of exasperation. Certainly, she was more than entitled to remind him that his previous forays into this territory had earned him a visit to Sir Michael Hillier's office. Instead, she looked at him almost approvingly, as if she saw in his unshakeable conviction about Santos's involvement something admirable.

She bent forward toward a small vanity mirror propped up on her desk, but then seemed to think better of it and stood to look at him directly, as if what she had to say next needed to be delivered head-on.

"I'm afraid the problem is, Domenic, with so much at stake diplomatically, HM Government is not going to have any patience for wishy-washy theories about parked cars and dodgy South American aliases. They're going to be much more interested in what you can say definitively about Santos's involvement. Is there anything?"

Jejeune said nothing.

Shepherd's tone softened. "The thing is, well, there's no easy way to put this, but I'm not sure you could find sufficient support in Whitehall anymore to float a theory like this. It's been a long time since your name was in the headlines, Domenic, and when set against the continuing cordial relations with a friendly nation, I'm afraid your star no longer burns as brightly in the Home Office firmament as it once did."

It was a lyrical phrase, at odds with Shepherd's prosaic day-to-day delivery, and Jejeune realized she had spent some time working on this speech, polishing it as she might an address to the Saltmarsh Golf Club at the annual awards banquet. It told him all he needed to know about how important she felt the message was. She let it sink in for a moment, leaning forward once more toward the mirror and applying her lipstick with exaggerated care.

"So we're agreed then? For the time being, we have our suspect and we have our motive. We think Jordan Waters killed Ramon Santos and Phoebe Hunter in the commission of a theft of a pair of valuable doves he could sell on the black market."

For the time being? What was Shepherd telling him? First Hillier's cryptic comments, and now Shepherd's; it was a sign of the tension being felt at the higher levels that everyone was being so circumspect and leaving their comments open to interpretation like this — or *mis*interpretation.

As was often the case, Jejeune's silence unnerved Shepherd. "Am I clear? Jordan Waters continues to be the main focus of our enquiries as we pursue all other leads. That's the party line, and that's the one I'll be delivering to Guy Trueman when I meet him for dinner tonight. In case you were wondering who all this fuss was for."

"Trueman's in town?"

"As a matter of fact, he is, though you probably don't need to sound quite so surprised that a man would drive all the way up from London to take me out for the evening. And don't give me that disapproving look, either. I don't plan on spending tonight discussing the evidence with him, if that's what you're worried about. I'm sure it'll be an evening of reminiscences about his good old days with Danny Maik. Amazing the conversations some women are willing to put up with to get a free meal, isn't it?"

Shepherd stood up straight and smoothed her skirt. She turned toward Jejeune and splayed her hands out in front of her. "Well?" she asked. "You know, it wouldn't kill you to acknowledge the effort I've put in here, Domenic."

"It's … fine. Great, really," said Jejeune uncertainly.

"There's something about Guy Trueman that bothers you, isn't there?" she asked. "I get the impression you don't trust him."

"It depends what with," said Jejeune.

She nodded. "Yes. And conditional trust is not really trust at all, is it?"

"I get the feeling he's very careful about how much co-operation he gives us. I think he knows more about the phone surveillance of the Obregón's than he's willing to share."

"He almost certainly does," agreed Shepherd. "But Guy's in a difficult position, Domenic. He is, in effect, playing for the other team here. But at the same time, I'm sure he's keen to help his old army pal Danny out as much as he can. For old times' sake, if nothing else."

"He doesn't seem the sentimental type to me," said Jejeune.

"There's a difference between sentimentality and loyalty. And in my experience, army loyalty can run very deep indeed."

She put on a jacket that had been hanging on the back of the door and looked herself up and down in the full-length mirror, shaking her head. "*Okay. Fine. Nice.* Honestly, Domenic, you must just sweep that girlfriend of yours off her feet with your compliments. I mean, absolutely leave her breathless."

22

Lindy and Jejeune sat side by side on a small rock, watching the swells rise and fall with a gentle heaving. Small whitecaps dotted the surface of the water, as if the passing winds had snagged the skin of the sea and teased out its white foam interior. When they had first come here to north Norfolk, the locals had talked about the character of the sea, its personality. Lindy was starting to understand what they meant. Today, on this lonely stretch of coastline in the middle of nowhere, the sea was a dark and brooding animal, an uneasy, moving thing.

"So the station is back to normal now? After all the excitement?"

Jejeune dragged his eyes away from the mesmerizing movement of the water.

"Constable Salter. Is she okay?"

"I think so," said Jejeune, considering the question. "Over the worst of the shock, according to Sergeant Maik. From what I can gather, it could have been much worse, if Trueman hadn't acted as quickly as he did."

"What a pity it wasn't Danny. From her point of view, I mean."

Jejeune gave her a querying look.

"To be saved by the man of her dreams? Oh, Dom, don't tell me you haven't noticed. I've only seen them together a couple of times, but it stands out a mile. She can barely take her eyes off him when they're in a room together."

Salter? And Sergeant Maik? Did these things really go on all around him? And were they so obvious to other people? *How many parts of how many other lives am I missing out on?* he wondered.

"Is it serious?"

Lindy shook her head. "I don't think he has a clue. I imagine he's about as thick as you are when it comes to these things. I shouldn't worry, though. Knowing Danny Maik, I very much doubt you're going to have an office romance on your hands." A thought seemed to strike her. "You probably didn't pick up the signs with Chippy the Woodworker, either, did you?"

"Carrie Pritchard?"

Lindy nodded playfully, unable to suppress a smile at Domenic's obvious surprise.

"Sorry to burst your bubble, darling, but she's seeing someone."

"I'm sure she said she was unattached."

"Gee, imagine my surprise," said Lindy sarcastically. But if she wondered how such a comment might have made its way into Pritchard's and Domenic's casual conversations about bird migrations on the north Norfolk coast, she didn't let it show.

"Could it be somebody younger?"

Lindy cast him a glance and gave the idea some thought. "Could be. There's a coyness about her, a playfulness that older women sometimes get when they're dating younger men."

Jejeune looked out over the water. The wind had died down and the whitecaps had disappeared, leaving the sea's skin once again smooth and unblemished.

"Young like Jordan Waters's age?"

"Jeez, Dom, I'm not psychic. I just have normal feminine powers of observation, that's all."

Based on past experience, it was not a distinction Jejeune would have been prepared to make, but he let Lindy's comment go. To the north, a grain of Sanderlings executed a series of tight swirls over the water before coming in to land at the shoreline. The towering backdrop of windswept saltmarsh grasses seemed only to heighten the fragility of the small birds. Lindy half-turned toward Domenic and watched him watching; alive, alert to every nuance of the birds' behaviour, every flicker of movement. She leaned in against his shoulder, just to remind him she was there, in case he got drawn in too deeply and disappeared into his birds.

"It's beautiful here, isn't it?" she said conversationally. "I can't imagine Burkina Faso has many spots like this."

"Sorry?"

"That stuff on your laptop. Come on, Dom, I'm an investigative journalist. *Journalist of the Year* three years ago, no less. Nothing since, I'll grant you, but I haven't lost all my skills," she said, trying to introduce lightness she didn't really feel. "You want to do it, don't you? This business with the Turtledoves, studying their feather isotopes or whatever. The work Phoebe Hunter was doing in Africa. You want to take over the project."

She was still leaning against him, staring out at the water, at its silky undulation. In front of them, a pair of Herring Gulls was engaged in a noisy discussion over the remains of a crab. Domenic was watching them quietly. *Poor Dom. He's wondering what he can say, what he can do, to make things better for me.* He didn't seem to realize that at times like this there was nothing in the world that he could have said or done, or even anything that she wanted him to. Sometimes, for all his genius, he seemed so lost in personal situations. She had been prepared to be angry with him, to fight, to argue. But now she felt only sadness for him, and a protectiveness that had no room for confrontation.

"I understand, Dom. Why you would want to do it," she said. "Really, I do. And now these other ones, the Socorro Doves, they just seem to make the work that much more important.

How did they become extinct, anyway? How does that even happen in this day and age?"

"Mostly because they lived only on one small island," Jejeune said. "The numbers would never have been that great to begin with. Even a natural disaster like a hurricane could decimate the population enough that it might never recover. In this case, it was introduced predators — rats and feral cats. It usually is on islands. Coupled with the inevitable habitat loss when humans arrived with their farm animals. It was a lethal combination."

"And nobody thought to do anything about it?"

"I'm sure they're trying an eradication programme now, removing the predators to preserve the island's other endemic bird species. But for the doves, it's too late. The habitat they need will be degraded beyond use, and they have nowhere else they can call home."

"So these birds still in captivity, and any more that are bred, they're consigned to a life behind bars forever?"

Jejeune nodded, and for a moment Lindy was overwhelmed with sadness for a species that could never know freedom again; a freedom granted even to these ragtag gulls squabbling away on the rocks in front of her. For the first time, she began to see Carrie Pritchard's Free to Fly programme in a new light.

"I don't know why anybody would want to keep birds in an aviary. Not a private one, anyway. But I suppose there will always be a market for rare things, and if there are no more of these doves left in the wild, I can see why some collectors would pay a lot for them."

"Yes, and as a motive for Waters, it makes sense. But for Santos," he shook his head, "I'm not so sure."

Lindy pulled back from him slightly in surprise. "Santos?" she said, "You're trying to implicate a diplomat from a friendly foreign country in this? Blimey, Dom, choose your enemies well. They'll be around long after all your friends have disappeared.

You have told DCS Shepherd about this, I take it? I imagine she's thrilled to bits."

"She doesn't think I'd get much backing from higher up if I tried to pursue it. According to her, as far as the media and the general public are concerned, I'm already yesterday's news."

Jejeune didn't sound too upset at the prognosis. Lindy knew he had always been uneasy with the media attention that had tracked him since he had rescued the Home Secretary's daughter. She knew if Shepherd was right, the waning public interest would come as more of a relief to him than a disappointment, even if his favoured status had undoubtedly earned him some leeway in the past, and allowed him to pursue lines of enquiry others might never have been permitted to follow. Exactly like this one, in fact.

"I'm sure she wasn't trying to be unkind. She's just pointing out that the stakes are high here, Dom, and politicians can have short memories when faced with the pragmatics of a potential diplomatic incident." She squeezed his hand in a playful gesture designed to lighten the mood. "I could see if Eric would let me do a feature about you in our rag, if you like. Jam you in between the reality show feuds and the celebrity liposuctions. Put you right back in the public eye."

He gave her a thin smile. "I just can't understand why a young man who has already secured all the benefits of a diplomatic career would risk it all to steal a pair of birds," he said.

"Maybe Santos just needed the money. It's the simple explanation. This Occam's razor thing, it really is a problem for you, isn't it? But he was married, right? You know what they say: 'It is a truth universally acknowledged that a man in possession of a wife must be in want of a good fortune.'"

Jejeune smiled. When they had first met, Lindy had been in her Jane Austen phase, and it had become one of their shared things. It had been in the early days of their relationship, when they had indulged each other's passions with more tolerance, and he had never quite managed to get around to telling her the appeal of eighteenth-century drawing-room dramas was, quite frankly, lost on him. As a result, he had sat through many hours of TV presentations, with Lindy snuggled contentedly against his chest, while he cast furtive glances at the great outdoors just beyond the window, thinking about the indescribable wild beauty of places just like this.

The sea had changed moods now and there was an ethereal glow to the water. It seemed to be glittering from within, as if it had trapped light, somehow, and was only allowing it to escape a little at a time in a silvery sheen. Lindy watched the Herring Gulls in front of them, so primal in their pursuits. How much easier Domenic's job would be if humans could be so uncompli-cated. Animals killed to satisfy their needs: protection, defence, hunger. *Humans are supposed to have evolved beyond that,* she thought. *But have we really? Was that not what murder was, the hunting of another human, killing to satisfy some need?*

She looked at his troubled features as he watched the gulls preening and fluffing on the rocks. At least two, he had told her at the cottage that day. At least two people were intent on stealing the birds from the sanctuary. Two paths to follow, then. Two stories to resolve into a single narrative, where people are mur-dered so birds can be stolen. It had seemed so absurd at the time that another man might have tried to convince himself that he must be mistaken. But such thoughts never seemed to occur to Domenic Jejeune. Once he had taken his readings, sifted through the evidence, he no longer seemed to have any doubts. It was one of the strange inconsistencies of the man beside her, that he could so lack a sense of his place in the world and yet have such unfailing confidence in his deductions. And now he had done it, identified them, these two people he had always known were involved. He was so good at this, and it meant so little to him.

"I don't expect policing will ever match your interest in bird-ing," she said, suddenly, "but maybe if you just gave yourself a chance to take some reward from being a detective, you know, see the upside everybody else sees in your work, the results you get. I expect there will always be a little part of you that hangs onto this dream about Burkina Faso. But it might just be time to acknowledge the truth of it, Dom. It's never going to happen."

Perhaps she was right. Perhaps it was his destiny to stay here on this windswept, beautiful coast and look for the reasons human beings chose to end each others' lives. All he knew was he could never settle to it, could never accept it, until he was certain that his chances for another life were over. And despite the best intentions of the beautiful young woman sitting next to him, that certainty had not yet come.

23

Perhaps there was some law, some hidden rule of quantum physics, that stated the chaos increased the farther it spread from the epicentre. Police units and rescue cars were slewed all across the road, haphazardly parked with two wheels on grass verges, tucked into gateway entrances and any other small niche they could find in the hedges that lined the lane. Around the periphery of the action, people were calling on mobile phones, shouting to each other, gesturing, discussing the new approaches with the crane operator, the tow-truck drivers, the structural engineers. But, at the centre of it all, right next to the beat-up panel van that was teetering precipitously on the wall of the bridge, a small knot of people stood calmly discussing the situation and looking for all the world as if they were chatting about Norwich City's prospects in Saturday's match. Of course, it helped if one of the people at the epicentre of chaos like this was Danny Maik.

He had seen Jejeune arrive, watched him park The Beast some way off and walk along the lane to where everyone was gathered. He had seen him pause suddenly, freeze, not once, but twice, each time obviously straining to listen to a sound coming from the marsh that stretched out beyond the bridge. *Even at a time like this,* thought Maik, *with a suspect's car precariously*

balanced between the lane and the marsh ten feet below, and
the suspect himself who knew where, even now Inspector Jejeune
takes the time to listen to a bird call.

As he approached, Jejeune paused again in mid-stride.

"Hear that?" he asked the small group.

Danny Maik had been holding court with Salter and Holland,
issuing short, succinct instructions in a low conversational tone.
Against the backdrop of gesticulating and histrionics going on
around them, Danny's performance was a masterclass in understatement. But even then, it apparently hadn't left any room for
Maik to cast an ear toward the marsh.

"Sorry, no."

"I think it could be a Baillon's Crake. It would be remarkable
if it is. It's an extremely rare find here in Britain. There was an
influx a few years ago and some of them seem to have stayed
on, but it's still a great bird."

"Ah," said Maik uncertainly, the only one of the group able
to muster even that feeble a response. "Erm, the crew is keen to
start recovering the van, but they've held off in case you want
to see it before they get started."

Jejeune looked around at the surrounding countryside. It
was a damp, cool morning, and wraiths of mist draped the hills
inland. In front of them, heavier mist lay low over the marsh,
leaving only tantalizing glimpses of the wetland, like some
heavenly landscape appearing between the clouds. The mist
seemed to muffle the sounds of the marsh, too; an eerie silence
hung over the land, in which the noises from the bridge behind
them, and perhaps that one other sound, seemed to echo.

"No sign of Waters," said Maik. "There is a single set of footprints, though, disappearing off into the marsh. If you look
closely, you can see the track where the reed stems are all bent.
Constable Holland has an idea this is not a single-car accident."
Maik turned to Holland to offer him the stage.

"That hairpin back there slows you down. You couldn't get up a head of steam going over Carter's Bridge if you wanted to. Waters was born and bred here. Like most of us, this road would have been second nature to him. I can't see him misjudging this, even in this fog. Not without some help."

"Only one set of footprints though, right?" confirmed Jejeune. "So if somebody did run him off the road, they didn't try to follow him into the marsh."

Maik couldn't be sure if Jejeune was dismissing Holland's idea or merely trying to fit it into the evidence. There was a call from a uniformed constable down in the marsh beneath the bridge. Gasoline from the ruptured tank of the van had begun running down the wall of the bridge and flowing into the marsh. The tank of an old van like this could probably hold as much as sixty litres of petrol, and that meant another headache for the recovery crew, another complication in the already difficult process of trying to drag the van back over the wall onto the road. Now, the sparks that seemed inevitable as the metal dragged against the stone wall would present a real danger. The crane operator came over to discuss whether the van could be swung out and away from the wall before being pulled up to the road surface. Salter climbed over the retaining rail and scudded down the steep slope to see what could be done to stem the flow of gasoline into the marsh.

Maik led Jejeune down a muddy track to the edge of the reed beds. "He was headed in that direction." Maik tilted a thumb toward the dark wall of pines that separated the far edge of the marsh from the beach beyond.

Jejeune looked out over the reed beds, as much as were visible through the mist. Normally, this was a swaying landscape of constant motion, but now a ghostly, unnatural stillness hung over it, as if the crash had scarred the natural world, too, leaving a wound as deep as the one the van had carved into the stonework of the bridge.

Maik watched Jejeune as he peered out over the marsh. *You think he's still out there*, thought Maik. *And I think you're right.*

"He can't have gotten far in this stuff. I could get the canine unit in. This mist — fret, the locals call it — should start lifting fairly soon. It'll make the job easier."

"No," said Jejeune. "No dogs."

"These rare birds, these crakes, they do fly, I take it," said Maik reasonably. "I mean, it would have gotten to this marsh under its own steam. So it would be able to get away again, if the dogs got too close."

"No dogs," said Jejeune again. "We can follow the tracks ourselves," he said, taking the first tentative steps onto the spongy surface beneath their feet. Maik was at his shoulder in a matter of seconds, and they began methodically pushing their way through the high grasses in silence. Off to their right, a faint metallic rattle caused a pause and an involuntary head turn from Jejeune. Maik waited, annoyed. "Concentration is your best weapon in this stuff," he murmured quietly. Whether Jejeune heard it as criticism or not didn't really matter. Even Danny's Motown had a time and place.

Maik realized he knew nothing about this Waters, the man to whom they had tied these murders. He was a name only, floated before them like a wraith of this mist. He had heard references to Jordan Waters down at the station, seen the name on reports. But what of the man? He had drifted into their consciousness only at his arrests. But what about the gaps in his life, those great empty spaces about which they had no knowledge? Had he picked up some special training, perhaps, like Danny? Would he, too, know how to use the high cover of a reed bed to steal up behind someone and snap their neck, before melting away into the cover, leaving the marsh to the dampness and the mist and Jejeune's rare bird? Maik heard a reed snap behind him and he spun around in a crouch.

Jejeune had heard it, too, and was bending forward cautiously, trying to peer between the reed stems. Perhaps, just perhaps, there was a shadow of movement in there somewhere. Maik made a circling gesture with his hand and moved off silently to flank the patch of reeds. Jejeune watched for another flicker of movement, a shimmer of disturbed light filtering through the reeds. He realized he was holding his breath. There. Another faint sound of pressure on wet reeds underfoot. There was no doubt now. But would Danny Maik be in position yet? Did he have a clearer view? The mist swirling all around them was so dense that Jejeune couldn't tell. Then, finally, a definite movement, barely visible in the mist-shrouded light. Maik burst through the reed cover from the far side, shattering the silence. Jejeune ducked half a second late as the object came toward him, shoulder height and rising fast. The heron's long legs barely missed him as it lifted off with a heart-stopping clatter of wings.

Jejeune made his way into the tiny clearing between them, where he found Maik still recovering his breath. "Well, at least we found your bird," he said.

Jejeune couldn't suppress a smile. "It was a Grey Heron, Sergeant. We could be five yards away and we would have virtually no chance of seeing a secretive bird like a Baillon's Crake in these reeds." He paused, and Maik could see Jejeune's silent acknowledgment. As conflicted as he might be, this way was far too dangerous. They should call in the dogs.

But before he could voice this or any other thought, there was the sound of tortured metal and a thunderous crash from behind them near the road and loud, alarmed shouts and cries; the sounds of panic. Without another word the two men began thrashing their way frantically back through the reeds. Whatever had happened back at the bridge, they knew they would be needed. Now.

24

"It's Lauren, sir," said Holland breathlessly, meeting the two men as they emerged at the edge of the marsh. "She went to put a container underneath the van to collect the petrol. She had just gotten under there when the van slipped off the wall. She was right beneath it. We think it has ..."

Maik brushed past him and mounted the steep bank in long, loping steps. Jejeune matched him stride for stride. A wall of stunned faces greeted them as they climbed back onto the road surface. Men and women trained to handle traumatic situations, facing them every day, were standing around in a daze. *When it's one of your own...,* thought Maik. He had been here before, too many times, and he knew all the training in the world couldn't prevent the shock from rising within you. All you could do was keep it in check, prevent it from taking over your actions. And do what you had been trained to do, as efficiently and dispassionately as your emotions would allow.

Maik began to issue commands, his tone urgent but controlled, directing the crane driver to move in closer to the bridge wall, so the two constables already down below could get enough slack to hook up the cables. "Bugger the harness, just get something on those axles so he can lift it," shouted Maik, "and make sure you're well clear when he starts to raise it. Everyone else, out of the way. Let him see what he's doing."

Other commands, orders issued, advice given. And all followed exactly, every one of them, as part of a single great ballet of
movement and action, choreographed by Grandmaster Danny
Maik from his parapet on the bridge. *In Danny we trust.* It was
Maik's direction they wanted at a time like this: Danny Maik, the
voice of authority, while he, Jejeune, stood motionless, watching it all like some casually unfolding drama, real-time actions
slowed so he could take it all in. It was as if he was behind a
gossamer screen from which he could see and be seen, but could
play no part, beyond peering over the wall, looking for any signs
of movement beneath the van. Of which there were none.

The heavy diesel engine of the crane roared as the operator
manoeuvred it into position, swinging a pair of giant steel
cables down to where the two uniformed constables stood
waiting. As soon as there was enough slack, they approached
and began attaching the cables to the van's exposed axles.

"Wait for the crane to swing the van off to the side before you
go under there," Maik called from up on the bridge. In these
circumstances, it would be all too easy for some would-be
rescuer to venture in too soon. The crane's engine, bellowing
with the strain of the added load, filled the air again with its
angry thunder. As the cables drew taut, the van rose slowly
from the ground. Without warning, the rear cable slipped off
the axle, slamming the van back into the earth with a sickening
crash. The crane continued to lift on the single cable, hauling
the front of the vehicle higher, where it began spinning in a
slow, terrible spiral, until it bounced against the half-collapsed
bridge wall, its metal skin squealing against the jagged stone.

"Drop it down again. Let's get that second bloody cable back
on, now!" shouted someone from the bridge. But not Danny
Maik. He was silent, his eyes fixed on the spot from where the
van had first lifted, where even from here he could still see the

remains of the steel container Salter had been trying to place to collect the gasoline. It was crushed beyond recognition. Beside the container lay the remains of one of the dislodged sandstone blocks from the bridge, pulverized into powder by the two tons of massive force slamming onto it directly from above. Nothing could have withstood such a blow, Maik realized. Not metal, not stone. Not human flesh. He summoned one of the medics over with a crooked finger and whispered quietly into his ear. The man nodded solemnly and moved off to the waiting ambulance. Over the roar of the crane, Jejeune couldn't hear Maik's message, but he knew what it was: prepare for the worst.

Side by side, the two men watched almost in a trance as one of the constables approached the twisted metal block of the van and began to reattach the rear cable. Perhaps Jejeune heard it first, his birder's ear attuned to sounds behind the animal roar of the crane. But if he picked it up a heartbeat sooner than Maik, his sergeant matched him stride for stride to the far side of the bridge, where they could see officers running across the road, shouting. Leaning over the wall, they saw a shock of blonde hair appear from beneath the bridge, framing a pale face streaked with blood and dirt. Salter's clothing was torn and filthy. Her shirt was soaked with blood and, even on all fours, she appeared to be dragging one leg. She tried to stand, but her expression morphed into a grimace of pain and she stumbled backward into the open and collapsed.

Maik directed the recovery efforts from the ground beside Salter. Even now, it seemed best to leave things in the hands of the one person whose instructions would be obeyed without question. Jejeune watched from the bridge. He heard the grunts of pain, and the single short cry as Salter was laid on the stretcher and covered with a blanket.

Maik watched the lights of the ambulance disappear along the lane before making his way back up to the bridge, breathing heavily after the steep ascent. "She made it," he said, his eyes shining with an emotion Jejeune hadn't seen before. "She was directly beneath the van as it started to fall, but she was able to dive back into the arch. Her left leg got caught, but they don't think it's broken."

"Internal injuries?" Jejeune wasn't asking for a diagnosis from Maik, just the opinion of someone who had been close to such situations before.

"She's making a fist of being upbeat, which is a good sign, but she's got a bit of fight to her, so it's hard to tell how much pain she's in or what the damage is. There's a fair bit of blood. I didn't get a good look as they were lifting her out, but there were plenty of cuts and bruises. The blood could always be from those." Maik paused for a moment, as if trying to convince himself of the truth of his statement.

The two men were silent for a moment with their thoughts. As always, an inquiry would find out what happened and how. And apportion blame, too, plenty of it, and no doubt aimed in Constable Lauren Salter's direction. But an inquiry wouldn't tell them why, wouldn't tell them what Maik and Jejeune already knew: that Salter was still trying to make up for her earlier mistake. Trying too hard. With Maggie Wylde no longer available to deflect the lances of her guilt, Salter had decided to confront them head on. If somebody didn't intervene soon, she might not get rescued a third time.

"I'll follow her to the hospital, if that's okay with you, sir. I don't think there's much more I can do here anyway. Waters is long gone by now." Maik let his eyes rest on Jejeune for a long moment. The DCI seemed troubled by something. Not Salter's situation, surely? As terrible as it was, this accident couldn't be laid at the DCI's feet. Maik doubted it was the reference to Waters, either. It hadn't been intended as criticism and surely

Jejeune knew him well enough by now not to take it as such.

He followed Jejeune's gaze to the van, now resting on its roof on the road, the cables still attached to the axles. The driver's door was clearly visible for the first time. Apart from the scratches and dents caused by the bridge wall, there was one other obvious and clearly identifiable mark: a long shallow scrape running almost the full width of the door.

Jejeune turned to see Maik looking at the same thing. "We've seen that shade of British racing green before, haven't we, Sergeant? You go on to the hospital. I'll stay on here a while and direct the clean-up."

Maik eyed him uncertainly for a moment. Jejeune had never offered to stay on at a scene before. But then again, there had never been a rare bird at a scene before, either. Although, perhaps that was unfair. Since the rescue efforts had begun, Jejeune had seemed reluctant to become involved, as if he felt like he didn't belong, that somehow it wasn't his place. Whatever the reasons for Jejeune's decision to stay, Maik was in no mood to dwell on them. Without another word, he ran from the bridge and got in his car to race after the speeding ambulance.

25

In the days immediately following Salter's accident, a cloud of disillusionment seemed to descend over the station, slowing any progress in the case and discouraging the investigators pursuing it. In the vacuum of inactivity, it was inevitable that the gossip about Salter's resignation occupied more of their time than any productive police work.

After Salter had been released from her two-day observation period at the hospital, Jejeune and Maik had squeezed into the sergeant's Mini and made the trip out to the tiny row cottage down near the quay that Salter shared with her son and her widowed father, Davy. Predictably, the journey had been soundtracked by vintage Motown: a collection called *Chartbusters*, though, frankly, if these tunes had busted the charts, Jejeune couldn't imagine what the competition must have been like. He only recognized one song — "You Keep Me Hangin' On" — and that through a much later cover version from the dawn of his youth. In truth, he preferred it to the original, though he didn't choose to share this opinion with his sergeant.

Seated at the Salter's ancient butcher-block table in the kitchen, cradling cups of tea made by Davy, her "live-in maid," as Lauren introduced him, the three police officers endured awkward, stilted conversation punctuated by uncomfortable pauses. That was, until Salter's announcement.

It had come out of the blue. One minute they were all sitting around talking and the next she was delivering the bombshell, quietly and reasonably, if not without emotion. She was resigning.

Max, thought Danny. The two recent brushes with death had made her stop and think about what life would be like for her little boy, already with an absent father, if he was forced to grow up without a mother, too, relying only on the kindly but ageing Davy for his upbringing. But Jejeune had a different idea and, as usual, he turned out to be right on the mark. Danny had seen it in her eyes when Jejeune had looked at her across the kitchen table and, for one of the few times Maik could ever remember, offered a piece of unsolicited advice.

"Guilt isn't like other emotions," Jejeune had said in that quiet, reasonable tone of his. "It doesn't diminish with the passing of time. You can wake up two years later and still feel as guilty as the day something happened. The thing is, Constable Salter, guilt will never let you go. You have to accept it, allow it to become a part of you. Eventually your life will begin to adjust to its presence."

The message had been delivered with such quiet earnestness, Jejeune not leaning forward at all, not gesturing with his hands, just looking frankly into Salter's eyes, that Maik could tell this was a subject his DCI knew something about. *The boy, the one who died during the rescue of the Home Secretary's daughter.* With all the hoopla surrounding the girl's safe return, no one else had paid much attention at the time. But Jejeune would have. It was the sort of thing he would carry around with him, if he felt he was to blame.

Salter listened quietly. "I don't think I can, sir." She shook her head slowly. "I just don't."

Neither man had said anything; neither pointed out that she couldn't have prevented the murders even if she had acted on Phoebe's phone call, or that the only person responsible for Phoebe's death was Jordan Waters. Nor did they urge her to reconsider, take a break, think about it before making any hasty decisions. They just sat there in silence, untouched tea going cold in the cups between their hands. Salter had excused herself politely, claiming tiredness, and limped out of the room, letting the men see themselves out.

Because Jejeune and Maik had never discussed it, in fact, never even referred to Salter's announcement at all, neither could be exactly sure where the gossip could have come from. But this was a small community, and cottage walls were thin, windows generally open, and neighbours often in the garden. It had gotten out, that was the important thing. It had become public property, and rumours were now swirling in many directions at once, the way they did when there were no facts of any sort to anchor them to.

So it was with something approaching shock that Jejeune had entered the incident room to find Constable Salter, detective first class sitting in the front row, left leg stretched out before her, sporting a walking cast that already showed signs of mileage. Her look could have conveyed a thousand things, but mostly her soft blue eyes said only one: *I'll try.*

Maik welcomed Salter's return, too, but despite her prominent position in the room, she seemed uncomfortable with the attention she was attracting, so he passed over all but the briefest of acknowledgements and launched straight into a summary of their progress so far, which wasn't much.

Uniforms had found Nyce's car later on the day of the crash, parked round the back of a local pub, sporting significant damage to the front passenger wing.

"Nyce claims his car was stolen that morning, but we can't place him at home. A neighbour called to talk to him about something, but there was no answer. He says he must have been out looking for the car at that time."

"And what do we think about that?" asked Jejeune, enjoying the look of distain on Danny's face.

"I think all that book learnin' doesn't seem to be much of a preparation for a life of crime. Do you want me to go and pick him up?"

"And charge him with what? Insulting our intelligence? No. For one thing, I don't think we have a motive."

This was new territory for the DCI. Normally, he didn't pay much attention to motive. In the past, it had always been enough for Inspector Jejeune to work out the *who*. He seemed content to let somebody else worry about the *why*; not too keen himself, apparently, to dwell in the dark recesses of the criminal mind.

Maik was itching to move, as much for the activity as anything else. Left to his own devices, he would have gladly arrested Nyce on a charge of failing to possess a personality. And probably made it stick, too. But Jejeune seemed reluctant to act, or even to explain why.

The door opened suddenly and a smartly dressed DCS Shepherd entered, with a spring in her step. Guy Trueman, who entered a moment later, also seemed to have a particular lightness about him this morning.

Shepherd regarded Salter carefully, as if trying to assess her state of mind. Some wounded officers wore their injuries like a trophy; others as if it was a badge of shame. But however they looked at them, Maik knew Shepherd was here to ensure that her officers did not start simply considering injuries to be part of their normal operating procedure.

He noticed Holland's eye roll; not a dramatic one for the paying customers, but a genuine look of despair meant just for himself. Like the others, he knew what was coming: a check on everyone's well-being; offers of counselling sessions or private chats Shepherd knew no one would ever dream of taking her up on. And then one of her addresses to the troops, reminding them of her unwavering faith in their professionalism and urging them to take this incident "on board" and learn from it.

Careful Danny, you're becoming as cynical as young Holland.

Maik turned to the room at large, taking up the discussion about David Nyce once again. "When we were with Nyce, he did everything he could to avoid checking texts and emails that were coming in. Now, normally, I might just put that down to good manners, but with Nyce ..." Maik shook his head. "He doesn't exactly strike me as the type to let a little thing like courtesy come between him and his work." He didn't pause for agreement. "I wonder if it might be worth having a look into his background, just to see if he's avoiding contact with the outside world for a reason."

"Good idea, Sergeant," said Jejeune, with uncharacteristic enthusiasm. "I'll have a word with the chairman of the Faculty Conduct Committee myself."

Maik eyed him carefully. If there was a reason his DCI was keen to spare Nyce the scrutiny of a formal police investigation, Danny couldn't imagine what it might be.

"It might be worthwhile looking into this set-aside business more closely, too," said Jejeune. "Luisa Obregón seems to have been prepared to entertain the idea. I have the feeling that wouldn't have gone down too well with her son."

"And so he killed Phoebe Hunter to prevent it happening?" Maik had not meant it to sound so sarcastic. But the message was clear: *as important as the conservation of Turtledoves undoubtedly is, sir, the residents of Saltmarsh are not going to resort to murdering one another over it. Not here in the real world, where the rest of us live.*

"Right, well," said Shepherd briskly, "I'm sure Inspector Jejeune has also decided that one of the first things we need to resolve here is the extent of Phoebe Hunter's involvement in all this. She had the birds' DNA tested. She would have known they were rare, and valuable. Presumably, she must have shared that information with Waters at some point. From what we know of Waters, he was hardly likely to get there on his own. So, a romantic link perhaps?"

Shepherd and Jejeune exchanged a glance, but it was quite clear she was going to pursue this avenue of enquiry whether Jejeune took any ownership of it or not.

"According to David Nyce, there was nothing special going on between Phoebe Hunter and anyone at the sanctuary," he said.

"Anything that he knew about. And one might expect that he would have been paying special attention, for obvious reasons." Shepherd paused to check that the reasons were as obvious to everyone else as they were to her. Apparently they were. At least, no one asked for a clarification.

"Still, even if Nyce is right, and there was nothing going on between Phoebe Hunter and Waters, she may have been naive enough to have mentioned it in casual conversation." Lauren Salter's voice sounded slightly uncertain, as if she was unsure how her first contribution to the discussion might be received.

"Telling a man with a history of burglary that there are some potentially valuable items in a cage to which he has the key goes a bit beyond naiveté, wouldn't you say?" asked Shepherd.

Jejeune shook his head uncertainly. "Phoebe Hunter dedicated her life to the welfare of birds. It makes no sense that she would be a party to them being sold to the caged bird trade, where who knows what kind of conditions awaited them."

"Fair enough, then," said Shepherd reasonably, "so we're back to naiveté." She scoured the whiteboard at the front of the room, which showed more white space than entries, and fastened on a small detail relegated to the far corner. "This written note left on the car in the hotel car park," she asked. "Anything more on that?"

Maik looked at Trueman. Despite his admiring glances in Shepherd's direction, surely even Danny's ex-CO must realize she was putting on this show for his benefit. You didn't get to be as successful a DCS as Shepherd was by micro-managing the daylights out of every aspect of a case like this. But Tony Holland seemed keen enough to indulge his DCS's interest.

"Strangely enough, ma'am, we don't seem to have a very big collection of writing samples from our local villains to compare it with." His tone implied that such oversights would never be permitted by a newly promoted Detective Sergeant Tony Holland, should that day ever come. "Of course, if the note was in joined-up writing, that alone would be enough to eliminate most of the rabble I could think of."

Shepherd didn't smile. "Right," she said curtly, "so not a viable line of enquiry, then. Where are we on the DNA tests on those fingernail fragments? If we've got a match with Waters, then even that milk-veined lot over at the CPS office would be willing to move forward with a prosecution, surely."

Shepherd seemed to want to give Trueman something definite to take away with him, perhaps to overwrite any lingering residue of Holland's earlier references to Mexican drug gangs, but an uncomfortable silence had settled over the room.

"We don't have Waters's DNA for comparison," said Maik finally.

"What? He's a convicted criminal, for God's sake. Surely his DNA must be on file."

"His records are missing. Mislabelled, they think. Or, you know … just gone." He shrugged.

Shepherd was staring at him as if she thought by the force of her sheer willpower alone she might change the sergeant's report. God almighty, if the public only knew the extent of the

A Pitying of Doves

bureaucratic cock-ups made on a daily basis in the nation's police stations, any scant trust they still had in their police forces would disappear in a puff of smoke.

"Ma'am, if I may," said Holland tentatively, using the sincere tone he went to when he wanted to make an impression with his superiors. "As the sergeant says, I know this Jordan Waters. I've lifted him a number of times over the years, as a matter of fact. The thing is, I can see him being involved in this somewhere along the line, but I can't see him killing anyone. He hasn't got it in him. I'm sure of it. I know him."

"*Knew*, Constable. In those heady days before the drug habit and the prison sentence."

Waters had done some genuine time, and prison, they all knew, had a way of providing inmates with an entirely new skill set. One of the first lessons anybody learned in prison was if you wanted something, you went and got it, and you didn't let anybody get in your way.

"Well if that's all, Guy ... Mr. Trueman and I will leave you to it. You'll let me know when anything turns up, Domenic?"

She didn't say *if.* She turned on her heel and, without a word or a backward glance, exited the room. Maik couldn't help noticing there was considerably less spring in her step than when she had entered.

26

They were due to meet on the bridge again, near the Clarence Gate entrance, but when Jejeune arrived Hidalgo was not there. Across the road, he could see the late-morning traffic beginning to build along Baker Street. Cars, buses, pedestrians preoccupied with thoughts of the coming day, perhaps, the tasks that awaited them.

Hidalgo emerged from the crowd and crossed the road, exercising the caution non-natives often do in an unfamiliar city. "Forgive me, Inspector," he said. "I was on the telephone with Ramon's wife. It was not a call I could end abruptly." He shook his head. "What could I tell her? Can you ever recover your enthusiasm for life after something like this?" He shook his head. "A terrible business. But you must forgive my discourtesy," said Hidalgo, seeming to shake off his sadness a little. "I forgot to enquire. Your constable, she is all right?"

Jejeune assured Hidalgo that Salter was recovering, and a soft smile of relief touched the older man's lips. "I am pleased."

They began to walk across the grass, heading for the bandstand. Hidalgo took in the view from the bridge, the same view they had enjoyed once before. He spoke without turning to face Jejeune. "I hear you have a suspect? This boy, Waters, did he commit this crime?"

"We're not sure."

"But you have managed to link him to Luisa Obregón?" Hidalgo paused and turned to look at Jejeune. "It may perhaps be better for me to hear of any involvement concerning Mexican citizens through unofficial channels first, if that is possible."

"Luisa Obregón says the Mexican authorities are to blame for her husband's death."

Whether the abruptness of Jejeune's comment was intended to take him off-guard, Hidalgo didn't know, but he doubted it. The inspector did not seem the type to play such games with people's emotions. He offered a wan smile. "Death was treated with great respect in ancient Mexico, Inspector. It was viewed as simply a phase, a portal to another stage of consciousness. Perhaps we should feel proud Luisa Obregón wishes to confer this honour upon us. You must understand, Inspector, *la viuda negra*, the black widow, is fierce in her loyalty toward her husband's memory. He was under contract with the Mexican military at one time. Her claim arises from their decision to terminate that arrangement. Nothing more."

"To withdraw the funding for his research, you mean?" asked Jejeune. "His genetic manipulation studies?"

Hidalgo searched Jejeune's face carefully, as if looking for something behind the words. "I am afraid the exact nature of the Mexican authorities' relationship with Victor Obregón is classified, but you must read nothing sinister into this. It is the normal way of such military matters."

"Is it normal for the military to ask an outside agency to continue monitoring the Obregón's telephone calls so long after the contract is terminated? Why would they want to do that, I wonder?"

"I think you will find that arrangement is now at an end," said Hidalgo carefully.

Now, noted Jejeune. "But what possible interest could they still have had in the Obregón family after all this time?"

Hidalgo offered an indulgent smile. "This is not the first time Mrs. Obregón has made such an accusation against the Mexican authorities. I cannot say in this case, of course, but such comments would normally be more than enough justification for someone to take an interest in her communications."

Jejeune hesitated for a moment, aware his next statement might determine the course of the rest of this meeting. And perhaps all his future meetings with Hidalgo. "It would help our enquiries if we knew if there was any connection between Mr. Santos and the Obregón family. He was in the military himself at one point, wasn't he?"

Hidalgo drew in a breath and placed a flat hand against his barrel chest. "I can assure you with all the honesty I hold in my heart, Inspector, I know of no connection between the decision to withdraw Victor Obregón's funding and Ramon's death at the sanctuary." He looked at Jejeune, challenging him to decide whether he could believe the diplomat's words.

They began strolling again, pausing again on the Long Bridge to scan the waters, then crossing the playing fields and moving on up toward the plantation. "All this green space for the people to enjoy," said Hidalgo, looking around him. "Of late, there is much economic optimism in Mexico. Our oil reserves have been opened to foreign investors. But do we not need to pause to consider what damage they will do, these foreigners, to the natural beauty of our land? There are laws, of course, to protect our environment, but some opportunities, they can tempt even the most honest of men."

As they crossed the grassy meadow approaching the golf and tennis school, a bird called out. Both men stopped and looked up into the treetops.

"It's a jay," said Jejeune, "but I can't find it. It's a pity. It's a striking bird."

"You have such birds in Canada, also, I think?" Hidalgo smiled at Jejeune's look of surprise. "The Toronto Blue Jays? Baseball is one of my great passions."

"Ah. Blue Jays are different, more bold and confident." Jejeune nodded up at the tree. "These British jays let out these loud calls every now and then, but they are generally fairly shy."

"The bold Canadians. The retiring British. The corrupt Mexicans," said Hidalgo thoughtfully. "Such generalities are easier to apply to nationalities than to individuals, I think." He paused and looked at Jejeune. "I understand you must pursue your enquiries wherever they may lead you, but even a hint of suspicion that Ramon was involved in anything illegal may cause the authorities to withhold his government pension. If they do, it will leave his wife and children without the money they need to survive. The family of such a loyal, honest man does not deserve this, I think."

Hidalgo lowered his gaze and stared unseeing into the base of the trees in front of the patch of woodland. *Santos listed a Ring Ouzel here,* thought Jejeune. *If he was honest. If his birding records could be trusted.*

"The ancient Mexicans were not correct about death, Inspector," said Hidalgo quietly. "Perhaps such propaganda simply made it easier to find sacrificial victims willing to volunteer for their fates." He shook his head. "Death is a terrible, evil thing, and even more so when it comes to one so young. I do not know what happened at the sanctuary that night, but I can tell you only this: Ramon Santos was not involved in any dealings with Luisa Obregón. Of this I am sure. Ramon's first loyalty was to his country. He would never have betrayed the trust that had been placed in him... Never."

Tears welled up in Hidalgo's eyes and he brushed them away with an angry, impatient gesture. Jejeune found something to occupy his gaze and give the diplomat the time he needed to recover his composure. *There are so many forms of betrayal,* thought Jejeune. Would he be able to issue such a sweeping statement about anyone, including himself, considering a career change even as he interviewed this man?

Hidalgo drew a breath and steadied himself. When he turned again to look at Jejeune, his eyes still held the mist of his earlier emotion. "Forgive me. For the Latin male, the machismo ethic is tested to its limits by the death of a colleague," he said. Both men stood in silence for a moment, staring once again up into the treetops. Finally, unable to locate the jay, they resumed their walk at a leisurely pace. "I wonder if a Canadian jay would thrive as well in this British climate as the celebrated Inspector Jejeune," said Hidalgo softly. "However much they like you here, you are still an outsider to the British, I think. How they must wish your success had fallen to one of them."

It was the second time Hidalgo had made a reference to Jejeune's background. He wondered why the counsellor had brought the subject up again. In Jejeune's experience, people rarely spoke about nationalities unless they had an agenda to promote. What was Hidalgo's? Solidarity, perhaps; two outsiders wandering around a park here at the heart of everything that was British — this city, this capital? Was this Hidalgo's way of trying to ensure fairness in Jejeune's investigations, to counteract any favouritism he might be feeling toward his adopted country? Or was it something else?

As they approached the Clarence Gate entrance to complete their circuit, Hidalgo paused to extend a farewell handshake to Jejeune.

"The service for Ramon at Westminster is scheduled for next week," said Hidalgo. "If you have no doubts about his innocence by then, I hope you will attend. Sir Michael Hillier is coming, I understand, and perhaps the chief constable."

Whether he had resolved his doubts by then or not, Jejeune would attend the service. Whatever he had been involved in during the final few moments of his life, Ramon Santos deserved the dignity of being mourned by everyone. Especially, perhaps, by the man who was trying to solve his murder.

27

Perhaps in deference to Domenic's unease in large groups, Lindy had taken to hosting smaller gatherings recently. Melissa the travel agent and Robin the cockney rhyming slang coach had occupied one such evening. Tonight it was Lindy's boss, Eric. Lindy was especially fond of Eric and had gone to great lengths to dress up their cottage with the inevitable plethora of candles and baskets. The fourth would be Carrie Pritchard. Lindy had no idea why Dom had insisted on inviting her, but it was okay with her that he had. Lindy had always bought into the old adage of keeping your friends close, and your enemies closer. And your rivals closest of all.

Eric was still taking off his jacket in the hallway when Carrie arrived. There was an instant frisson of mutual discomfort that was all the more noticeable between two such normally gregarious people.

"Eric," said Pritchard, trying and not quite succeeding to keep a note of uncertainty from her voice. "I had no idea you were going to be here."

"Nor I you," said Eric. He looked at Lindy carefully, as if he suspected this might be some contrived social engineering experiment of hers. But it was clear she was as surprised as anyone at the situation.

"You two know each other?" asked Lindy, ignoring the atmosphere with an act of will that was almost visible.

"We used to date," said Eric simply.

"Well, I suppose that would make introductions a bit daft, then, wouldn't it? So why don't you come in and let Dom get you both a drink. I'll just grab some snacks."

And with that, Lindy disappeared into the kitchen, leaving Jejeune to take coats and drink orders. Pritchard and Eric settled into chairs close enough to be social but distant enough to avoid discomfort. Jejeune was so desperate for ice-breaking conversation that he was even considering resorting to discussing the north Norfolk weather when Lindy reappeared carrying a tray of crabcakes. She set them on the table and sat down next to Jejeune on their buttoned-leather couch.

"Well, this could hardly be more awkward, could it?" said Lindy brightly. She had a way of confronting difficult situations by accelerating into them with as much force as possible, hoping, perhaps, that they might just disintegrate on impact. It was such a wonderfully optimistic approach to life's problems that it never failed to make Jejeune's heart glow a little.

"I do hope you parted on good terms at least," said Lindy, passing around plates and napkins. She seemed determined to underline the fact that this situation was complete happenstance, and had no intention of letting it ruin a perfectly good dinner party.

"I believe we did," said Eric. He turned to Pritchard. "I think we both simply decided that a life of desperate, unrelieved loneliness was better than seeing each other anymore."

Pritchard's laugh was a beautiful, musical thing, and she accompanied it with a playful toss of her hair. The tension gone, an air of grateful relaxation settled over the room. A bell dinged somewhere behind a closed door and Lindy got up to attend to something in the oven. When she returned, the two men were hovering on either side of Pritchard, peering at something on her iPhone. It was the earlier bird sculpture, now fully painted.

"Still no?" she said to Jejeune.

He shook his head. "Not with those cinnamon wing linings."

"A clue, then. Think Canada."

"The national bird?" ventured Eric.

Jejeune shook his head. "Canada doesn't have one. We have provincial birds. For Ontario, it's the Common Loon."

Lindy held up a hand. "I'm saying nothing."

"It's called a Great Northern Diver over here," Pritchard reminded him. "I can't always understand why they change the names of some birds from one place to another, but with that one, at least, I can see their reasoning."

Dom did the honours once more with the wine bottle. As he leaned over to pour, Lindy saw Carrie Pritchard do that ear-curl thing with her hair. *Carrie the bird sculptor,* thought Lindy, *dedicated to conservation, conversant in birding matters. Dom's identikit woman.* Another bell from the kitchen stopped her pursuing the thoughts any further.

Lindy returned this time with a platter of potted Cromer crab with caper sauce, served on a bed of samphire. Lindy's embrace of all things Norfolk included the cuisine, and she rarely missed a chance to trot out an authentic Norfolk recipe when they were entertaining. However, past experiments hadn't always worked out exactly as planned, and while this dish at least looked palatable, Domenic would still approach it with a certain amount of caution.

Pritchard got the conversation ball rolling by quizzing Domenic on his latest sighting. If that was what you could call it. "What is this I hear about a possible Baillon's Crake out in Carter's Marsh? A record, I note, you have not reported to the rare bird hotline."

"There was a suspected double murderer in the area," said Jejeune simply. "Encouraging birders to come out there didn't seem the most responsible course of action."

"Oh, Dom, I think you should at least have invited Carrie." Lindy at her most mischievous could assume an expression of such wide-eyed innocence that only those who had seen it before could detect the undercurrents. Carrie Pritchard didn't know Lindy very well, but from the way Eric lowered his eyes and smiled slightly into his wine, Jejeune suspected that Lindy's editor had seen her act before — likely many times.

"So you didn't mention it to any of the local birders at all?" pressed Pritchard.

Jejeune looked guilty. "I emailed Quentin Senior."

Carrie made a face. "And what did Quentin say? That he would abandon his birding tour group in the middle of the Steppes and hop on the first plane home?"

"He asked if I had ever heard a Marsh Frog."

"And?" Carrie Pritchard scrutinized Jejeune's face intently.

"It wasn't a Marsh Frog," he said simply. "He also pointed out that Baillon's Crakes normally call at night. It was daylight, early morning, when I heard this one, but it was quite foggy and overcast."

Carrie Pritchard considered Jejeune's account in silence. "You should at least submit a report," she said finally. "Now that access to Carter's Marsh is open again, it would be up to others if they wanted to check it out, but I think at least they should have the option."

Jejeune's agreement was so nonchalant it caused Lindy to cast him a glance. From what she was hearing, this Baillon's Crake was potentially a very rare find, and yet he didn't seem overly bothered about having it recorded. But Domenic could be like this about his birding at times. Just before they moved up here, he had been part of a group of a dozen or so birders who had seen a bird tentatively identified as the U.K.'s first wild Azure-winged Magpie. By all accounts, it was an astonishing record; one of which he should have been extremely proud, but she doubted if he had even mentioned it to the birders out here. He seemed almost embarrassed by it, as if he felt that he hadn't really earned the sighting, merely being present when other, better birders had found it. The irony was, of course, that as someone who was appearing on the news almost nightly at the time, giving Britain updates on the case involving the Home Secretary's daughter, Domenic's word had lent particular credence to the claim, which was still in the process of being verified by the British Birds Rarities Committee. And now, here he was again, nonchalantly shrugging off a record of a Baillon's Crake. Perhaps Quentin Senior had shaken his confidence in his identification, after all, or perhaps the previous year's Ivory Gull rejection had left a tang of distrust of the local Rare Birds Committee, of which the scrupulous Carrie Pritchard was once the secretary.

"Interesting lot, birders," said Eric. "A couple of my close friends in Hong Kong were extremely keen. I never really saw the appeal myself, but they were always threatening to take me out and show me the error of my ways. I sometimes regret that I never took them up on their offer. Any pursuit that can arouse that kind of enthusiasm is clearly worth a closer look."

That comment reflected so much about Eric, thought Lindy. Regardless of whether he had any interest in birding himself, he still wanted to understand what it was about it that others found so compelling. It was this kind of curiosity about life, this embrace of human enthusiasm in all its many forms, which had first attracted Lindy to work for him, despite many other offers. It was a decision that she never regretted, even if the day-to-day machinations of life at the magazine could sometimes drive her mad.

"So, Eric," said Lindy, with an energy that suggested she was prepared to shift the conversation on from birding with a front-end loader if necessary, "I take it you haven't been man enough to admit your mistake to them yet?" Both Pritchard and Jejeune turned quizzical looks on Eric.

"I allowed someone to use the word *overexaggerate* in a piece this week," he said simply.

"What's wrong with *overexaggerate*?" asked Pritchard.

"It's redundancy," said Lindy bluntly. "*Exaggerate* about covers it, don't you think? Did you ever hear of anyone *under-exaggerating*?"

"Redundancies have their place," said Eric reasonably. "Look at Proust. *Remembrances of Things Past*. It could hardly have been *Remembrances of Things in the Future*, could it? But I think you'd agree *Remembrances of Things* hardly has the same ring to it."

"It's called logomachy, isn't it?" said Domenic, in an apparent effort to remind the others that they weren't the only ones who had taken some English courses at university. "A dispute over words."

"Never heard of it." Lindy took a flamboyant swig of her wine. "Are you sure that's a real word?"

"Cited by none other than Samuel Johnson, in his dictionary," affirmed Jejeune.

"This would be the same Samuel Johnson who claimed a tarantula bite could be cured by music, then? Not to mention his surreal definition of the boramez: *a vegetable lamb*?" Lindy looked around at the others. "God knows what they must have been putting in the ale at the Cheshire Cheese the day he came up with that one."

"Wasn't it Johnson who defined a penguin as a fruit, too?" asked Eric.

Pritchard nodded. "I believe he also thought swallows

hibernated in the mud in winter," she said, piling on good-naturedly. "I'm not sure he's an entirely reliable source, Domenic."

Jejeune gave them all a look that suggested he had slipped his learning into a mental box labelled SELF: ITEMS FOR THE FUTURE HUMILIATION OF, and firmly closed the lid.

"Great word, though, regardless," said Eric, belatedly coming to Jejeune's rescue. He turned to Lindy. "You'll certainly be hearing it at the office from now on. After all, *logomachy* is a lot more polite than any of the other words I can think of to describe our editorial meetings."

As the meal drew to an end, Pritchard began to gather the empty plates. "I'll give you a hand washing them if you like," she said to Lindy. "We can do them the old fashioned way, at the sink, so you don't have to empty the dishwasher in the morning."

"Oh, surely that's not necessary," said Jejeune with an enthusiasm that caused Lindy to cast him a glance. "I can give Lindy a hand with that later on." But even if Domenic seemed unnaturally keen to spare Ms. Pritchard's delicate artist's hands from the ravages of dishwashing soap, Lindy's past experiences told her that such help from him rarely materialized. One call from the station and Domenic would be gone, leaving all his good intentions in the sink alongside the pile of dirty dishes.

"If you insist, Carrie," said Lindy. "You two go off and do your male bonding thing, and we'll discuss all the ways we could improve men if only they would listen to us."

Jejeune and Eric rose and carried their wine glasses outside. She watched them go; two men so much alike in their layers of complexity and their dark corners. There weren't many men around with such qualities. David Nyce was another, from what she had heard, which made Carrie Pritchard somewhat of a collector of men like this. "Let's get to those dishes, Carrie," she said briskly.

The men stood on the porch, side by side, not speaking. A single pool of light from the kitchen window fell at their feet, but in front of them stretched only the vast canvas of the sky, black and grey, with ragged clouds scudding on the winds, as if they had been dragged across the night to polish the twinkling constellations beyond. Jejeune closed his eyes for a moment and felt the salty tang of sea air on his face, carried in by the night breeze.

Eric lit a cigarette and took a long drag, savouring it as if it was something he had been waiting a long time to do. "I thought our girl acquitted herself pretty well tonight. Carrie can be a pretty formidable female presence in a room, but Lindy certainly held her own in there."

Dom hadn't realized Lindy had become shared property, but he took Eric's comment in the spirit it was intended. For his own part, he had seen a couple of stutter steps, one or two out-of-place comments from Lindy, who normally hit her social marks with unerring accuracy. He could think of no reason why Carrie Pritchard's presence should have made her uneasy; himself, yes, but not Lindy.

Eric took another long, luxuriating pull on his cigarette. "I suppose I really should give these up," he said, holding the cigarette in front of him and staring at the tip, glowing red in the darkness. "One of our journalists has just done a story on the cigarette industry in the U.S. Did you know cigarettes cause about one death per million smoked? At about one cent in profit for every cigarette sold, that fixes the value of a human life to a cigarette maker at a rather neat figure of ten thousand dollars."

Jejeune held up his wine glass, allowing the moonlight to filter through it in a liquid glow. "I'm sure alcohol has a terrifying kill ratio, too, if one bothered to analyse the stats."

"Yes, somehow not quite so quantifiable though, is it?" Eric laughed and shook his head. "Makes me wonder sometimes about the world we live in, where the value of a human life can be fixed so precisely on a balance sheet. Still, I suppose you come across people all the time in your job who place an even more dubious value on human life."

Jejeune smiled to acknowledge the comment, but said nothing. He turned to watch the two women through the kitchen window. They were standing side-by-side at the sink, Lindy washing and Carrie thoroughly drying as Lindy handed each item to her. They chatted easily, unaware of Domenic's gaze — at them, at the counter, at the dishes and glasses piling up on it, each one clean, polished, and without a single fingerprint on it.

28

Shepherd stalked out to the parking lot with a short leather jacket on, heels clicking on the cobbled surface. She was seething; her complexion still flushed with a mix of anger and humiliation, her jaw muscles tweaked with vexation.

"It's not just one thing, you understand, Colleen. It's the gradual accumulation; the injuries to your constable, the involvement with Hillier, this business with the canine unit."

Peter Albrecht, the newest in a long line of assistant chief constables she had dealt with, had spread ample hands before him on her desk and studied them instead of looking her in the eye. He was a career desk jockey; more used to conducting his business over chilled Chablis and starched white tablecloths in refined clubs. The kind of copper who wouldn't know a piece of hard evidence if it came up and kicked him in his bony backside.

"I'm sure I don't need to articulate to you what the concerns are. Or where they are coming from. But you are obviously going to be held accountable for the actions of your staff."

The fact that he had come down here, to her office, was a sign of some kind of concession in the power pyramid that was the North Norfolk Constabulary these days, she supposed. But it was no compensation for the message he brought with him. He had looked up, making eye contact finally. *"We wouldn't want to lose you, Colleen.*" He had actually said that, the lanky, feckless cretin. However, the very fact that he had mentioned it at all was an acknowledgement that they were prepared to do exactly that, if this case was not resolved with the speed and, more particularly, the result they desired.

Jejeune had followed Shepherd outside after she had crooked a finger at him in her march past his office, and he was standing expectantly now, looking at her over the top of Nyce's green Jag.

"In the car, Domenic. We're going for a ride."

"In this? It's material evidence?"

"They only want a scraping of the paint, for God's sake," said Shepherd irritably. "Apparently Norwich Central can't get a transport unit up here until tomorrow, so I said we would save them a trip and take the Jag down there to them. Jump in. We can talk on the way."

Jejeune blanched. He had experienced numerous trips with DCS Shepherd behind the wheel, and they had been interesting enough without her being so obviously upset. He had secured his seat belt before she rounded the sleek green front of the vehicle and slid behind the wheel.

"Still, chain of evidence and everything," said Jejeune uncertainly. "I'm not sure the CPS will be too happy."

Shepherd flipped on her sunglasses, grabbed the wheel, and turned her head to face him. "Well, they can just bugger off then, can't they?"

She pressed the starter and the engine leaped to life with a throaty roar. There was a slight lurch as she slipped the clutch and sped out of the parking lot into Saltmarsh's late-morning traffic.

"We'll take the scenic route, blow the cobwebs away. A high-performance job like this shouldn't be sitting around for as long as it has been."

Although Jejeune was a more than competent driver himself, he had never quite come to terms with being a passenger on the left-hand side of the road. At least when Lindy was driving, though, he had the chance to scan the hedgerows and fields for birds. With the DCS behind the wheel, the north Norfolk countryside was flashing by in such a blur he would have been hard pressed to spot a racing pigeon.

"So Domenic, do we need to talk about why you refused the canine unit?" She was giving her driving the utmost attention, eyes locked on the road ahead, arms extended in speed control mode. "It didn't come from Danny Maik, by the way, in case you were wondering."

Jejeune wasn't, but he could not help admiring the way that even in her annoyance she was careful to preserve the harmonious relationships of her team, so carefully assembled under her personal direction.

"I couldn't take the risk that the birds would be harmed."

It was enough to get Shepherd to fire a sidelong glance at him. "You don't think there's just the slightest chance that your hobby is compromising your professionalism?"

Not my hobby, he thought. *Other things, maybe, but not that.*

"Not the Baillon's Crake," he said, "the doves. They are the only connection between everybody in this case — Phoebe Hunter, Santos, Waters, Obregón … even Maggie Wylde. The Socorro Doves are the magnets that draw everyone together. If they were killed by the dogs, or escaped in the chase, all those connections would disappear. Besides, Waters was long gone. He wasn't about to hang around to give Nyce a second chance."

Shepherd wondered whether the last part sounded just a little bit like someone trying to convince himself of something. "I see," she said after a long pause, giving the distinct impression that, in this case, seeing wasn't necessarily believing. "Then let's leave that aside for the moment. Anything come of your conversation with the Faculty Conduct Chair? Presumably you were waiting for just the right moment to tell me you had gone to see him."

Shepherd afforded herself another quick glance over at Jejeune, but the DCI could see only his own reflection in her dark glasses.

"He was very careful not to make any accusations," said Jejeune, "but the word *plagiarism* did come up. Apparently, the early papers are much more sophisticated than Nyce's later ones, which is a pretty clear flag. I mean, presumably nobody gets less intelligent the longer they spend in an academic institution."

"It's quite clear you've never spent any time in an English comprehensive school," said Shepherd drily. She checked her mirrors and moved out to accelerate past a tractor trundling along. Jejeune jerked back in his seat a little as the car leaped to obey her command. In an instant they were past the tractor and Shepherd eased the car back into the inside lane, backing off the accelerator. A little.

"So what? We think he pinched his early stuff and Phoebe Hunter found out. Just the sort of thing to base a relationship on — one in which he helps out her career while she helps out his mid-life crisis."

"That's the thing," said Jejeune. "According to the Chair, there was no suggestion of any impropriety between Nyce and Phoebe Hunter. None at all."

"Which just means he's careful," said Shepherd, "or clever …"

"Or innocent," said Jejeune. "There was some kind of relationship between them, clearly, but, I don't know …" Jejeune shook his head. "His reaction. It seems, well … wrong for a distraught lover."

"Wrong? What exactly is the right kind of reaction? You could argue that Efren Hidalgo's reaction is not normal. Grief is not a normal human condition, Domenic."

"True. But Hidalgo's is mixed with remorse, for failing to protect someone who was his responsibility. Nyce's response doesn't seem to have any connection to Phoebe Hunter's death. It's more like anger, bitterness."

"It's all very well for you, Domenic, in a nice stable relationship with a wonderful young woman, but for some of us who are … well, I'm just not sure that affairs of the heart are as easily encompassed by your normal sweeping generalizations, that's all."

Shepherd checked her mirror again before moving out to pick off another hapless kerb-crawling victim and drifting effortlessly back into her lane again. The rural landscape had gradually given way to small outcroppings of residential development, following the meandering course of a wide, flat river. A pretty pub appeared on the horizon and moments later Shepherd wheeled the Jag into the forecourt.

Shepherd parked and removed her sunglasses, slipping them into her handbag along with the car keys. "Come on, you can buy me a white wine. I need one after the morning I've had," she said. "And come to think of it, you look like you could do with a drink, too."

29

"I'm not sure this is a panini," said Jejeune, dubiously regarding the sandwich on the plate in front of him. A placard outside the pub suggested that the building had been around since the time John Cabot set off on his first voyage of discovery to Jejeune's homeland, but the pub's menu reflected Britain's embrace of all things modern and foreign.

"Of course it's not a panini. Do you think the locals would stand for prices like these if the sandwiches didn't have foreign names? Besides, I didn't bring you here for the food. I thought you would like these."

She nodded toward the water just beyond the patio on which they were sitting. A flotilla of Mute Swans were drifting sedately past, perhaps as many as thirty of them. Jejeune was aware that he shouldn't approve of this; birds living off an artificial food supply of bread thrown to them by the pub's customers. It couldn't be good for the river's natural ecosystem either. But almost despite himself, he found the beauty of the birds mesmerizing — their pure white plumage, the noble bearing of those sensuously curved necks. Watching them now, it was impossible not to admire the majesty of the effortless gliding over the surface of the dark water.

"What do they call a flock of swans anyway?" asked Shepherd, watching them as intently as Jejeune.

"A *lamentation* is one common term. Some people say a *bevy*."

DCS held up her glass. "A bevy, then" she said, taking a drink. She leaned back slightly, as if to take in the view — the water, the cottages on the far bank, the people at the other tables basking in the weak spring sunshine.

"You might be interested to know that Constable Holland, too, is less than convinced that Nyce's attempt to kill Waters is the revenge of an anguished lover. He came to see me a couple of days ago. God knows where you were. Busy, I suppose, or off birding somewhere. He wondered if perhaps you might have overplayed your hand a little when you questioned Nyce, and inadvertently identified Waters as our prime suspect." She held up her hand. "Yes, I know, I've already spoken to Danny Maik. But even if you didn't mention Waters by name, it's possible that Nyce picked up on it. Don't give me that look, Domenic. It happens. Nyce is a very bright chap. A university professor, for God's sake. You can't always be the cleverest person in the room, you know. If he was able to identify Waters as our suspect, well ..."

"Well, what?" asked Jejeune defensively. "If Nyce could give us our suspect, albeit dead, then we could all just pack our bags and go home?"

"Holland does have a point. There are plenty of questions that wouldn't ever be asked if we had our number one suspect on a slab in the mortuary. It might well be enough to justify closing the case. After all, who is going to keep digging if we already believe we have our man?" She spared Jejeune the details of Holland's mischievous, conspiratorial glance at this point, the one that had seemed to say, "except perhaps, for one pain-in-the-arse Canadian chief inspector."

Shepherd took a sip of her wine and watched the swans float along the river. "All swans in Britain are the property of the Queen, aren't they?" she asked.

Jejeune nodded. "All unmarked swans in open water, I believe it is. I doubt she cares much, though."

But you do, thought Shepherd. *The custody of these wild birds matters a lot more to you than this bloody job ever will.* "Of course," she said, "this business about Nyce all comes about because Holland is absolutely convinced that this Jordan Waters is no killer. Ergo, he needs to find someone else who is. I'm not sure how much stock we can put into Holland's intuition, to be honest. Guy Trueman tells me he's seen boys you would trust to babysit your children turn into ruthless killing machines when the circumstances called for it. Personally, I think almost anyone would be capable of killing in certain situations. But either way, it's one more reason you need to find Jordan Waters. And quick."

Shepherd paused to look out over the water again. She seemed to reach a decision, and when she began speaking again, she did so slowly, quietly, as if she didn't quite trust her voice to convey her thoughts out in the open like this.

"It has been made clear to me in no uncertain terms that Ramon Santos should no longer be considered a person of interest in this case."

Jejeune was quiet, watching the swans, not looking at her as she spoke.

"The irony is, of course, that they would love him to be involved," said Shepherd. "It would take a lot of pressure off the Home Office diplomatically, to have a Mexican suspect tied to all this. But it means if you were to make a case for Santos's involvement, however small or tenuous that involvement might be, they would seize upon it. They would take the idea that Santos was somehow complicit in his own death as fact, Domenic. They would blow it up and announce it as certainty, remove any suggestion that Santos was just an innocent victim of a crazy, drug-addled Brit. They wouldn't be content to let you go out into the press and say it's just a theory, just another one of your convoluted thinking-out-loud exercises. They would be looking to nail this idea to you like a cross. You would need to be able to prove a connection unequivocally. And I don't think you can do that, can you?"

Jejeune still said nothing.

"I know you rather too well to expect that you're going to let this line of investigation go, Domenic, regardless of what I, or Michael Hillier, or DAC Peter Albrecht might feel is in your best interests. So I suggest you bury it in an avalanche of other enquiries for now. But I won't wait forever. If you don't bring me something soon, this avenue of investigation *will* be closed. Permanently. Understood?"

She tilted her wine glass back to drain it before standing and gathering in Jejeune's glass. "My shout, I believe." She saw his look. "Relax. The boys from Norwich will be here at any moment to take the keys to the Jag from me. Tony Holland said he will meet us here and take us back in the Audi. He's in town, seeing some new girlfriend, no doubt."

Jejeune drew a breath. *Relax?* Holland threw his Audi A5 around these narrow lanes in a way that would make the DCS look like a Sunday morning grandmother. It said something about Jejeune's predicament when he was half-hoping Shepherd might ask if she could drive the Audi back herself.

"That drink?"

"Can you see if they have any Crown Royal?"

"Premium Canadian rye in the middle of the day, Inspector Jejeune? Are you sure you don't want me to make it a double?"

If there was any faint sarcasm behind the DCS's question, Jejeune seemed to have missed it. With the prospect of the daredevil automotive feats that awaited him on the drive home, he was half considering asking Shepherd if she would mind just bringing the bottle.

30

Wraiths of mist lay across the low-lying countryside like twisted ribbons, leaving heavy dew that held the police officers' footprints long after they had passed across the wet grass. The early-morning fret was more common in the autumn, but a cool spring morning like this one could still produce a good covering.

By now, the man's body had been recovered from the narrow culvert and hauled up to lie on the gravel road. Although Jejeune normally made a point of seeing bodies where they lay before they were moved, it would have been pointless to leave the bent, battered body of Jordan Waters where it was. The DCI couldn't have seen anything by looking into the darkness of the culvert, and there was not enough room for anyone to have gotten in alongside the body. Besides, cause of death was obvious enough, even for someone normally as cautious about jumping to conclusions as Danny Maik. A single stab wound to the chest. The other cuts and scrapes would be the result of the body having been dragged to the end of the culvert and shoved in.

There was a slight tremor of disturbance at the perimeter of the crime scene and Maik looked up to see Jejeune ducking under the blue-and-white tape. He watched him approach with his usual easy stride, taking in everything along the way, missing nothing, and all the while seeming as if he didn't have the slightest interest in this case, or any other.

"Found by a man taking his dog for an early-morning walk," said Danny as Jejeune drew near. "He saw the car and the pool of blood. His dog got the scent and led him toward the culvert, but the man stopped when he saw where it was leading. Understandable, I suppose. He said he had an idea what he might find and he wanted to spare himself the sight."

"Wise man," said Jejeune. He looked around at the mist-draped landscape emerging slightly through the morning light. "How far are we from the Obregón's property here?"

Maik nodded his head slightly in admiration. They banged on a lot at the station about Jejeune not being from around these parts, but he certainly had his geography right when it mattered.

"A couple of miles. The car is registered to Waters's mother. No trace of the birds."

Jejeune nodded. "Any idea on a time of death?"

"The ME hasn't arrived yet, but the wound …" Maik made a face. "I've seen them like this. I'd say a couple of hours, three at the most. Let's say early this morning, at least, rather than last night. I'd imagine the body hadn't been there all that long when the man came upon the car."

"A single knife wound?"

Maik nodded. "But something big. Carving knife, hunting knife maybe."

Not a pocket knife, he was implying, though he would have called it a penknife anyway. In any case, not the sort of thing someone might carry around with them on a casual basis. Something that you would choose with care, and bring with you deliberately to do a specific job you had in mind.

Jejeune walked back and stood over the body of the dead man.

"I asked a couple of uniforms to drop round and invite David Nyce to come into the station for a chat. I thought you might have wanted a word," Maik said.

Jejeune raised an eyebrow.

"He's not at home," said Maik. "His neighbours haven't seen him for days."

"I see." The DCI seemed preoccupied with thoughts beyond the news Maik was delivering. "Mr. Waters," Jejeune gestured toward the body. "I wonder, could we ..."

Maik looked down at the body. It had been placed in a way that skewed the head round at a grotesque, unnatural angle. The pose was similar to the one in the photos Maik had seen of a young man who had died in another case Jejeune had worked on. Jordan Waters was almost the same age and build as the boy who had died when Jejeune had rescued the Home Secretary's daughter. Jejeune had waited, then, that was all Maik knew. Jejeune had waited and no one knew why. He had never explained it, and in all the euphoria over the girl's rescue people had forgotten to keep asking. There would have been a reason, a good one, but for a man like Jejeune, perhaps that wouldn't have been enough, despite the world telling him he was free of blame. It was why he was able to speak so compellingly to Lauren Salter, tell her all about guilt and how it would never let you go. Jejeune was a clever lad; one of the cleverest Maik had ever worked with. In most things, he was sensible and well-grounded enough that Danny would have trusted his judgment without question. But guilt in one area, he knew, could spread like a disease, and he would be on the lookout to ensure the DCI knew that there was only one person responsible for Jordan Waters's death, and that was the person who had stabbed him and shoved him into this culvert. Maik placed his latex-gloved hands gently under the dead man's lolling head and straightened it.

With the sun rising higher, the mist was slowly releasing its grip on the land, clinging on only in the valleys and depressions that disappeared off in the direction of the Obregóns' property. A Curlew flapped lazily over the fields, issuing a single mournful cry as it passed. Otherwise, birdsong was absent. Perhaps they, too, felt the vague sense of unease that the sea mist brought to this place.

"I'll go and see the Obregóns," said Jejeune. "You can stay on here until SOCO and the ME arrive."

"No need," said Maik, "they'll know what to do. I'll come with you." Maik hadn't intended to make it sound like he was offering protection against a man who knew no fear, but sometimes, trying to couch things too delicately only made matters worse.

Jejeune called over one of the uniformed constables. "I assume nobody has let Jordan Waters's mother know about this yet," he said. "I think somebody local might be best."

Maik knew it wasn't a case of Jejeune shirking the responsibility, merely another example of his sensitivity, trying to find a way to soften the blow of the stark, terrible darkness a son's mother was about to descend into. But the constable hesitated for a moment, looking at Danny Maik before wordlessly walking away and getting into his car.

What am I doing here, thought Jejeune, *when they turn to Maik whenever they need direction?* He looked around him at the mist-wreathed fields. He was still not a part of this place, he realized, no matter how much he loved the coastal landscapes and the birds and the big, open skies. He wondered if he ever would be.

31

"I never did ask, what with all the excitement over Lauren ... Constable Salter ... and all. Did you ever see that rare bird of yours, the crake?"

"No," said Jejeune, looking out at the passing fields. For once, there was no music coming from the audio system in Maik's Mini. Combined with the sergeant's rare foray into small talk, it was a sign that he was concerned about coming up against Gabriel Obregón again. Not *afraid*. Jejeune suspected that word was almost as foreign to Maik's vocabulary as it was to Obregón's. But police training was designed for situations, and people, with patterns of behaviour that could be anticipated. It was unpredictability that worried police officers most. And a man like Gabriel Obregón, who was incapable of knowing fear, was about as unpredictable as they come.

"If you don't mind my saying so, you don't seem as, well ... pleased, as I thought you might be. You said it was a very rare find." Maik had been with Jejeune a couple of times when he had seen rare birds, and witnessed the DCI's shiny-eyed excitement first hand. A thought seemed to strike him. "The rare bird lot, Carrie Pritchard and the rest, are they refusing to accept the record? I did hear the call. If you played me a tape, I might be able to verify it, if that would help."

Jejeune smiled his thanks. Maik had been around when Jejeune had his Ivory Gull sighting rejected. Despite Jejeune's protestations to the contrary, the sergeant had obviously picked up how disappointed his DCI had been at the time.

"I have reported it, but I won't be adding it to my own life list," said Jejeune simply. He shrugged. "It's just a personal choice. To list a bird for the first time ever based solely on a noise somewhere in the middle of a marsh ...? It doesn't seem ... well, enough, somehow."

Not for the first time, the vagaries of Jejeune's pastime left Maik befuddled. Shouldn't there be some standard set of guidelines that everybody followed? Either hearing a bird counted or it didn't. How could you keep score, have lists and what-not, if everybody just made up their own rules as they went along? But Jejeune's mood, he suspected, had roots beyond failed bird sightings. A young man had been murdered, and no amount of small talk was going to take the DCI's mind off that. Death scarred him, each one carving a little deeper into the soft tissue of his humanity. There were days when Maik wondered just what would happen when there was no more flesh to tear at, when the DCI had nothing else left to give to the job. What then? Maik wasn't sure, but he had more than a passing interest in the question. His own future, he knew, rested just as much upon the answer as Jejeune's did.

Maik wheeled the Mini into the Obregón's driveway, grimacing as the small wheels rattled across the cattle grid. At least it could have been that. Over by the barn, Gabriel Obregón was leaning against the fence, holding a metallic object in his hands, turning it around carefully. It was about the size of a bread bin and looked like it could have been the skeleton of some long-forgotten piece of machinery. Maik thought it looked vaguely familiar, though he couldn't quite place it until Obregón raised it to eye level. It was an old gin trap, rusted and worn. But the jaws were still sharp and it was primed to snap.

Maik turned off the engine and the men unfurled themselves from the car. Maik continued to stare at Obregón. Though he was still looking down at the trap, he seemed to sense Maik's attention. Slowly and deliberately, Obregón placed his hand between the jaws and began tapping the rusted footplate, lightly at first and then slightly harder. He withdrew his hand and smiled at Maik, making as if to offer the trap with a look which said "your turn."

Luisa Obregón emerged from the house. Her dark hair was gathered in an untidy bun at the back of her head, and her drab, loose-fitting clothes were streaked with dirt. It was the uniform of a woman who had been working in the fields. Jejeune had seen the look many times since he had come to these parts, but in this case there was something particularly striking about a woman who was willing to sacrifice so much natural beauty to the demands of her work.

She seemed to understand his look.

"Organic farming is hard work, Inspector," she said, brushing a stray strand of hair back from her face with her wrist. "It requires much …" She turned and fired a term at her son in Spanish.

"Micro-management," he supplied from the far side of the courtyard, without looking up from the trap.

"Organic farming is a long term prospect, but life has taught me to be patient. Things are more rewarding if you wait for them. Do you not think so, Inspector?"

Jejeune offered a non-committal smile. Including revenge, perhaps?

"I imagine things must have been very difficult when the Mexican government withdrew its funding for your husband's research."

Luisa Obregón tossed her head slightly, as if she had forgotten that her long black tresses were secured behind her head and no longer free to swirl around. It gave the gesture an empty awkwardness. "My husband tried to ensure we would be secure financially."

Gabriel Obregón began to approach slowly from the far side of the courtyard. From this angle, Jejeune couldn't see if he was still carrying the trap, but Maik's reaction told him that he wasn't. The sergeant stirred only slightly, just enough to make the young man pause in his approach, close enough to watch proceedings carefully but far enough away to pose no threat.

"Do you mind if I have another look at the aviary?" asked Jejeune. "From the outside will be fine."

Luisa Obregón gave a non-committal tilt of her head and led the men around to the side of the house where the aviary came into view. From here the true scale of the structure was apparent, extending back and out from the house in all directions. The glass in the windows seemed secure, but the frame was showing signs of wear and neglect, with paint peeling and many rust patches.

"It doesn't look like anyone's done any maintenance around here in while," said Maik. "It's a shame, an elaborate set-up like this."

"I am too busy with my work on the farm."

"Your son doesn't have much interest?"

"Gabriel sees in it only a place where his father spent many hours alone. It has, for him, not pleasant memories. But perhaps it is simply the normal way of things. Children so often despise the passions of their parents. I do not know why this should be so, but it is."

Maik didn't know either. Too much parental attention lost to the pastime? Too much enthusiasm encouraged, too much information force-fed? All he knew was it wasn't an uncommon story, and it was probably as old as parent-child relationships themselves.

Jejeune was staring into the aviary intently, though from this angle Maik could see no signs of life. The birds were still in there, he supposed, the ones he and Jejeune had seen on their previous visit, but he could see no flickers of movement at all.

"Your husband obviously loved birds very much," said Jejeune. "I wonder, did he ever go birdwatching, take a book with him, make notes, that sort of thing?"

Obregón nodded. "Sometimes, yes. I gave his binoculars to Gabriel. His notes and bird guides, too. I hoped perhaps he might show some interest. But ..." She shrugged.

"Does your son still have them?" asked Maik.

"I am not sure. He became depressed once and gave away many things, sold them. His illness, it can make him do such things."

Maik looked at Jejeune to see if he wanted to take this any further. He didn't.

"This aviary," said Jejeune, "you say your husband built it to pursue his work. I wonder why you continue with it, now that your husband is no longer here."

"A wife who has lost her husband must think every day of the good things," said Obregón, seemingly unable to tear her eyes away from the aviary, "of the very best her husband was. She must hold on to this, these memories, and preserve them, store them away forever. She cannot allow anyone to take them away from her. This aviary is all I have of my husband. This is why I can never allow Carrie Pritchard to close it." Her voice seemed to falter a little.

It's this place, thought Maik. It would take a lot to knock someone as poised as Luisa Obregón off her stride. He had seen plenty of other coppers try their hand with suspects in interview rooms; if they liked to be on their feet, have them sitting; if moving around unsettled them, be all over the place. But such methods seemed crude and unsophisticated when you were in the presence of a master like Domenic Jejeune. Why go to all the trouble of dragging Luisa Obregón to the manufactured discomfort of an interview room, when you could simply bring her over here and stand her before her husband's aviary, her place of maximum emotional turmoil and pain. Jejeune would have hated to be thought of as calculating or manipulative, Maik knew, but at the business of interviewing suspects, he was a natural.

"The man who called about the doves was named Jordan Waters," said Jejeune suddenly. "His car was found not far away from here. From the direction it was facing, he could have been on his way here. Do you have any idea why?"

Obregón had a survivor's wariness about her, the kind that said you didn't answer a question until you fully understood the implications of your answer. Maik was expecting a lot of silence from Luisa Obregón now that she knew the true reason for their visit. But she surprised him.

"It is possible he was coming here to sell me the birds," she said, staring unwaveringly at the still-life aviary. "He was supposed to bring them to me on the night they were taken from the sanctuary, but he did not show up."

"Do you know if your husband ever had any connection with Phoebe Hunter?" The question came suddenly from Jejeune, and perhaps it was this that added the accusatory tone.

"Why do you ask this question?" Luisa Obregón's raised her voice angrily. "My husband was a good man," she continued, still shouting, "an honest man, faithful, decent. Why would he have interest in this girl? She would have been barely more than a child when he disappeared. I will not allow you to ask such questions on my land, here, near his memory."

Gabriel Obregón appeared round the corner, not at a run, but fast enough to cause Maik to step forward and block his way. "It's time you left," the young man said. "She has no more to say to you."

He stepped closer and Jejeune sensed Maik tensing slightly. "I'm sorry, I meant no offence," said Jejeune. "We will leave now."

Danny Maik saw the clouds of uncertainty in Jejeune's face as he led the way past Gabriel Obregón back toward the Mini. He could feel the eyes of both Obregóns on them as they left.

32

Danny Maik stood next to Guy Trueman at the window of his hotel room, looking down into the square below. A small group of people were making their way across the pavement, dressed in mottled greens and browns, carrying binoculars and scopes. Probably headed out to Titchwell, Maik guessed, where a report of something called a Black-winged Pratincole had sent Jejeune haring off earlier that morning.

"Tell me something," said Trueman, watching the procession, "these birders, this business with the camo gear? They're not expecting the birds to start opening fire on them, are they?"

"Probably more concerned with being surrounded on all sides from elevated positions, I imagine."

"Ah, well, if they're going to let the birds gain a tactical advantage like that, all the camo gear in the world isn't going to help them, is it?"

The levity over, Trueman turned to Maik in earnest. "So, what do you want, Danny? You made it sound important."

"Did I? Need to clear up a couple of things, that's all." Trueman noticed that Danny hadn't exactly denied it was important. "I never did ask you," said Danny, "why the Mexicans?"

Trueman shrugged. "You know how it is in our business. Somebody knows somebody. I saw a bit of action in Central

America. Brushed up on my Spanish. Made a couple of contacts."

He turned from the window and took a seat on the room's only chair. Maik had the choice of the bed or to remain standing. He chose the latter. "A diplomat's military records are sealed, but I understand Santos was in the Mexican army for a time," said Maik conversationally. "I wonder if he ever saw any action in Central America."

Trueman eyed him cautiously. "He never struck me as the type. Lots of people do military service, Danny, but as you and I know, not all of them turn out to be combat material. He was more the sort to go home and record his feelings in a journal, if you ask me."

Maik nodded and noted something down in his book. "The problem is," Jejeune had said, "everything we know about Santos has come through the Mexican Consulate. What we really need is some independent information, someone who knew Santos and could offer another perspective."

Another perspective. One that might explain why he was trying to steal doves from the sanctuary that night. Nobody could talk about Santos as a potential suspect; that much had been made clear in the directive that had come down from on high. But the chief constable's office couldn't prevent their DCIs from thinking things, much as they would like to. And if Domenic Jejeune wasn't in the habit of thinking out loud very much, well, then it made those moments when he did so all that more noticeable. Maik had fancied he had heard a clock ticking in the background somewhere during the pregnant pause that had followed.

"Okay," he had agreed finally. "No guarantees, but I'll ask him."

Back in the present, Trueman was making a point. "Listen, Danny," he said, "this Santos was everything they're saying he was — loyal, faithful, honest. No criminal record, not even a breath of scandal or suspicion about him." He looked at Maik frankly. "You can tell your DCI he's barking up the wrong tree. That kid had nothing to do with any of this."

It occurred to Maik that it would be easier to offer such an emphatic denial if you knew who *did* have something to do with it. But Danny didn't feel like pushing it just now, especially with the other tricky ground he still had to cover with his ex-CO.

"It's a long drive up from London, especially in that traffic, that time of night. Tiring. You must have slept like a baby after you got here."

Trueman looked puzzled. "Awake at oh six hundred, as usual." A momentary pause passed between the two men, like the space between heartbeats. "Am I a suspect, Danny? In Jordan Waters's death?"

"I just need to know where you were that morning. You arrive in Saltmarsh, and somebody who took out one of yours dies soon after. You know I've never been one for coincidences." Whether Trueman realized it or not, it was a measure of Maik's esteem for the man that he had furnished even this much of an explanation for his line of questioning.

Trueman gave a sigh, trying for amusement and not quite making it. "On the morning Jordan Waters died, I was in this very room, watching the picturesque seaside village of Saltmarsh come to life. Pretty sight, too, dawn breaking over the boats in the harbour, gulls flying about all over the place, the early risers setting out their stalls."

"And after?" Maik was letting the act of writing notes in his book take up all of his attention.

"After? Bloody hell, Danny! I made myself a coffee on that machine there, and settled in to read the paper until I could hear sounds of movement next door." Trueman nodded toward the wall. "Hidalgo's an early riser too, and he likes to get a start on the day as soon as his feet hit the floor."

Danny was still making his meticulous notes, staring down at his page. He said nothing. "As it happened," said Trueman peevishly, "there was an early-morning call; some diplomatic crisis brewing back at the consulate. As soon as the chauffeur had Hidalgo in the car, and they were safely on their way, I went downstairs to have breakfast. I suppose I could have ordered room service, but I wanted to make sure I had an alibi in case my old sergeant came by to ask me if I had murdered anybody that morning." The angry smile did nothing to disguise the bitterness in his voice.

Maik finished writing and looked up from his notebook. He treated Trueman to an entry from his slender repertoire of expressions, but it was so enigmatic that as far as the other man was concerned it might have been regret, contempt, or just about anything in between. Nevertheless, when Trueman spoke again, some of the terseness had gone from his voice.

"If that was your idea of role play, I can tell you, the job's already yours," he said. His tone softened further still. "That's why I need you, Danny. I know you won't go missing in action when the dirty work needs to be done. You won't be afraid to ask the hard questions." He looked at Maik steadily. "Let's face it, all this ..." he spread his hands; an expansive gesture that encompassed the room, Saltmarsh, perhaps even Maik's life itself, "... playing second fiddle to the force's pin-up boy, while your DCS flits around putting up the bunting in case the TV cameras show up, it's not really your scene, is it, Danny? You need something to stretch you, put you at the pointy end of the action every now and then."

Danny seemed to find a spot on the wall behind Trueman's shoulder on which to rest his gaze. *The trouble is,* he thought, *the more I get stretched these days, the harder I'm finding it to rebound to my original shape.*

"I thought you liked DCS Shepherd."

"I do, Danny, I do. She's a smart woman with impeccable taste in men, and she's good company. And her ambition has got nothing to do with me, as long as it stays separate from our relationship."

"Is she the reason you're still here?"

"What's that look for? It's just a couple of unattached people having a bit of fun. It's what adults do. Women like Colleen Shepherd, or that nice Constable Salter, they're what we need, Danny, battered old bastards like us. Somebody who will take us for what we are, and be okay with it. Women who under-stand what we have done, the baggage we carry. Somebody to nurse us through our dark nights, when the memories come, eh? You should try letting your own guard down a little some time. You'd be surprised what can happen."

A thought seemed to be playing behind Danny Maik's eyes, but if Trueman was waiting for the sergeant to give voice to it, he was disappointed.

Trueman looked at Maik seriously. "Hidalgo wasn't down here to sample the delights of a day on the beach at Cromer, Danny. He was here to see the assistant chief constable. If that boy of yours keeps trying to implicate Santos in his bird cage murders, sooner or later the guano is going to hit the fan."

"If there is nothing to it, Jejeune will let it drop. This DCI is not the kind of bloke to wrap it up and put a bow on it just to get a pat on the back from the Home Office."

"Whether he's right or he's wrong, all I'm saying is, if your boss keeps trying to tie this to the Mexicans, somebody's going to rock his world. Hard. No matter how much juice he thinks he has in Whitehall, it's nothing compared to the amount of pressure a foreign country can bring to bear on the British Government. We both know what happens to people who play with hand grenades, Danny, and I'm telling you, you don't want to be anywhere in the blast radius when this one goes off. There's going to be a lot of casualties. Come with me, into private security; leave them to sort it out — Hidalgo, Shepherd, Hillier."

"And Jejeune?"

"He's a big boy. There's nothing you can do to stop this. You're a brave soldier and a loyal one. One of the best I ever served with. But you were smart, too. You always knew when the time had come to stop defending a lost cause and get out and save your own arse. It's why you're still here and so many of those other poor buggers we served with aren't. Listen to me, Danny, not as your ex-CO but as a comrade in arms. You need to get out while you still can."

A faint breeze from outside stirred the curtain beside the open window. Somewhere a car horn sounded, and from far away a gull issued a haunting plea for Danny to listen to Trueman's advice. Maik tucked his notebook in his pocket, and with one final enigmatic glance at his former commanding officer, he opened the door and left.

33

"You're a hard man to find, Dr. Nyce," said Danny Maik.

"That's generally the idea of a retreat," said Nyce. His tone was testy, but nowhere near as self-assured as it had been in the past. The sergeant's considerable frame filled the doorway of the small cottage, and it took a moment before Nyce realized the sergeant had not come alone. "Well, I suppose you'd better come in, since you're here." He stepped aside and allowed Maik and Jejeune to duck in through the low opening.

The cottage was small, even by the parsimonious standards of north Norfolk accommodations. It seemed to consist of two rooms only — a cramped bedroom tucked away at the back, and this one, a combination living room and kitchen. A stone fireplace was flanked by a pair of dilapidated armchairs with a low coffee table between. One of the two windows in the front wall sat above a simple wooden desk and chair, while farther along the wall the other window looked down onto a steel sink with a single tap. A row of low wooden shelves ran all around the walls, many of them showing gaps where their contents, books and journals, had once been. These now sat in untidy piles on the coffee table, the desk, the floor. It looked like some ragged 3-D plan of a city Nyce was envisioning for the future. Items of clothing lay strewn around the room, fighting for surface space with mugs half-full of cold tea. Nyce himself looked haggard, his eyes red-rimmed from lack of sleep, his cheeks covered with the unchecked growth of a few days' beard. All indications were that the carefully ordered world of dashing David Nyce was casually falling apart at the seams.

"So how come you chose to hide out here?" asked Maik pleasantly. "All that book learnin' getting too much for you?" Jejeune could see that Maik sensed a vulnerability in Nyce here, one that might be fruitfully exploited by a little needling, perhaps. Unless, of course, Maik was just enjoying himself.

"I'm not hiding. Merely treating myself to a bit of hermitage. There is a difference. *Hiding* carries connotations of guilt."

Jejeune looked around the room. He could see no telephone, no computer, no television. A pair of propane lamps stood on the desk, and there were a few candles placed strategically around the room. He crossed to the small sink in the corner and turned on the single tap. Running water, just. Cold, but it meant that somebody could live here for a few days if they chose to. Jejeune bent to peer out of the window above the sink. A long, unbroken vista of flat farmland stretched away from the cottage. On their way here they had passed a small heath clad in gorse and low shrubbery. Along with the cliffs on the far side of the cottage, the area would provide habitat for a wide diversity of bird species, especially here in north Norfolk. He said as much to Nyce now, and the other man nodded.

"I used to come here when I was a birder, spend a couple of days up here at a time, if I could get away with it. I had my route all planned out, followed it religiously, same one, twice a day. Saw all manner of species." He paused suddenly and gazed into the middle distance, as if trying to peer back into a time that had long since disappeared.

"How do you mean, when you were a birder?" asked Maik. "That licence plate — AVES — I thought ..."

"I am an ornithologist now, Sergeant. I study birds only in the context of conservation. They are my subjects. Your DCI will understand the difference. I'm afraid for me the enjoyment of the pastime has long since disappeared. In fact, I suppose that's true of most things. Sad to say, but there you are."

He took a seat on the couch, leaving the men to stand awkwardly where they chose.

Jejeune began to wander about the room. He dragged his hands casually along the rough whitewashed interior of the walls. "Stone walls do not a prison make," Richard Lovelace had written of his own incarceration. But according to Lovelace, in order to take them for an hermitage, one needed a mind innocent and quiet. Jejeune suspected Nyce's mind was a very long way from either.

"The bicycle against the wall outside, you use that to go to the shops, I take it," said Jejeune.

Nyce's failure to respond didn't seem to trouble the inspector and he lapsed into a silence of his own again. One of the many things that bothered Maik about this case was that most of the time he didn't know exactly where he stood. In the past, the sergeant and his DCI had settled into a nice routine. He would do the heavy lifting early on, while Jejeune just pottered around the room, listening. Then, at some point, when he had covered the standard questions, Jejeune would step in and take things off in the direction he actually wanted them to go. Maik didn't always like it, but at least he usually knew where he was. But with this case, Jejeune was in and out like a fiddler's elbow, questioning one minute, the next slipping off into a thoughtful silence, then back into the fray again. It was the birding angle that was doing it, no doubt. But it was still disconcerting. In Maik's experience, the most productive interviews happened when the police officers, at least, knew what was supposed to be going on.

"We were wondering how your car might have come to be stolen," said Maik conversationally. "Those new Jags have pretty sophisticated alarm systems, or so I'm led to believe."

"It wasn't set, I'm afraid," said Nyce meekly.

"You didn't leave the keys in it, as well, by any chance?" Maik had probably just about managed to keep the sarcasm at bay, but Nyce picked up on the tenor of the question anyway.

"Cars *can* be hot-wired, you know," he said tersely. "Happens all the time, apparently. The result of insufficient police vigilance, I suppose."

"Not these new ones. Not without expertise far beyond the scope of a few teenage joyriders out here in Saltmarsh, anyway."

"Jordan Waters is dead," said Jejeune with an abruptness that brought everything else to a stop. He was standing on the far side of the room, near the sink, but he was looking directly at Nyce as he spoke, watching for a reaction.

Nyce spent a long time staring at his hands, not speaking. "Will the charge be murder?" he asked finally. His voice was small and distant.

Both Jejeune and Maik fixed him with a stare. "We're still trying to establish exactly what happened, but we believe it was murder," said Jejeune carefully.

The two detectives continued to stare expectantly at Nyce, but he didn't look up from his hands. Although he appeared deeply troubled by the news, he said nothing. He tented his elbows on his knees and rubbed his forehead with his hands. When he did finally look up, for the most fleeting of moments, both Maik and Jejeune had the impression he was going to confess. But Nyce seemed to gather himself at the last moment. "He killed Phoebe."

Was there something behind Nyce's words, some attempt at justification? Or was it just an academic, clarifying the facts so he could come to terms with the situation?

"Our investigations are proceeding on that basis," said Jejeune carefully, "but until we know what happened at the sanctuary that night ..."

"Oh, he killed her," said Nyce, his voice shaking with emotion. "Whether you can prove he was there that night or not, whether you have evidence that it was him who pushed her onto the branch, Jordan Waters killed her. And for what? His greed and his tawdry, money-grabbing little schemes."

Tears began to roll gently down Nyce's cheeks and he did nothing to check them. "That poor child. All she wanted to do was to make the world safe for her birds. But he couldn't let her do that, he had to destroy her, take away everything with his criminal filth. He deserved to die."

"No," said Jejeune quietly, "he didn't."

"It was justice. Jordan Waters killed Phoebe, and for that he paid with his own life."

They were close now, Maik could feel it; a few more seconds. Let him talk and it would all be over. And yet, here it was again, this strangely connected disconnect between Nyce and Phoebe Hunter. It was as if something was duelling with his sense of guilt, trying to convince him that he had been justified in his actions. But Nyce's reaction lacked the palpable viciousness, the outrage, that might lead to an act of vengeance. Whatever the reason David Nyce had hunted down Jordan Waters and killed him, it wasn't to avenge Phoebe Hunter's death. Maik was convinced of it.

Nyce rubbed his eye sockets angrily with the heels of his hands, leaving dark smudges around his eyes.

"Forgive me," he said, recovering himself a little. "Embarrassing really. Look, as you can see, I've got a lot of work, so if you have no further questions, I'd rather like to be left alone now to get on with it."

Despite himself, Maik almost felt sorry for Nyce, here in his solitary existence, no one to award his full marks to, no one to bludgeon with his searing intellect. A solitary man on a lonely stage playing to his invisible audience. "If you're sure there's nothing else you'd like to tell us."

"What? No, nothing that comes to mind."

"Very well, then," said Jejeune politely. "Please let us know if you plan to move from here, relocate back to town or anything like that."

"Oh, I have no intention of leaving, Inspector. You may rest assured of that."

Outside the cottage, Maik and Jejeune stood shoulder to shoulder on the edge of the cliff. A gunmetal grey sea moved uneasily under a bank of low clouds. "Storm's coming," said Maik. He let his eyes play over the sea. "We should bring him in. He's ready."

Jejeune shook his head. "No, I don't think he is. Not yet." There were other questions he could have asked in the cottage, questions of plagiarism and sexual misconduct, but in Nyce's current state of mind, denial was the only defence he could have mustered and he would have used it, constructing a fortress of angry indignation against the charges. Like Maik, Jejeune could sense there was something hidden, something that lay tantalizingly below the surface, like an object half-buried in the sand, just beyond the reach of their outstretched fingertips. It was this, this secret, this hidden truth, that was keeping Nyce from confessing. And until they could discover what it was, the detective doubted Nyce would be willing to admit to anything.

Below them, a Common Gull glided past, riding the air effortlessly. When Nyce was pursuing his boyhood birding here, it might have been a Fulmar. But time and the elements had crumbled the cliffs and taken away the strange, tube-nosed seabirds' nesting habitat. The Fulmars had moved on, and were rarely seen in these parts anymore. *That's what time does,* thought Jejeune. *It slowly erodes what used to be, until one day you look around and find there's no longer anything about your past life that remains.*

The wind picked up, buffeting the two detectives. Maik was right. A storm was coming. It would produce excellent birding later, as the onshore winds drove the migrating flocks out of the skies and stacked them up along the estuaries and coastlines to wait out the worst of the weather. But for once, Jejeune wasn't too concerned about the birding forecast. He had other things on his mind. The two men turned away from the sea and headed toward the car in silence.

34

"Useless, that Saltmarsh library!" Tony Holland slapped his bag down onto his desk.

"What's up, Tony?" asked Salter. "All the colouring books checked out again?" She looked across at Holland and smiled. Their periodic spats notwithstanding, they had presented a more or less united front in the past against the varying moods and whims of the North Norfolk Constabulary's upper echelons. She knew part of the tension between them this time had been that, if ever there had been a case primed to blow up in their faces, it was this one. And, as always, it would have been the lower ranks — the Lauren Salters and Tony Hollands of the policing world — that would have suffered the most. Fortunately, though, if the rumour mill was to be believed, they had new DNA evidence that linked Waters to the sanctuary murders, and Nyce's conviction in Waters's death was little more than a formality. Things looked to be resolving themselves nicely in the cases, despite Jejeune's efforts to complicate matters.

"There's not a single Mexican phrasebook anywhere in that library," said Holland peevishly, continuing his earlier complaint. "They've got everything else — German, French, Italian."

Maik made a small tutting noise. "Probably Spanish, too, I imagine," he said, pointedly avoiding eye contact with Salter, who was discreetly covering her mouth with her hand. "That's how it is in these parts," continued Maik. "Too little contact with the outside world, see. Mention foreign culture to most of this lot and they think you're talking about Greek yoghurt. Who were you planning on speaking Mexican with, anyway?"

"Now that this case is just about sorted, I thought I would tell Luisa Obregón I'd be willing to look into her husband's disappearance again. On my own time, of course. See if I can provide her with a bit of closure."

"That case is as cold as Obregón himself undoubtedly is," said Maik. "If he had wanted us to find him, we would have done so by now. He took himself off somewhere so we couldn't prove suicide. He wanted his family to get the insurance money."

"Still ..."

"Never mind *still*, Constable. You'll want to be bringing your towering intellect to bear in the investigation of more recent cases, like this open one before us. There's still plenty to be done — putting Nyce at the Waters murder scene, for one thing. Since he doesn't seem particularly inclined to do it himself, it looks like we're going to have to do it for him. Inconvenient, I know, but that's the life of a village copper sometimes."

Salter had recovered her composure enough to look at Holland. "Luisa Obregón is not one of your starry-eyed community service temps, Tony. If she suspects even for a minute that you're using her old man's disappearance to get her into bed, she's going to give you some closure of your own, probably with one of her threshing machines. Not to mention that her son likely wouldn't take very kindly to your intentions."

Maik nodded his head sagely. "A man without fear is a dangerous prospect, young Holland. Your warrant card wouldn't even make him think twice. You want to be giving that family a wide berth." It was clear that, whatever jocularity had gone on before, Maik was deadly serious now. He wasn't offering this as a piece of advice; it was an order.

Any response Tony Holland was intending to make was stilled by the sudden entrance of Domenic Jejeune. He looked harried and a little more ruffled than usual. Normally, no matter how much was going on around him, the DCI exuded an air of calm, as if he could retreat to some distant inner core and observe everything like a spectator, perched on one of the desks at the back of the room. It was where he headed now, as the reason for his discomfort followed him into the incident room in the person of DCS Shepherd.

She was elated, and made a point of ignoring Jejeune's obvious discontent as she informed the rest of the investigating team assembled in the room exactly how she felt. They had a match between Jordan Waters's DNA and the broken bits of fingernail under Phoebe Hunter's lapels. It put Waters not only at the scene, but with his hands on the actual body of the victim. Add to that a syringe covered with Waters' fingerprints and traces of Ramon Santos's blood on the needle, and the laboratory's earlier DNA test results of the birds' feathers, both recovered from the wreckage of Jordan Waters's transit van, and you had your classic three-point tie between the suspect and victims. Unequivocal evidence didn't get much better than that in murder cases.

"All we need now is to secure David Nyce for Waters's death and we can all go home and get a good night's sleep." She looked around the room expectantly. "I take it we aren't quite there yet."

"No, ma'am, but we are getting closer," said Maik. "For the first attempt on Waters's life, at least. The onboard EDR in Nyce's Jag shows that after leaving his home address that morning, the car went to Stiffkey, where it was stationary for a while before taking the road to Carter's bridge, registering a collision, and ending up in the pub car park where we found it."

"What's at Stiffkey?" she asked. Both she and Maik had pronounced it *Stewkey* as the locals did, and she could tell from Jejeune's expression that he was remembering Holland's uncontrolled mirth when the inspector had first given the word its phonetic pronunciation.

"Waters's grandmother had a house there. It's derelict now, but somebody mentioned that Waters had taken lady friends up there on occasion."

"Another graduate from the Tony Holland Academy of Romance," said Salter. "You must be so proud."

Holland's smile said he would let her have these pops, what with her being just back from sick leave and all. Despite her misgivings, she was obviously making some progress in getting over her guilt over Maggie Wylde, especially now that matters seemed to be resolving so clearly in other directions.

"I never even thought about his granny's place," said Holland. "It's barely standing now. But if Phoebe Hunter had ever mentioned those rumours to Nyce, he might have thought to look for Waters there."

"Which is why he was able to locate Waters so easily when we couldn't, you mean?" said Shepherd, a touch more indulgently than might have otherwise been the case if they weren't all so buoyed by these new developments. "Well then," she said brightly, "let's get Nyce in and wrap this up. Unless you have any contributions to make, Domenic?"

It was over, he knew. They had their killers, and they had their motives, however weak and incomplete they seemed to him. Any other unanswered questions would be swept away as soon as the case was declared closed. But he couldn't allow that yet. They were so far from the truth.

"I believe Constable Salter has some information on the doves in Obregón's aviary," he said. It was irrelevant now, he knew, but it would buy him some time to come up with an objection to delay the closure of the case. "Constable?" he invited.

Salter shuffled through a sheaf of notes on her knee and sighed, like someone not knowing where to start. "The dove species you saw at the aviary are all part of something called a nested clade," she said. "But two of them, the Eared Doves and the Mourning Doves, are also part of something else, called a superspecies."

"Come with a cape and mask, do they?" asked Holland to some general laughter from the rest of the room. But Salter was not about to be sidetracked. Since Jejeune had approached her and asked her to take on this research, she had put in a lot of effort, and for a time it had looked like it might have been in vain. Even if this stuff was all gibberish to her, she was grateful to be given the opportunity to present it. "There's a third species that's also a part of this dove superspecies," she said. "Socorro Doves."

She concentrated on Jejeune, studiously avoiding all the other eyes on her, including Shepherd's. "Honestly, sir, when you asked if I had any interest in biology, I thought you meant helping Max collect tadpoles so he could watch them grow legs. None of this makes the faintest bit of sense to me." She offered a smile. "Even without the painkillers, I doubt I'd be able to understand it."

"What does any of this mean, Domenic?" Shepherd's tone was testy, but for once, Jejeune's reply matched it. He was fighting for his life here, as far as any further enquiries into this case were concerned, and he wasn't prepared to roll over just because it suited everyone else's sense of convenience.

"Well, it explains the presence of all these species in Obregón's aviary collection, for a start. Nested clades share a great many genetic similarities, and I'm assuming superspecies must be even more closely linked genetically. Obregón must have been using the birds in his studies somehow. We need to get a genetic specialist in to look at all this."

Shepherd took a short intake of breath to steady herself. It was clear that her patience had run out. Whether it was Jejeune's inability to explain the significance of Salter's findings or something else, in a way that none of the others could quite understand, something had tipped the balance for her.

"It's time to bring this whole sorry episode to an end," said Shepherd. "Pick up David Nyce and bring him in, Domenic. If he's as fragile as you say, he'll confess to Waters's murder soon enough, and I want you to stay on him until he does."

Her look at Jejeune held a special message, one meant exclusively for him. "You've had your chance," it said. "I've given you all the time I could to make a connection, to bring me something concrete. And you've failed to produce even one scrap of evidence to show Santos was implicated in any way. So now, it's up to me, to wrap up the case and save my job, save all our jobs."

The problem was, thought Jejeune, if he was right, arresting Nyce wasn't likely to achieve any of that. In fact, it just might have the opposite effect.

35

They pulled into the car park at the sanctuary. Lindy wasn't surprised. Domenic had suggested a drive out into the country as if it had just occurred to him, but she had been with him too long to suspect that he was acting on impulse. Domenic always had a plan. It saddened her a little that he had so little capacity for spontaneity. It was part of what drove him to always follow the same route when he was birding, she knew. It was part of what was holding him back on committing to their holiday, even now that the case seemed to be drawing to a close.

The interior of the sanctuary was dark when they entered, and as it flickered to life under the glare of the fluorescent lights, Lindy wondered if perhaps that had been no bad thing. A scene of sad desolation unfolded before them; unwashed dishes lay abandoned on the tops of cabinets, half-opened bags of seed gaped forlornly on the floor. They picked their way through the debris and made their way to the cages. Jejeune looked at the birds, sitting perched, unconcerned. Their food and water dishes were full. Volunteers had been allowed back in for a few days now, and even if they showed no interest in the heart-breaking task of trying to restore the sanctuary to the neatness and organization it had known under Phoebe Hunter, at least they were taking care of the birds.

Lindy stood beside Jejeune and peered around at the mess. *This is his work,* she thought, *picking through the wreckage of other people's lives.* It must be a sad, haunting experience to have to face broken dreams and shattered promises over and over again. What a toll it must take on him.

"Why are we here, Dom? What are you looking for? I thought the case was as good as closed."

"We have answers to the big questions, admittedly. But ..."

But, for Dom, that wasn't quite the same thing as closing the case, Lindy knew. It was the answers to the small questions, the unasked questions, even, that would continue to trouble him. She looked at the birds in the cages. What had they made of the dark pools of pungent liquid that had spilled on the floor of the cage beside them, she wondered? What had been their response to the stench of death? In the wild, it would have been flight. Spilled blood was a warning. Danger was present, you needed to flee. But these birds were caged; they couldn't escape the death next door. So how long had it been, then, before other instincts kicked in, to feed, to drink, to sleep? To carry on, in short, the way things were before death had interposed itself between them and the rest of their life? *If only it was the same for humans,* she thought, *that after a short period of shock we simply rebounded from the death of another person, to carry on as before. Why must it linger with us, become a part of our consciousness, our lives?*

Jejeune picked something up off the floor and stared at it intently. It was a photograph, with sticky notes around the frame. Phoebe Hunter, smiling in the sunshine of Burkina Faso. The scene seemed such a stark counterpoint to the darkness Lindy felt spreading over her. She placed a soft hand on his arm.

"I'm so sorry, Dom. You do wonderful things. You bring killers to justice and solve cases. Only it's not enough for you, is it?

I'm sorry that the only thing that could ever really bring you happiness is never going to happen."

"It wouldn't be forever," he said quietly. "The field work blocks are only about eight weeks long."

Anger flooded over her, at his stubbornness, at his refusal to see reason. "It can't ever happen, Dom, surely you can see that. It's a dream, a fantasy. This is our world *here*. This is where our friends are, our home, our life. I have a career here. I can't just abandon it to trot around behind you carrying your safari kit, while you sit in swamps all day watching birds. What am I supposed to do out there? Maybe write a travel guide? Tell the readers where to buy all that authentic Burkina Faso craft work? How about a blog? 'Burkina Faso is, like, such a cool country. They have different money and food and stuff. They even talk differently. LOL.'"

Jejeune hadn't asked her to sit around in swamps, or carry his kit. They had barely discussed the job at all, and even then only in the vaguest of terms. He sometimes felt as if Lindy used her own inner torment as a furnace from which the truth might emerge, pure and beautiful, purged of its impurities. But what was the truth in this case? Jejeune wasn't even sure he knew himself.

Lindy picked up on his look of uncertainty and confusion. "Or wasn't I even supposed to go? Perhaps I wasn't part of your travel plans. Perhaps I am not a part of your plans at all."

Her anger spent, she moved to the far side of the room, not so much to be away from him, but to make sure he didn't try to comfort her. Because he couldn't, could he? He couldn't say he wasn't thinking about it, wasn't constantly working out permutations and possibilities in his head, wondering if it might, just might, be possible to grab this one last chance to have a career studying birds, before the dream finally faded into a younger man's world. And that was the only comfort she could have used just then.

The sound of a car door slamming fractured the heavy silence that hung between them, startling them both. Moments later, Carrie Pritchard appeared in the doorway carrying an open sack of bird seed. She seemed surprised to see them, even though The Beast was parked directly out front. Or perhaps it was just Lindy she was surprised to see. The lingering tension between Lindy and Jejeune seemed to hang in the air like a cloud, but if Pritchard noted it, she affected not to.

"Domenic … and Lindy. What a nice surprise. I just came down to try to tidy the place up a bit. As terrible as this has all been, we need to start getting things back to normal." She stopped suddenly. Perhaps she had been about to say *Phoebe would have wanted it that way*, but if so, she thought better of it.

She set down the sack of seed and stooped to retrieve an upturned dish from the floor. She set it on a desk, as if marking the place where she would begin her task. What she made of the awkward, stilted silence that greeted her remarks wasn't clear, but it wasn't enough to stop her from pressing on. "If there is to be continuity with Phoebe's research, a decision on her replacement will need to be made very soon. I haven't been able to contact David recently. He has a tendency to drop off the radar every once in a while, but the last time we spoke, he seemed more than willing to go with my recommendation. I can tell you we will very soon be inviting expressions of interest." She stared frankly at Jejeune, as if checking to see whether he had anything to say.

Did she know, wondered Lindy. Had she sensed, somehow, the tension between them and guessed its cause? She could not have twisted the knife into Lindy any more cruelly, and yet, for all her many faults, Carrie Pritchard wasn't a malicious person. Calculating, certainly, and not afraid to use any of the weapons in her considerable arsenal to get what she wanted. But not given to wanton spite. Even in her current distress, Lindy was prepared to concede that much.

Pritchard toyed with the bowl, running her finger around the rim and letting her eyes follow the movement. "Since it appears the decision is pretty much mine to make, I should tell you that my philosophy is that it may be time for a fresh approach, a new set of eyes on the problem. Someone from outside the realms of academia, even."

She looked up and tried a coy smile. It didn't work for Lindy, but she doubted she was the intended target anyway. She felt her emotions welling up inside her, but she would not give them the satisfaction, either of them, of seeing her in that state. She excused herself for a moment and went outside.

Jejeune watched Lindy go, helpless to stop her. He saw the sack of seed on the floor at Pritchard's feet. Brought in from the porch outside to protect it from marauding wild birds. And yet, if those same wild birds were brought into the santuary as rescues, they would be given all the seed they wanted. *How irrationally we guard our possessions,* he thought. *And how passionately.* Possessions and passions; take them out of the equation and you would eliminate just about every motive for murder there was. Perhaps even for these murders.

Pritchard surveyed the room and the corridor beyond. "I hear you've managed to find out who was responsible for all this ..." she hesitated, "sorrow." She looked sad. "I didn't know the boy at all, but still, you never dream it could be someone close like that, do you?" She walked a short way and let her eyes rest on the empty cage at the end of the corridor. "You haven't found the birds yet, I take it. Sadly, I suspect they're already dead."

"The doves are worth a considerable amount of money on the underground market." Jejeune's voice sounded uncertain, as if it was rusty from lack of use. His mouth felt dry, the residue of the anguish from a few moments before. "Whoever has them now, it would be in their interests to keep them alive."

Pritchard shook her head. "Caged birds are extremely fragile. They adjust their metabolism to a regular food source, at regular times, and come to depend on it to a very great extent. Sometimes, even the slightest disturbance in their routine can be enough to send them into decline. That said, I'll keep my ear to the ground. If I do hear that a pair of Socorro Doves has surfaced anywhere, I'll certainly let you know."

At Luisa Obregón's, she meant, where possessing a pair of birds stolen in the commission of a double murder would certainly be enough to have her aviary closed down by the authorities. "I've been wondering," said Jejeune carefully, "that sighting in Hunstanton. How could you be so sure Luisa Obregón had Mourning Doves in her collection?"

Pritchard waved a careless hand. "Industry tittle-tattle I picked up from somewhere. I'm afraid I can't remember where exactly." She looked at him significantly. "But I was not wrong. Whatever that woman may claim, she did have Mourning Doves in that aviary."

Jejeune was sure it was true. But he was equally sure that someone who was purchasing birds from illegal sources would be very careful about letting information about her collection become industry "tittle-tattle."

Lindy returned to the room, offering Pritchard a flicker of a smile but avoiding eye contact.

"I was just about to tell the inspector how impressed the community is with him, Lindy," said Pritchard brightly, "for having solved this terrible crime so quickly. We are very fortunate. One gets the feeling Domenic could be a success at whatever he turned his hand to." She smiled at him. "And yet, here he is, policing for us in our little community of Saltmarsh."

Lindy smiled again but said nothing. *For now,* she thought sadly. *But for how much longer?*

36

Jejeune was first there because he was closest. By far. He had just returned to The Beast, parked in the car park at Sidestrand, and as he checked his phone messages he caught a glimpse of himself in the rear-view mirror. He was smiling, the first proper smile he had treated himself to in days. And why not? He had been watching a Kestrel, hawking and hunting its way across the clifftop. He had stood there for a long time on the cliff edge, perhaps fifteen minutes, just watching the bird hovering, suspended as if on wires, head moving from side to side, before a dramatic swoop to snatch something — a dragon-fly, a grasshopper — and then a rapid climb again to hover once more on the blustery updrafts rising from the cliff face. For a quarter of an hour his mind had been nowhere else, not at a blood-stained bird sanctuary, nor a neglected aviary, nor even the wide, everblue skies of West Africa. Just here, on this coastline, with this bird.

One text message, his phone said, two minutes old: *Emergency – Call Station.* So he had. A man, tentatively iden-tified as David Nyce, had been spotted on a cliff ledge at Trimingham. It was less than five minutes away. Jejeune advised the desk sergeant he would respond and had The Beast in gear and moving so quickly that the sergeant's advice that Jejeune should wait for the rescue services met only with the steady tone of a disconnected line.

At Trimingham, Jejeune bounced The Beast over the curb of the clifftop public car park and drove parallel to the cliff itself, examining the grassy edge for a spot where someone could have descended to the rocky face below. There was only one place. The recent rains had destabilized a small section of the cliff, and a fresh white scar marked the site of a recent collapse, where chalky scree and rubble had descended into a steep runnel beneath.

Jejeune slewed the Range Rover to a stop and got out, scrambling to the edge to scan the cliffs below. There! Nyce was standing on a narrow ledge about forty feet below him. A hundred feet farther down, an angry sea foamed around the black fangs of half-submerged rocks. Nyce was looking out over the sea as if transfixed by something on the horizon. He was wearing the same clothes Jejeune had seen him in a couple of days before — khaki trousers and a thin blue denim shirt, now rippling in the fierce winds that scoured the cliff face. He was barefoot, a pair of battered sandals discarded beside him on the ledge.

Jejeune didn't know what to do. "Doctor," he called. Nyce gave no indication that he had heard. Jejeune called again, louder, battling the winds that threatened to snatch away his words. "Dr. Nyce. Please. We need to talk."

Nyce's frame seemed to tense, but he did not turn from his intense study of the sea. "Too late for a chat, Inspector," he called over his shoulder. "The decision's been made, I'm afraid."

"There have been claims, sexual impropriety." Jejeune was desperate, pulling things out of the air. There were no such accusations as far as he knew, merely rumours, but the truth hardly mattered now. Jejeune was in a desperate struggle to save a man's life. And what man of Nyce's vanity, what innocent man, could refrain from defending himself against such charges? Unless Jejeune's words would turn out to be enough, in Nyce's fragile state, to convince him that everything really was lost. Jejeune had no way of knowing. But he was out of options.

Nyce responded by backing away slightly from the edge. He let out a derisive, sneering laugh, but he still didn't turn around.

"My God, you people really are incredible. You're talking about poor Phoebe, I take it? Well, let me set your mind at rest, Inspector. There was never anything like that between Phoebe and me. Do you understand? Never." He stepped forward again and for a sickening moment Jejeune thought the battle between the will to end life and the will to preserve it had been lost.

"Then tell me your side," called Jejeune urgently. "Let me come down there so you can set the record straight. People should know the truth."

"This is idiocy, Inspector. You are absolutely wrong." Frustration seemed to overtake Nyce at his inability to remove this stain from his character. But he backed away from the ledge again. Safe, for the moment anyway.

Jejeune edged cautiously onto the narrow channel between the rocky outcrops. The loose, unstable scree made the footing treacherous, and he turned his back to the sea, scrabbling for handholds, clutching the tiniest of knots and crevices as he descended. Twice, clumps of rock came away under his grasp and crumbled to powder in his hands. He could see the scuffs and skid marks from when Nyce had come down this same crevice. Neither man had paused to consider if it would be possible to ascend by the same route.

The wind was a physical force on the ledge, tearing at Jejeune's hair and clothing and filling his ears with a roaring, singing sound. Nyce was at the other edge of the ledge, ten feet from Jejeune, three feet from death. He was staring down, seemingly mesmerized by the pulsating movement of the sea roiling over the rocks below. Finally, he withdrew his gaze and looked at Jejeune. The inspector made no move to approach him.

"How did I get here, Inspector? How did I go from what I was to what I am now?" He gave a little laugh. "It was sudden, I'll tell you that much. One minute, on top of the world, the next," he spread his arms, "this. You can't stop me, you realize, though that is undoubtedly your intention. You are a good, decent human being, and you want to stop me." He laughed a little again, an unsteady, dangerous sound. "You want to save me from myself. It's too late for that, I'm afraid. That boy, Waters, he has seen to that. He took away everything. There's nothing left."

A cascade of loose rubble broke free, the small pebbles pattering onto the ledge like rain, and then spinning off into the infinity beyond. Over Nyce's shoulder, Jejeune could see a line of people on the far headland. They were too far away to help, but it meant that others, the coast guard, the rescuers, would know where they were. If Jejeune could keep Nyce engaged, keep him telling his story, just until help arrived … Then what? He didn't know. He only knew he couldn't release his grip on this strand of narrative, this fragile thread that was tethering Nyce to him, to life.

"But how?" he asked. "How did Jordan Waters destroy you? I mean, it was Phoebe who was blackmailing you. Did she tell Waters about it? Did he threaten to expose you, your earlier plagiarism? Is that why he had to die?"

Nyce looked shocked.

"Earlier?" He gave another laugh, richer this time, fuller, more genuine. "You know, I'm so glad you dropped by, Inspector, I really am. At least now my early reputation, my shining jewel, will remain intact. No, Inspector Jejeune, the earlier work, that soaring intellect, that breathtaking, beautiful mind, that was me, in full flow, synapses firing on all cylinders. It was the later stuff

I was copping off Phoebe. Dried up, you see. Couldn't produce the goods anymore. If only someone could create a Viagra for the mind, eh? Make a fortune. As it was, for the past few years I couldn't come up with a single original idea if you paid me. Which they continued to do, of course. Quite well, in fact. No, it was Phoebe who produced those later papers. She really did have a wonderfully fertile mind, and her intellectual curiosity, well, it knew no bounds. She could come up with more viable lines of enquiry, piece together more intellectual data in a single afternoon than I could in a month of Sundays. Couldn't write worth a damn, of course, despite all my coaching, but she did have that one irreplaceable quality: modesty. She didn't really want any acclaim. She was happy to turn all her ideas over to me to submit under my name as long as she got my support — my full support — for continuing her research work. A perfect arrangement for both of us."

"No, Doctor. Not for both of you," said Jejeune. "Phoebe Hunter had changed the name on the paper I saw."

"Ah, yes, the first stirrings of ambition in our Phoeebs. Wanted a bit more recognition, she said; peer respect she called it, in that charmingly naive way of hers. But I could have handled that. She had her Achilles heel, you see. Like all of us."

"The set-asides," said Jejeune. "That's why you kept withholding your approval for the project." He was careful to keep any note of disapproval from his voice. It was about building connections, creating a bridge across which Nyce could step again to find human compassion, understanding, forgiveness. The accusations and recriminations could come later, if there was to be a later.

"There were genuine concerns," said Nyce reflectively, "but I knew that she would never risk losing the possibility of set-asides over some petty academic dispute. Those Turtledoves really did mean everything to her. It was remarkable the lengths she was willing to go to in order to protect them. The conditions she endured in West Africa …" Nyce fell silent for a moment and then suddenly shook his head, dramatically, over-vigorously, like a man expelling voices no one else could hear. "No, things would have been fine. But then Waters killed her. Took away my little ghostwriter, exposed me to the world for what I am — a charlatan, a fraud, a washed-up empty shell of an academic."

"Why don't you tell me what happened the day Jordan Waters died?"

Nyce gave a small ironic laugh. "What, just between the two of us, you mean? And you'll promise to keep it to yourself, will you?" He gave another sneer, but something seemed to settle over him, a calm Jejeune had not seen until now: resignation; the final slow walk to the end. It was not a good sign. "Firstly," said Nyce, "I don't want you to think that I sat down and coldly mapped it all out before hunting Jordan Waters down and killing him. There was no plotting, no forethought. But I did it, Inspector Jejeune. I murdered Jordan Waters. That's what you need to hear, isn't it? I murdered Jordan Waters, then I retreated to watch from a distance. I saw you lot arrive, do your thing. And then I drove away, knowing I had taken the life of another human being, deliberately and purposefully. Do you know what that feels like, Inspector? That knowledge that you have taken another life? It takes something from your own life. You die a little inside. Melodramatic, I know, but certainly we are in the place for it, aren't we?" Nyce spread his arms and half-spun to encompass this tiny windswept stage high above the north Norfolk coast.

He was almost there, recognized Jejeune. Nyce was ramping himself up, preparing, steeling himself for that one final act of supreme courage, the one final plunge into … what? Peace? Darkness? Emptiness? Whatever it was that awaited Nyce, its draw was proving stronger than life, coaxing him ever closer to the crossing point. Jejeune began inching almost imperceptibly along the ledge toward him.

"Exposed to the ridicule of all those fools, watching my academic reputation turn to dust before my eyes." Nyce shook his head sadly. He was not looking at Jejeune now, but was again staring out at the sea, as if heeding some distant, silent call. "I had thought these things would be intolerable. But it was the knowledge that I had taken that boy's life that stole from me the final ounces of will I had to carry on."

Nyce had shuffled nearer to the edge of the rocky platform now. Jejeune silently closed the gap between them, willing even his breathing shallower.

"So there you have it, Inspector. At least I know you will report my sins honestly. There is some comfort to be had in that, perhaps."

Nyce took the final step toward to the edge of the rock shelf and Jejeune realized that this time, there would be no stopping him. As he lurched across to grab Nyce's arm, his shirt, anything, a deafening crack from above caused both men to spin around instinctively, just in time to see a rocky outcrop break away from the cliff face and fall toward them in an explosion of scree and dust and flying flinty pellets. Jejeune raised an arm and the rock glanced off it, striking a glancing blow across his shoulder before smashing into the ledge where Nyce was standing. A chunk of the ledge disintegrated like dust and Nyce's feet slid over the edge. He grappled desperately for a handhold, tearing his fingernails from their beds in a bloody trail. But he found no purchase, and his body had already begun to slip into the open air when Jejeune's hand reached out and grabbed his wrist.

37

He had known that Nyce would struggle; that he would claw and grab and snatch at any chance to live. The instincts would always fight against a fall, even in a potential suicide. Now, dangling from this ledge, with the cruel sea foaming like a rabid animal below him and the jagged, lethal rocks ready to rip his flesh and snap his bones, Nyce's survival instinct had taken over.

Until it was stilled. Jejeune had been leaning far enough over the edge to see into Nyce's eyes; the terror, the fear as his body swung violently inward under Jejeune's desperate grip. And he had seen the light go out of them when a second falling rock smashed into Nyce's face, striking his temple with a sickening blow. Jejeune felt the body slump, the weight now one of unconsciousness, or death. His own arm muscles were burning white hot with the strain. The sharp edge of the rock shelf cut into his chest as he fought to keep his body from being dragged over by the weight of his burden. With a massive effort, Jejeune reached his left arm over the edge and scrabbled for purchase on Nyce's collar. He felt the relief flooding into his right arm as some of the strain was shared, but immediately the material of Nyce's shirt began to tear from his hand. Jejeune edged his torso farther out over the ledge. He could see the sea and the rocks below, like gaping jaws waiting to claim their victim. *Victims.*

With a desperate lunge, he reached down below Nyce's back and grabbed his belt. Gradually, with every muscle in both arms tearing and burning in protest, he managed to raise Nyce to the point where he could slide an arm under his armpit and around his back, clasping him to the ledge. Jejeune had no idea if Nyce was still alive. His head lolled loosely to one side and a thin trail of blood was seeping from a deep puncture wound between his eye socket and his ear. Jejeune reached out and slid his other arm around Nyce's body. The detective knew that if he was to slide forward now, they would both plunge to their deaths together. He would not be able to let Nyce go. The intimacy of this life hug was too strong. He would hold on to him all the way down.

With Nyce's body pressed against the ledge, Jejeune some-how found the strength to inch backward, the razor-sharp rocks cutting into his arms, scraping them, urging them to abandon their burden to its fate. And then, as suddenly as the fall itself, the other man's upper body had crested the edge and slumped over it, enough to outweigh the still dangling hips and legs, enough to allow Jejeune to drag the limp form all the way onto the ledge. To safety.

"Chief Inspector Jejeune. My name is Colin. I am with North Norfolk Coastguard Rescue. If you can hear me, raise your left hand."

The voice had drifted down to him through the haze of fatigue and pain. Who actually placed the call to the rescue squad, to whom, in reality, he owed his life, Jejeune never found out. There were rumours that the rescue services were already on their way, alerted perhaps by an earlier call to the media outlets from Nyce himself; one final act of narcissism, to have his suicide recorded for posterity. All Jejeune knew was that, injured, exhausted, spent, he would never have been able to get off that ledge alone.

How long he had been slumped here, with the still-unconscious form of Nyce by his side, he had no idea. He could hear the sea, and feel the sticky wetness of the salty winds upon his skin. And in the distance somewhere, the call of a single seabird, sad and mournful.

"Your left hand, Inspector. If you can hear me, raise your left hand."

Left hand. The non-dominant hand, for most people. The one it would take that extra second of concentration, of focus, of conscious effort to raise. The muscles in Jejeune's shoulder burned so much they prevented him from raising his arm above eye level.

"Very good." The relief in Colin's voice seemed to transcend any training about keeping a calm and measured tone. "All right, Inspector, we are here to get you to safety, but you will need to follow my instructions exactly. You are both in an extremely dangerous position at the moment. Do not move or do anything unless I tell you to. Do you understand these instructions?"

More burning from the shoulder muscles.

"That's good. Is Mr. Nyce conscious?"

Jejeune's arm stayed by his side. Even in his exhausted, over-wrought state, he realized that the extended beat of silence from above meant that this was not good news.

"Are you injured yourself?"

Jejeune raised his arm, and there was another beat of silence, longer this time. Jejeune may have drifted off into a daze again. Colin's voice, when it came, startled him slightly.

"Inspector, we are going to have to get the Search and Rescue squad in from Lakenheath to airlift Mr. Nyce off the ledge. We can't risk bringing him up the rock face."

Because it's too unstable, thought Jejeune through his hazy logic. *Because it may crumble and send loose rocks cascading down on top of anyone still left on the ledge.* On the headland to the north, he could see the group of figures he had seen before. Their numbers seemed much greater now, their ranks swelled by those who had gathered to watch the proceedings. Domenic Jejeune, sideshow for the public once again.

"Search and Rescue advise us that the overhang is too great to lower anyone onto the ledge from the helicopter," called Colin. "If we lower a harness down to you, would you be able to secure it around Mr. Nyce? Raise your left arm, please."

Jejeune looked at the inert form lying on the ledge beside him, and for the first time he detected the slight swell of Nyce's chest. Suddenly, there was a new urgency to get him off this ledge and to the safety of a hospital bed.

Jejeune wasn't sure how long it was from the time he raised his arm until he heard Colin's voice again. It seemed only a short while, a heartbeat, the single contraction of a human muscle. But he was aware, too, that time had passed unaccounted for. He realized he must have drifted out of consciousness again.

"Inspector, we are going to lower the harness now. If at all possible, try to get back into a niche beneath an overhang, just in case it dislodges some debris on its way down." Colin waited, but Jejeune did not move.

From out of the air above, a canvas harness attached to a thick steel cable descended and nestled onto the ledge a few feet from Jejeune. He realized he needed to grab it now, before the winds snatched away the straps and sent the harness floating out over the sea. But he could not compel himself to move. His muscles ached, his body would not raise from its slumped, seated position. With a supreme effort of will, he reached out and scrabbled his fingers toward the canvas webbing.

"Okay," said Colin, "that's good. Now it is very important that you attach this harness onto Mr. Nyce exactly as I say. We'll stop at each point and you can give me the okay before I move on to the next step."

Jejeune carefully followed each measured, precise instruction shouted down from Colin until Nyce was secured in the harness and all fastenings were double-checked. The detective's upper body was still heaving with the strain of his exertions when Colin's voice came again.

"In a couple of moments a helicopter is going to take off from up here and appear above you. The downdraft will be tremendous for a couple of seconds until it gets out over the sea, so be prepared, and stay well back against the rock face. As soon as the slack on the cable has been taken up, Mr. Nyce will start to be pulled off the ledge. This will be a bit shocking to see, but do not try to stop it, or grab hold of him in any way. Do you understand this instruction, Inspector Jejeune?"

A pause. Colin was apparently not going to go on until Jejeune had raised a weary arm one more time. Still more people had gathered on the northern headland, a large crowd of tiny, dark silhouettes watching the drama unfold with studious intensity. Jejeune saw the flash of a couple of pairs of binoculars and a lucid moment allowed him to acknowledge the irony before Colin's final communication came drifting down to him.

"The helicopter will move out to sea as quickly as possible to prevent Mr. Nyce from swinging back against the rock face. As soon as he is safely on land, we will be coming back for you. Do you understand?"

Mr. Nyce, registered Jejeune finally. Not *Dr.* Just a man, a human being in trouble, in need of the help of others. How Dr. Nyce would hate the indignity of it all. Jejeune raised his arm for a final time and within seconds the overloud whirring of blades chopping the air appeared above him.

———

The news footage that night was mostly of the compelling visuals of the rescue; Nyce's body swinging out from the cliffs and twirling dangerously over the roiling, angry, grey-white sea. But the single image that went viral, the one the newspapers and social media fastened on, beamed around the country, around the Internet, around the world, was the one of Domenic Jejeune on the narrow ledge, legs outstretched before him, back slumped against the craggy wall of rock. His face was scraped and bloodied by his encounters with the rocky platform and his neck and collar were bathed in the blood that was still flowing from some unseen shoulder wound. As Tony Holland peevishly pointed out to his mates gathered around the television in The Boatman's Arms that night, you could hardly have found a more marketable image of a gallant police hero if you had drafted in a Hollywood director to stage it.

38

Jejeune had been in the media spotlight before, but this time there was something different about it. Whereas the previous news coverage had at least concerned itself partially with the events of the case, providing some sort of context for Domenic's celebrity, this frenzy seemed to want to concentrate solely on Jejeune himself. What were his memories about the events on the cliff? How did he feel about saving the life of a murderer? Did he ever think about letting Nyce fall? The attention was suffocating and Lindy knew that it wasn't just the injuries that were keeping him cooped up in the cottage like this.

She looked out from behind a lace-curtained window. A crowd of reporters and other onlookers had gathered at the bottom of the driveway. A few had even ventured onto the property itself, until Danny Maik had arrived to explain to them in terms they were easily able to understand that it was going to stop. Now. But although they ceased their trespassing, they had not given up their right to peaceful assembly, and they were camped out now, sharing banter and sandwiches and flasks of hot tea, casting the occasional glance toward the cottage, alert for any signs of life.

"This is bloody ridiculous," Lindy declared. "Come on, let's go for a drive. Are you up to driving The Beast?"

The uniformed constable on duty at the bottom of the driveway looked less than happy with his lot, but he managed a smile when Lindy waved to him from the passenger seat as they passed.

"All of a sudden, that vacation doesn't seem like such a bad idea," said Jejeune, as The Beast bounced out of the rutted driveway and onto the paved coast road. He had meant it as a joke, but Lindy seized on the comment.

"I'm glad you said that," she said, "because I've booked it. We leave a week from Tuesday. St. Lucia. Gatwick to Hewanorra direct. Eight and a half hours and we're in the sunshine."

Jejeune concentrated on his driving, saying nothing. He tried hard to look enthusiastic, but there was a shadow behind his response.

"For God's sake, Dom, it's a holiday, to a beautiful Caribbean island. It's not like I bought us two tickets to watch Norwich City play." She saw him fighting his reluctance and she moved in for the clinching argument. "I want this, Dom. It's important to me."

He tried a few lukewarm enquiries about the plans, but it was clear that his heart wasn't in it and they spent much of the drive in silence. Eventually he wheeled The Beast into a car park near a wide expanse of beach and turned off the engine. "Thanks for arranging everything. I know it will be great," he said.

Lindy eyed him warily. "Okay," she said, taking the light route, "but just so you know, we are going to do more than just chase birds. I want us to have a proper holiday, a break from everything. Clear?"

But it would be a birding trip. Like this drive she had suggested, designed to remind Dom of the wonders the world's other birding hotspots could offer, and show him how Burkina Faso might pale in comparison. Lindy realized that the incident with Nyce on the cliff was the sort of thing that caused people to evaluate the priorities in their life. And their careers.

They got out and began a slow stroll toward the far end of the beach, where a spit of land curled around, as if protecting a bay in its single-armed embrace. Smoky clouds lay low in a sky the colour of pewter. Only a few brave shafts of sunlight pierced the cover, laying their light on the surface of the water like ribbons of silver. It had been a blustery day, spitting rain on and off, and there was just enough coolness in the air to remind the optimists that summer was still some way off. Far out to sea, the harsh two-syllable call of a Common Tern rolled toward them. Jejeune paused and watched it for a moment as it put on its dazzling display, hanging above the waves before plunging in to claim its prey. So fragile, and yet so fearless. No thought of the consequences, of what unseen dangers might lie beneath the rolling waves.

A small bird sped over the surface of the water and Jejeune snapped his bins up, tracking its rapid, stiff-winged flight, waiting for the glide as it swooped and skimmed, *sheared* the surface of the water. He followed the bird's progress all the way out to the horizon, only lowering his bins when it was no longer visible.

"Good bird?" asked Lindy.

"Manx Shearwater," he said. There was always a chance of see-ing one out here in rougher weather, what the locals call a bit of dirt in the air, but it was still a bird he enjoyed watching. "They're fantastic long-distance travellers," he said. "One female was recorded as having flown over one million miles in her lifetime."

"Finally," said Lindy, twisting her head to free her face of wind-blown hair, "a female with more miles on her than Carrie Pritchard." She kicked her flip-flops playfully through the lively surf that was shuffling the pebble beach with a gentle music. "Why did you ask if she could have been seeing Waters? Did you think she might have asked him to grab those birds, to prevent them from falling into Obregón's hands?"

Jejeune shook his head. "There's no evidence that she had any part to play in all of this."

"No." Lindy drew the word out generously. "Absent the fact that you always say people rarely lie just for the thrill of it. Why would she tell you she's not seeing anyone if she is? Why would she tell me the same thing? Innocence needs no secrecy. All I'm saying is I've seen people fly to the top of your suspect list for an inconsistency like that." She stopped and threw up her hands at his expression. "Hey, just a casual observation from some know-nothing journalist, that's all."

Had he really based past suspicions on inconsistencies like this? It bothered him that he couldn't be sure. He prided himself on being objective, but was he, in this case? Had he really been able to ignore the fact that filling the research position lay squarely in Carrie Pritchard's hands? Or was it there, in the back of his mind, colouring his every decision, his every interpretation concerning her? Certainly, there were inconsistencies in Pritchard's story, but there were inconsistencies in the stories of every person Jejeune had ever interviewed — misremembered facts, confused dates. Couldn't it be just that with Pritchard? Or was it something more?

On the far side of the bay, they saw a single figure walking briskly in their direction. Jejeune felt a momentary stab of disappointment. After the claustrophobic attentions of the media, he had hoped they would have this beach to themselves. As irrational as it was, he looked upon this other person as an intruder into their space. The person waved at them and Lindy waved back.

"It's Gavin," she said.

Jejeune's mood wasn't helped by the fact that Lindy didn't seem to share his desire for solitude.

"What are you doing here?" she asked as they approached. "Not another oiled bird, I hope."

"Fishing line." He had a large grey bird in a towel tucked under one arm, resting it on his hip. It was an attitude Lindy had seen neo-natal nurses use with babies. Never careless, but just completely at ease with something so fragile and vulnerable. The bird offered a perfunctory struggle every now and then, but it seemed to have already accepted that it wouldn't be escaping from this human's strong, expert grip.

"Lesser Black-backed Gull," said Gavin. He held up a heavily gloved hand. "Biter, too, this one. They aim for that little flap of skin just between your thumb and forefinger. It can really smart. I guess they're not so good at telling good intentions from bad ones." But there was no bitterness in the comment, just a gentle amusement. "I managed to cut its legs free from the line, but it looks a little emaciated, so I'm going to run it back for a check-up." He paused. "I heard about that guy from the sanctuary," he said. "That's too bad." There was something genuine about his sadness, the same kind Lindy saw in the eyes of Domenic at times, and Danny Maik, too. Such confidence with fragile things, and such compassion; Gavin would make a good dad, she thought, irrationally.

"Did you know him?" asked Jejeune.

Gavin shook his head. The gull squirmed slightly and he laid a gentle hand on it to still the movement. He shifted the bird slightly on his hip. "Not really. I saw him hanging around the place a couple of times when I took birds in. He seemed okay, kind of quiet, inoffensive, you know?"

No, thought Jejeune, *I don't know*. And that was the problem. He didn't know anything about any of the victims in this case. Not really. What could he say about the personalities, the dreams, the lives of Ramon Santos, or Phoebe Hunter, or Jordan Waters? He was learning about these people now, in death, but about them in life, he knew nothing. What kind of a job was it where you only learned about someone, got to know them, after they were dead?

"Looks like that Black Guillemot is going to make it, by the way. The one we pulled off the beach at Snettisham. You should both come out when I release it. It's a great feeling. After all, you guys helped save it."

"I'd like that a lot," said Jejeune.

Lindy saw the light in his eyes; the one that came at birding times and was so noticeably absent otherwise. She knew she needed to rein in Domenic's enthusiasm, to stop thoughts of Burkina Faso surfacing again. Of what might have been ... might still be.

"Still, I suppose it must be very hard when you come across ones you can't save," she said. "That oil slick recently, the one off Yarmouth. That killed a lot of birds, didn't it?"

Gavin nodded sadly. "I must have collected twenty bodies off the beach that day. Great species, too — Gannet, Pomarine Jaeger, even a Razorbill." He turned to Jejeune. "Birds we would have happily travelled the length of Lake Ontario to see if we were back home." He fell silent with his thoughts for moment, shaking his head finally. "It was a tough day," he said.

Lindy felt guilty that she had used this man's sadness as a foil for her own private contest with Domenic's career aspirations. But was there not a point here, too? Deaths did affect Domenic. He wore them, carried them around forever after. Jordan Waters's death, for example, had brought back memories of another boy, another death that haunted Domenic still. "You can't save everyone, Dom," she had told him more than once, "you can only make yourself eternally sad by trying." Would it not be the same, even if only to some small extent, it if was birds' lives that Domenic was not able to save. Or a species?

"Oh, hey," said Gavin, brightening suddenly, "I Facebooked one of my friends back home the other day and mentioned that I had met you. I guess that was your brother who used to lead those tours out of Toronto? Nobody has seen him around for quite a while. I suppose he doesn't do it anymore, eh?" He seemed to pick up something in Jejeune's expression, some sense of uneasiness, of evasion. "I hope you don't mind my bringing it up. It was just chat, you know. I wasn't checking up on you or anything."

Jejeune assured him that he understood, that everything was fine, but the awkwardness of the moment lingered. "We should go," he said to Lindy. He turned to Gavin. "We're heading out for a vacation soon and I've still got some packing to do," he said by way of an explanation.

Lindy looked uncertain, but she played her role. She looked out over the grey leaden sky. "Tropical paradise, meet Lindy and Dom. I can hardly wait."

They had been driving along the high-hedged lanes for some moments before Lindy broke the silence. "Your brother is the reason you're over here, isn't he?" she asked tentatively.

"I'm here because I like it," said Jejeune simply. He didn't let his eyes wander from the road.

And it was true, she knew. He liked the English approach to life, the glorious eccentricity of putting one-eighth mile distances on footpath signs, the inexhaustible courtesy at traffic islands. He liked the TV commercials that made him wonder aloud whether everyone in the country shared some mild form of brain damage. But if it was true, it wasn't the whole truth. She really wanted Domenic to start opening up about those other parts on his own. However, she was an investigative journalist, a bloody good one, as a matter of fact, and she was sure she would be able to uncover the truth about what had really brought Domenic here, and why he had stayed, if she wanted to. But that was the key, wasn't it? Whether she really wanted to know. Because you could never unlearn what you had found out, no matter how desperately you might wish to go back to your former state of innocence. You were stuck with knowing the facts, however disturbing and unpleasant and troubling they might be. And, as she had already learned in her young life, there were some things it was simply better not to know.

39

The two gatherings, the first informal, the second less so, had taken place within a matter of days. But if Jejeune seemed merely uneasy at the first, by the second, for different reasons, he was decidedly edgy.

On the first day of his return to work, he had entered the incident room to a light smattering of sarcastic applause. Whether he realized it or not, it was the same sort of response Lauren Salter had received a few days earlier. Not quite the reception Danny Maik might have gotten, perhaps, but it was a sign that something may have changed between the inspector and the others at the station.

A general euphoria seemed to float through the room; the helium of success. Someone had ordered pizzas, and a generous array of baked goods and opened wine bottles was laid out on the tables near the front. A sense of relief was normal at the conclusion of a murder enquiry, from both the police officers and the general public, but this result seemed particularly to have lifted a cloud from the place, and, like a new day emerging from an overnight storm, everything seemed charged with the brightness and freshness and optimism of a new beginning.

A buoyant DCS Shepherd approached, cradling a glass of white wine, as Jejeune gingerly inched himself up onto his customary desktop perch at the back of the room. She had noticed Jejeune declined the offer of a glass on his way through.

"Well, as unlikely as it once seemed, you appear to have conjured up a result with which both H.M. Government and the Mexican authorities can live. And in the process, you've done your own reputation no harm either, I might add."

She offered him a significant look, but Jejeune met her comments only with a faint, uncomfortable smile that showed more embarrassment than gratitude. *The injuries, perhaps,* she thought. His ribs were still heavily strapped and his breathing was shallow. Beneath the collar line of his shirt, she could see the bruising that she had heard extended all the way to his shoulder. On his head, too, redness and swelling spread beyond the bandage that covered the laceration above his eyebrow.

"I'm glad you've decided to take a break. I would have ordered it anyway if you hadn't. When do you leave?"

"Tuesday. The day after the ... you know ... the thing."

The ceremony. So perhaps that was what this was all about, this reticence, this reluctance to involve himself in the general celebrations. She knew he was uncomfortable with public acclaim at the best of times, but on this occasion especially, it seemed as if he was deliberately trying to distance himself from it. Still, he must have known the chief constable would insist on some sort of public ceremony, given the huge media interest in, and since, the rescue. Once again, it was to be Detective Chief Inspector Domenic Jejeune, long-time golden boy of the police service, front and centre.

Shepherd regarded him carefully as he scanned the room, taking it all in, eyes moving, listening, but not really being a part of it at all. Was he really so disillusioned with police work that even accolades could make him so unhappy? He had led the team to a spectacular result; a victory of justice over crime. It was not too much of a stretch to say it might have been beyond most investigators to draw all the threads together, to see the interconnecting pathways, the intricate interdependence of clues, from Nyce, to Waters, to Phoebe Hunter. It just seemed a shame, to have such a gift and yet not be able to glean any pleasure from it. Most people, Shepherd knew, lived lives of quiet frustration, eking out the odd victory against a general tide of small defeats. Trying to avoid making cock-ups, and then, when they couldn't manage that, trying to dodge the blame for them. To be really, genuinely talented at something, at anything, was a rare privilege. He really should accept his gift, and the rewards that came with it, with better grace.

"Yes, well," she said uncertainly, "at least it will be a chance to relax, have a few drinks, spend a bit of time with Lindy. You've earned it, Domenic, truly you have. You've done a wonderful job on this case. I'm sure while you are off chasing round the jungles looking for your birds we can tidy up the few loose ends that are left. First and foremost, of course, that will involve charging Nyce. I'm told they will be bringing him out of the coma in a day or two."

Jejeune nodded, but said nothing. Despite his own injuries, he had asked to be kept informed of Nyce's condition. He knew concerns about swelling on Nyce's brain had caused the admitting doctor at the hospital to induce a coma. But the prognosis now was that it was safe to resuscitate him. David Nyce would suffer no permanent injuries, to his body at least.

"The optics aren't great, I'll grant you," continued Shepherd, unnerved by Jejeune's silence. "Having to arrest him in a hospital bed. There's some public sympathy for Nyce out there. Despite the fact that he murdered Jordan Waters, a lot of people seem to feel there was some sense of justification." She shook her head. "But this needs to be wrapped up as soon as possible."

Jejeune nodded again, as a person does to acknowledge they have been listening. There was nothing in the gesture to indicate any sort of agreement or approval. Sometimes Shepherd wished Jejeune would just get over his damned Canadian politeness and argue with her. Instead, all she got was this non-committal silence that suggested he had already brought his own infallible logic to bear on events, and was content to let you voice your opinion although it would not be having the slightest effect on his own point of view. Exasperating did not even begin to cover it. But it was clear that Domenic Jejeune was in no mood to contribute to the celebratory atmosphere today, and Shepherd was buggered if she was going to let him spoil the day for her, so with a few more perfunctory congratulations, she left him to observe proceedings from his aerie on the desk and drifted off to join the party.

The other event followed so hard on the heels of the first that the euphoria had no time to dissipate. In fact, in the general way of things, perhaps it had even increased slightly in the intervening period, if in a far more staid, dignified way.

It wasn't an ideal setting, a little cramped and segregated into different rooms like this, but the award ceremony had been hastily convened, and a local venue had been deemed important. At such short notice, pickings were slim, and when the offices of Sir Michael Hillier were volunteered, the offer was gratefully accepted.

Danny Maik stood to one side, nursing a local craft beer of dubious quality and watching the proceedings carefully. Lauren Salter was standing by his side, telling him about a day trip she and Max were planning to take, as soon as this lot was all over. It was a sign she was recovering a little, getting back into the normal swing of things, but while this pleased Maik, he was only half-listening to the details. He was on observation duty today; self-imposed but nonetheless important for all that.

Jejeune was standing in a corner of the room, looking sheepish and uncomfortable in front of a hail of flashbulbs and microphones. Lindy was a glittering jewel at his side, shimmering in her simple, figure-hugging emerald-green dress.

Over by the big picture window overlooking the square, Hillier and Hidalgo were chatting amicably. It should have been a ludicrous pairing, the politician's tall, slightly inclined frame towering over the Mexican, dwarfing him, diminished him in some way. But Hidalgo retained a dignified bearing, standing an extra half-step away to allow him to look at his speaker without seeming to peer upward. Maik noticed the easy friendliness between the two. To them, it had been a contest, nothing more. Nothing personal in it: we'll battle it out for the watching public and then meet afterward for a quiet drink. *Acting out their roles,* he thought. Guy Trueman flashed Danny a smile as he passed, looking as much at home in a black tie as he had ever looked in fatigues. How easily some people drifted between different worlds. He saw Trueman approach Shepherd, standing closer than casual acquaintances did, and watched as he reached down to surreptitiously squeeze the DCS's hand. Maik noted, too, the ghost of her smile as her eyes followed Trueman when he moved off across the room.

Someone from Hillier's staff ushered Jejeune over toward the MP and the diplomat, Lindy in tow, and Hidalgo turned to address them both. "A satisfactory outcome, I think, Inspector, if one may use such a term in a tragic case like this. I know you understand how important it is that Ramon was exonerated. For this, particularly, I thank you."

Jejeune tilted his head in acknowledgment.

"Once again you demonstrate that your reputation is justified, Inspector," said Sir Michael Hillier in his rich baritone. He raised a glass. "I congratulate you. You must be extremely proud of him, young lady."

"Always," said Lindy, slipping her hand through his arm. Jejeune winced a little.

"I hope your injuries are not too serious." There was genuine concern in Hidalgo's voice. Jejeune assured him they were not, and deflected further enquiries by inviting Hidalgo to explain the duties of his position to Lindy. The diplomat inclined his head gracefully.

"Mexico is a place of many beauties, but it faces many challenges, too," he said. "Did you know, almost a quarter of a million people once lived on floating islands on Lake Tenochtitlan, the site of modern-day Mexico City? When the Spanish arrived, they drained the lake, but today, water being removed by wells from the lakebed is causing Mexico City to sink forty times faster than Venice. I cannot think of a more heartbreaking metaphor for my country's fate. Mexico is like our precious planet Earth, Ms. Hey; it is under threat from all sides. To our north we have an established industrial giant, to our south an emerging one. We have the latent Asian tiger to our west and the might of Europe to our east. No country, I believe, faces a greater threat to its culture. So, like this planet, my country needs champions to preserve all aspects of its dignity, its environment, its heritage. My role is to make some small contribution to this effort."

"I'd like to visit Mexico one day," said Lindy, "but I could probably only get Dom to go if you promised him that there were birds there."

Hidalgo shared a knowing smile with Jejeune. "Those who know about these things inform me that over one thousand species of bird can be seen in Mexico."

"Blimey, Dom," said Lindy, turning to him. "I guess we know where you'll be going when you die. If you're good, that is."

Jejeune smiled, but it was clear he was content to let the conversation swirl around him. He was mentally preparing himself for what was to come — the speech, the gracious acknowledgement of the accolades and compliments, the humble acceptance of the bravery award. The show, in other words, that was about to begin. Maik, watching from the sidelines, saw Domenic Jejeune set himself. In a few moments he would stroll to the microphone and become the master of it all — his speech, his subject, the room. He would captivate them, as he always did. And only a few, Lindy, Maik, perhaps Shepherd, would know how much of himself Jejeune was holding back, how reluctant he was to become a part of this event thrown in his honour.

Shepherd's raised voice caused a hush to fall over the room. Her introduction was uncharacteristically brief and uneffusive, and then it was the chief constable's turn to step up and shower Domenic with praise before presenting him with the medal in a velvet box.

Jejeune waited patiently behind the podium for the applause to die down. After the initial acknowledgements and thanks, he turned to the TV cameras, as if in the dispassionate glass lens he could find an understanding for his points he might not from the expectant faces in the room.

"People constantly try to find rational explanations for why a person would attempt to commit suicide," he said. "But to attempt suicide in itself is not a rational act, so it's perhaps only by looking past the rational explanations that these people can find their answers." The audience was hushed, unsure of where he was going, but willing to follow him anyway, wherever he led them. "I'm not sure what drove the man I saw on that ledge to his act of desperation, and to be honest, I'm not sure he knew himself. In his mind, David Nyce saw the taking of his life, committing the ultimate act of penance, self-murder, as the price he should pay for his actions. But the person I saw out there was a deeply troubled, confused person for whom the rational world seemed a long way off. Whatever it is we know, or think we know, must be considered in this light, too. The victims in this case, Ramon Santos, Phoebe Hunter, Jordan Waters, and those left behind to mourn them, deserve answers to all the questions. But the only way we can be sure those answers will come is if we can finally settle the truth about why David Nyce wanted to kill himself. I am happy to report that he is recovering, so let us all hope that, in the next few days, he will be able to supply those answers for us himself. Thank you."

The applause when Jejeune descended from the podium was generous but brief, and the room fell into a quiet hum of conversation more quickly than might have been expected. Shepherd had watched the proceedings with a guarded expression. If there was to be controversy, she knew, it would centre on Jejeune including Waters among the victims, counting his loss as equal to the others. But there were things in the speech that troubled her far more than that. And they would speak of them, if not before Jejeune left on his holiday, then definitely after his return.

Lindy approached him with an uncertain smile. "Nice job, darling, even if it was a bit deep for an acceptance speech," she said. "Next time, maybe just thank your agent and the members of the academy and leave it at that." Jejeune accepted her fleeting kiss on the cheek and then made his way over to where Danny Maik was standing.

"Off tomorrow, then," said Danny over-brightly. "A bit of birding, Lindy tells me. That'll be nice. A chance to recharge the batteries a bit, come back fighting fit." And then, having established that there was no reason for anyone to be paying any particular attention to their conversation, he waited for Jejeune to get to what it was he wanted to say.

"Just a couple of loose ends to tie up," said the DCI, with a strangely frank look at Maik. "I wonder if I could ask you to take care of them while I'm away."

Maik looked around the room, at Trueman, at Hillier, at Hidalgo, at Shepherd. Which one of them didn't Jejeune want eavesdropping on anything he might have to say to Danny? He turned his gaze back to Jejeune.

"You'd like to be kept informed, I take it?" He was beginning to understand Jejeune's cadences, and he realized that these unspoken communications between them marked the first steps toward a true partnership. But with partnerships came commitments that could put you in jeopardy. Jejeune seemed to hesitate, as if he was aware that once he had drawn Danny into his plans, there would be no going back. They would both be complicit from this point on, wherever it might lead. It was a heavy burden to lay on someone without their approval. Danny gave it to Jejeune with a look.

"I'm going to buy a prepaid phone for the trip," Jejeune said. Unregistered, he meant. "Save taking my own. I could buy one for you, too, if you like. It seems unfair to have to run up long distance bills on the station's plan. Wise use of resources and all that."

Danny nodded. "Trouble is, a careless bugger like me, chances are I might lose this new phone sooner or later." *And with it, any evidence that we had been in contact.* He saw that he had guessed correctly. Jejeune moved in and told him what he needed him to do.

"Look at you two, huddled over here like BFFs," said Lindy as she approached them. The men exchanged a glance of understanding, brief, but not unmissed by Lindy. "Honestly, you are developing such great shorthand between you," she said.

A strange way to put it, perhaps, but she wasn't wrong.

40

Lindy leaned on the balcony railing, looking out at the tropical morning emerging from the sea. On the horizon, daybreak was unfurling a pink and grey tapestry beneath a bank of low clouds. Domenic joined her, a cup of steaming coffee in his hand.

She turned around and kissed him, letting her hand rest on the stubble on his cheek. "You know, every day I spend in places like this makes me wonder why I don't spend every day in places like this. How about you? Having fun?"

He was. She could see it. She looked at him now, with a couple of days' beard, sporting a loosely woven fedora and a blue-patterned shirt with parrots on it. Dom was like a different person whenever he was away. Not in that daft non-literal way that Lindy's mum used the phrase, but in a real, almost transcendent sense. It was as if he shed a skin, shrugging off not only the oppressive weight of the cases he was working on, but the job itself; as if his existence as Domenic Jejeune, police detective, was nothing more than a bad dream from which he had suddenly emerged. It was, of course, why he always crashed so spectacularly toward the end of their trips, descending into a mood of brooding silence. But it was a price Lindy was always willing to pay.

They had spent the previous day, their first on the island, driving around the coastal road, drinking in the sights and sounds of the island: the warm, tropical light; the soft, sandy shorelines; the luxuriant vegetation. Lindy wondered whether the locals ever became blasé about it all. Probably not, she had decided.

Only once had a cloud appeared on her tropical horizon. They had stopped at a small market, and the assault on the senses was overwhelming; the fetid odours, the vivacious colours. And the noise, a dreadful, wonderful cacophony of car horns, made-for-tourists reggae musak, shouts, gestures, disputes, greetings, embraces. Lindy loved it all. She browsed the stalls and found a trinket, a souvenir of St. Lucia that would be perfect for the little niche above their fireplace.

Domenic pulled a face. It was a conversation they had bandied between them many times before. Why would someone who disliked dust as much as Lindy spend so much of her time shopping for things that would collect it? But he had smiled indulgently. That is, until she reached into his pocket for his credit card. He had snapped his hand down, pressing hers flat.

"Blimey, Dom, take it easy. I'm not going to steal it. I left mine in the safety deposit box."

"Sorry, I would just prefer to use cash."

"You realize they are going to tell you they have to give you East Caribbean dollars as change?"

"I would expect no less," he said, his smile not disguising his desire to move on from the incident as quickly as possible.

Later, as they sat nursing drinks at a small outdoor café, watching the passing parade of street life, he had leaned in and suddenly become serious. "If anything was to happen down here, you should go to the British authorities, not the Canadian."

Lindy stopped sipping. "Anything like what?"

"I'm just saying."

"What's going to happen, Dom? You're scaring me here."

"Nothing." He laughed, but to Lindy it sounded a little bit forced. "No, it's just that I hold two passports, Canadian and British. I just wouldn't want it to be confusing. I mean, I could pass for British now. I've had my lessons from Robin, *Jump in the old jam jar, off dahn the frog n' toad for a pint in the rub-a-dub-dub. Sorted, innit.*"

Lindy exploded a spray of fruit juice across the table, turning red and flapping a hand helplessly as she tried to stop herself from choking.

"Oh, God," she said as she eventually surfaced for air. She dabbed her eyes. "That's the best Am-glish I've heard since Dick Van Dyke in *Mary Poppins*." And then she went off again, dissolving into a fit of giggles that earned stares from passing pedestrians. The uncomfortable exchange of earlier passed and she had all but forgotten about it until dinner that evening, when she saw his expression in an unguarded moment as he eased the bill toward her to sign, that same look of uneasiness.

But today was a new day, and after a leisurely breakfast in the sun on the hotel patio, they got in the rented Jeep and headed up into the hills to visit a bird reserve Domenic had on his list. How strange, thought Lindy as the Jeep wended its way farther and farther up toward the rainforest-cloaked interior of the island. At home, the bird reserves were all tucked along the margins between the land and sea, with human habitation penning them in. Here it was the resorts that were penned in, and the wide expanses of wilderness that stretched inland.

Eventually they saw a hand-painted wooden sign to the Des Cartiers Trail and turned off down a steep dirt track. There was only one other vehicle in the lot when Jejeune pulled the Jeep to a halt. They got out and strolled along a path dappled by the bright sunlight that filtered through the tangle of leaves high overhead. In a small clearing ahead of them, a man was standing at the base of a large tree, his binoculars trained on something up in the canopy.

"The people you meet when you're walking through the rainforest," said Jejeune.

The man started a little at Jejeune's greeting, turning to face them almost defensively. Then his face broke into a wide smile. "Well, damn, JJ. Long time, no see," said the man delightedly. "What the hell are you doing here? Damn," he said again. The two men shook hands warmly and Jejeune made the introductions.

His name was Traz, and he gave Lindy a frank, appreciative look that she found flattering and yet honest at the same time.

"Saw you on YouTube," said Traz to Jejeune. He hummed a few bars of dramatic theme music before breaking into another of his broad, infectious smiles.

"*Star Wars*?" asked Lindy.

Jejeune pulled a face. "Indiana Jones, I think."

Lindy laughed. It wouldn't take very long at all to get to like Traz. For one thing, he was possibly the neatest field worker she had ever seen. Despite wandering around in this wilting tropical humidity, his khakis looked pressed and unsoiled, and his dark hair was clean and neatly brushed. Even his boots showed few traces of mud. Lindy had taken Dom to parties looking less well turned-out than this.

"Traz?" asked Lindy inquisitively.

"Short for Alcatraz. As in Birdman of. It's from an old movie, a true story about a convict named Robert Stroud who used to care for birds. Somebody tagged me with it in college, probably numbnuts here, and it stuck. My real name is Juan Perez. Proud second-generation Canadian." He smiled.

"And JJ?"

"Jejeune junior."

She looked at Domenic. "So who's Jejeune senior, then, your dad?"

"No." Jejeune looked uneasy, guilty almost.

Lindy looked back to Traz. "You know Dom's older brother?"

"A little, yeah," said Traz guardedly. The men exchanged a glance and something flickered between them for a brief moment and was gone. Upbeat, lightweight talk between the two friends took its place. Somewhere in the space it had taken Lindy to recover herself, Dom had asked Traz about his work.

"The overall goal is to measure the impact of human disturbance, pesky tourists like you, on the forest birds. We have some great trails here in St. Lucia, but they can see a surprising amount of traffic. In order to know how the birds react to disturbance, I need to find out how they react when there isn't any. Only ..."

Jejeune nodded. Only in order to study how birds react when no humans are around, you have to be around. Traz saw that he understood.

"I try to have as little impact on the natural rhythms as possible, to let it all flow on around me. I collect my data in the morning and evening, but for the rest of the time I pretty much just sit around and watch nature being nature. I just, literally, try to do as little as possible."

"Sounds like the perfect job for you," said Jejeune, smiling.

Traz looked Jejeune up and down, as if he couldn't really believe his old college friend was actually here in front of him. "Man, it's good to see you, JJ," he said sincerely.

JJ. We are so many different things to so many people, thought Lindy. Like Phoebe Hunter. Who would Domenic have been to this man, this kid, when they were at college together? She thought about her own college friends. What reaction would they have if they knew literary brainiac Lindy Hey was out stomping through the Caribbean rainforest in her hiking boots looking for birds? Pity, probably.

"So, let's see." Traz held his hands to his head like a prophet channelling a message. "Foreign birder, this part of the island. You want to see the endemics."

"The St. Lucia Parrot especially," said Lindy. "Dom's been banging on about that one ever since we landed."

Traz shook his head. "Too late. In this part of the forest, early morning is your best bet. If you can come early tomorrow, we'll take a walk up into the hills. I know a few spots. There are other endemics around now, though," said Traz, "like that one over there, for example. St. Lucia Warbler."

He and Lindy laughed as Jejeune grabbed his bins and darted along the trail, cautiously approaching the thicket into which the little bird had disappeared. They watched him holding his bins at the ready, primed to be snapped into action the second the tiny bird reappeared.

"It's funny," said Traz, tossing his head in Jejeune's direction, "we all thought it was a lock that he would become a field researcher. He was always talking about it. I sometimes think I only got into it in the first place because he was so enthusiastic about it."

"So why didn't he?"

Traz shrugged his shoulders. "Too many people told him otherwise. He doesn't like to contradict people."

"He's getting better at it," said Lindy with a half-smile. "But I know what you mean. If somebody says something he disagrees with, he rarely argues with them."

Traz raised his eyebrows. "Perhaps he should have. If there was ever a time to speak your mind, it's when other people are planning your future for you. Dom never did, though, so he ended up doing what everybody else thought he would be good at."

And they were right, thought Lindy. But that didn't mean Domenic wouldn't swap places with his old college friend now — in a heartbeat.

Jejeune returned, beaming.

"Get on it?" asked Traz.

He nodded.

"Diagnostic looks?" asked Lindy, drawing an appreciative glance from Traz. She knew how important it was for Dom to be able to distinguish the field marks on a new bird. Someone as familiar with the species as Traz could tell him with absolute certainty that it had been a St. Lucia Warbler, but Dom would want to have seen it clearly enough, and for long enough, to be able to identify it himself.

He smiled. "Beautiful. That *V* on its head and the little black eye-stripe ..." he stopped, still smiling. "You've seen them before."

Traz nodded. "Once or twice," he said with heavy sarcasm. But it was clear he understood Jejeune's delight. Listing a "lifer" had made his friend's day. The residue of excitement was still coursing through him, and would stay with him for a while yet.

"Come on. Let's see if we can find you another one. I'll bet it's been a while since you had a two-lifer day."

It turned out to be a three: a fleeting glimpse of a St. Lucia Peewee, and a slightly better, if distant view of a St. Lucia Oriole. Though Jejeune and Traz had discussed the sightings at length as they shook hands and firmed up plans to meet the following morning, Lindy had little doubt she would be hearing about the birds again, likely many times, on the drive back. But that was okay. She'd been given a glimpse into Domenic's past today, and in a way she couldn't quite explain, she felt like a barrier between them had started to come down. Dom could chat about St. Lucia's birds as much as he liked on the way back. For once, she would be happy to listen.

41

Luisa Obregón's grey-blue eyes grew slightly wider as she opened the door.

"Sergeant Maik. You have come to tell me these cases are solved, that I and my son are no longer suspects?"

"We believe we know who committed the murders," said Maik carefully. "There are just a couple of questions ... if you don't mind." He peered behind the woman into the house. He had not seen Gabriel Obregón anywhere around on his approach to the house, and that fact did not fill him with ease.

Luisa Obregón held the door open and invited him in. Filling in the blanks, Jejeune had called it. Now that they had their killer in custody, albeit in a hospital bed, and all the evidence they needed against Jordan Waters, Shepherd would have seen it as just more of Jejeune's pedantry if she had been made aware of Maik's assignment. For that reason, he had let it slip his mind to inform her where he was going today. Danny Maik knew his DCI well enough by now to know that he wouldn't have asked if he was completely satisfied with the way things stood. Something was still bothering Jejeune, and if Maik hadn't figured out what it was yet, that knowledge on its own was enough for him to take his request seriously.

"I hope you have forgiven my son for his earlier behaviour," she said, leading him through the hallway into the large living room. "He has had no father to show him how a man should behave. His only role models growing up have been movie thugs and Internet game heroes. Perhaps his life would have been different if he had been able to have someone like you to guide him toward manhood."

Maik had little doubt both of their lives would have been different, but he let Luisa Obregón's observations pass without comment.

"You have questions?" she asked. Whatever they were, she appeared ready to answer them honestly, as if she had nothing to fear from him any longer.

"Your husband's research," said Maik cautiously, "you mentioned it was to do with doves. He could be surrounded by his work, you said."

"To do *with* them, yes. But *about* them, no."

"Forgive me, but your son's condition, it's a genetic disorder, I believe?"

Luisa Obregón regarded Maik's face carefully. "Such an intelligent man, Sergeant."

Not me, thought Maik. *But the man who wanted me to ask this question, and the one before it? Now there was a clever man.*

She gestured for Maik to sit, and settled her delicate frame on the big leather couch opposite him. "In Urbache Weithe victims, the membrane sheath does not form properly. Something about the DNA codes ... I do not understand." She shrugged. "I know only that it makes my son's life very difficult." She gave a shake of her long hair, as if to dismiss the thoughts that threatened to engulf her. "My husband wanted to study the genetic codes of this family of doves. Of course the DNA of birds is quite different from humans, but as part of the superspecies, these doves have only very subtle genetic differences. This is what interested him. He wanted to study closely related gene sequences to see if these differences could be manipulated, repaired somehow. Or controlled."

Luisa Obregón's everyday English had run hot and cold on a couple of occasions when Maik had interviewed her in the past. But these things, gene sequences, membrane sheaths, superspecies, these she got right. It was the legacy of living with them, he realized, of countless hours of thinking about them, discussing them, reflecting on how they were controlling the lives of her family.

"And originally the Mexican government was happy to fund your husband's work?"

She nodded, her dark hair shimmering in a silken cascade. "At first, yes. But then later it became clear that they wanted to take possession of his research."

Luisa Obregón sighed slightly, but it was the release of more than just pent-up breath. It was the release, also, of secrets, of lies and deceptions that went back many years. The release of emotions, too, possibly, though there were plenty of those still in her eyes as she continued.

"My husband feared they wanted to use it for their own purposes. Instead of finding a cure for Gabriel's condition, perhaps they would wish to know how to create such a condition in young men. You cannot imagine such evil exists in the world, Sergeant, but it does."

Maik, who could have probably written a Ph.D. dissertation on the evil that humans were capable of, said nothing. But he did not doubt the truth of Luisa Obregón's words. Armies of young men without the capacity to feel fear was the stuff of science fiction. But anywhere along that scale, any research, for example, that might one day lead to a vaccine to suppress the human fear response, even temporarily, that was something that any military establishment in the world would be interested in. But Maik knew, too, that if the Mexican military had been denied Victor Obregón's research, they would want to make sure no one else was going to get their hands on it either.

It explained why Luisa Obregón's telephone conversations were still of interest to them, even after all this time.

"They said if he would not agree to turn over his research, they would end his funding. How could they do this, Sergeant? How could they take away my husband's work, prevent him from looking for a cure for his son's illness? I asked him to agree, to give them what they wanted. But he was such a good man, so decent, so honourable. He said he could not bring himself to do it. I gave him much guilt over this. In the end, too much."

Maik could see the regret in Luisa Obregón's eyes, and he knew that her black widow's heart was broken in two.

"Gabriel was growing more uncontrollable as the illness progressed. I saw in my husband the frustration that he could do nothing to prevent this. At first, he tried to continue the work on his own, spending hours in the aviary every day, trapping the birds and taking samples from them, anaylzing the results himself. But of course, he could never do all the work he needed to alone. He started spending entire days and nights in there, all the time slipping farther and farther away from me … from us. And then, one day, he was gone. So yes, Sergeant, I do believe the Mexican authorities killed my husband. I do think it was them who left me a widow, who left my son without a father."

Behind Luisa Obregón, Maik thought he detected a faint shadow, a subtle change in the light falling into the aviary, as if someone was up on the roof. She noticed his furtive glance back toward the plate glass window, but misinterpreted it.

"The Socorro Doves are not here, Sergeant. Once I thought I would have given anything, done anything, to possess them once again. Birds my husband knew, had worked with, had held in his hands. But I would not have bought them from that man, not when I knew he had killed to steal them."

"Do you know where they are?" asked Maik.

She shrugged. "The world is not kind to the weak and timid, even more so in a strange land. And yet, they survived until now, so perhaps … I would like to think they are alive still, somewhere."

It had taken the better part of three interviews for Danny to be treated to a smile from Luisa Obregón, but the genuine article, when it finally came, was well worth waiting for. It was a thing of such pained beauty it made his heart seem to skip a beat.

Maik started as he heard a noise. He saw another shadow through the glass of the aviary's roof, clearer now, definite. He stood quickly and began to make his way toward the back door.

"Ms. Obregón, where is your son?"

"He is up there, on the roof of the aviary. There was a leak. Rain was getting in. I have asked him to fix it. I do not want the birds to become ill."

"He's up there, on the glass? That ribbing will never hold a man's weight. What is he tethered to?" There was urgency in Maik's question, and genuine concern.

"My son uses no safety equipment, Sergeant. He simply climbed up using a ladder."

"That wet glass will be like ice," said Maik, his voice rising as he looked for a way to alert Gabriel Obregón to come down. "If he goes off into that ravine, it's a forty-foot drop. Worse, he could come crashing through that glass at any moment." He turned to her earnestly. "You have to get your son to come down from there, Ms.Obregón. He is in real danger."

Luisa Obregón looked at Maik with sadness in her eyes. "He will not listen to me, Sergeant, or to you. What is danger if you do not have the capacity to fear it? It is like love — a meaningless word only if you cannot experience it for yourself."

Maik saw that it was hopeless. He could do nothing but leave Gabriel Obregón on the roof, suspended between life and death, supported only by a membrane of thin, transparent glass.

And yet, he thought, *perhaps margins like these are all that ever separate any of us from the dangers in our lives.*

He drew his eyes from the roofline and found Luisa Obregón looking at him. "I do not know how much longer my son will be able to survive," she said quietly.

"The illness?"

"Possibly. But it is more likely he will find himself in a situation from which there is no escape. I cannot protect him forever. This I know. I try, but one day he will go somewhere dangerous, as fearless as ever, and he will not return. This will happen, I am sure of it. And when it does, the only memory I will have of my family, of my husband, my beautiful son, of the life we used to have together, will be this aviary."

"Is that why you wanted the birds? These Socorro Doves?"

"My husband has gone. I have no body to bury, no grave to mourn at. All I have of him is his aviary. I want to rebuild his collection, to have it back as it once was, when he … left. As it was before the storm came and took away all of his birds."

Maik saw tears appear in her grey-blue eyes. Blue, the recessive gene, he remembered, from some long-ago biology class. And here it was, having battled all those generations of dark genes in her native heritage and emerged victorious. The tenacity of Luisa Obregón, the survivor, on display for all to see.

"You are a good man, Sergeant. You care so much about the welfare of others." Her expression morphed into one of pain and regret. "This man who was killed at the sanctuary, Ramon Santos, he was married?"

Maik nodded.

"His wife will never recover. To lose a husband to divorce or infidelity, somewhere back behind your heart, you know he is still there, maybe there is even a hope he will return. But to have a man you love taken away from you forever …" She faltered, and tears started to her eyes again. "Her life will never be as it was. Although I have never met this woman, my heart is full of sorrow for her. Please tell her this."

Danny nodded ruefully. "I won't be seeing her myself, but I will make sure it is passed on."

She knew he would.

42

Though it was still early morning, the shimmering surface of distant Caribbean glittered in the intense sunlight. They had risen at first light to make the long drive up into the hills again. From the Jeep's passenger seat, Lindy took in the sights and sounds of a country still awakening. She watched the stalls being opened and produce being meticulously arranged, and she caught the smell of coffee and fresh baked goods hanging tantalizingly in the morning air.

The sun had already climbed above the highest of the horizon lines by the time they pulled into the car park and headed out along a trail that led down to a wide inland lake. They found Traz standing at the edge of the water, looking as neat and dapper as the day before. He was bending to peer through a telescope set up on a tripod, but he seemed to sense their approach.

"We can head up into the hills in a few minutes," he said without taking his eye from the scope. "I'm just finishing up some population counts, doing a bit of citizen science in my spare time. It's a good spot here." He straightened up and indicated the flat expanse of glistening water in front of them, where dark shapes were scattered out as far as the eye could see.

"Anything special?" asked Jejeune.

STEVE BURROWS

"Green Heron, Greater Yellowlegs, a few Northern Shovelers."

"All of which I might see on a stroll around Sam Smith Park in Toronto," said Jejeune with mock distain.

"But not in such erudite and charming company."

Lindy laughed and asked Traz about his counting.

"Today will just be estimates. You get an eye for it over time. See that colony of Laughing Gulls resting on the mud over there, for example. How many would you say?"

Lindy took a quick look. "Twenty or so."

Traz looked at Jejeune.

"Thirty five?"

"Not bad," Traz conceded. "Probably just over forty."

Lindy looked surprised. "Really? That many?" She took a moment to count. Forty-two.

"How about that congregation of Black-bellied Plovers coming in now?" he asked. He turned to Domenic. "Or Grey Plovers, as you no doubt refer to them now your British citizenship has come through."

Lindy shielded her eyes from the glare as she tracked the group of birds speeding in over the water. They flew in an astonishingly tight formation, all but disappearing from view at times as they twisted and swooped almost as one, until the silvery light caught them again as they banked at a new angle.

"I would have said at least sixty," she pronounced confidently.

"Probably closer to a hundred. The tendency is usually to underestimate, the more so if they are on the wing. I've seen some seasoned birders get numbers spectacularly wrong." He stopped suddenly. "Wait," he said dramatically, holding a hand to his head and staring up into the sky, as if communing with some higher power, "I sense that, in a moment, all these birds shall rise as one."

On cue, the birds lifted from the water and began a slow, lazy spiral around the lake, swirling in the air in a majestic ballet of gently beating wings.

"How on earth could you predict that?" asked Lindy in astonishment.

"Being out here," said Traz solemnly, "I have acquired the ability to connect spiritually with nature in a way that city folks like you simply cannot comprehend."

Jejeune rolled his eyes and Traz laughed out loud. "Plus of course, I saw that Peregrine coming in. It landed on that tree over there. C'mon, let's go find some forest birds."

The foliage around them was alive with birdsong as they hiked up the trail into the forest. Traz looked around and smiled appreciatively. "Plenty of noise," he said. "Always a good sign. You take point, JJ. The birds often hang over the trail at this time in the morning and I get the feeling Lindy won't be quite as heartbroken if she dips on something you scare back into the undergrowth."

Lindy smiled. Was her lack of interest really so evident? Was it the way she trudged along the trail, rather than bouncing forward on the front foot like Dom, his body as taut and tense as a golden retriever about to be let off the leash? Or perhaps it was the way she kept her eyes on Traz as she was speaking to him, rather than having them flit all around the skies and trees surrounding them as they conducted their conversation. Either way, Traz's easy smile showed that there was no judgment in the comment, only perhaps a gentle amusement that two such obviously mismatched hikers should be with him here on the path this morning.

Jejeune set off at a leisurely pace, scanning the treetops around him, peering into thickets, immersing himself in his environment. Lindy saw his joy at being out here, birding in this wilderness, with nothing else to care about. *This is who he is,* she thought sadly, *all he will ever be.*

"So, this case you're working on," said Traz, "those birds that were stolen, they were an island species? Endemics?"

Jejeune nodded. "Socorro Doves. They're from an island off the coast of Mexico. Why, do you know of them?"

Traz shook his head. "I've barely even heard of them, but one of the guys I work with down here is an island endemics expert. That's why he's here. I could ask him."

"Couldn't hurt," said Jejeune, "especially if he's heard anything unusual about their genetic makeup." A thought seemed to strike Jejeune, completely out of the blue. "I was wondering, Traz, this research you do yourself, does any of it involve stable isotope studies?"

Lindy didn't know how long it had been since Traz had heard Dom's attempts at casual disinterest, but she was betting even he could pick up that the question wasn't entirely as unimportant as Domenic was trying to make it out to be.

With Traz behind him in the line, Jejeune couldn't see his friend shake his head. "It would take a long time to establish a programme like that," he said. "You could come armed with all the previous data you like, but to do any kind of isotope research effectively you need to know the land, really know it, know which isotopes were accumulating where and under what conditions, what synergies were going on between them, external influences, weather patterns."

Jejeune was quiet for a few moments, only the sound of his hiking boots crunching over the leaf litter breaking the silence.

"You have to realize," said Traz, "not everywhere is like Canada or the U.K., where things are open and on record and government legislation is for the most part observed without question. People in other places aren't always keen on foreigners coming in and prying into their business. Maybe they don't want to tell you what fertilizers they are using these days, maybe the local government doesn't even want you to be taking soil samples, in case you find something nobody wants to talk about."

Traz shrugged. "It takes time to build those relationships on the ground — a long time. Okay, this is a good spot," he said, stopping suddenly at a space with a view over the densely forested hills below. He peeled off his day pack and sat down on the edge of the trail, letting his legs dangle over the side. Lindy followed suit. There was not a breath of wind, just silence, a peace in which Lindy fancied she could hear the beating of her own heart.

"I'm going on up ahead a little way, see what I can find," said Jejeune.

"Knock yourself out," Traz called after him. "I'll shout if anything interesting drops in back here."

They watched him until he had disappeared around a bend in the trail and off into the thick curtain of green.

"So, is he the same as you remember him?" asked Lindy.

Traz considered the question seriously. "A little more subdued maybe. That boy who died, when he found that politician's daughter, that sort of thing would stay with the Domenic Jejeune I knew."

"He doesn't say much," said Lindy, "but he still thinks about it. It was getting better, I think ..."

"Until this new kid, Waters?" Traz saw Lindy's expression of surprise. "I try to follow his cases as much as I can. Whatever you do, don't tell him, though," he said with a lopsided grin.

Lindy nodded. "Waters was about the same age. Dom's not conflicted over his death, particularly, but it brought back, you know, memories ... I think ... I don't know," she said uncertainly. "He doesn't talk about it much."

"That sounds like our boy."

"But something else has been bothering him since he's been here. He seems on edge sometimes, uneasy. He even seemed a bit reluctant to come here in the first place, and he's had me book everything — the hotel, the car — in my name."

From up on the trail, they heard the sound of Dom's footfalls returning. Traz turned as he came into sight. "Maybe he's just worried about the media following him around if they find out he's here. He's a pretty well-known guy these days. YouTube, the Net. It could be that."

Lindy didn't know if Traz had a girlfriend, but if he did, she certainly hoped he didn't try to deceive her very often. He was even worse at it than Dom. Well, as bad anyway.

"Oh, hey," said Traz suddenly. "Looks like Dom's on something up there."

He got to his feet and quickly crossed to the far side of the trail, where he joined Domenic near the edge of a steep drop-off. The two men began staring intently across the valley through their binoculars. Possibly Dom had found something of note. But Traz spent his days in these forests, and had undoubtedly seen most things here a hundred times. So he must have thought Domenic was on something pretty spectacular indeed. Unless there was another reason he had found it necessary to interrupt his conversation so abruptly and put some distance between him and Lindy.

Jejeune was quiet on the drive back. Though they had enjoyed a good day of birding — productive, Dom called it — they had not seen the St. Lucia Parrot, or St. Lucia Amazon, as Traz corrected them. He had heard one calling far off, deep in the forest, and Traz had pointed it out to them. Dom had sportingly pretended it was enough. But he had fooled no one. Looking at the studious intensity on his face as he negotiated the winding mountain roads, Lindy wondered if there might be something else on his mind, though.

As she began to shrug off her hiking things in the cool comfort of the air-conditioned room, Jejeune walked out onto the balcony and stood staring out at the sea. Lindy joined him and handed him a cold beer from the bar fridge. They sat on their cane chairs, cradling beers and listening to the warm evening breeze stirring the fronds of the palm trees below. Lindy put her bare feet up on the balcony rail.

"So, what do you think of Traz?" asked Jejeune.

It was his way of saying he didn't want to talk about anything else, and Lindy didn't push it. There was no point in spoiling a beautiful Caribbean evening. "I like him," she said. "He's fun. Plus, of course, he's so clean. I don't think I've ever seen anyone who managed to stay so neat and tidy."

Jejeune laughed. "Yeah, he's always been like that, even in college. He's just one of those people that dirt never seems to stick to."

"It's good to see you two together," she said simply.

Jejeune swigged on his beer and nodded. "Yeah, it's nice to see him doing so well down here."

He fell silent, staring out over the sea again. On the horizon, the sky was turning a spectacular shade of orange as the sun bade the island goodbye for another day. But Domenic's gaze seemed to rest far short of the sunset, somewhere in the middle distance. He was thinking about what Traz had said, she knew, about the knowledge of the *place*, for which all the research and learning and studying could not substitute. It would take a long time to acquire that knowledge — time Domenic no longer had.

Lindy took his hand and squeezed it gently. "Is everything okay?"

He smiled at her. "A cold beer and a sunset like this?"

"And me," added Lindy.

"And you," agreed Jejeune. "Apart from a St. Lucia Amazon sighting, what else could a man possibly ask for?"

43

Maik had brought Tony Holland along, not so much for company but because he thought Holland's past connection with the family might come in handy when he spoke with Jordan Waters's mother. As before, he had made no mention to DCS Shepherd of where he was going, and he had been equally forgetful about informing Holland whose errand they were on. They had driven out together in Maik's Mini, chatting amicably enough until the moment when Holland had asked the name of the song that was playing.

"'Heatwave,'" said Maik.

"I heard my granddad mention this one," said Holland. "It was one of his favourites. He loved all those old Ethel Merman show tunes."

With a consummate wind-up artist like Holland, you could never be sure whether he had genuinely confused Martha Reeves's doo-wop classic with the 1930s Irving Berlin song. But to even compare Pistol Allen's driving backbeat and Mike Terry's scintillating sax work with a ditty about a can-can dancer who started a heatwave by letting her seat wave was enough to cause Maik to give Holland one of his special stares. They had completed the rest of the journey in silence.

"Anthony," Mrs. Waters had said in surprise when she answered the door, "it's good of you to stop by. Come in. Let me get you and your friend a nice cup of tea."

Which is why Tony Holland and his friend were now sitting side by side on a chintz sofa in a tiny room at the front of the house, waiting for this small, huddled woman to reappear from the kitchen where she had gone, *popped* was her word, to put the kettle on.

Danny Maik was comfortable being the lead at a questioning. Basically, he thought wryly, all you had to do was think about Detective Chief Inspector Domenic Jejeune's technique and do the opposite. Sit still, pay attention, and ask questions. But Maik didn't mind giving Tony Holland a bit of leeway in this interview, either. Holland was, after all, well acquainted with Mrs. Waters, even if he hadn't realized until now quite how well acquainted.

She returned with tea and an assortment of biscuits arranged on a floral plate with a chip in the rim. *Even at times like this,* thought Maik, *even in her grief, such care, such kindness.*

"I'm glad you came, Anthony," she said pouring the tea and handing them their cups. The two policemen cradled them as they looked for a place to set them down. The cups were the same pattern as the plate. Perhaps the saucers had not survived the journey down through the ages.

Mrs. Waters seemed not to notice. She settled back into her worn, overstuffed armchair with its quilted blanket draped over the back, and stared blankly into the empty fireplace. "At a time like this, it's nice to remember the good days." She turned to Maik. "Thick as thieves, the two of them were, Sergeant, back in the day. Of course, they drifted apart later on, when Anthony joined the police, but for a time, they were a proper couple of cowboys. Just lads being lads, though, I suppose."

Holland looked uncomfortable. He turned to take in the room, frozen in a time from another era. It would have looked like this back then, guessed Maik; such a comfortable, normal base of operations for two young cowboys to launch two such divergent careers.

"I hear you have arrested the man who took our poor Jordan." She shook her head and looked at Maik through watery grey eyes from which all anger had long since gone. Now there was only sorrow, and a strange kind of sadness mixed with bewilderment. "How could anybody do it? Will you ask him that for me? This man. Will you look him in the eyes and ask him how he could do something like this?"

She seemed to sense Maik's compassion, his ability to share her loss, however slightly, as someone who, too, had seen young men buried before their time.

"Those questions will be asked as part of the formal arrest and charge process," said Maik, tempering the formality of the words with just the right amount of personal investment. "We still have a couple of other matters to clear up, if you feel up to it."

She seemed surprised "About our Jordan? I'm afraid he didn't tell me very much about what was going on in his life, but anything I can do to help."

"Did your son happen to mention that he might be coming into some money soon, anything like that?"

Mrs. Waters shook her head. "Not in so many words. He did ask me if I still wanted to see Athens before I died. He said he was going to take me. Just me and him, he said, the two of us together." She paused for a moment. "I would have liked that," she said, nodding to herself. "We never had a proper holiday together. And now we never shall." A flicker of sadness crossed her features. She was rocking back and forth in her chair, Maik realized, the movement so slight it was barely noticeable. "But how was he going to manage that on his money? Still, you know Jordan, Anthony, always the dreamer." Not for the first time, her eyes flickered toward the doorway, watching for a son who would never walk through it again.

"What did Jordan do when he wasn't working at the sanctuary, Mrs. W?" asked Holland. "Where did he spend his time?"

"He was mostly down that club the two of you used to hang out at. They've reopened it now, you know. They call it *The Retro*, whatever that means."

"*Retro*," said Holland. He shook his head. "My youth, somebody else's nostalgia. Now I know how the sarge must feel when *Downton Abbey* comes on."

He offered a cheeky grin at Maik, whose own expression suggested that while he wouldn't be wholly opposed to the idea of Holland giving up his day job, he probably shouldn't do it for a career in comedy.

"Don't you pay any attention to him, Sergeant. That's how they are these days. No respect for their elders." But it was all said with a kindly smile, one which morphed into soft sorrow as a thought visited her briefly. "Jordan was just the same, bless him. But he didn't mean anything by it. He was a good boy at heart, Anthony. You know that. A bit wild, but a good boy at heart."

Holland shook his blond locks. "No, he wasn't, Mrs. W. We had some good times together in those early days, but if there was ever any trouble around, Jordan would find it. Or vice versa. Jordan was a lot of things, Mrs W., but he was never a good boy."

A flash of pain crossed her features. "No, you're right. But it wasn't all his fault. He never had much of a father. He was hardly ever around, and when he was, he was not a good influence on young Jordan."

Holland nodded in agreement. "You know, I never really cared for Mr. Waters."

"Nor did I, truth be told," said Mrs. Waters. "He was a bad one, and I suppose the apple never falls far from the tree. But this business the police suspect Jordan of, you know he would never harm a girl, Anthony, you know that."

Holland was silent, but he couldn't resist a sidelong glance at Danny.

"Jordan never mentioned that he was seeing an older woman, did he?" asked Maik. "He never came home with any presents, carvings, wood sculptures, anything like that?"

Mrs. Waters shook her head, bemused. "No. I don't think he was, well, attracted to older women."

Maik nodded, mentally checking off the last item on the list Jejeune had given him.

"I think he really liked that girl he worked with, to tell you the truth," said Mrs. Waters. "I could tell by the way he talked about her. Who knows, if he had met her earlier, instead of running about all over the place ... Well, look who I'm talking to. The two of you were as bad as each other. This should make you think, Anthony, about that lifestyle of yours. It's not healthy, and besides, what kind of a future is there in it, running around from one girl to the next all the time?"

Maik stirred uneasily but Holland made a point of ignoring his sergeant's presence. "I had one mum, thanks, Mrs. W.," he said with more than a touch of bitterness. "She wasn't much good at it, but one was enough."

Maik, who had found something in his notebook to occupy his attention during the exchange, decided now might be a good time to give Constable Holland a few moments to recover himself. He thanked Mrs. Waters for her help and left to wait outside.

He was leaning by the Mini, fiddling with a side mirror that didn't need any attention, when Holland emerged from the house. He didn't meet the sergeant's eyes for a moment and Danny waited until Holland had regained his composure. This being Holland, it didn't take long.

"This Jordan Waters, you didn't say you knew him that well, Constable."

"I did, Sarge," said Holland simply. "More than once. It's just that nobody was listening."

"Well enough to think he was incapable of murder." It wasn't a question, but Holland treated it with his customary wariness just the same. When you didn't know where Danny Maik was going, it was a good idea to leave your options open.

"I would have said *no*. I realize everything points that way: the fingernail, the phone call. I can't just ignore all the evidence. I'd be as bad as ... But murder?" He shook his head. "I know you've heard it all before, Sarge, but I don't see it. It's not in him to murder anybody."

Not murder, perhaps, thought Maik. *But killing; now that's a different thing.* To protect someone, to save the one you love, everyone's got that in them, somewhere deep down inside. Anybody could kill, if the motivation was strong enough.

Holland took Maik's silence as disapproval. "It does sound like he had a buyer lined up for the birds, though. That trip to Athens and all. Although, let's just say, if Jordan Waters was going to Greece, I doubt he would have left a forwarding address. Take his mother as cover to avoid any suspicion, send her back alone after a couple of weeks and disappear among the Ouzo and bronzed bodies on the local beaches. Now that sounds more like the Jordan Waters I knew."

Maik stood for a moment beside the car. He had gotten Inspector Jejeune most of his answers, but none of them seemed to have any impact on the overall outcome of the case. Only one more question remained. But the answer to that one, he suspected, might change things a lot.

44

Danny sat across from Lauren Salter in the pub. Even though it was a beautiful spring morning outside, he had chosen this inside table, in a quiet corner, tucked away near a window.

"So," said Salter brightly. "It looks like it's all wrapped up, then."

Danny took a slow draw on his beer, "It looks that way."

"It didn't turn out to be Maggie, after all." It was a simple statement, obvious, unnecessary. But Salter meant something more by it, and Danny understood. How could they have ever considered a frail little thing like Maggie Wylde as having the strength to shove Phoebe Hunter onto that branch with enough force to impale her? Maggie, now dribbling into her soup in a secure facility, waiting for her court date on a charge of assaulting a police officer, so she could tell the judge how much she loved her babies and wanted them back. It was a sign of how desperate they had been to solve this case in the beginning, all of them, for their different reasons. And now it was over. But if so, why was this unregistered phone burning a hole in Danny's pocket, waiting for Jejeune's call?

Maik reached for his beer glass and spun it slowly. He spoke without raising his eyes. "Constable … Lauren, I've got something to talk to you about." He paused. Was he waiting for her to say something, encourage him on? Salter's uncertainty kept her silent.

"The thing is, for some of us ex-military types, relationships can be difficult. Some take to it like ducks to water, of course. Great husbands, great dads, but for others it's just not that easy." He was looking around the pub now, at the comings and goings of the mid-morning traffic. Why was it so difficult for him to look at her? Was it because of what he was leading up to, what he was going to say next? Salter's heart jolted. Her mouth felt dry.

"The thing is, being in the military, it can give you a bit of a different view of things. You learn to see things on more of a day-to-day basis. Grab what you can now in case it gets taken away from you tomorrow. It's the same with relationships. *Carpe femina*, I heard Guy Trueman call it once." For the first time, Maik looked at her. He tried a grin that didn't quite come off, but Salter met him half way.

Carpe femina. Tony Holland would like that, she thought. Though he'd want it translated into English — *seize the skirt* or something like that. But where was Danny going with this?

She reached for her wine but thought better of it. She would just sit still and wait. Hope. Pray.

"As you can see, I'm not much good at this sort of thing," said Maik. He took a long time taking a drink of his beer.

"No, Sarge … Danny, you're doing fine."

Why did she have to wear this ratty old two-piece today? She should have dressed up a bit, a nice blouse and skirt. If only she'd known.

Her heart was pounding as if it might explode out of her chest. She could hardly breathe. Danny was staring at his hands splayed out on the table in front of him. Scarred, battle-hardened hands that had protected him from who knew what horrors. She looked at them, too. *Would they be capable of tenderness?* she wondered.

All at once she was thirteen again, sitting across from Ashley Morgan in the park, spotty, gangly Ashley Morgan, waiting for him to stop faffing about and get to the part where he invited her to go to the dance with him, so she could smile and say yes and set her heart free to sing with joy.

Come on, Danny, get to the part you brought me here for. Ask! We can work out the fine print later.

"As I say, even if we want to get into a relationship, some of us, we might not know how to go about it properly. Things could get messy, even if there was no intent." He raised his head again but turned to stare out of the window beside them. "Guy Trueman, for example," said Danny quietly, not looking at her. "I'd trust him with my life, but in a relationship with someone I cared about …" He shook his head.

Guy Trueman? Why were they talking about Guy Trueman?

Salter searched her memory for any hint she may have given that she was interested in Trueman. She was staring at Danny now, unable to unlock her gaze from him. But he didn't notice, couldn't notice. He was still staring out the window.

"Guy and the DCS are starting to see a lot of each other." Maik held up a hand as if to ward off an objection. "I'm not saying there's anything in it, or that it will lead anywhere, but, well, she's not had the best of luck with her leading men in the past."

Finally, he looked at her, a wan smile on his face. Salter continued to stare at him, smiling back, showing nothing of an internal landscape turning to dust as empires of dreams collapsed in on themselves.

"I was wondering if you could have a quiet word with her, just to put her on guard a bit. I wouldn't normally go anywhere near anything like this, as you know, but … I just wouldn't want to see anybody get hurt."

Too late for that, Danny, much too late for that.

But Constable Lauren Salter just sipped on her drink and smiled easily at this clumsy ex-military type who had just casually carpet-bombed her emotions.

"Relationship counselling, Sargeant Maik? Bit of a new line for you, isn't it?" It sounded like the voice of another person, distant, frail. "Sure, Sarge, leave it with me." She drank her wine again, drained it. "I'd better be getting back."

She left hurriedly, taking her crushed hopes and her trampled dreams with her, to a place where even an Extra Super Power Hug from Max might not be enough to mend a broken heart tonight. And if Davy Salter walked past her bedroom later that evening and noticed her sadness, how was he to know that it wasn't the flashbacks of her attack now, or her accident with the van? How was he to know that his little girl's anguish was coming from a completely different cause this time?

Maik was sipping his beer thoughtfully, musing about Salter's sudden need to depart in such a hurry, when his phone rang. It was Jejeune. The men didn't waste much time on pleasantries. Maik started slowly. He knew what he had found, but he didn't know what it meant. Not yet, though he suspected he soon would.

"No record of any car rental at all, not even as far out as Norwich. And Nyce didn't borrow one from any of his friends, either. I checked. So what now?"

There was a silence for a moment from Jejeune's end. "We need to stop DCS Shepherd from bringing a charge of murder against Nyce," he said finally.

Maik's own silence suggested that it might be a touch difficult. "She has his confession," he said eventually. "With respect, sir, she's going to need something more than just your say so before she's willing to give that up. Especially in this case."

"David Nyce's car was already in our pound when Waters was murdered. He had no way of getting all the way out to the Obregón property, and certainly no way to have driven away after, thinking about how he had just murdered somebody. Nyce was never at the scene of Waters's murder. It was

Constable Salter he saw, at Carter's Bridge. It was *that* scene he was watching, probably from that hill to the west. He must have seen Salter being loaded into an ambulance and thought it was Waters. With the fret, the fog around, he couldn't have had a clear view from any great distance, so he just pieced together what he thought had happened."

Across the miles, Maik nodded to himself. And after, Nyce had retired to his cottage, gone dark, as they said in the military these days, off the grid. He would not have heard any news updates about the incident at Carter's Bridge. Or Waters's murder. His only truth would be that which he thought he already knew.

"Remember his question to us? 'Will the charge be murder?' He thought whoever had been taken away in that ambulance had died later, of his injuries. And he thought it was Jordan Waters."

Maik did remember that question, the strange cadence of it, and the unusual syntax. Now, isolated like this, it seemed so bloody obvious. But at the time, it had been just a few more words in a miasma of others. Only Jejeune could have picked them out of that jumble and found their significance.

"There's something else, too. Nyce told me that he hadn't planned to kill Waters, but the killer took a large knife."

"Nyce has a pretty powerful motive for lying, sir. He was trying to duck a charge of premeditated murder."

"Not when he was on the ledge," said Jejeune. "He was expecting to die. He was dictating his suicide note to me. I just can't see why anybody would lie under circumstances like that."

There was another long pause. "Shepherd might buy it," conceded Maik carefully. "But she won't be happy. Not unless you have someone else in mind to offer her in exchange?"

Jejeune was silent for a long time. "Not yet," he said finally. "But I believe I will have soon."

45

Domenic Jejeune was quiet as they followed the narrow, winding road up into the hills. Up here, away from the tourist facilities that fringed the island's coastline, life in St. Lucia took on a more pragmatic edge. Village after village appeared along the fringes of the road, as if they had sprung up from so much broadcast seed. Each bore the scars of the harsh reality of trying to eke out a living in the hinterland of a tropical paradise.

Lindy knew that, for once, Dom's silence was not because he was thinking about the case. Traz had passed sentence on Dom's dream, and he was coming to terms with it. She had woken in the night and seen him sitting out on the balcony, tipped back in the cane chair with his feet on the railing. He was sitting perfectly still, just staring out over the black sea into the darkness, into nothing. The brave sadness of a man watching something precious disappear. They should discuss it, she knew. It needed to be talked about. She didn't want to spoil their holiday, but not to acknowledge something this big seemed awkward, ridiculous, not at all how serious partners went about handling difficult subjects.

She turned on the radio; the local news channel in English. It was the standard fare of human commerce everywhere

— unfairness, inequality, injustice. And behind it all somewhere, a plea for someone to put it all right.

"Can you find any music?" asked Jejeune pleasantly.

So quickly? she thought. *To put it behind him?* Perhaps he had known all along, in his heart of hearts. Perhaps he just needed to hear it once, from someone he trusted, before he was prepared to let it go. But if he was going to put his disappointment behind him for the moment, to get on with the business of relentlessly enjoying the rest of their holiday, then so would she. They could discuss his broken dreams later, once they returned home, once paradise was no more than a memory.

They found Traz standing on the edge of the car park. "Morning," he said. "You might want to check that trail down there," he told Jejeune, pointing. "I heard a couple of interesting things on the way in."

With a look at Lindy and a smile, Jejeune set off down the track. "Come on," said Traz. "There's something I want to show you while he's off chasing the avifauna of St. Lucia."

They climbed a steep path that led up off the main trail, the stones still slick with the early-morning moisture. It required concentration and neither of them spoke until they reached the top. They emerged into a small clearing. It was like a stage, no more than twenty feet in diameter. All around them dense green vegetation crowded in, so much so that Lindy couldn't even see the trailhead they had just stepped off. But out in front of them there was a gap in the foliage and the vista was open. Far below in the distance a tiny blue bay glittered in the sunshine.

"Beautiful, isn't it?" said Traz. "That's St. Francis's Bay down there. The only way in or out is by boat. Hardly anybody knows about it. I try to keep it that way."

"But you'd share your secret with Dom, of course," said Lindy, looking out over the landscape. "Just like he'd share his secrets with you." She realized that if ever there was going to be a window into Domenic's past, it would be here, with his good friend, in this exotic place, with its island rhythms and its tropical cadences so different from the orderly elegance of the north Norfolk coast and its polite restraint and its decorum and its careful observations of other people's privacy. It would be here she would need to push for answers. Here or nowhere.

"I don't know him like I used to," said Traz guardedly. He turned to look at the trees behind them, or anywhere, it seemed, that wasn't Lindy's eyes. "It's been a long time, you know, a lot has happened to both of us. All I can tell you is, if it was me and I found myself in the middle of something good, I wouldn't want to risk losing it. I mean, I wouldn't want something that happened in the past to be a problem."

"You mean his brother, don't you? What happened, Traz?"

He looked at her finally. "Look, Lindy. It's not my place. All I can tell you is he got himself into some trouble down here."

"Here in St. Lucia?"

"Here, Peru, a couple of other places in between." Traz held up a hand. "Nobody thinks Dom was involved, but the Jejeune name, it doesn't have the greatest pedigree in this part of the world."

She nodded. It had been there, she recognized now, in that first greeting. She had a good ear for such nuances, honed by years of interviews with subjects, when the truth was evasive, masked by other things. And if she had wondered at the time whether she had just imagined it, she was convinced now that she had not. What the hell are you doing *here*? Traz's question, the emphasis on the last word, not the pronoun. Not a surprise that Domenic had appeared, but that he had come here, to this place of such painful associations for him? *And I brought him here,* she thought. *Why on earth didn't he say anything?*

"If he hasn't talked about it to you, I suppose he just wants to be sure he's not going to be judged on the basis of his brother's actions, that's all."

"He should bloody well know that already," said Lindy, anger rising within her.

"Maybe," said Traz reasonably, "but it's not like it hasn't happened before."

Lindy looked at Traz, but his eyes were fixed on the landscape again. There would be no more, she knew. He had gone as far as his kind of friendship would allow, perhaps farther. It would be up to her to take it from here. If she wanted to. If she dared to.

They stood for a few moments more, looking out at the view, though neither was really seeing it anymore. Then they began to scramble back down the steep path. Jejeune was waiting for them at the bottom. "Antillean Crested Hummingbird, Grey Trembler, and Pearly-eyed Thrasher," he announced with a grin. "A grackle, as well. I suspect Carib rather than Greater Antillean."

"Ya think?" asked Traz with heavy sarcasm.

Jejeune looked perplexed.

"St. Lucia's in the Lesser Antilles. The Greater Antillean Grackle is found in, well, the clue is kind of in the name."

Lindy loved the way Traz bantered with Domenic. He was the first person she had ever met who was not in awe of his intellect in some way, who didn't seem to revere his intelligence or his knowledge. Domenic Jejeune was, to Traz, just a friend from college, and that seemed to suit them both. Perfectly.

"Are you this good with the birds of north Norfolk?" asked Traz with a smile. "Maybe I should come over and give you a hand."

"You'd love it," said Jejeune. "It has some of the widest, emptiest beaches you'll ever see, and the skies can throw you a million different moods. And the bird life, Traz. It's incredible. Tens of thousands of Knots, as many Pink-footed Geese. When they take off against a red sunrise, words can't do it justice. It's as amazing as anything I've ever seen."

This is a man talking about a home he loves, thought Lindy, *a place he wants to stay.* Dom was trying so hard to be that person today, to want to be there forever and never go off on research trips to Africa. But even if he couldn't quite sell the sincerity yet, she loved him so much for trying that she thought her heart would burst.

"I talked to my friend last night," said Traz. "He didn't know much about Socorro Doves, but that island sounds like a pretty interesting place. I guess they're into a pretty heavy eradication programme out there."

"Just as you predicted," said Lindy, all joy now, despite the heat and the humidity and the troubling shadow of Traz's revelations. "Clever old you." She turned to Traz. "Dom said they'd try to get rid of the cats and rats to save the other endemics."

"Not just rats and cats, though. Sheep and goats, too."

"Farm animals?" asked Lindy, "What's wrong with these people, nothing else left to kill out there?"

But Jejeune was staring at Traz with an intensity that she recognized all too well, and Lindy was aware she had missed something important.

"Sheep and goats?" he confirmed.

Traz nodded. "I could have told them they're probably wasting their time, but strangely, the Mexican conservation authorities didn't think to consult some nobody bird researcher working in the middle of the Caribbean about any of this." He shrugged. "Their loss."

Jejeune was quiet for a moment, and Lindy and Traz stood on either side of him on the trail in an awkward, suspended silence. But she knew. Whatever it was that Jejeune had heard in Traz's report, Lindy knew it had made a difference. *The* difference. Dom had put things together and now he would hone in on his target like an arrow. Nothing else would matter — not birds, not St. Lucia, not his brother's past. How could Dom say this was not his calling, when the solution to a case consumed him so completely like this?

Jejeune had taken out his phone and was holding it aloft as he headed for a clearing on the edge of the trail. "Any chance of a signal up here?"

Traz shrugged. "On a good day, with the winds blowing in the right direction and the clouds just so, maybe the faintest signs of life. Otherwise, the only bars you're going to get out here serve cold beer, and the nearest one of them is about a mile away."

Jejeune returned and turned to Lindy. "We have to go. Come on." He flapped a hand at Traz as he hurried away down the trail. "Take care, Traz." A thought seemed to strike him and he stopped so suddenly Lindy almost bumped into him. He returned and extended a hand. "It's been, you know ..."

Traz nodded. "Yeah, me too."

46

Jejeune did not wait to get back to the hotel. He drove with the phone in his hand as he gripped the steering wheel, risking a brief glance whenever the steep, winding road down the mountainside straightened out for a moment. As soon as he saw bars appear, he pulled over into a small siding and dialled.

Danny Maik answered on the second ring.

"What do you see when you look around you, Sergeant?"

"The dashboard of my Mini. Cars parked around me. Constable Holland sneaking a quick smoke round a corner. I'm okay to have a quiet conversation, if that's what you're asking."

There was a heartbeat of hesitation, so rare in Dom that Lindy looked at him, concerned. From their vantage point, Jejeune could see the sparkling turquoise waters of the Caribbean Sea far below. North Norfolk seemed a long way off, an impossibly long distance from this spot up here in these mountains to a place where he needed to destroy something that could never be repaired.

"We need to arrest Guy Trueman."

There was a long silence, but Jejeune didn't need to ask if Maik was still there.

"Charges?" The voice sounded distant, defeated.

"None yet. But he wasn't in that hotel room the morning

Waters was murdered. You need to arrange to have him arrested immediately and taken into custody."

"I don't need to *arrange* it." Maik sounded angry now, bitter. "I'll take care of it myself."

It was Jejeune's turn to be silent. Was there something in his sergeant's voice that suggested he had known this, already found the flaw in Trueman's alibi, if only he had been willing to let himself recognize it. Perhaps it was a mistake to let Maik handle this, to let him place this burden on himself. Jejeune's thoughts flickered to Traz. Could anyone set aside their shared past at a moment's notice, place it in a box and put it on a shelf, just like that?

"The thing is, we'll need to offer Efren Hidalgo blanket protection right away. This is very important, from the exact moment Trueman is taken into custody. Even if Hidalgo protests, do not take no for an answer, and make sure whoever is on duty does not let him out of their sight. As soon as you can, I'd like you to get over there and take over his protection detail personally."

Maik had recovered his composure by the next time he spoke.

"If you could just specify the nature of the threat, sir, or at least which direction we are supposed to be looking ..."

"Just stay close, Sergeant, as close as you possibly can. Night and day. I'll be there as soon as I can."

Maik cradled the folded mobile phone with exaggerated care, as if afraid of crushing it to dust in his large, powerful hands. He sat in the tiny car, taking in what he had to do, the enormity of it growing by the second now that the initial shock had worn off. He remained still, staring down at the phone, taking a few minutes to regain his composure. Drawing a breath, he got out of the car and looked around him. The car park was empty. Holland had finished his smoke and sloped off back into the station unobserved. Somewhere across two continents, across an ocean and the infinite spaces in between, Danny Maik recognized that there was more than one reason Inspector Jejeune had asked if his sergeant was somewhere quiet when he took the phone call.

They were each subdued as they packed, but there was no anger in their silence. Domenic was a policeman. End of. The job, whether he wanted to do it or not, came first. And Domenic's expression as he drove down through the mountains after his call to Danny Maik told Lindy all she needed to know about the seriousness of the situation back home.

Only once had he broached the subject after he told her they would have to cut the holiday short and return to the U.K. right away. "It's been good," he told her. "I'm glad we came." And she could tell that he was. But it had not all been good, and she could see the trace of sadness behind his eyes.

"I'm so sorry, Dom," she said sadly. "Maybe it's not too late, if it's what you really want to do ... work with birds. Maybe there is some other way you could be involved, when we get back home. There are lots of organizations; that citizen science Traz was talking about ..." Her arguments petered out as she acknowledged their futility.

Their packing was interrupted by a knock on the door. It would be Lindy's new friend, the desk clerk, with the details of their flight. Five hours from now, thought Lindy, if she remembered her research correctly. George F.L. Charles to London via Bridgetown, Barbados. She had played the Detective Chief Inspector card with the clerk when she stopped by the desk, just to make sure there was room on the flight. So, five hours. Time to do a little shopping on the way to the airport perhaps, eat at one of the roadside cafes, grab a couple of last little bits of St. Lucia to take home with them from this brief, strange, enlightening holiday.

She padded to the door barefoot, readying a smile for the girl she had connected with over the course of their short stay. How strange, she thought, the way people pop into our lives and assume such importance and then are gone again, most likely forever.

But it wasn't the desk clerk. Three policemen stood in the hall, two in the smart white starched shirts and peaked caps of the St. Lucia constabulary, and one behind, smaller, but clearly the power, in his lightweight peacock-blue linen suit and dark wraparound sunglasses.

"Royal St. Lucia Police Force." The man in the blue suit offered a name, but in her shock she missed it. The three men entered the hotel room without asking for permission. Blue Suit removed his sunglasses before he spoke.

"Domenic Jejeune?"

"Inspector Domenic Jejeune actually," Lindy answered for him. "Chief Inspector." She looked at Domenic, who had stopped packing but was still hovering over his case, making no move at all.

Blue Suit was impassive. He showed no signs of discomfort despite the tropical heat in the room, where Lindy had turned off the air conditioning and opened the windows wide to allow the St. Lucia climate free rein one last time before they left.

"You will need to accompany us to the station." His delivery was dispassionate. It didn't seem to leave much room for argument, but Dom seemed to be accepting it particularly meekly. Professional courtesy was one thing, but Lindy didn't owe a thing to these men who had pushed themselves into her hotel room at the end of her vacation.

"We have a plane to catch," she said bluntly, looking away from the men and making a show of resuming her packing.

Neither Blue Suit nor the other officers reacted. They just stood there, waiting for Domenic Jejeune, Chief Inspector Domenic Jejeune, actually, to decide what he was going to do next. There was no hostility in their demeanor, but no reassurance either; not a single smile or softening of an expression to reduce the tension. The other two were still young; perhaps friendliness might be construed as a sign of weakness out on the mean streets of Castries. But Blue Suit was a veteran, his hard face lined with the experiences of a lifetime of imposing law and order on this tropical island. He could have afforded a slight smile and gotten away with it, a small gesture of mollification. He offered nothing. Lindy had caught Domenic's act a few times and she had always thought he had the professional detachment thing down pretty well, but he could take a few lessons from this one. There weren't many cold things on this island, but this man's demeanor out-cooled anything else by some distance.

"Flights leave the island daily for the U.K. If you miss this flight, arrangements can be made to take a later one," he said in the same neutral tone as before.

Arrangements can be made. But not by him. Lindy had been around power often enough to recognize it when she saw it. You wouldn't find this one rounding up the tourists who had committed crimes after a few too many Piton beers and shipping them back home. That would be the purview of these happy chappies in the white shirts. Blue Suit would be back in a well-appointed office somewhere, planning schedules for visiting dignitaries, not playing travel agent for a visiting copper.

"May I have a couple of minutes?" Domenic sounded polite, but not contrite.

"You can take a few moments, but you may not be alone."

"Just what the hell is going on?" Whether Lindy's fire came from the fact that she didn't know, or that Domenic seemed to, wasn't clear. She turned to him in frustration. "Is this about the case?"

"It could be. I'm not sure." Jejeune paused, sighed almost. "No," he said finally, "I don't think it is."

Realization fell from the sky and landed on Lindy with a crushing force.

"It's about your ..."

Jejeune's look stopped her cold. There were a thousand messages in his gaze. *You need to not know. You need to be able to say you don't know, that I have never told you anything. It needs to be true.*

Lindy reached for her bag. "I'm coming with you."

The two uniformed officers looked at their commander uncertainly. He gave a disinterested shrug.

"No," said Jejeune urgently. "Stay here and wait for me. Finish packing. I'm sure we will work all this out and I'll be back in no time." He looked toward the commander as if seeking some reassurance, but the man's face remained impassive.

Lindy reached for the room telephone. "Then I'm calling the British High Commission, right now."

"Don't call anybody," said Jejeune. "Please. Just wait. I'll be back. Check into other flights, the next one. Just in case ..." he added weakly. "It's okay, Lindy, honestly. Everything is going to be all right."

And when I get back I'll explain everything, he didn't say. *We'll have a laugh about all this over a couple of drinks, about how it was all a mistake, just some crazy, typical police cock-up.* He didn't say any of it, because it was clear that it was no mistake. It was about the only thing about this entire mad, frightening business that was clear to Lindy. Blue Suit hadn't built a career of policing on this island by barging into the hotel rooms of visiting police officers and hauling them off to the station by mistake. Whatever was going on, it was Domenic Jejeune they had come for. And it was Domenic Jejeune who, with one last lingering backward glance that was meant to be reassuring but fell short on so many levels, was going with them now, leaving Lindy with nothing to do but sit on the bed and let all her anger and frustration and concern well up inside her and release itself as tears.

47

Gabriel Obregón was slumped against the kitchen cabinets when Maik and Holland burst into the farmhouse. From the angle of the boy's shoulder, Maik guessed it was probably a broken collarbone. Luisa Obregón was kneeling beside him, dabbing his bleeding mouth with a towel.

"Is he still here?"

She nodded. "In the aviary. He came in demanding the doves. Gabriel tried to stop him." She looked down at her son. "He was so brave."

Holland had known this call was something different, something tricky, when Maik had grabbed his shoulder as he headed out of the station. "With me. Now," he had said urgently. Holland understood now why Maik had looked so troubled by the call he had received moments earlier.

"Why did he want the doves?" Holland looked at Maik, but it was Luisa Obregón who answered.

"He said the police would hesitate, think twice, about arresting him if he had the birds as a …" she struggled for the phrase.

Her son offered it through swollen lips. "Bargaining chip," he said weakly.

Why hadn't she called 999, or the station? Why him, on his mobile? Did she know, somehow, the connection between the two men, or had he said something, mentioned Danny, as he was using his dark arts to neutralize Gabriel Obregón?

"Sergeant, my son." She reached down and tenderly stroked his cheek.

Maik snapped out of his reverie. "Are the birds here?"

"I have already told you this. I have not seen those birds since they disappeared during the storm. Sergeant, my son needs help. He must go to a hospital."

Maik turned to Holland. "Get an ambulance out here. But tell them no police. We're here, it's under control. No backup required. Got it?" And then to Obregón again. "Was he armed?"

She shook her head. "I did not see a weapon, but perhaps, this man ..." She turned again to look at her son. Both Maik and Holland took her meaning. *Perhaps this man did not need weapons.*

Maik moved toward the door. "I'm going in to the aviary," he told Holland. "You stay out here. Under no circumstances come through that door. You wait out here for me to tell you what to do next."

Holland nodded and reached for his phone as Maik moved off. Listening to the ring, he looked down into the face of the young man lying at his feet. He was the image of his father, the man Holland had seen in the missing person files: the dark hair, the features. And the eyes, dark fluid reflecting pools into which Luisa Obregón could immerse herself, as she was now doing, reliving her past. Holland regarded her carefully. It was as clear as a written statement: Luisa Obregón was still married, faithful to a man who had disappeared from her life and was never coming back. Even an eternal optimist like Tony Holland could see that he would never have stood a chance with her.

Danny Maik strolled out onto the elevated walkway trying to project a confidence he didn't feel. The afternoon sun was streaming in through the glass panes on the roof of the aviary, and a sticky, cloying heat filled the space. All around him, birds beat the air with their wings as they escaped to the safety of the treetops. But not below. When Maik reached the observation platform and leaned over the rail to tentatively scan the overgrown vegetation below, he could see nothing moving at all.

"You shouldn't have warned Colleen Shepherd off, Danny. A dead giveaway that I was in your sights." The voice came from off to the right somewhere, indistinct.

"You weren't even a suspect then, Guy. You were just wrong for her. That's all." As he called out, Maik scoured the dense undergrowth for signs of movement. There were none.

"You ought to open one of those online dating services, Danny. Make a fortune."

Maik craned his neck to see over the railing. A different location now, farther back, behind him somewhere. He had seen nothing, though, not even the shimmer of a single branch as Trueman had moved through the tangled foliage.

"Those stolen birds aren't here, Guy," called Danny. "They never were." The heat was oppressive now. Maik wanted to remove his jacket, but he was concerned about making any unusual movements, at least until he knew where Trueman was. And if he was armed.

"Not about birds anymore, though, is it? We've got other business to sort out now, you and me."

Over to the left again. Always moving but never giving a sign of it. Trueman hadn't lost any of his skills, by the look of it. But Danny knew he couldn't say the same about himself. Finally, he detected a flicker, a shimmer of movement, almost directly beneath the platform. If Trueman did have a weapon, he had a bead on Danny from here.

"This is not us, Guy, shouting at each other through the treetops like this." Maik eased back from the railing carefully. "I'm going to take my coat off, no sudden movements, nothing up my sleeve. And then I'm coming down."

No response this time. Silence was unnatural, even in this man-made jungle in the middle of the north Norfolk country-side. But it wasn't comforting. When Guy Trueman was around, silence was your enemy.

Maik removed his jacket and loosened his tie, then began to climb down the ladder, discreetly tucked against one of the supporting pillars. Facing the ladder, he had his sweat-soaked back exposed to the aviary. If Guy Trueman was going to attack him now, Danny would have no defence. Maik reached the ground and spun around. Nothing. Just a wall of green — thick, dark, impenetrable.

Maik began to pick his way through the vegetation, moving slowly, carefully. The heat was even greater down here, and he blinked the sweat from his eyes as he moved through the undergrowth. He felt gravel beneath his feet and found himself in the centre of a small clearing. There were feeding stations and a stone water fountain, long dry and now all but claimed by mosses and climbing vines. On the ground, a few old feeding dishes lay overturned and broken. *It would have been an open space when the doves used to feed here,* thought Maik, *exposed, offering no cover.*

Maik heard a rustling behind him and turned to find Guy Trueman standing on the far side of the clearing. He was in a combat-ready stance but his hands were free of weapons. A single shaft of light from above penetrated the overgrowth and fell on the gravel between them.

"Well, this is a situation, isn't it, Danny? Bet there's no Motown tune to cover this one."

They had been here before, surrounded by foliage in heavy, tropical heat. The clothes were different, though. Civvies, now, Danny in his shirtsleeves and Guy Trueman in a golf shirt and sharp slacks, looking as if he had just stepped off the course at the Saltmarsh Golf Club. And the danger, of course, that was different, too. Before, it had never come from within.

Trueman made a show of taking in their surroundings. He spread his hands before him. "So, what happens now? Mano-a-mano?"

"Be a bit embarrassing, wouldn't it? Two old buggers like us rolling around on the ground." Maik made it sound light, but both men knew the truth of it. With the skills they possessed, it could be more than embarrassing. For one of them, it could be fatal. "You weren't in your room, Guy. Not when Jordan Waters was killed."

Trueman looked at Maik with interest, but he said nothing.

"We have a changeable climate out here in north Norfolk. You never know what you're going to get from one day to the next. Especially on a spring morning. We've been getting a bit of sea fog lately. Fret, the old timers call it."

"Long way to come just to give me a weather report, Danny. You got a point?"

"This fret, it burns off as soon the sun comes up, most of the time. You'd never even know it's been there. But when it rolls in," Maik shook his head sagely, "sometimes you can't even see your hand in front of your face. Certainly from your hotel room you couldn't see the picturesque seaside village of Saltmarsh come to life, dawn breaking over the boats in the harbour, things like that."

Trueman stayed silent still, but Maik could see his body squaring, shifting his balance just that little bit, to where it would need to be if he was going to launch an attack.

"There was a lot of fret about at oh six hundred on the morning Jordan Waters died," Maik said, slowly, evenly, keeping his voice as flat as he could. "I know, I was out in it, recovering Waters's body from a culvert."

"A bit of fog?" Trueman's laugh had all the anger and contempt he could muster. "That's what this is all about? Come on, Danny, you're embarrassing yourself here." Trueman tensed slightly as he eased into another stance. It was one Danny recognized. Guy Trueman was tipping forward ever so slightly onto the balls of his feet, readying himself for action. "You always did think you were one up on me, didn't you? The rest of them," Trueman held up a little finger, "round here, no problem. But not Danny Maik. I never minded that. When you're in charge of a unit, there's always going to be one, somewhere down the ranks, who's smarter than you are. Now a good CO, he might even welcome that, as long as this man knew how to keep it in check. But you've overstretched yourself here, old son."

"You're going to have to come in with me, Guy," said Maik evenly. He felt a bead of sweat trickle down his cheek.

"And what if I don't want to? What then?"

"The kids today," said Danny quietly, "they have a saying — *I don't think it would end well.*"

"How d'you mean, me doing time for assaulting a police officer and you in a hospital bed somewhere? Not well like that, you mean?" Trueman raised his voice angrily, but he didn't move.

They stood in their arena of green, two ageing gladiators separated by a shaft of sunlight, the heat like a physical force around them. Trueman seemed to be considering things, weighing his options. *He hasn't decided yet,* thought Danny. *He hasn't made his mind up which way this is going to go.* But it would be up to Trueman. It would be his decision. Danny would be content to let him make the first move. It was the last move Danny was more concerned about. He just hoped he would be making that one.

"What is it now? Forty-eight hours you can hold me?" said Trueman conversationally, so suddenly it made Maik flinch slightly. "So I'll just sit it out, shall I? And on hour forty-nine I'll pick up my gear and skate off into the sunset. And then where are we, eh? Hard feelings all round, and nobody's really any farther ahead. Come on, Danny, it's not too late to put this right. This is not even reasonable suspicion you've got here. You couldn't hold your worst enemy on this. I know it, you know it, and your flirty DCS knows it, too. All I see here is a bit of doubt, some desperation, and a handful of jealousy thrown in for good measure."

Maik had his own anger now. So far he had been prepared to defend himself only. But Trueman's attitude, the careless disconnection he was showing to the death of Jordan Waters changed all that. Now it was Danny who was poised to attack.

"He was just a kid, Guy," shouted Maik, barely able to control his rage, "barely older than some of those squaddies who used to look up to you."

Trueman saw the anger, the same raw, primal fire that he had seen in Danny Maik when other young men had died. He knew that something had changed, that Danny would fight him now, if necessary, with all the strength and courage he had shown beside Trueman on the field of battle.

"I'm sorry the boy died, truly I am. But you've got this all wrong."

The sun had crept ever so slightly around the clearing, closer to Trueman. But Danny was prepared to wait until it had completed a full rotation in the sky, if necessary. There was no rush. Now that he had come this far, time didn't matter anymore. In truth, not much of anything seemed to matter anymore.

Trueman gazed around the clearing. Looking for what? A means of escape? The only way was through Danny Maik. And Guy Trueman wasn't prepared to take that route today. He fixed Maik with a resigned look.

"Do what you have to."

Holland led Trueman away unresisting, past the ambulance with its silently flashing lights, past the staring ambulance drivers loading Gabriel Obregón solicitously into the back, past the watching Luisa Obregón.

Maik watched Holland ease Trueman into the back of his car. Neither man gave Danny a backward glance. He turned away, and headed to his car, ready to obey the second and final part of Jejeune's directive.

48

Lindy hadn't expected chapter and verse from Dom, not right away. She had known him too long for that. Even a closed book like Domenic Jejeune had predictable ways of responding to situations, and Lindy had come to learn them. He would think about it first, assess the situation, then explore the possible outcomes from this point on. He wouldn't dwell on what had happened; that wasn't his style at all. So, analysis first, and then, perhaps, an explanation, of sorts. Lindy could wait. She had done so before, on other less serious matters, so if it took him a little bit longer this time, took a little more analysis before he got to the point where he could talk to her about it, that was okay. Because he would talk about it eventually. Though how much, in this case, she didn't know. Domenic would never lie to her. She knew that with the certainty that all women have about the honesty of the men they love. But that didn't mean he would tell her everything, either.

They were in economy class, cramped in tiny seats somewhere near the back of the plane, even these secured for them only through the influence of the Royal St. Lucia Police Force. They had missed the flight they had planned on taking, just as Blue Suit had seemed to know they would; missed it by more than fifteen hours, in fact. But as a tiny, feeble act of apology for all their inconvenience, a police car had picked Lindy and the luggage up at the hotel and driven her to the airport, where Domenic was waiting for her at the gate so they could scramble onto this flight: Hewanorra to Gatwick. Eight and half hours, direct. But it promised to be a long eight and a half hours, with Domenic brooding thoughtfully beside her and the same in-flight films she had seen on the way over.

She sighed and looked around for a flight attendant. She would be giving the in-flight bar service some serious attention on the way back. If she could disembark without assistance, Lindy would be greatly disappointed with her efforts.

They had been in the air about twenty minutes when Domenic turned to her with a weak smile. It was one of his special ones, sadness and regret and apology. You could get a lot of mileage out of a smile like that. Yes, Lindy would wait.

"Do you have my charger in your purse? I need to make a call and my phone is dead."

Lindy looked puzzled. "You can't use your mobile phone on a plane."

"I'll use the plane's phone to call. I just need the number of Danny Maik's new phone. I didn't bother to memorize it, but it's in the phone."

"I don't have the charger."

"Where is it? In the other bag?' He made to get up and reach for the overhead storage compartment.

"No Dom," said Lindy. "I don't have it. When the police came to pick me up at the hotel, I just piled all the bags in the back of their car. I put your charger in your computer bag, but they whisked me right through security and took the bags to check them through for me. Your computer bag was with them. It's in the hold."

She had only seen the expression a couple of times before. Deep, genuine alarm. And something else: panic.

Jejeune got up slowly and spoke to one of the flight attendants, quietly, urgently. Then he strode to the front of the plane, disappearing from Lindy's view. When he eventually returned, he was working the rows, stopping methodically at each, talking to everyone, waking them, even, if they were sleeping, explaining his situation, polite but not smiling, showing them his phone and his warrant card, asking if they had a compatible charger, the same model phone, even, so he might, on official police business, take out their memory card and insert his, even for one brief, flickering instant, to recover the number of Danny Maik's unregistered phone. But head after head swayed regretfully from side to side, and he returned to his seat desolate.

"Can't you just call him at the consulate?" asked Lindy. It didn't seem likely Jejeune had overlooked this possibility, but perhaps now, if he was desperate enough, out of all other options, he would consider it again. "Even if he's not there, they'll know where he is if he's on protection detail for Hidalgo."

But Jejeune shook his head. "I can't do that." There was resignation in his voice now. He asked for Lindy's phone, to compose a text on it. It would be faster, he said, to just plug his phone in when they landed, and dial Maik's number from Lindy's phone, sending the already-composed text. *Surely,* she thought, *this is just Domenic finding something to do, some activity to make him feel less helpless, less trapped in his situation. Surely, things couldn't be so desperate that the few seconds this preparation would save would really make a difference. Could they?*

Lindy looked at him, alarmed at how seriously he was taking this. "Jeez, Dom. We'll be landing in about eight hours; you'll have the phone in your hand in nine. Whatever it is you need to talk to Danny Maik about, surely it can wait that long. Can't it?"

"No," said Jejeune simply. "It's already been almost a full day. An additional nine hours is too long. It could be the difference."

"Between life and death?" She was trying flippancy to snap him out of it, but then she registered the look on his face.

Perhaps it was the trauma of being held at the station for so long. She had checked him out as closely as she was able without him noticing and she hadn't seen any signs of rough treatment. But the psychological scars wouldn't show. She didn't know what they had asked him about his brother, or perhaps even what new information they had told him. But she did know that Domenic never went for the melodramatic. Ever. So only one of two things was true: either what had happened at the station had left him with a sudden flair for the theatrical, or this situation at home, this event he was powerless to stop for the next few hours, really might end up in more death.

Lindy didn't touch a drop of alcohol on the flight. She just watched Domenic, sitting, staring silently at the phone in his hands, as if urging it to spring to life by sheer force of will. As the plane finally started its descent, a new obsession seized him, checking his watch every two minutes, every one minute now. For only the second time since she had known him, she saw in Domenic's face the look of someone dealing with catastrophic human error. His own. She reached over and squeezed his hand. "Soon, Dom, soon."

But it was not until the next day that he would eventually get his phone charger. And by then, Domenic Jejeune had long since come to the realization that even had he been able to send his message from the plane, he would have been too late.

49

Lauren Salter was waiting at the gate. She hurried over. "We have a situation, sir. It's Danny — Sergeant Maik. He's been injured. We don't know how badly. We have a car waiting. We have to go now."

Without waiting for an answer she began sprinting through the concourse, passing the startled travellers. Jejeune kept pace easily, Lindy, too, with her lithe athlete's stride.

Salter's police car was parked at the doors of the terminal, lights spiralling their warning to everyone. She drove fast. As the outskirts of London sped by and they headed toward the city proper, Lindy heard only snippets of the conversation in the front seat. Salter, eyes locked on the road, answering only what Jejeune asked, wanting to give him the complete picture, but afraid to let her mind wander over what exactly the complete picture might be, the horrors it might hold. Instead, she put her emotions into her driving, speeding the car through the labyrinth of London streets until they reached their Mayfair destination.

She pulled sharply up to the kerb outside a white building with delicate small-paned windows, four storeys high. Other police cars were already there, ambulances too. Even a fire engine stood at the ready, its long ladder primed for use. The narrow street was barricaded at both ends. Uniformed officers in yellow coats shepherded onlookers to the far side, where a small but growing crowd was gathering.

For a second, Lindy thought she detected a slight hesitation before Domenic reached for the door. But Salter wasn't waiting. Danny was inside, and he was injured. That was enough for her. And then, suddenly, Jejeune was out of the car, too, disappearing from sight through the elegant doorway. As Lindy tried to follow him up the steps, only to have her way politely but firmly barred by a uniformed officer, she knew that the thing Domenic had feared throughout their flight awaited him here, on the other side of these doors to the Mexican Consulate.

The morning sun was still low in the sky over this part of West London, painting long shadows on the ground far below. But no one on the rooftop was taking in the view. It was the scene before them that held all their attention, the same scene that had stopped Jejeune and Salter literally in their tracks as the doors of the service lift had opened.

At first glance, it seemed to be a wire aviary. At least that was what Jejeune had taken it for, a large cage, slightly hidden behind the massive air conditioning unit on the roof. But then he saw the transformer and generators inside, and he realized it was a safety cage, a perimeter of wire fencing encompassing an auxiliary power supply, one that ensured the Mexican Consulate would have electricity to run emergency services if the mains supply was ever interrupted accidentally. Or otherwise. The entrance gate of the cage appeared to be locked by a handcuff bracelet. There were two figures inside the cage. One of them was slumped on the floor, attached to the other handcuff bracelet: Danny Maik.

"You have come, Inspector. This is good. Now it is time to end this matter, I think."

Efren Hidalgo's voice was weary. He looked dishevelled, his immaculately groomed hair tousled by the wind up here, his open shirt torn and stained. On the floor of the cage at Hidalgo's feet, Jejeune could see a pool of dark fluid. He saw a deep gash on Maik's slumped head, the hair around it matted and wet. A sharp intake of breath at his side told him Salter had seen it, too.

"You have done brilliantly, as they say in this country. Unfortunately, however, it has brought us to this." Hidalgo looked around the small cage and gestured helplessly with his left arm. He was holding something in his right hand, dangling by his side, but Jejeune couldn't see what it was. Maik looked like he might be conscious, but if so, he wasn't making an attempt to get up. He was still sprawled on the floor of the cage, his left arm extended up awkwardly to the height at which Hidalgo had handcuffed it to the wire gate. His face was bathed in the blood from his wound. There was a lot of it.

Salter and the other policemen on the roof had begun to stir. Previously frozen, it was as if they had become emboldened by Jejeune's appearance, somebody who could talk to this person, engage this madman who was locked in a cage with a police sergeant he had handcuffed as his prisoner. Holland and two other officers began to move stealthily, ready to take up strategic positions. But Jejeune saw Hidalgo's eyes flicker toward them and he stilled their movements with a gesture of his hand.

"I think there is no way for us to resolve this situation, but I would like us to talk for a while." Hidalgo gestured around at the rooftop. "I do not think either one of us can have anything more pressing."

Jejeune said nothing. He had used Hidalgo's speech to make his way slowly toward the cage. He stood before it now, looking in. At the back, on the floor behind Hidalgo, tucked under a low concrete shelf, Jejeune could see a small cage with two birds in it.

"My sergeant needs emergency medical treatment, Counsellor. You must allow us to come in and help him."

Hidalgo's eyes reflected his inner sorrow. "I am sorry for the injuries your sergeant has suffered. I did not intend to harm him. This you must believe. I added a sedative to his water bottle. It should have rendered him unconscious for the short time I needed. But he saw that I had come up here and, drugged as he was, he followed me. I did not know if he had seen the birds, but I could not take the chance." Hidalgo shook his head sadly. "Even after I had struck him, he somehow found the strength to lock the gate with his handcuffs and throw the keys outside." He looked down at Maik. "Your sergeant, my Ramon. I wonder, Inspector, do we deserve the loyalty of men such as these?"

Jejeune looked at Maik, too. Men like this knew better than to offer their loyalty to people. It was to ideals that they stayed loyal; ideals of fairness and truth and justice. He could see the handcuff keys lying on the ground just outside the cage. There would have been a second blow, he realized, to subdue Maik further, to allow Hidalgo to fasten the other end of the handcuffs onto his wrist. Two blows, it explained the amount of blood. But Jejeune couldn't see the second wound. And that worried him.

Suddenly, Salter burst forward, ready to make a grab for the keys, but Jejeune put an arm out to stop her. He could see the heavy wrench lying on the floor at Hidalgo's feet. But it was the weapon in Hidalgo's right hand that had the DCI's attention.

Hidalgo raised the loose cable he had been holding down by his side. It writhed and spat like an angry serpent, sparks flying from it as the electricity arced toward a metal plate, hissing as they burnt out. "I will, of course, not allow anyone to touch those keys, or approach the cage. When this ends, it will do so as I decide. You will allow me this, I think."

The cable writhed in his hands again, and his meaning was clear. One touch against the wire fence and four hundred kilovolts of electricity would course through Danny Maik's body.

"My sergeant needs medical treatment, Counsellor," repeated Jejeune. "There can be no discussions of any kind until he receives help."

But Hidalgo was in some other place, not listening, merely regarding Maik with his sad, sorrowful eyes. "I asked only for ten minutes of privacy, but he said your instructions were that I should never be left alone. This was when I realized that you knew. After that, it was simply a matter of waiting, was it not, Inspector? Waiting to see who would give in first, who would care most about the welfare of the birds."

Hidalgo spread his hands, the cable missing the fence by a hair's breadth. He didn't seem to notice, or perhaps care. "So intelligent, Inspector, leaving me no alternative but to relinquish my diplomatic immunity in order to save the doves. I was quite sure you would relent, that you would not be willing to sacrifice the life of these birds, to starve them to death, to force my hand. But as it got later and later, I realized I was wrong. I had misjudged your priorities. Your commitment to your profession was stronger. I do wonder, though, could you have lived with the idea that you had been responsible for the deaths of two such important birds?"

Salter stirred. She needed to get to Danny, to save him. If Jejeune could not do it through talk, she would do it by action. She tried to judge the distance to the keys, calculate the time it would take to get to Danny, unlock his handcuff, save him. *Too long.* She needed Hidalgo away from the fence. Jejeune was approaching the cage now, closer, more purposefully. Had he realized it, too? Was he working toward a distraction?

"Close enough, Inspector. I am sure you will have the good grace to spare me the details of how you discovered my guilt, but please permit me to ask one thing. How long have you

STEVE BURROWS

known? It is strange. The idea that you knew I was lying when we spoke distresses me almost more than anything else."

Politicians and diplomats, thought Jejeune. Getting caught in lies seemed to be the biggest sin of all.

"After our walk around Regent's Park," said Jejeune, "the second time. You stopped at all the same spots. You were looking in places where you had seen things before: Chiffchaff, Smew, Ring Ouzel; birds you had recorded in *your* guide. You couldn't help yourself. It's a birder's reflex. We follow the same routes, check the same places. I compared the places we stopped with the sightings you had listed. They all matched."

"Such a small thing," said Hidalgo quietly.

But enough, the watching officers knew. Enough to get Jejeune looking in the right direction, to begin asking all those what ifs. And then, it was all just a matter of time. He was like one of those water dowsers, always twitching and twisting in the right direction, not perhaps heading straight for his target, but always inching ever closer, drawn inexorably by some primeval gift, as inexplicable and mysterious as the water dowser's craft itself.

Jejeune took another step toward the cage, and the four hundred kilovolts of death that Hidalgo held in his hand. The diplomat watched him carefully but made no move to raise the cable.

Salter stirred almost imperceptibly. *That's it, sir; you keep his eyes on you. So I can reach those keys and get to Danny, get him away from the wire, away from danger.* But she knew she never could. Hidalgo would touch the cable to the wire as much by instinct as anything else if she moved. She knew there would be no time. She couldn't leave Danny like this, at the mercy of a madman who had already declared he was going to kill himself, kill them both. But she couldn't save him either.

Salter readied herself to move, but it was Jejeune who took a final step forward. He extended his arms to his sides and linked his fingers through the chain-link fence.

Hidalgo hesitated, unsure what to do, the cable hanging loosely at his side. Jejeune locked his eyes onto Hidalgo's, knowing that he had to. If he let their gazes slip apart, even for a moment, it could mean death for all of them.

"Please step back, Inspector." Hidalgo seemed on the verge of tears, his eyes watery, his lips trembling.

But they knew that Jejeune would never do that, Holland and Salter and the others. They knew Jejeune would never unfurl his fingers from the fence and step back to safety. Not while Danny Maik was still shackled to the same fence. He would stay there, his face inches from the wire, staring at Hidalgo, imploring him not to raise the cable, not to commit the one final act of madness, of despair, that seemed his only exit from this nightmare he had brought upon himself.

"I do not want to harm you, Inspector." Hidalgo was almost weeping now, with frustration, with regret. "I have caused enough pain. There is no other way for me, or for this brave man here. It is the price we must pay for the situation we find ourselves in, the situation I have brought upon us all. But it does not deserve your sacrifice as well."

He was close to the edge. Salter could see it. Surely, Jejeune must see it, too. Hidalgo gripped the fence with his own free hand now, the black, writhing serpent of the cable sputtering as the exposed terminals arced to the wire again. The act may not even be deliberate now. The slightest gust of wind could tug the cable, bow the wire fence. It would not matter. The result would be the same.

"If we die on this rooftop tonight, so will your dream," said Jejeune quietly. "The birds will be taken away and given to a private collector, a petting zoo, somewhere, anywhere. Those doves will die in captivity, Señor Hidalgo, their precious, pure genetic material will be lost forever. But if we walk down from this place together, you and me and the sergeant, I give you my word I will not let that happen. I will make sure the birds go to a Socorro Dove captive breeding programme, as you intended. They will contribute to the gene pool, strengthen it, and one day, their offspring will return to Socorro Island. That was what you wanted, wasn't it? To see the species reintroduced into the wild, to restore one small piece of Mexico's lost heritage. That's what all this has been about."

"It was my dream to be there when the first doves were released back into the wild. I will never see this moment now, I think."

Tell him he will, urged Salter silently. For God's sake, for Danny's sake. Tell him anything. Tell him about legal appeals, about early release programmes. Confirm the only thing that will be able to salvage this situation, the only hope we have of getting off this roof with everybody still alive.

"No," said Jejeune, "you will never see it."

Hidalgo nodded. It had been a test, one final check to see if Domenic Jejeune would tell the truth, no matter what the circumstances, what the stakes. Hidalgo smiled as if he had always known how the detective would react. He turned and moved toward the fence, raising the cable. "Then the time has come, I think, to end this."

"But the day they are released, Ramon Santos's legacy will be enshrined forever. You can ensure that, Señor Hidalgo, you can honour Ramon, honour his loyalty, a loyalty that sent him to the sanctuary for you, to do what you asked, to steal those birds, even though he knew it was wrong. The loyalty he paid for with his life."

Jejeune could see the tears on Hidalgo's cheeks now, flowing unchecked. His hand was trembling, the cable quivering so near the cage sparks were arcing from it constantly.

On the spiderweb of roadways far below the rooftop, life went on. People hurried to work, to meetings, to shops. Those beyond this street didn't know what was happening on this roof, likely never would. There were no cameras this time, no media. Just people, whose lives hung in the balance, a hair's breadth from death.

"So much wrong I have done," said Hidalgo. "So much."

Jejeune still hadn't unfurled his fingers from the cage by the time Salter unlocked the handcuff from the fence and led Danny Maik, groggy and stumbling, to the service lift. Holland waited outside the cage for Hidalgo to come to him. There was no need to restrain him. With Holland in tow, the diplomat walked slowly toward the waiting lift, his head bowed. He entered without looking back at Jejeune. As the doors began to close, a uniformed officer squeezed in, gently cradling the bird cage. One final journey for the doves, to safety. Somewhere far from this rooftop. From Hidalgo.

Jejeune peeled his fingers slowly from the wire and went to wait for the lift to return. It would only be five flights if he chose to take the stairs down. On a normal day, he would have welcomed the exercise. But just now, he didn't feel as if he could trust his legs.

50

"Are you denying you knew it was Hidalgo before you went to St. Lucia?" Shepherd eyed him dubiously across the vast expanse of her paper-littered desk, but there was indulgence in her tone. Things had gone well, when they could have gone so terribly, catastrophically wrong. And she had Domenic Jejeune to thank for it.

"I didn't know for sure. I couldn't understand why he would have done it. Not until I learned about the reintroduction plans. Then it made sense."

"Really, Domenic? This made sense to you?" Shepherd managed to keep any note of contempt out of her voice.

"His interest in conservation, his first love, he called it, it would have allowed him to recognize the incredible importance of new, pure genetic material to the Socorro Dove captive breeding programme. Perhaps on its own even that might not have been motive enough to steal them, but with plans in place to reintroduce the doves to Socorro Island, Hidalgo saw his chance to recover one tiny piece of the Mexican environment that has been lost."

"And he still followed conservation issues that closely, all these years after abandoning his studies?"

"Once it has a grip on you, I don't think it ever lets you go," said Jejeune.

"Still, you might have mentioned your suspicions, instead of telephoning them in to Sergeant Maik. Even if I couldn't appreciate all the nuances of this whole reintroduction scheme. I may not appreciate fine art either, but I could certainly understand a motive of someone who killed to prevent a precious sculpture being destroyed, lost to the world forever. This is much the same thing, isn't it?"

But Jejeune could tell she didn't need him to explain why he hadn't confided in her. She knew already. She looked at him with an expression that seemed to hold both regret and sorrow, one that told him the price she had paid for ignoring Jejeune's instincts about Guy Trueman and listening to her heart instead.

"And you think recovering those birds was Hidalgo's only motive for killing Waters?" She was ready to move on, to find solace in the details of the case, and Jejeune was happy to let her.

He shrugged. "The new genetic material was too precious to allow it to disappear again into a private collection, especially that one. He knew that if Luisa Obregón ever got possession of those doves again, birds that had once belonged to her husband, she would never part with them for any amount of money. But he claims he didn't go to the meeting with the intention of killing Waters, that it wasn't revenge for Santos's death."

"I know what he said, Domenic. I was here, remember? I'm asking if you believe him."

Jejeune shrugged again. "He took a knife with him." As he had taken a heavy wrench to the rooftop, heavy enough to disconnect the cable, heavy enough to strike two glancing blows to Danny Maik's head, for which the sergeant had been under observation at the local hospital for the past twenty-four hours. Jejeune had no doubt Hidalgo believed what he said. But perhaps for Hidalgo, innocence only meant you weren't conscious of those intentions, those forces driving you. And who knew, perhaps that was all innocence could ever really mean.

Jejeune had not asked why the formal booking interview had taken place here, in Shepherd's office, or why Shepherd had taken the unusual step of sitting in, even leading the proceedings at times. Perhaps she thought the more comfortable surroundings and the obvious deference to Hidalgo's standing might encourage the Mexican Counsellor for Culture and Heritage to co-operate on the extent of Santos's involvement. If so, she had been disappointed.

Santos was innocent. Of everything. That was the price of Hidalgo's confession.

"He was there to commit a crime, Señor Hidalgo. Burglary," Shepherd had said irritably. Having made the concessions she already had, the DCS was in no mood to be pushed around.

"And you gave him your bird guide to help him commit that crime," Jejeune had told Hidalgo. "Santos was no birder. He wouldn't have known what a Socorro Dove looked like. You knew there were also Turtledoves in the sanctuary. So you gave him your book, bookmarked at the page. He was supposed to bring you the doves that *didn't* look like the birds on that page, the ones that *weren't* in the book."

Hidalgo had shrugged indifferently. "Ramon was following my instructions only. He had no idea he was being asked to do anything illegal. This is to be part of my confession. Otherwise, you will be left to prosecute me on the evidence. A case built on birding walks in Regent's Park ..." Hidalgo had spread his hands at this point and let his eyes flicker toward Shepherd, as if perhaps his diplomat's antennae could detect the path of least resistance.

In the end, Shepherd had relented. Ramon Santos was innocent; another victim of the tragic circumstances in this story, all stemming from the attempted theft of a couple of birds. It still seemed incredible to her. Nonsensical. But of course it was more complicated than that. Human motives always were. This was about immortality, having your contributions live on long after you were gone. The ongoing survival of a once-extinct species. It was a lofty ambition. Shepherd had regarded Hidalgo, sitting there, defiant, desperately trying to preserve his failed dignity. Such ambitions caused the fall of so many people.

But other than the level of Santos's involvement, Hidalgo's version of events had enough of the ring of truth to let them pass relatively unquestioned. As soon as Hidalgo had realized Waters had the birds, he had called him, using the telephone number retrieved from the surveillance tapes, and offered to buy the birds. They had agreed to meet at a remote location on a dirt road near the Obregón's property. But when Hidalgo got out of the car, Waters had seen only a Mexican. Though Hidalgo did not know it, Luisa Obregón had already refused to buy the birds, and Waters thought she had now sent a compatriot to take back her property by force — "The curse of the Latino complexion, Inspector." But there was bitterness in Hidalgo's sad smile. Waters had panicked and threatened to release the birds. He even opened the door to the cage. If Hidalgo had not killed him, "the birds, Inspector, would most certainly have escaped."

"What chance would they have had out there?" Hidalgo had asked them both plaintively through moist eyes, the only time he had shown any emotion during his formal confession. "They would surely have perished."

Shepherd picked up the report on her desk. Words. To explain humans killing each other over birds. She slapped the paper down again irritably. "Tell me, what you said to Hidalgo about the reintroduction project, is that true? Are the chances of success really that remote?"

"You must know," Jejeune had said to Hidalgo, "that a great many things have to go right for any reintroduction programme to be successful."

Hidalgo had offered a smile, the only genuine one they had seen during the interview. For a moment all the guilt left his face, all the pain, the sadness. "We idealists must be allowed our fantasies, Inspector. Our dreams are all that separate humans from the animals we seek to save."

Jejeune pulled a face at the memory and looked at Shepherd. "Even after the last of the foraging goats and sheep are removed, it will take a generation or two before the natural vegetation produces the seeds and fruits a reintroduced dove population would need. Then there would be many years of delicate work for that population to become self-sustaining, if it ever does."

"So all this," said Shepherd, "the deaths, everything — it was probably all for nothing?"

No, not for nothing. And perhaps a Colleen Shepherd in a less damaged state might have recognized this. But she had taken a chance on a relationship again and been punished for it. It was probably easier to distrust optimistic outcomes today, to see only the darkness instead.

Jejeune's only remaining question was why she had summoned him to her office today. They had already rehashed most things in the immediate post-mortem of Hidalgo's arrest and confession. She would need to have her story straight when she went before the head table, but she was clever enough to think on her feet, to memorize the stuff they knew and ad lib the rest. And Shepherd's failure to ask about the incident with the St. Lucia Royal Constabulary undoubtedly meant that she had not been informed about it. Jejeune had no intention of changing that. Lindy had been supportive, indulgent, patient about the episode. Any eventual explanations, such as they were, would surely be owed to her alone. Jejeune watched Shepherd lift a piece of paper from the desk and replace it in exactly the same position. He supposed it gave her something to do with her hands and her eyes as she spoke.

"I judged you unfairly, Domenic. In the Jag, that day, when I questioned your priorities. I want you to know, I recognize, we all recognize, what it must have cost you, to be willing to risk letting those birds starve to death to force Hidalgo's hand. As he said, it was the only way we were ever going to get him. With his diplomatic immunity, had he not confessed, we could never have touched him. But it can't have been an easy decision for you. I just want you to know it has been noted, at the highest levels, that you did not let your concern for the welfare of those birds compromise your sense of what needed to be done."

Her speech over, Shepherd brightened finally. "Right, well we have our result. The diplomatic fallout will be considerable, of course, but none of that is our doing. That said, I'm still extremely grateful we are on the outside of this one looking in. Can you handle the media briefing? I've told the chief constable I think it's warranted in this case, given the work you've put in."

"I'd like to wait on that for the moment." Jejeune had struck a tone somewhere between a request and a statement. As far as Shepherd could tell, it was one all his own. And it never failed to make her look up at him.

"Is there anything I should be aware of?"

Jejeune shrugged. "Fine art. I need to identify a bird sculpture."

51

"So I'm free to go, I understand? Nothing to hold me on. Don't worry, Danny, old son, I'm not the type to say I told you so. Oh, looks like I just did."

Guy Trueman gave Maik a mirthless grin. He was sitting at a desk, hurriedly tucking his things into his pockets — wallet, phone, keys — not bothering to check them. On the desk between them was a large manila envelope, torn untidily across its entire length. *Redirected anger, Guy? Frustration? Or just a desire to get your belongings and get out of here as quickly as possible?*

Maik sat down at the desk opposite him. Trueman's eyes found their way to the bandage on the side of Maik's head. Danny had tried to get by with the smallest dressing possible on the day of his return to work, but there had been some weeping from the site of the larger of the two wounds, and Lauren Salter had sat him down unceremoniously at his desk and affixed this monstrosity, with orders that it not be removed. It had been a strange encounter, Salter at once solicitous and yet distant, as if she couldn't prevent herself from helping him, even if she wasn't particularly impressed with herself for doing so. It was probably this, the fact that she had so obviously acted against her own instincts, which prevented Danny from removing the bandage as soon as he was out of her sight. He knew that if she saw him again later and the dressing was gone, she would feel betrayed in some way, disappointed in him. It had affected them all, Danny realized, this case, scarred them all in ways perhaps none of them really yet understood.

"Looks like you took a fair old wallop to the noggin," said Trueman. "Still, at least they didn't get anywhere important."

He thinks it's okay, that he can just turn it on, that mega-watt smile and the old school charm and we'll be back to normal. Mates again, comrades in arms, water under the bridge. But what had been broken, for Danny, could never be repaired. Perhaps his expression told Trueman this, because his ex-CO stopped smiling, sitting there now, hands loosely resting on the desk, waiting to say his farewells.

"Efren Hidalgo claims he wasn't overly quiet when he left that morning," said Maik. "He said he half-expected to have to make up some story for his personal security executive on his way out. But that his personal security executive never stirred."

Trueman looked at Maik, the playfulness gone now, replaced by a look of resignation.

"It's the pictures, Danny. When I close my eyes at night. The things I've seen, we've both seen. And the noises, all those sounds, the cries, the explosions, the … the noises. I can't get them out of my head. During the day you can keep them at bay, stay busy, don't think about things too much. But at night, when it's quiet, when there's nobody around to turn them off … How do you shut them out? Or have you just learned to live with them? You're a lucky man if you have."

Lucky? No, Maik didn't think so. But however he dealt with his own memories, that was not why he had sought out Guy Trueman before he was released.

"So what was it? Pills? Drugs?"

Trueman pulled a face. "I'd never touch that junk. A few months ago somebody told me about these hypnosis tapes. You listen to them as you're going to sleep and they put you right out. No dreams, nothing. Deep sleep, just like a baby. The only trouble is, it can be hard to wake up sometimes. Not ideal for somebody who's supposed to be providing round-the-clock personal security, but I thought, what harm can it do? It's a straight babysitting job anyway, most of the time. I'll see Hidalgo in safe for the night, tuck him in. A persistent phone call can get through the haze enough to wake me up if there ever was a problem. As long as I'm up before him in the morning, nobody's any the wiser."

"So you didn't hear Hidalgo leave to go and meet Waters?"

Trueman shook his head regretfully. "When I got up, I went straight in to see Hidalgo as usual, but he was already gone. Left me a note at reception saying he had gone back early to deal with some budding crisis at the consulate. I know now he had taken the birds back to London with him."

"You didn't know before?"

"You're asking if I knew he had killed the boy. I didn't, Danny, I swear to you. I had no idea."

There was a cold silence between them. Maik looked at Trueman steadily. "I wonder if you suspected, though," he said quietly. "I wonder if you thought about coming to me with your suspicions. Or did you just think, instead of telling me about your tapes and your deep sleeps, and your not being able to say where Efren Hidalgo was on the morning Jordan Waters was murdered, you might just drop a hint to Hidalgo every now and then, instead. Remind him that his alibi might not be as rock-solid as he thought. A man could get a lot of career mileage out of a reminder like that, hypnosis tapes or no hypnosis tapes."

It was over. Trueman could read it in Maik's eyes. But he tried once more anyway, for old times' sake.

"I helped you, Danny. Put you on to Waters, told you about the call to Obregón."

He was asking Danny to leave his ex-CO's role out of his report.

To take pity on him. A wave of sadness swept over Maik. Major Guy Trueman, reduced to the indignity of begging like this, knowing that the facts would be enough to end his lucrative career. A private security executive who slept through his boss's nocturnal wanderings. It might even be funny if it wasn't so pathetic. The truth was, it wasn't Danny's decision to make, but he didn't insult Trueman by hiding behind that fact. Both men knew he could make it all disappear if he wanted to. Both knew, too, that he wouldn't.

Trueman's expression showed that he had already accepted the fact. "You always were a cold-eyed bastard, Danny. No real attachment to anybody, not even yourself. Probably what made you a good soldier. But it won't do you any good in the long run, this lonely Joe routine. Danny Maik, man of steel, the solitary crusader, with only his Motown to keep him company. Take my advice, Danny, find somebody to be with, somebody who is going to make life seem important, vital again, like it was when we were out there together, where it mattered."

Maik was silent. There didn't seem to be much of anything to say anymore.

Trueman stood up, the scraping of his chair overloud in the stark, unfurnished room. "Do something for me, will you. Tell your DCS I meant it. All of it. Can you tell her that for me, in case I don't get the chance myself?"

Trueman looked around the room as if checking out his incarceration one last time. He managed a laugh. "Bloody hell, though, eh, Danny? All we've seen, all we've done together, and it all comes to an end over some doves. You'd hardly credit it, would you?"

"Pitying," said Maik. "That's what they call a group of doves, apparently. A pitying."

He gathered up the torn envelope on the table in front of him and stood up. Though they locked eyes, neither man said anything more. It seemed as if their goodbyes had all been said a long time ago.

52

Carrie Pritchard opened the door of her cottage and greeted Jejeune with guarded friendliness.

"Domenic, how nice."

From somewhere behind her, Jejeune heard the sound of a shower being turned off, and the woman noted it registering with him. "Well, I suppose you had better come in. Now that this business is finally over, a little openness can't hurt, can it?" Her eyes searched Jejeune's face for a response, but she found nothing there.

Jejeune walked toward the sculptures and picked up the one she had challenged him with.

"*Think Canada*," he said. "Fred Bodsworth, you meant. *The Last of the Curlews.*"

Pritchard smiled. "I knew you would get it eventually. The Eskimo Curlew, possibly the most significant bird in the history of the New World. It really should mean a lot more to North Americans than it seems to, don't you think? Not just birders, of course. Everyone."

The Eskimo Curlew's place in North American history was tenuous, Jejeune knew. A comparison of dates and migratory patterns had caused some people to speculate that it may have been Eskimo Curlews that Christopher Columbus had seen, alerting him, after sixty-five days at sea, that land must be nearby. The evidence was sketchy; circumstantial at best. But sometimes that was all you had to go on. That, and your instincts. Now the birds were gone, extinct, unable to compete with the stresses brought by the European populations that they may have guided to the shores in the first place. As a tragic irony, it sat high on the list of things that disturbed Jejeune's sleep at times. But it was not why he had come to Carrie Pritchard's home this day.

Music came from the kitchen, and the sound of food being prepared. Jejeune looked up through the open doorway.

"You know your compatriot, I understand," said Pritchard quietly.

"Hey, Inspector," said Gavin Churchill with a confident smile. He tilted his still-wet hair toward the iPod. "A real blast from the past, eh? Remember the Hip? Ever been to Bobcaygeon? Watched those constellations revealing themselves one star at a time?"

Jejeune did remember the Tragically Hip. And he had been to Bobcaygeon. But it seemed like a long time ago now. It belonged to another age, one of innocence, of campfires by the lake with Traz, of beers and laughter and the endless promises of a life that stretched out before you, unfettered and uncompromised, like a pathway out among those constellations, paved by only boundless dreams and expectations and hopes for the future. When had it all changed for him? he wondered. When had his life become a place where it was his job to stand in people's living rooms and bring their lives crashing down around them?

"You don't seem surprised, Inspector," said Pritchard. "We thought we were being very discreet."

No, not surprised. Not even disappointed. Life seemed to have lost its capacity to disappoint Jejeune recently. Something to do with expectations and hopes, he realized, the lack of them.

"You told Lindy about the skin in your freezer," he said quietly, "the Arctic Skua. It's an uncommon bird. Someone commented recently about how birders can always remember the first time they saw a particular species. The first Arctic Skua I ever saw was when my brother drove me to Van Wagner's Beach in Hamilton. Of course, being in Canada, we called it a Parasitic Jaeger, as you did, Gavin. But you were quite right; it was worth driving half the length of Lake Ontario to see."

Jejeune paused, but he had no need to look at their expressions to know that they recognized where he was leading them. "Even though it must have been Gavin who gave you that skin, you both made a point of denying you knew each other. But why hide your relationship? You're both single, unattached. Innocence needs no secrecy. So it had to be something more." He turned to Pritchard. "I think you wanted to protect a potential source, someone who could gain access to Obregón's property every now and again and tell you if any black market birds were finding their way into her aviary."

"Gavin could go up there whenever an exotic bird was found and ask Luisa Obregón if it had escaped from her collection. She had no qualms about letting him look around her aviary," said Carrie breezily. She wheeled away and poured herself a glass of wine, settling herself comfortably on her couch. "There was nothing illegal in it, Inspector. Had they known, perhaps the local busybodies might have seen it as Gavin trading information for the love of a good woman, but surely, that is amongst the noblest of exchanges civilization has yet developed."

Gavin shrugged. "Glad to be of service," he said with a smile.

"Yes," agreed Jejeune sadly. "Only it's not an exclusive service that you offer, is it, Gavin? You hired yourself out to Luisa Obregón, too."

"What?" Gavin turned to Carrie. "That's crazy."

Jejeune seemed to be listening to the Hip song again; waiting as the constellations continued to reveal themselves.

"The music we grew up with always seems to stay with us, doesn't it? Like our accents."

Gavin faltered, no longer looking Carrie in the eye.

"You were there that night. At the sanctuary. It was you who left that note reporting the murders on the car windshield. You couldn't call it in, not with that accent." When he had reached this point in his deductions, these weren't questions for Jejeune anymore, so there was little point in phrasing them as such.

Gavin didn't say anything. Carrie was staring at him. The playful glimmer of a few moments ago had disappeared from her eyes, replaced now by the empty desolation of the betrayed lover.

"Your prints aren't in the database over here, but I'm sure we can find a set somewhere to test against those on the filing cabinet," said Jejeune reasonably.

Gavin took a step back, as if distance might help to relieve some of the pressure. "She wanted the DNA results. She knew Phoebe had sent the samples in for analysis. Waters told her when he called. That's how they knew the doves were pure Socorros. She wanted to know if the DNA samples were a match with those her husband had taken from the birds in his collection." Jejeune's eyes followed him as he began pacing around the room. "She's obsessed with rebuilding that collection, and the idea that these might actually have been her husband's own birds ..." He shook his head, "She would have paid Waters twice what he was asking. More. But she needed to be sure first. So she sent me there to get the results."

The other two stared at Gavin in silence. He stopped pacing and held up his hand.

"Oh, no. Wait. You've got this wrong. I told you I was there, but that's it. That's the truth. The filing cabinet was locked so I went to see if the keys were still on the hook by the cage, where they usually are. Those two were already dead when I found them." Gavin was beginning to panic, his breathing quickened and his movements were becoming agitated. "You saw that cage. The blood. Everywhere. And the smell, too. I mean, I've seen dead animals before, but this was different. Jeez, I mean, these were people. But I never touched that cage, I never went near it. I swear. I just got out of there as quickly as I could."

"Without even wiping down the filing cabinet."

Gavin shook his head, his damp hair flopping forward. "As soon as I got outside, I realized my prints would be on there. But there was no way was I going back into that place, not to see that again." He cringed at the memory. "I should have stuck around; I know that. I should have called it in and waited till the cops arrived. But I just wanted to get away from there. So I wrote the note and stuck it on the car at that pub. I was just acting out of …"

Desperation was probably the word he was going to use, but neither callousness nor calculated self-interest seemed beyond the repertoire of the man now standing before Jejeune. Though to admit to either would have needed more candour than Gavin was willing to show in front of Carrie.

Jejeune said nothing more. Carrie Pritchard had been looking on in silence, shrouded by her anguish. She turned to Jejeune, mustering a display of dignity that must have taken all her reserves of strength. "I'm sure you two will have further matters to discuss, Inspector, but I wonder if you could give us a few minutes."

Jejeune tilted his head to acknowledge her request and made his way toward the door. "I'll be down by the estuary," he said, "checking if those Knots are still around. Take all the time you need."

53

Shepherd was staring out of the window at the rolling Norfolk landscape, golden in the late afternoon sunlight. She was deep in thought.

"So Gavin Churchill has admitted to being at the scene." She nodded. "A plausible explanation, you think? It certainly answers our questions about the anonymous tip. Well done, Domenic. The chief constable is not a fan of loose ends anyway, and for this case in particular it is especially important to wrap everything up."

His silence caused her to look up at him.

"Something?"

"He can't be sure the cage door was locked."

Shepherd remained staring at her desk for a long moment. Should a bombshell really land so quietly? It was some time before she looked up.

"The official report is that Santos was killed by Waters during the commission of a crime. I have to tell you the HO will not look favourably on any attempt to challenge this finding."

"It means they may have been dead before Jordan Waters got there."

"Yes, I know what it means." Shepherd was quiet. "Leave it, Domenic."

But he couldn't leave it. Wouldn't.

"It makes sense," said Jejeune. "Phoebe Hunter surprised Santos in the act of stealing the doves. She panicked and attacked him with the closest weapon to hand, a syringe used to put medication into the doves' water dish. The neck wound wouldn't have killed him instantly. It would have taken a few moments. He turned and pushed her away, onto the branch, maybe an accident, maybe deliberately."

Shepherd was still silent.

"That was how Gavin Churchill found them. And left them. When Waters arrived, he saw what had happened and tried to pull Phoebe off the branch, not push her on to it. That's how he tore his nail. Performing the actions of a man his mother said cared for her, a man Tony Holland says didn't have it in him to kill. When Waters saw the syringe in Santos' neck, he must have realized what had happened, that Phoebe had stabbed him. He wanted to cover for her, so he removed the syringe and took it with him, grabbing the birds and locking the cage when he left."

"And the DNA records? The ones Gavin couldn't find and we couldn't find? The ones that turned up in Waters's panel van?"

"Maybe Phoebe Hunter had them with her in the cage. Gavin didn't approach the cage closely so he never saw them. Waters would have recognized their importance if he was going to sell the birds, so he took those too. It all fits."

"A lot of things fit, Domenic. It doesn't make them true." Shepherd fell silent again. She seemed to take a breath before speaking.

"It's preposterous," she said finally. "We know none of this, can prove none of it. A person could come up with any one of a dozen other explanations, equally plausible, without having to satisfy the burden of proof." She looked at Jejeune. "That's what they'll say, Domenic. That and more. They have their result.

They're not interested in other interpretations of the evidence. Those can be left to decay with time, unexplored, unanswered."

"Not even to get to the truth?"

"They have their truth, or at least the version of it they're happy with. And that's always the problem with the truth, isn't it? People just seem to choose the version that suits their needs. A British subject killed a Mexican diplomat and a Mexican diplomat killed a British subject. As twisted and sick as it is, it is the balance they need. They can all go off and be publicly outraged and quietly satisfied. The last thing they want now is somebody complicating things."

"Even if it means Jordan Waters is going to be thought guilty of two murders he didn't commit? I mean, I'm not claiming he was an innocent party in all this, by any means. He stole the birds, but …"

"I don't think any of us are innocent. Fools with good intentions; that's what we are, all of us." She looked at him sadly. "They will not allow you to open this up again, Domenic. You have to let it go. Gavin Churchill may have thought the cage door was open, but could he say so definitely? More to the point, *would* he say so, if he had his options explained to him by the collective weight of the U.K. and Canadian governments, and the Mexicans thrown in for good measure? Or would he just, do you think, reconsider, and decide that perhaps that cage was locked when he looked in, after all? At which point, it all goes away — your theory, your unanswered questions, your truth. And with it will go your career. And mine. And anyone else's who has been foolish enough to let you air this version of events in public."

She looked sad, as if she recognized that having to tell Jejeune this, having to explain the facts of life to him in this way, was going to change something. He would never again believe that uncovering the evidence, or finding the guilty party, was enough. It would affect the way he approached his job, his search for the truth, unfettered, unadorned, unadulterated. It would shatter any lasting illusions he might have about the value of his work as a detective, the pure, simple *rightness* of what he did. And for a man so disillusioned with this career anyway, it may be the final blow. She hoped not. He was too valuable an asset to lose. But she would understand if it was. And in some ways, she wouldn't blame him.

But Jejeune said nothing. He didn't rail around cursing about the injustice of it all. He didn't melodramatically draw his warrant card from his wallet and silently lay it on the table between them. He said nothing. Perhaps it didn't really matter enough to him, after all.

He looked at her, through her, and she knew he could see, as clearly as if she had been made of glass, that the uncertainty troubled her too. But the result must take precedent for now, for the sake of everybody, to ensure the continued existence of her department, her team, her station. When the doubts came in the small quiet hours, she would deal with them privately. Publicly, this case was closed.

He was on his way from the room when she called out to him. "Domenic, those doves? Do you know what became of them? Did they ever go to the captive breeding programme?"

She had turned to the window again, so Jejeune delivered the message to her back. "They are still trying to nurse them back to health. The male is likely to make a full recovery, so it looks like he will be able to contribute to the gene pool. But the female was gravid. She lost her clutch and there is some question as to whether the stress on her body may have permanently damaged her reproductive system." He paused. "There could be considerable dangers to the bird in using her in a captive breeding programme. I imagine there will be a lot of discussion about whether they want to risk her or not."

"For the greater good of the species?" said Shepherd, staring out at the fields beyond her office. "I have no doubt that they will."

Jejeune left her to seek the solace of the world outside her window, to consider, perhaps, how often the burdens of making sure life goes on seemed so often to fall upon the female of the species.

54

Jejeune sat on a dune near the entrance between the pines at Holkham, staring out at the expanse of pale water before him. Rafts of birds floated far out on the horizon, gulls and ducks, but the numbers of shorebirds were fewer now, and the movements less. The vast transit of migrating flocks was slowing down, and most of the birds that had arrived here lately would be staying on, spending their summer along the north Norfolk coast, seeking shelter among its bays, foraging along its wide, fertile mudflats, retiring to its wetlands and salt marshes to breed and raise their young. It was the end of a season; the birds settling to a new equilibrium after the upheavals of the previous weeks. Not calmness, not comfort; life for the birds on this coast was never that. There would still be the daily struggles, battles to be waged against the elements, against competitors for food, for territory, for mates. But it was a sedentary life for a few months, at least, without the perils of long-distance travel, with all its uncertainties, its threats seen and unseen, its dangers man-made and natural.

Jejeune watched as a flock of Black-tailed Godwits flew in from the west to settle on the shore. New arrivals from West Africa. Even these robust shorebirds seemed so fragile to have made such a long journey. And yet, here they were, nestled between a soft pastel sea that stretched out behind them and the endless infinity of a blue Norfolk sky. As they would be next year, and the year after that, and every year for as long as humans preserved their summer homes and their wintering grounds, and the important resting places in between. But who would do that? Who would work to guarantee that these birds, and others like them, would always have these places? Would the Turtledoves, who must follow the same route as these Godwits, find refuges and safe havens at the end of their epic migration route? Jejeune had not seen a Turtledove in the wild this year, but he knew he would, at some point. Out here in north Norfolk there would be Turtledoves to be found, if one looked long enough and hard enough. But would future generations of birders be able to find them? Or would they be left to see them only in captivity, in aviaries, in breeding programmes destined to produce only more generations of captive Turtledoves? Once it had been Phoebe Hunter's role to provide answers to these questions. Once he had thought it might become his. But he knew now that it would not.

An unfamiliar chirrup came from his pocket and Jejeune belatedly remembered that Lindy had handed him her phone on his way out, since he couldn't locate his own. He read the text:

> Found your phone — obviously, since I'm texting
> you from it. Dinner at 7. Hope the birding is good. X.

As he went to turn off the phone, he noticed the draft folder. He opened it and saw the message he had composed on the plane. Fifteen words, that was all they were now, stripped of the emotion, the panic, the despair in which he had written them. Fifteen words that had been stilled, rendered irrelevant by Salter meeting them at the airport gate and their frantic, breathless rush to the consulate, where the words had no place anymore, no meaning. And never would again.

Jejeune looked at the message again:

> Effective immediately. Withdraw all protection
> on Hidalgo. Advise him no further monitoring
> of his activities.

Tell him to save the doves, he was saying. The message would have defined his stand between his two worlds forever, spelled it out for all to see. Domenic Jejeune was willing to allow Hidalgo to provide the necessities of life to a pair of rare and precious doves and still preserve his diplomatic immunity, still avoid confessing to a murder Jejeune knew he had committed.

It was a price Jejeune had been willing to pay. If he had sent the message. But would he have sent it, finally? Or would he have looked down at those words one final time before pressing the button? Heard in them Danny Maik's disapproval, Shepherd's outrage, Lindy's disappointment? Would they have caused him to rethink, to hesitate, to re-evaluate the lives of two birds against the larger justice owed to Jordan Waters, to Phoebe Hunter, to Ramon Santos? Jejeune didn't know. He suspected he never would now.

He pressed the button.

Permanently delete this message?

How easy it was to make words disappear, to erase them so that the only place they existed, would ever exist, was in some shadowy recess of the writer's heart.

He pressed the button again.

Folder empty.

Domenic Jejeune shut off Lindy's phone and headed home.

THE
EUROPEAN TURTLEDOVE

It is estimated that European Turtledove (*Streptopelia turtur*) population in the United Kingdom has declined by more than seventy-five percent in the past forty years. Today, fewer than 45,000 pairs return to breed each year in the U.K. The problems are manyfold, but include inadequate protection of the African wintering grounds and intensive arable farming practices in the U.K. Such practices remove the weed seeds that constitute a major portion of the European Turtledove's diet. Another major factor is hunting, both legal and illegal, of the species during their migration. As many as four million birds are shot or trapped as they pass through Europe and North Africa.

A number of groups, including The Royal Society for the Protection of Birds (RSPB) and the British Trust for Ornithology (BTO), are now lobbying for better enforcement of the EU Birds Directive, which limits the hunting season, and seeking additional legal protection for this declining species. To learn more about the efforts to protect European Turtledoves, please visit www.rspb.org.uk or www.bto.org.uk.

THE
SOCORRO DOVE

Once a species has disappeared from the wild, only a large-scale, multi-faceted effort can restore it. In 2013, more than four decades after the last member of the species was seen in the wild, six captive-bred Socorro Doves (*Zenaida graysoni*) were transferred to breeding facilities in Mexico. These birds are part of a project designed to support the eventual reintroduction of the species to Socorro Island. The project involves thirty-three organizations in twelve countries, including the National Autonomous University of Mexico Institute of Biology, the Island Endemics Foundation, and Mexico's Instituto de Ecologia. To learn more about the work of the Socorro Dove Reintroduction Project, please visit www.zeroextinction.org.

Turn the page to read the opening of...

A CAST OF FALCONS

The gripping third installment in the

BIRDER MURDER SERIES

The threat from above casts a dark shadow...

PUBLISHED SEPTEMBER 2016

1

The noise. The deafening, terrible noise. The sound of air, rushing through his clothing, tearing at his hair, clawing his lips back into a grotesque grin. Ten seconds? Perhaps. Thirty-two feet per second, per second. A memory. School? Shadows. Sadness. Anger.

Lightheaded now, lungs unable to snatch the air rushing by. Panic. The rock face a grey curtain hurtling past at one hundred and twenty miles per hour. Terminal velocity. Another memory. School? Or college? Good times. Laughter. Women. Bars. Five seconds? Terminal! *I'm dying.*

He had seen the angel, a brief glimpse as he released his grip on the rock face. On life. Pure, white, beautiful. An angel that had brought him death. Angels. Heaven. Too late? Never too late, his mother said.

His mother. Regrets. Words not spoken. Actions not taken. Taken. Birds. Fear, now. Plunging down through open space. *I'm going to die.* Repentance. The key. *God, forgive me. For the birds. For—*

The man watching through binoculars fixed the body's landing place against the scarred granite backdrop, and then swept the horizon in either direction. Nothing else stirred. He focused again on the rock face and relocated the crumpled form, remembering the sickening flat bounce as life had left it. He lowered his binoculars and sat, deep in thought, seeming not to notice the fierce buffeting of the winds that scoured the bleak landscape. After a moment, he tucked his bins into a canvas bag resting against his hip, careful not to damage the other item inside. Things had changed now, but perhaps there was still a way; and perhaps this other item, now nestling gently against the bins, held the key. He rose from his crouched position and began to make his way toward the towering presence of Sgurr Fiona.

He moved with haste over the uneven terrain, beneath a sky that was grey and leaden. Swollen rain clouds were riding inland on the onshore winds. A fierce Atlantic squall was on its way and the exposed heath would offer no shelter once the storm arrived. The man wore only a heavy fisherman's sweater, denim jeans, and walking shoes. He had no coat or waterproofs to ward off the horizontal rains that would soon drive across the landscape.

He had estimated the distance to the rock face at a quarter of a mile, and he could tell now, as he crossed the ground with his steady, purposeful gait, that he'd been about right. Even experienced walkers underestimated distances in these parts. The stark, featureless landscape seemed to draw in the mountains on the horizon, making them appear closer. But the man had spent enough time in the natural world to be alert for its deceptions. It was those of the human world he found harder to detect.

He moved over the tussocks easily, barely noticing the sprigs of gorse and brambles that snatched like harpies at his trouser cuffs. Once or twice he stumbled over the craggy, moss-covered mounds, but for the most part his progress was sure-footed, even in the flimsy, well-worn soles of his walking shoes. On the horizon, the grey mass of a low cloudbank had begun its inexorable time-lapse march across the landscape. He would need to work quickly if he was to find shelter before the storm came. He had a window, a tiny chink of opportunity: The coming storm would discourage others from venturing out here. But squalls passed over these coastal areas quickly, chased into the inland valleys and hill passes by the relentless coastal winds. Behind the storm would come the clear white-blue skies of the North Atlantic. And then the walkers would return to the trails. It wouldn't be long before the body was found and reported. He must do what had to be done long before that happened. He needed to be far away by then.

The last of the vegetation died away and he emerged onto a slight slope of scree that led up to the base of the rock face. Sgurr Fiona towered above him, its peaks already lost in the greyness of the clouds. He stopped for a second to take in its grandeur, and as he looked up, he paused. Until now, only the images of the death, the violent impact of the man's body hitting the ground, had occupied his thoughts. But the initial shock was starting to wear off, and he began to recognize a meaning behind what he had seen; an explanation, perhaps. Had the other man recognized it, also, in those last, long terrifying seconds? Had he, too, acknowledged what it might mean? Either way, it was just him, now, standing alone on this desolate, windswept heath, who possessed this wisdom, this secret, entrusted to him by another man's death. He looked up at Sgurr Fiona once again, but the sky below the clouds was empty.

He approached the body and forced himself to look down at the broken, rag-doll form. It was clear the man had died on impact. The damage seemed to be mostly to the head and face. It was difficult to even make out the features now. He shook his head. It was as if the fates themselves had determined to cloak the death in a double layer of mystery: not only of who the dead man was, but of what he had looked like in life.

The man felt a momentary wave of sadness for the empty shape at his feet. All that was left of Jack de Laet, with whom he had drunk, and laughed, and swapped lies — and unknowingly, a few truths too — over the previous weeks. He was a bad man, Jack, one of the worst. But he had been a person, a living, breathing human being. And now he was ... what? The man didn't have time to consider the question. Musing about the afterlife, the great beyond, was for a warm pub, where he would head after this, for a hot meal and a glass of single malt whisky and the comfort of a gently burning fire. Out here, at the base of a granite rock face, under a low, roiling, gunmetal sky, he had work to do.

He knelt beside the body and slowly began to withdraw the day pack from beneath Jack de Laet's stiffening form. He worked with great care. He couldn't see any blood coming from under the body, but if there was any, he knew the small pack could disturb it, smear it, perhaps in a way that a good forensic examiner might be able to detect. He breathed a sigh of relief when the pack finally slithered free showing no traces of blood. He lifted it to one side and peered in. "Ah Jack, you lied to me," he said quietly, without malice. Using a handkerchief, he withdrew a book from his canvas shoulder bag. It was battered and dog-eared, with a long-faded cover from which the images of a couple of birds, well-drawn and easily identifiable, stared back at him. He took a pen from his pocket and wrote two words on the flyleaf, holding the cover open with the handkerchief. Then he leaned forward to delicately lift the flap on one of De Laet's jacket pockets. He slid the book in.

He patted the pocket slightly as he closed the flap and rose from his kneeling position clutching the small day pack.

"See you soon," he said. But he wasn't talking to Jack de Laet.

2

Death had won again. As it always did in the end. Another man had challenged it, tried to face it down and defeat it with his frail human courage. And he had lost. In this case, Death had stalked its victim, pursued him silently through this leafy forest glade, treading the path parallel to this one that ran farther down in the ravine. At some point, it had moved ahead of the man so it could scramble silently up to this footpath, and lurk, hidden from view, until the man rounded the bend. To find Death waiting for him. A short struggle, perhaps, and then Death had claimed another victim, and dragged his soul off to its lair. And now it was up to Danny Maik to find out who had been Death's foot soldier this time, and to bring that person in to face the justice that Death itself never would.

They knew the choreography, and little bits more, from the trail of clues, footprints whispered into the woodchips of the two trails. But it was not enough to tell them who had been following the man, so they were still no closer to knowing who had decapitated him and left his body lying here in the centre of the path, and the head a few yards off, in the bracken to the right.

In this strange twilight aftermath of the event, not now fresh enough to be shrouded in shock, but recent enough that the horror had not yet faded completely, it was the jogger that

Danny Maik felt for most. The emotional trauma of those Philip Wayland had left behind would be understandable; their grief and despair justified. No one would consider it unusual if any of the family or friends fell apart for a few days. Or longer. But the jogger who had found the body was not in their circle, not really entitled to any of the emotions his death engendered in them. And so, this unremarkable woman, who had done nothing worse than decide on this path for her morning jog, must now deal with her own feelings only in the shadows. Maik could hardly imagine the shock she had endured. One minute enjoying the woods, hearing the rhythmic pounding of her running shoes on the trail, treating her lungs to the fresh, clean woodland air, and the next, happening upon the worst, most horrifying sight she would ever see in her life.

She seemed so shaken, so utterly traumatized by her discovery, as she was led away, trembling and sobbing into Constable Lauren Salter's sympathetic embrace. When the police arrived, they had found her standing beside the body, over it almost, as if unable to draw herself away. Or perhaps it was just that she was unwilling to leave the victim, feeling that someone should stay to watch over him, even in his brutalized, incomplete state, until the medics could come and treat him with the care and dignity the last moments of his life had denied him. If so, the woman's compassion would cost her dearly. Days and nights of images, things seen when her eyes had been inexorably drawn to the horror at her feet on the path; images that may never leave her. How could you confront such a sight — the headless body of a person — out here in the silence and the solitude of the woods, and not be damaged by your discovery? Domenic Jejeune, too, had seemed to recognize the toll the woman's discovery would take, had already taken, on her. The DCI made sure he organized her care and treatment before turning his attention to the body on the path. In truth, there had been no need to rush on that score. Both Detective Chief Inspector Jejeune and Sergeant Danny Maik had already long acknowledged the truth of the situation. Death had won again.

Maik looked along the trail again now and then turned his gaze to the right, peering through the undergrowth as if trying to judge exactly how far he was from the compound. Though this path was a public right of way, the battered sign on the fence made it clear to anyone veering from it that they were entering onto PRIVATE PROPERTY.

Public access through private land. Maik could hardly count the times as a beat constable he had found it necessary to go over the concept with tourists: *Yes, the path does go through private property. Yes, you are allowed onto it. No, you don't need the owners' permission. No, I don't understand it either.* And when the new foreign owners had acquired this particular property, the "Old Dairy" as they now called it, Maik had been present at the earliest briefings, when the questions about public access to private property had become even more pointed. *What exactly does the concept of land ownership mean in this country, when the public is granted rights of way into perpetuity?* But if the legal representative of Old Dairy Holdings had expected Detective Chief Superintendent Colleen Shepherd to quail under his withering glance, he was disappointed. Shepherd had told him politely that it meant whatever the Highways Passage Act meant it to mean. The discussion had ended there.

The world being the way it was, Maik had probably always known if any major crime was ever going to be committed around here, it would happen on this path, where jurisdiction and rights were at their most nebulous. Now, it would require all of DCS Shepherd's considerable diplomatic skills to get them the access and co-operation the investigating officers were going to need from Old Dairy Holdings to pursue their inquiries into this case.

Maik looked around at the glade again, drinking in its tranquility, the tangy hint of bark on its breezes. It had happened at dusk, the medical examiner had determined, at the far end of daylight's arc, when any protesters had long since gone home and the woods had returned to silence. *What brought you here, Mr. Wayland, to this path beside the place you had not worked at in more than a year? What, if anything, did it have to do with you being killed in such a disturbingly brutal way?* Maik smiled wryly. He was pretty sure his absent DCI would approve of these questions about Philip Wayland's final moments, even if he might not be too impressed by the high-minded affectation with which Danny's subconscious was composing them.

Absent, thought Maik. His *absent* DCI. Even for the famously disengaged Inspector Domenic Jejeune, the absence was puzzling. The call had come in from the Highland Constabulary just as the first analysis of the physical evidence in this case was starting to materialize. Not the ideal time, one would have thought, for the inspector to go haring off up to Scotland. Not at all the actions of a DCI fully engaged in the business of solving Philip Wayland's murder. Jejeune had certainly been invested enough in the case during the early days, even if his detached approach might have suggested otherwise. So when did a trip up to the Scottish Highlands suddenly take precedence over an active murder inquiry? When did investigating a book, a bird guide no less, found on the body of a fallen climber, become more important than pursuing a killer? Perhaps today was the day Danny would get some answers. Perhaps there would be a message waiting for him at the office, or an email, telling him the DCI was on his way back to north Norfolk.

Maik looked around the glade now, seeing the last remnants of the police incident tape flapping from one or two trees and the fresh bark chips on the trail that replaced the blood-stained ones gathered as evidence. It seemed inconceivable that this spot could have been the scene of such violence and brutality a scant few days ago. Shafts of light were beginning to filter through the leafy canopy, dappling the forest path into tawny patterns. Beneath the giant beeches on both sides of the path, patches of bluebells awaited the warmth of the early morning sun. This was a place of tranquility again now, a place that seemed to have gathered up the horrors of the past and laid a blanket of quiet over them. Nature providing a balm for the crimes of humans, forgiving them once again, as it always did.

Maik turned and headed back to his car, but not before pausing for one quick look back. The corner of an office was barely visible through the vegetation, the only evidence one could see of the research compound on the other side of the wire fence. DCI Jejeune had spent a long time staring at that office the last time he was here. *Just what was it you were looking at?* wondered Danny. *And why does it make you distrust the only witness statement we have in this case?*